DARK IS THE NIGHT

a novel

Mirriam Neal

MIRRIAM NEAL

This Mirriam Neal paperback edition October 2019.

Printed in the United States of America.

Cover design by Oliviaprodesign.

ISBN - 978-1-64669-494-5

ALSO BY MIRRIAM NEAL

Monster (Shieldmaiden Publishing)
Paper Crowns (Mirror Publishing)

*This book is dedicated to
every supernatural creature
in South Carolina.
I owe you one.*

CHAPTER ONE

South Carolina gave the term 'God-forsaken' an entirely new meaning. It wasn't just the black water and tall brown grass sucking at his boots with every step. It wasn't the thick, hot air or the loud buzz of unseen insects.

It was the long, chilling howl that cut through the stillness like a blade and hung there, even after the sound passed.

It was a familiar sound, but it didn't belong in this state. Heck, it didn't belong on this side of the country. Skata tapped the smooth barrel of his sawed-off shotgun and continued forward, faster than before. Flat, soggy marshes were a bad place to be attacked, with uneven ground and nowhere to hide but in plain sight.

Another howl sang from somewhere, not far enough away for comfort. It was joined by a second howl, the noises twined together in the distance. Skata knew it could still be only one lone wolf, changing the tone of its voice and undulating, tricking him into thinking it had a pack.

Still, he reasoned, *best to be on the safe side.*

He drew his gun, the barrels pointing ahead as he finally broke free of the marsh and moved into the tree line. In Montana, trees grew straight and strong, like natural monuments. Here, they spread and twisted and hung themselves with pale, ragged moss. They gave the impression that they were watching him, lurking in their own shadows.

"Idiot," he muttered. His voice was quiet, but his ears had grown unaccustomed to it over the past week and the single word might have been a shout. He stopped and slid his finger around the trigger.

A branch snapped. He knew by the sound it was a small branch, possibly a twig, and broken by a light step. He crouched down on one knee and waited for something to appear. A long breath, and then two small spots of light blinked to life less than ten yards in front of him.

The wolf growled and lowered its head, its unblinking eyes watching him, waiting to see if he was interesting. If it was just a wolf, the chance that it would attack was small, at best. In the Deep South, in late spring, there would be plenty of smaller and less threatening food for a wolf to find.

C'mon, make your move.

The wolf crouched, muscles coiling under fur before it launched into the air. A shot blew out from Skata's rifle, taking the wolf down in the middle of a leap that would have landed it on top of him. The animal collapsed to the ground with a muffled thud. Blood stained gray fur in patterned spots. It had been close enough he could see a burn mark smudging the fur across its chest from the hot explosion of gunpowder.

He rose to his feet and waited, sure it was nothing more than an animal, but thinking it best to make absolutely certain. After a long and silent minute, he placed his gun back in the holster strapped around his thigh.

Just a crazy loner with nothing better to do. Killing an animal he didn't intend to make use of seemed sacrilegious somehow, but there wasn't anything he could do about it.

He kicked it with the toe of his boot, a last check. Definitely dead. He moved around it and resumed walking, placing his steps carefully around the roots that ran along the ground like arthritic fingers.

The weight came out of nowhere and knocked him down. The ground rose up to meet his back, pushing the air from his lungs and leaving him unable to breathe or react for several seconds. It was long enough; he felt pressure around his arm as if someone had it in a vice-grip, and blood spilled, warm and wet and thick across his chest.

There was no pain yet, but the realization that he had been bitten forced him to act. He reached down and withdrew his gun from the holster with no thought except to get the animal off him. He fired, but the first shot went wild. He fired again, and the shot was met with a squeal of pain.

He heard the steps of the animal retreating into the distance, and stillness returned. No sooner had things gone quiet than pain rolled along his body, twisting his mind into the realization that he had been badly injured, was in a forest in the middle of nowhere, and he was going to die if he continued to lay there and do nothing.

Breathe, he told himself. *In and out. You do it all the time.*

He clenched his teeth and pulled himself to his feet. As soon as he was standing on two legs, he took a ginger step. He staggered, dragged his fingers along a tree until they caught on a branch. Bark left splinters along his fingers and in his palm.

A small part of his mind told him the creature might not have been fatally injured, that it might be watching him now from a safe distance, waiting until he was too weak to move. Being eaten alive was not in the top five on his list of ways to go, but if he was unconscious when it happened, it might not be so bad.

"Come on," he urged himself, his voice weak and breathless, but working. At least something was working without causing him pain. "The forest can't last forever. There's got to be a road somewhere."

He pushed forward, not caring if he crashed through the night like a wounded buffalo. Life first, stealth afterward —if only he hadn't lost his phone in the blasted riverbed crossing into this cursed state. If only he'd had the sense to buy a new one for emergencies before he dove back into chasing someone who was probably laughing at him from a four-poster bed in a room with a view.

Irritation flamed inside him and kept him going, for minutes or hours. He wasn't sure, and he didn't care. It was longer than he could keep his eyes open or keep the signals moving from his mind to his body, telling his legs to move, his arms to reach out and stop him from falling.

He felt the collision when he hit the ground, but there was no pain. He was past that. Everything was numb, and the only thing that hurt were his lungs, pumping in spasms between his ribs. His face pressed into the thick, loamy dirt. The earthy, green smell of new leaves and damp ground filled his nostrils, and it felt so good to close his eyes.

It's only for a minute.

Just a quick rest.

Just a quick...

* * * * * *

A rushing sound, from somewhere, like a river under his head—quick footsteps approached, and a voice said, "Whoa, whoa. What happened to you?"

He caught a glimpse of something—a watch around a wrist. Someone had a hand on his shoulder, another on his arm. The ground fell away, and the world tilted.

"Easy," said the voice. "Come on."

A car door slammed.

Blackness.

CHAPTER TWO

Something wasn't right.

The entire feeling surrounding him was one he didn't recognize, and he was alarmed before he opened his eyes. His next emotion was relief when he discovered that he was neither in heaven or hell, but what appeared to be a small living room in someone's home.

The walls were painted the color of dark chocolate and set with several large, white-trimmed windows. The largest was behind the couch where Skata had ended up, and someone had opened it to let in a sluggish breeze. The sky was beginning to lighten, and somewhere, a bird was hailing the arrival of dawn.

He turned his attention away from the window and tried to grasp the details in the room around him, to get a grip on where he was and whose house he was in. The couch was long and too soft for Skata's taste, in contrast with the bare wood floors. A bookshelf stood up against the wall to the left, although half the shelves were taken up with vinyl records in paper sleeves. No pictures hung on the walls, but on the coffee table were large, flat books with titles like *The Best of National Geographic* and *A History of Warships*, as well as a leather-bound Bible with worn edges and a faded gold cross embossed on the cover. A small cactus grew in a pot to the side of the books.

Skata could see the wooden floors continued out into the hall, and there were two places to go—left, down a narrow hall, or straight and then right, into a kitchen. He could see the corner of a counter and cabinet, and a coffeemaker. From the noise, he gathered that the pot was in the process of filling up.

His coat and weapons were nowhere to be seen.

He pushed himself up in preparation to stand, but a series of burning pains across his upper body quickly changed his mind. Looking down, he could see someone had bandaged him with several large gauze patches, and he had started to bleed through half of them. His left arm was also bandaged, wound around with some kind of thick, sticky surgical tape.

Footsteps sounded in the hall, and Skata sat up again, setting his teeth against the pain that told him he was injuring himself. A man stepped around the corner. He was perhaps a few inches shorter than Skata himself and looked as non-threatening as it was possible to look in bare feet, a button-down shirt with the sleeves rolled up, and nape-length hair combed back from a face that could not belong to someone older than twenty-three or twenty-four.

If only appearances were reliable.

The man stepped down into the slightly sunken living room and stopped when he saw Skata watching him.

"Ah…hi." He smiled, but it was a cautious smile, the sort you gave a person when you weren't sure whether they were a friend or a murdering madman preparing to attack. His eyes moved to Skata's bandages and the blood blooming from the center of each one.

For a moment, Skata thought the stranger was going to tell him he should lie down, but after several seconds, he only blinked and said, "I'm Absolon Cassis. You can call me Cassis."

"Sure," said Skata.

Cassis crossed over to the couch and reached around the arm. When his hand reappeared, it held a first aid kit.

"I found you," he said, opening the box and pulling out a bottle of aspirin, a handful of paper squares, and a small tube of antibacterial ointment. It took Skata a second to realize he was talking about him and not the kit. "You were on the side of the road."

"Do you usually stop for roadkill?" Skata asked, wincing as Cassis pulled off one of the bandages and frowned at what he saw underneath.

"Only when I'm hungry," said Cassis lightly. He bit off one end of the paper from a square and tore it away, then put the fresh gauze patch over the gash. "I was full, but you looked pitiful."

"Thanks."

"Which isn't to say you'll stop looking pitiful once your skin's stitched back together," Cassis added, replacing another patch.

Trying to focus on something other than his current pain each time a patch was taken off and replaced, Skata said, "You could've taken me to a hospital."

"Could have, but didn't," said Cassis.

"There a reason for that?"

"I imagine it would have raised a handful of awkward questions, since when it comes to torn-up strangers carrying an arsenal of weapons and no cell phone, it's hard to keep quiet."

Skata grunted. "Thanks, I guess."

"You're welcome, Mr....?"

"No 'mister.' Just Skata."

"First or last?"

"None of your business."

Cassis seemed to be a non-confrontational individual; he only nodded and exited the living room, only to return a moment later with a mug of coffee in each hand.

"I hope you like it black." He held it out, handle first, and Skata took it with grudging acceptance.

"Thanks," said Skata.

Cassis sat on the edge of the coffee table and regarded him in silence, running the edge of his thumb around and around the rim of his mug. Finally he asked—abruptly, like he was afraid he wouldn't get the question out in time—"What are you doing in Salvation?"

"You don't mean to tell me this place is called Salvation," said Skata incredulously.

"It is."

"Funny name for a backwater ditch."

"You haven't even stepped outside," said Cassis, sipping his coffee.

"Don't need to. I've been traveling around this state for near a week now, and I haven't seen much to recommend it. Besides, I haven't got time to play tourist; I'm looking for someone. I've lost too many hours already."

"Does this have to do with the deconstructed Remington and other lethal paraphernalia you were carrying?"

"It might."

"You're avoiding my question. I asked what you were doing in Salvation."

Skata eased back against the cushion. "I wasn't aiming for it, if that's what you're asking."

Cassis got to his feet. He did not seem agitated, exactly, but tension showed in the lines of his body, the way he rested both hands against the belt on his hips so they were neither curled into fists nor loose and useless. "Let me rephrase. What's a vampire hunter doing in Salvation?"

Skata immediately moved to stand up, but suddenly Cassis was shoving him back down with one hand. There was an unnatural strength in the gesture, and Skata groaned.

Come on. "You're a vampire?"

"Not really," said Cassis. He picked up his cup of coffee and took another drink, like this was some sort of get-together between buddies. From his behavior, Skata half-expected to see hot wings on a plate and a football game playing on a television somewhere. "Just a dhampir."

Skata's fingers curled in the air where his shortened Remington 870 should have been. "A half-breed." Dhampirs were a rare kind item; half-human vampires who lived only several hundred years and were vulnerable to human illnesses. They were much weaker than strigoi or moroi, and while they had no need to consume blood, their heightened strength and speed—along with their fangs—made them far more dangerous than the average human.

"Relax," said Cassis, with a friendly smile. "I wouldn't have bothered to fix you up if I was going to kill you."

"What makes you think I won't kill you?"

"In your condition?" Cassis laughed a little, shaking his head. "You're not a threat yet."

"Don't bet anything important on that," said Skata.

The dhampir cocked his head. "I'm not a threat to *you*, hunter."

"That's for me to decide."

"Is it," said Cassis, in a musing voice. Then he asked, "To what Guild do you belong? Venator? Helsing?"

"I don't do Guilds."

"You had a nice array of stakes and poisons for an unsponsored hunter."

Skata frowned at the dhampir's use of past tense. "You better not have thrown them away."

"They weren't mine to throw away," said Cassis, "although you won't need them for a few weeks anyway."

"Why not?"

"You may have noticed," said Cassis dryly, "the bandages currently covering half your body."

"I've been bit by a wolf before," Skata muttered, his mood darkening with every passing second. "Probably won't be the last time."

"I hope not," said Cassis. "Be glad you aren't a vampire, or you'd be dead now with a bite like that."

The bite of a natural wolf couldn't kill a vampire. The bite of a werewolf could.

"Well, that's just peachy," Skata muttered, trying not to rake his fingers across the bandage on his arm. It was already beginning to itch. "I hate to be the one to tell you this, but I think Salvation's infested."

"Lucky for you, it didn't want to finish you off, although you might deserve it. Traveling across a marsh during a full moon."

"I drink wolfsbane. A bite won't turn me. Besides, I didn't exactly figure on South Carolina being werewolf country," Skata retorted. He moved to stand and gave the half-breed a warning look before he said, "I'm standing up. Don't touch me."

Cassis folded his arms as if physically restraining himself. "I'm going to have to change the bandages again at some point."

Skata brushed over the remark. "How long until I'm good to go?"

"Two weeks," said the dhampir. "Minimum."

Skata snorted. "Right. That's not going to happen."

"Of course," said Cassis. "Pardon my thoughtlessness. You have someone you need to kill."

Skata squinted, searching for signs of mockery, but the dhampir wore an impenetrable poker face. "Yeah, that's right."

"You seem very set on this, for someone who isn't in a Guild," said Cassis evenly. "Are you a bounty hunter?"

"Close, but no cigar."

"Revenge, then. Are you hunting down another man for personal reasons?"

Skata stepped closer, his fingers curling into his palms. Through his teeth, he replied, "He's not a *man*, half-breed. He's even less of a man than you are. He's the genuine article, and I'm not going to stop until I've put a stake through his heart."

To his credit, Cassis seemed unruffled. "Well, you can get back to your revenge in two weeks."

"I already said that's not going t—"

"Two weeks."

"You can't keep me here."

"Can't I," was the flat response.

"Listen." Skata lowered his voice, partly to keep from shouting and partly to add to the menace he felt. "I appreciate what you did, but come sunup, I'm gone. *Comprende?*"

"Yes," Cassis said mildly. "If by that you mean sunup two weeks from now." He picked up the mugs, one empty and the other still full of lukewarm liquid. "I'll get you some more coffee."

I need to get my weapons back, thought Skata.

CHAPTER THREE

The house was far too small for two men.

"I've seen dorm rooms bigger than this," said Skata, leaning his good hand against the stained-wood top of the small island.

Cassis opened one of the cabinet doors and pulled out a package of instant oatmeal. "Are you allergic to cranberries?"

"You listening to me?"

"I'll take that as a no, you aren't allergic." Cassis shut the door and bent down to pull out a pot from under the sink. "I hope you're all right with oatmeal. I don't usually shop for anyone but myself."

Skata leaned over the island as far as he could. "Hey. Half-breed."

"Yes?" Cassis sighed and poured the package of oatmeal into the pot.

"I've been here for five hours, and I'm already going stir-crazy."

"I'm sorry for the inconvenience," said Cassis and managed to make it sound like he meant it. "But I don't think I know anyone else who would be willing to take in a stranger who was bitten by a werewolf and may or may not be about to undergo an uncomfortable and potentially dangerous transformation into lycanthropy." He added water to the pot and switched the burner on.

"I already told you, I take wolfsbane in my coffee every morning. There's no way I'm turning."

"Be that as it may," said Cassis pointedly, "try telling that to a stranger."

Skata shifted his jaw, but the dhampir had a point. "Then I'll move into a motel. This is a small town; you have a motel, right?"

"Was that humor?"

"No."

"Could you get the bowls?" asked Cassis, interrupting their conversation to take the pot off the burner and motion at Skata. "They're in the cabinet behind you."

Skata frowned and opened the cabinet. Four bowls were neatly stacked in twos, and he took the left stack out, knocking the doors closed again. "I'm a grown man, dhampir. I've stayed in motels before."

"I'm sure you have, but not when you're planning to walk right out the back door as soon as I turn around," said Cassis. He dished the oatmeal into two bowls and nudged Skata's toward him.

Since screaming like a preschooler would have been counter-productive, Skata frowned and stabbed the proffered spoon into his oatmeal instead. Around a mouthful of the hot cereal, he said, "Then find someone who'll bunk me for a week."

"Two weeks. You look like you might actually start howling."

"That," growled Skata, "has nothing to do with being bitten."

Cassis sighed again. Reluctantly, he said, "I know one or two people I guess I could ask. But not until you finish your breakfast," he added, glancing at Skata's full bowl.

"Seriously?"

"Don't test me."

Skata decided not to make a fight out of it and took a bite. "So who are these folks?"

"Non-human ones."

Skata straightened slowly. "Why?" he demanded.

"Because the only humans who know about *us* here are the mayor, the sheriff, the preacher, and a couple other prominent figures. I can't go putting you with prominent figures. Everyone in town would know about you before tomorrow morning."

Skata grimaced. "I hate small towns."

"I'll find someone," said Cassis positively. "I don't have a guest bedroom, anyway. So why are you hunting this person?"

Skata pointed his finger at the dhampir. "First off, he's not a *person*."

"Vampire?"

"Yeah."

"Strigoi?"

"No." Skata wished aspirin were stronger; the wounds across his torso gnawed incessantly. "He's a moroi. Name's Samuel." Cassis continued to look genuinely interested, so after a brief moment, he continued. "I've been looking for him for a little more than a year now."

Cassis whistled. "Why?"

"None of your business."

"Even guilds don't tend to worry about moroi." Cassis twisted the watch around his left wrist with a methodical absentmindedness that said it was a habit. Turn, pause. Turn, pause. Turn.

Cassis was right—shadowy Guilds took it upon themselves to keep a widespread eye on inhuman activity, and strigoi vampires were seen as more of a threat then the more controlled moroi. Moroi were the highest class of vampire—they could survive without blood, and should a moroi bite a human, there was a fifty-fifty chance of the bite infecting the victim.

When a person was infected, they either became a malkavian—insane, ravenous creatures who usually died after a few weeks—or they became strigoi, the dangerous lesser vampires with an insatiable craving for blood. The more they killed, the more humanity they lost, until they were no better than animals who looked like people.

"Yeah, well," said Skata. "This one's not like most."

"You look upset," said Cassis.

2 5

"Actually, this is my happy face," said Skata.

Cassis paid no attention to the remark. "You should rest. You've been on your feet for almost half an hour."

A sound more groan than chuckle grated from Skata's throat. He rubbed the bridge of his nose with his thumb. "I never was very good at being an invalid."

"Time to improve," said Cassis. "Use my room, it's just down there." He pointed down the hallway leading away from the kitchen. A single door stood at the other end.

The room was larger than the kitchen and considerably more comfortable. Two small windows framed either side of the bed, and on the table next to the bed was a haphazard pile of torn envelopes. Another Bible, this one pocket-sized, leaned against the bedside lamp.

"I'll leave you alone," said Cassis, after he had ushered Skata inside. "And you're too big to get out through the windows, so don't bother."

Skata grunted. "I'm tired after standing on two legs for half an hour. I don't think I'll be planning a prison break for a few days, anyway."

"I'm not a jailer," said Cassis with a faint, amused smile in his wide brown eyes. "I'm just trying to help."

"Yeah, well, thanks," said Skata, in a tone that could be interpreted in a variety of ways.

Cassis closed the door with a faint click, and Skata stood for a moment, listening to the dhampir's retreating footsteps. They faded, and the only sound he was left with was the ticking of the clock on the dresser.

* * * * * *

In his dream, he was jogging up the stairs to the bedroom. "Em, darlin', are you home?"

The Honda was still parked in the driveway, but she might have gone for a walk or maybe out to the pasture for a quick ride. That gave him enough time before they left to shower and change his clothes into something more appropriate for a fancy dinner.

He turned the knob and walked into his room, in the middle of shrugging off his Carhartt jacket, when he paused. "Em?"

His wife sat on the edge of the bed, angled away from him. Her dark hair was tangled in undone waves, hanging over one shoulder and making it impossible to see her face. Her hands were in fists, clenching and unclenching in her lap.

"Em, is everything okay?"

She lifted her head and turned her face toward him, the movement slow and doll-like. Only then did he notice the open window. The chill that shivered through his bones had nothing to do with the winter air.

"Baby, you're home."

* * * * * * *

He sat up with a breath that left his lungs as reality came to life around him. It was just a dream. An obnoxiously frequent dream.

He pushed the blanket away and sat on the edge of the bed.

Stop it. Just stop it.

The windows.

Without thinking, he stood up and slammed the window closed, then strode around the bed and slammed the other window. He pressed a fist to the glass and looked through his reflection to the other side. The street was lit with dimming sunlight as the sky began to darken.

He shuffled out of the room, back into the hallway. Cassis had left his bag somewhere; he just had to find where.

He could hear the dhampir's voice coming from the kitchen, but he slowed down as the words became more intelligible. He came to a full stop before the corner and leaned against the wall to listen.

"He seems like he can take care of himself; he just needs a place to stay...no, he says he's not with a Guild. He told me—I searched his bag. He had a driver's license, but no Guild license. No credit cards, either. Yes—some moroi named Samuel. Really, that's all I know."

There was a long pause before Cassis asked, "You're sure?"

The incredulity in his voice grew. "That's it? All righty then, I'll bring him over in the morning before service. Yes, I'm sure he'll appreciate it, although I can't imagine he'll be more comfortable with you than me, even if your house is bigger." He laughed, then said, "Thanks again," before hanging up.

Skata rounded the corner and walked into the kitchen, scratching the back of his head.

The dhampir turned, sliding his cell into his back pocket. "You must have really needed that sleep."

Skata indicated the phone with his good hand. "Who was that?"

"Someone I know," said Cassis. He blinked, as if remembering that it was partly Skata's business to know as well. "Angel. He has plenty of rooms in his house; he says you can stay with him until you're well enough to travel."

"What kind of a name is Angel?"

"His," said Cassis.

"I hope it's not a reflection of his character," muttered Skata. "'Cause he and I won't be getting along."

"Trust me," said Cassis, "you two getting along will have nothing to do with his name."

Skata grunted before asking the million-dollar question. "All right, lay it on me. What is he?"

Cassis suddenly stretched and picked up the towel. "I'd better get din—"

"He's a vampire," said Skata. It wasn't a question.

Cassis ran a hand through his hair. "Moroi. I don't know him that well, but with the moon being full and the only other moroi refusing, he was better than nothing."

"I doubt that," said Skata.

CHAPTER FOUR

C assis gave him his pack before dinner. It was a large leather kit bag worn with hard use, and it carried Skata's basic necessities: a change of clothes, a flashlight, a journal to keep track of his search, a small photograph of Em, and a few smaller odds and ends. The weapons were gone, but Cassis assured Skata he would have them back the next day.

"I'll take you to your new roommate before church," he told him, handing him a plate of fried chicken and mashed potatoes.

They sat down at the cramped table in the dining room before Cassis said, "If you have questions, now is a good time to ask them."

Skata grunted—this was the first time he'd enjoyed a home-cooked meal in nearly a year. He was reluctant to interrupt it by talking, but after taking another bite he said, "Fine, then. Tell me about Salvation."

"You seem to need it."

Skata gave him a flat look before going on. "If I'm going to be stuck here for a week—"

"Two weeks," said Cassis.

"—then I need to know what kind of place it is," Skata finished.

"You could come to church with me in the morning and find out."

"Thanks, but I don't do church."

"You could still come."

"I'll skip it."

"Anyone is welcome," Cassis began.

"They can be welcome to stay away from me," interrupted Skata. "Just tell me about the rest of it. Who knows about vampires and stuff?"

Cassis wrinkled his nose at being called 'stuff' but held up a hand and counted down on his fingers. "The mayor and his wife. The sheriff, the sheriff's daughter, most of the deputies. The preacher. Plus the council."

"Who's on the council?"

"The old families."

"Old as in walkers and hearing aids, or old as in 'been around here a long time'?"

"Descendants of the families who founded Salvation back in the eighteen hundreds. Most of them aren't friendly toward anyone who doesn't classify as a *homo sapien*, but it's all right."

"Mm. How many inhumans live around here?"

Cassis made an *uh-uh* sound in his throat. "Not yet. Angel and I are putting our necks on the block for you, but no other inhuman has any obligation to do the same thing."

Skata thought for a minute before shrugging. "Fair enough."

* * * * * * *

The next morning, Skata was awoken by the sound of a female voice calling, "I ever have to do something like this again, you're going to owe me a seriously large favor."

Skata pulled a spare shirt out of his bag and tugged it on over his head, working it carefully around the bandages on his arm and torso before leaving the room.

There were only four rooms in the house as far as he knew—the bedroom, the bathroom, the kitchen, and the living room—so it was easy to tell the voice was coming from the latter. He stopped before actually stepping all the way into the living room, because a girl stood by the coffee table. Her arms were folded, and her eyebrows arched as she noticed him.

His weapons and his coat were on the coffee table. "These are yours, right?" she asked, pointing at them.

Before Skata could answer, the door to the bathroom opened and Cassis hurried out. His hair was still damp, dripping onto his forehead, but he was clearly dressed for church in slacks and a button-down shirt, with the sleeves rolled all the way down this time.

"Oh, hi, Shannon," he said, as if people turning up in his living room were a common occurrence. "Did you meet Skata?"

She snorted. "If by meet him, he just stood there, yeah. Look, my dad caught me sneaking these out of the trunk, and he thought I was hopping off to join a Guild somewhere, so if he asks, just explain, right? He thought I was skipping college and everything. They're his, right?" She jerked her chin toward Skata.

"They're mine," said Skata, raising his good hand. "Hi."

"They're his," Cassis affirmed, and touched Shannon's shoulder in a conciliatory way. "Sorry about the trouble."

Her annoyed expression faded slightly. "You, sir, would be lost without me. Also, we're going to be late for church if we don't get a move on."

"Oh, right—Skata, this is Shannon, the sheriff's daughter. Shannon, this is Skata, the stranger in town."

"Hi," said Shannon offhandedly. "Come on, Cas. I left Maylee in the car."

Cassis nodded and moved past Skata with a brief, "Get your stuff."

They filed out of the house a minute later, Skata with his pack, coat, and weapons. They climbed into the old Lexus, and as Shannon settled into the driver's seat, she said, "Cassis, can you sit next to Maylee? No offense," she added, this time directing her words toward Skata, "but you know. Random guys with guns and all."

"No problem," he said, settling into the passenger seat. The thought of Maylee being this teenager's daughter hadn't crossed his mind—the little girl in the back seat was maybe two or three, and Skata felt suddenly awkward and cramped with the three strangers in a small space.

He glanced back at Maylee, who waved at him. Skata cleared his throat uncomfortably and faced the windshield.

"Not a kid person?" Shannon asked, pulling out of the driveway. "She seems to like you. She doesn't wave at just anyone, you know."

"I thought everyone in the South waved at everyone else," Skata grunted.

Shannon rolled her eyes. Suburban homes flashed by, growing larger and more varied the farther into town they drove. "She's thirty months old. She can't hurt you. Go on, May. Say hi to Skata."

From the back, Maylee's whisper-soft voice said, "Skafa!"

"She wants you to tell her hello," said Shannon. She glanced in the rearview mirror and smiled at her daughter. "You should be thrilled. She doesn't talk much."

"Why's that?" asked Skata, not so much out of curiosity as to keep from having to interact with the kid.

"She just doesn't."

He grunted again.

"So say hello."

"Fine," snapped Skata. It was only to keep the dhampir and Shannon from harping on him the whole drive that he turned and nodded at Maylee. "Howdy."

She grinned to show two rows of perfectly small, white baby teeth without a single empty gap. *No, losing teeth wouldn't be for a few years,* Skata remembered. He hadn't dealt with kids since he babysat one of them a decade ago.

Shannon smiled. "That wasn't so hard, was it?"

Skata cleared his throat and looked back out the window. They drove for a few more minutes, and the only sound was Cassis playing quietly with Maylee in the back seat. The car turned left and drove down a long gravel driveway that ended in front of an impressive 1920's Tudor.

"He has money," said Cassis after several seconds of silence had passed. "Come on."

Skata and Cassis climbed out of the car while Shannon called, "Hurry up, guys," as they walked up to the front door. It was an impressive oak affair with a wrought-iron doorknocker, which Cassis bypassed in favor of the doorbell.

"This is a bad idea," said Skata.

Cassis didn't have time to argue. The door swung open, and Angel, who could easily have passed for a bad-boy of thirty or thirty-five, leaned against the doorframe.

"Angel, this is Skata."

"Skata what?" asked Angel.

"Angel what?" Skata retorted.

"Touché." Angel's eyes were the pale blue of an Alaskan sled dog, designed specifically to strike fear into the hearts of enemies and love into the hearts of unsuspecting females. He sounded so friendly when he held out a hand and said, "How's it going? It is an absolute *pleasure* to meet you," that Skata knew he was putting on a show for Cassis's benefit.

Skata reluctantly shook the vampire's hand. It was cooler than a human hand, but the grip was strong. A little too strong for a purely friendly greeting. For a brief moment, all they did was look, unblinking, into each other's eyes, and Skata could tell Angel was forming a quick impression of him.

Two can play that game.

"Well! Cassis." Angel clamped his hand down on the half-breed's shoulder. "Thanks for bringing him over. Aren't you going to be late for church?" he added, with a look of intense concern.

Sarcastic and cocky, doesn't much care if people see past it.

"Yes…listen, if there are any problems…" Cassis looked from Angel to Skata.

"Now don't you worry," said Angel warmly, patting Cassis on the back. "You skedaddle! It's not polite to leave a lady waiting."

"Just——" Cassis stopped himself and sighed. "Have fun."

"Oh, we *will*," Angel confirmed with a wide smile and eyes narrowed just a little too much.

I can't believe this guy. How does anybody believe a word he says?

With another worried glance at the two of them, Cassis left the vampire and the vampire hunter standing on either side of the threshold. Angel opened the door wider and swept his arm in a wide welcoming gesture. "Right this way."

Skata rested his hand on the butt of his gun as he stepped inside. The ceiling rose at least twenty feet, and a curving staircase led from the far side of the foyer up to the second floor.

"Okay, listen up," said Angel, shutting the door. "Obviously since this is my house, you abide by my rules."

Skata narrowed his eyes but asked, "What rules?"

"Don't make a mess."

Skata waited for more, but no more came. "That's it?"

"Don't make a mess…and—oh!" Angel snapped his fingers. "I hope you're not allergic to cats."

CHAPTER FIVE

Skata followed Angel up the stairs. "Big place."

The vampire grinned over his shoulder. "Thank you; it's been in the family for generations."

"Vampires don't do generations."

"I didn't say it was my family. Don't jump to conclusions, now."

Angel pushed open a door and waved Skata into a room that seemed bigger than Cassis's entire house. A large window led out onto the roof and then down. It was strangely clean for a room in a bachelor's house. "Here you go, home sweet home. Feel free to look in all the medicine cabinets and whatever, but don't make a mess."

"You said that already," said Skata, setting his pack down on the bed and draping the coat over it.

Angel frowned at the weapons. "That's because I meant it."

Skata thought about replying, but Angel had exited the room and shut the door before he could. Skata shrugged and stepped into the walk-in closet and the enormous bathroom, both of which were empty. He shoved his pack into the top drawer of the large chest of drawers and went back downstairs.

Angel was nowhere to be seen, which was fine with Skata. He would rather explore without someone watching over his shoulder. The kitchen sported a red Kitchen Aid, a double oven, and an island large enough to put a mortgage on.

Something hissed behind him, and he jumped, spinning with his right hand in a ready fist. A cat looked up at him, tail swishing like a fluffy gray banner in a low breeze. It hissed again, ears flattening in obvious dislike.

Skata glared. "Scram."

The cat yawned and stretched, tail still twitching. Skata sneezed, and this time it was the cat's turn to give him a startled stare.

"Now, now, Morticia." Angel sauntered into the kitchen. "Don't scare the new guy. He's a guest."

"Morticia?" Skata looked over at the vampire. "Really?"

"Like you can talk," said Angel, giving Skata a once-over. "What kind of name is Skata?"

"It's better than the stripper name you go by," Skata retorted.

Angel pushed his lower lip out and tilted his head to the side in a look of agreement.

Skata glanced down at Morticia, who had crossed the kitchen and was sitting next to Angel's foot. The moroi grabbed a handful of fur and picked her up, settling her in the crook of his arm. "Was he mean to you? It's okay. Not everyone knows how to treat a girl right." He stroked his finger down her forehead to the tip of her nose.

"Explains why all you can get is a cat," said Skata.

The vampire looked up at him. "Cute. But since I'm in such a good mood, I'll get you some Zyrtec next time I stop by the drug store."

"Thanks," said Skata, "but no thanks." He was already beginning to feel like he needed to sit down before he got lightheaded.

"Too late, already made up my mind." Angel put the cat down and crossed over to the sink. He turned the hot water on, pumped two pumps of soap into his palm, and proceeded to scrub his hands like he had just been handling toxic waste. "I need to go out later anyway." He turned the water off and dried his hands with a towel. "You should come with."

Skata twisted his mouth. "Why would I want to do that?"

"Oh, I don't know." Angel tossed the towel over his shoulder and the corner of his mouth lifted in a wide half-smile. "There might be something interesting in it for *you*, though."

Skata folded his arms, ignoring the sting of the werewolf bite under the bandage. "And what's that?" he asked, making sure the vampire knew he was humoring him.

"Are you coming or not?"

"Not until you tell me why I should."

"It's a drive into town, not a six-hundred-mile road trip."

"Nope."

The vampire sighed. "Well, Mister Control Freak," he said, putting emphasis on the *k*, "I just might happen to know someone with dirt on a certain vampire."

Skata unfolded his arms. "Samuel?"

Angel pointed at him. "That's the one."

Cassis had mentioned Samuel to Angel over the phone, but Skata couldn't imagine why the vampire would offer to help without an incentive. "What's in it for you?"

Angel managed to squint with only one side of his face, making him look doubly incredulous. "Oh, it's on the way, and I'm trying to be a good host. It's a new experience for me."

"Yeah, right," Skata scoffed.

"Offer's open for…" Angel glanced down at an imaginary watch on his left wrist. "Thirty seconds. Going once…going twice…"

"All right," said Skata. "I'm sick of house arrest already."

"Oh, go easy on yourself." Angel patted Skata's shoulder as he walked past. "It's not *every* day the magnificent hunter gets bitten by the big, bad werewolf. You should lie down. I'm sure the wear on your ego must be *exhausting*."

****

Two hours later, in spite of his better judgment, Skata was seated in the passenger seat of a red Oldsmobile Starfire. He glanced up at the afternoon sun before putting his sunglasses on.

The vampire was tapping his fingers on the steering wheel in time to AC/DC's "Highway to Hell" blaring from the radio.

"I miss the good old days, when I thought all vampires burned in the sun," said Skata under his breath.

"I heard that," said Angel. "But as a moroi, I bear the nice distinction of surviving sunlight."

"Too bad," said Skata.

Angel grinned and turned a corner so sharply that Skata had to grip the sides of his seat to keep from slamming into the door. "Honestly, I miss the days when people thought vampires slept in coffins and turned into bats. Now *that* was fun."

Skata let out a sigh of relief when they stopped at a red light in the middle of the town square. Green, carefully tended trees shaded either side of the street, and the brick buildings lining the sidewalks were like something out of an updated Mayberry reproduction.

"My driving bother you?"

Skata leaned back and attempted to look more relaxed. "Just remember that your passenger isn't immortal."

"There you go, making me all nostalgic for humanity. Oh, oh— nope, there it goes."

He sped forward as the light turned green, and Skata

clenched his teeth, hoping a deputy would show up and arrest the vampire for speeding.

"You don't miss being human at all, huh?" he asked, trying to keep his mind off the vampire's ridiculous driving.

"Pros of being a vampire," said Angel. "Super speed, super strength, the ability to compel people to do whatever I want, and— oh! Not dying. Pros of being a human? Eh...."

"Not wanting to eat other people?" Skata suggested.

Angel held up a finger. "Cannibals, my friend."

"I like them better."

"I didn't know there was a cannibal problem in...wherever you're from."

"Montana."

"Ahhh," said Angel, as if that explained everything.

They finally parked next to a wide alley. Angel turned the engine off and climbed out of the car, running his fingers through his hair.

Skata slammed his door. "What is this place?"

Without answering, the vampire walked down the alley, leaving Skata no choice but to follow. They came out on the other side of the street and saw velvet ropes lining the empty walk up to the front door. The neon sign hanging above them said, *The Diamond Straight Bar & Lounge.*

"You brought me to a bar?"

"A special bar. Be excited, I never come here." Angel ducked under the rope and motioned for Skata to follow him. He did, but they were stopped by the bouncer standing outside the door. He was a massive specimen, his muscles filling every inch of what Skata was positive was an XXL tee shirt.

"We're not open until eight," he growled.

Skata lifted his eyebrows and looked at Angel, who smiled, unperturbed.

Angel's bicuspids lengthened into fangs, and the blood vessels around his eyes turned a dark red, entering his eyes until they were horribly bloodshot. The vampire's true appearance faded as soon as it had appeared. "See? Vampire. Rukiel called me."

The bouncer scowled, but Angel seemed to have uttered the right words, because he said, "Fine" and stepped aside. "No trouble."

"Never." Angel waved his hand at Skata. "Come on."

Skata followed him inside. It looked nothing like the outside suggested. It was all polished wood and diamond patterns. The unmistakable smell of cigar smoke hung in the air.

"This way." Angel led Skata over to the bar and straddled one of the stools. Skata sat down on the stool next to him and leaned against the counter, every nerve in his body on end in spite of the fact the place was empty. He leaned toward Angel and lowered his voice. "Cassis didn't mention the bouncer or this Rukiel person."

"This particular establishment is very inhuman-friendly," said Angel, by way of explanation. "But Rukiel prefers to keep himself set apart from the usual riffraff like the council."

"Well, if it isn't my favorite vampire—and coming to me for once!" A beautiful, dark-skinned woman in her forties strode behind the bar, smiling widely.

Angel rose off the stool and met the woman's enthusiastic kiss across the counter.

"You are just as glorious as ever," said Angel, sitting back down and leaning his chin on his hand.

"Aw, thanks, beautiful." The woman turned to Skata and held out her hand. "I'm Zoe, the best bartender this side of the Bible Belt. Are you a friend of Angel's?"

"No," said Skata.

"Glad to hear it," said Zoe seriously. In a loud whisper, she added, "I'd stay away from him if I were you. He's no good."

"Slander," Angel protested lazily. "Lies."

"You know you love it," she said, reaching across the bar and running her fingers through his black hair. "Mmm-mmh. You're still just as fine as the day I met you."

"And you're twice as delicious."

"Stop trying to make me blush," Zoe scolded, but her eyes were full of warm affection when she looked at him, and from the way Angel brushed his thumb over her knuckles, they knew each other fairly well. "So tell me, what are two such beautiful men doing here at this time of day?"

Skata had been called a lot of things, but 'beautiful' was a new one. He turned his attention to Angel, who folded his fingers together and said, "I told the bouncer that Rukiel wanted to see me."

"Let me guess," said Zoe. "It was the other way around?"

"I think yes," said a new voice, congenial and as sharp-edged as a razor. "Tell me, Angel, what makes you think you're welcome in my place?"

CHAPTER SIX

It was obvious from the orange glow of his eyes that the speaker was inhuman. Not a werewolf, but Skata guessed some other kind of shapeshifter.

"Rukiel!" Angel hopped off the stool and held out his hand.

The shifter angled his head upward to give the vampire a smile, but his hands remained resting on his diamond-tipped swagger cane. "You brought a human into my lounge. Why?"

"Oh, don't worry." Angel slung an arm around Skata's shoulder. "He's house-trained."

Skata shrugged Angel off as Rukiel turned to give Skata his full attention. He was a strange creature to look at. Darkness shadowed the corners of his eyes underneath sharp eyebrows, and his lips were a slick, bloody red. His suit was a plunging v-neck affair with a patterned jacket and trousers, low-heeled leather shoes, and gold rings decorating every finger.

It made him seem over-the-top, and Skata knew from

experience that people who went out of their way to exaggerate themselves were either insecure or dangerous.

"You must be Skata," said Rukiel. "I've heard so much about you. Small towns," he added at the look of surprise on Skata's face. "What are you doing here?"

Skata glanced around. "Is there somewhere private we could talk?"

"Ouch," said Angel, looking sideways at Skata. "Remind me to schedule some trust exercises."

"Follow me," said Rukiel, walking away.

Skata followed him through a beaded curtain that separated the bar from the lounge.

The room was dark, lit only by the red glow cast by a few small, ornate lights hanging from the ceiling. They crossed the lounge and entered another room off to the side. It was smaller than the lounge, but gave a grandiose impression. A desk and two leather chairs sat in front of a large, cold fireplace. Bookshelves lined the walls, except for the space reserved for an enormous map of Salvation.

Rukiel sat down in the larger chair and motioned to the one opposite. "Sit down." Skata sat. "What is it you want to know?"

For someone who couldn't be over five and a half feet and looked as delicate as a collector's item, Rukiel should have been dwarfed by the chair he sat in. Instead, it became a throne and he the king, completely confident and in control.

Skata twisted around to look again at the map on the wall.

"What are you, some kind of small-town security?"

Rukiel grinned. "You could call me that. Really, all I do is trade. And run the *Straight* in my spare time."

"What do you trade?'

"Again, I ask—what is it you want to know?"

Skata shifted uncomfortably in the chair. "Ever heard of Samuel Lemeck?"

"Yes," said Rukiel and waited for Skata to continue.

"Do you know where he is?"

Rukiel leaned back and tapped his chin with two fingers. "Why?"

"Because."

"You don't know much about trading, do you?" Rukiel asked, tilting his head.

"Not really."

Rukiel laughed. "Well, here's how it works. If you want me to give you something, you have to give me something in return. Otherwise you've gained, and I've not made a profit."

"Yeah, well, I'm a stranger in town. I don't have anything you'd want."

"I think you soon will." Rukiel smiled faintly. "Do you know the Montgomery brothers?"

"No," said Skata. "I'm only interested in Samuel."

"You should be interested in the brothers." Rukiel crossed his legs and leaned back. "They're the most powerful family in

Salvation. The younger brother, Jackson, has recently stolen something from me."

So Rukiel was powerful, but not exactly omnipotent. "What was it?"

"A stake."

"So carve up a table leg," said Skata, shrugging. "Run to Home Depot. Find a big toothpick."

"Do you want to know where Samuel is or not?"

Now Skata had a choice. He could walk out now and search for Samuel himself once his wounds were healed, or he could go along with Rukiel's proposition—which apparently involved re-theft. "How am I supposed to get the stake from this guy?"

"Not my problem."

"Helpful."

"I will be helpful once you get me the stake," said Rukiel calmly, smoothing his thumb over the top of his cane.

"I don't think you know how to trade, either."

That elicited a laugh. "Do we have a deal?"

"Do I have a choice?"

Rukiel rose from his chair with a crooked smile. "I'm the only one who can help you. That being said, I'm being polite by giving you an option. I could always get someone else to retrieve the stake for me."

"Then why don't you?"

Rukiel grinned in a nasty way. "This way I don't need to hire anyone." His teeth were pointed and very, very white. "So we have a deal, yes?"

Skata stood and grudgingly held out his hand. "Looks like."

The shifter clasped his hand briefly. "As soon as I have my stake back, you will have your information. You have my word."

"Right," said Skata. "What does the stake look like?"

"It's red and pointed at one end," said Rukiel and ushered Skata out of the office before shutting the door behind him.

Skata made his way back to the bar, where he finally released a deep breath. Angel was spinning a shot glass, but he looked up as Skata leaned against the counter.

"How'd you do with the Godfather?" asked Angel.

Skata sat down one stool away from the vampire. "Whiskey," he said to Zoe.

"Sure thing." Zoe set a bottle half-full of alcohol in front of him and walked away, leaving them alone to talk.

Angel lifted an eyebrow as he eyed the bottle. "Not great, huh?"

"I did well enough." Skata lifted the bottle to his lips and took a long swallow that left his throat burning and his mind clear. "Hey, do you know the Montgomery brothers?"

Angel lifted his shot glass and peered through it. "Sure do," he said, with false cheer.

"How well?"

"We have special moments where one of us shows up and the other one leaves."

"They're good judges of character, then," said Skata, taking another dose of whiskey.

"Let's just say we're not about to go on a camping trip and sing Kumbaya together."

Skata set the bottle down and stood up.

"Are we leaving?" Angel asked.

"Yep."

They left through the front door. Angel gave the bouncer a broad smile before they went around the corner and down the alley. "Congratulations," said Angel, nudging Skata with his elbow. "I think you're the first human to step foot in that place."

"What's Zoe?"

"A Tinker." Angel tossed his head back and squinted at the waning moon. "Makes plants grow greener, makes drinks taste better. Things like that. Personally, I always thought she'd do best in a big city, but hey. Live and let live, I say." He pulled the keys from his pocket and unlocked the car. "What makes you so curious about the Montgomery brothers, anyway?"

Skata climbed into the passenger side and slammed the door. "Because apparently the younger brother took some kind of special stake from Rukiel, and Rukiel wants me to get it back before he'll tell me where Samuel is." He did nothing to hide his irritation at Rukiel.

"Ohh." Angel winced. "Fun."

"Yeah," said Skata. "Fun."

"You know what you need? A chill pill. No—a bottle of chill

pills. A lifetime supply." It was quieter now, with only a few people still outside. Most would probably be eating dinner about now. "I don't usually say things like this, but you are *way* too uptight."

"I'm always like this."

"Euch. Sounds exhausting."

"Don't worry about it."

They passed a home with the curtains parted, the family visible around the dining room table, and Skata realized he hadn't eaten anything since breakfast. "I need some food."

"I'm way ahead of you, brother."

They turned into a parking lot outside a low retro building with neon sign that said *8Track's Diner.*

"Let me guess," said Skata. "Fifties?"

"Sixties." Angel climbed out of the car and stretched his arms. "Not my favorite decade," he added, with a dark look that flickered across his face and was gone.

Skata removed his sunglasses from his head and hung them on the neck of his shirt. "Does it bother you to know that you're actually an old man?"

Angel drew his eyebrows together and curled his lip. "I stopped aging at thirty-four. How old are you?"

"Thirty-two."

"Oooh, you're going to pass me up soon. Then we'll see who's laughing."

He pulled open the door, and they stepped into a rush of cool, conditioned air. Everything from the booths to the silver stools to the jukebox was designed to look like it had been lifted from the sixties.

They sat down at a booth near the window, the red leather seats just squeaky enough to be annoying. Angel picked up a menu from behind the napkin dispenser and flipped it open. "I hope you like milkshakes and fries."

Skata opened the second menu and searched for something with meat. He settled on a plate of ribs, which didn't seem very sixties. From the jukebox, the Lovin' Spoonful was asking if he believed in magic.

Across the table, Angel moved his lips, mouthing the lyrics. He caught Skata giving him a death glare and sang louder, only barely carrying the tune. "If the music is groovy and makes you feel happy like an old-time mov—"

Skata kicked his shin as hard as he could under the table.

"Ow," said Angel. "Why would you do that?"

"You sound like a goat."

Angel quietly groaned and massaged his leg under the table, even though it had been like kicking a brick wall and Skata knew the vampire wasn't hurt at all.

A waitress walked up to the end of the table, wearing a pink-and-white checkered apron. "Good evening! My name is Easton, and I'll be your…Leslie?"

Skata lifted his head, shocked. "Easton?"

He stood up, and the girl fairly jumped into his arms. "Leslie! Oh my gosh, what are you doing here?"

Angel leaned on his elbow and watched, his eyebrows rising. "'Leslie?'"

"Call me that again, and I'll kill you," said Skata through his grin.

Angel waved a hand and smiled like the threat was a fly he could easily swat away. "Who's the girl?"

"Easton," said Skata, too surprised at the turn of events to be totally coherent. "She's, uh…"

"Easton Everett." The waitress was an attractive girl of twenty-one or twenty-two, with waist-length brown hair and wide hazel eyes. "I know him. Well, knew him. It was a really long time ago." Her face was bright when she looked at Skata before she asked Angel, "I'm so sorry—who are you?"

"Angel." He took her proffered hand, but instead of shaking it, he pressed his lips to her knuckles. "It is a *pleasure* to meet you."

Skata glared at the vampire over Easton's head and mouthed *off limits.* Angel put a hand to his ear, miming deafness.

Confusion entered Easton's smile as she looked back and forth between them. "Is something wrong?"

"Not a thing," said Skata, grinding the words out through his teeth. "Just happy to see you."

"What are you *doing* here?" she demanded.

"Just passing through."

"I'd still like to know just how you two know each other," said Angel.

Easton squeezed Skata's arm. "This guy used to babysit me when I was a kid."

"Way to go, Super Nanny," said the vampire with an overdose of astonished pride. "I'm impressed!" He eyed Easton, and his smile took a suggestive turn. "I might take up babysitting myself."

Skata nudged Easton's shoulder. "Can I have a second?"

She nodded, her face like someone coming out of a dream into the real world. "Yeah, yeah! I'll go get your order. What *did* you order?"

Angel lifted a hand. "I'll take the Greased Lightning."

Her hand lingered on her notepad, but she did not write anything down. "What flavor milkshake?"

"Strawberry," he said, and to Skata's amazement, managed to make the word sound like an innuendo.

"Got it." She gave him a lingering glance that could either have been curious or bewildered. "Leslie? What did you get?"

"Ribs," he said. "And water."

She nodded and flashed him another smile. "Okay! I'll be right back with your orders." She hurried across the near-empty diner and disappeared through the kitchen door.

Skata immediately leaned down across the table and put a fist in front of Angel's face. "Don't even think about it."

Angel fixed his gaze on Skata's fist. "Don't think about what?"

"Anything," Skata growled. "She's like a sister to me."

"A sister you haven't seen since you were *babysitting* her."

"I mean it."

"Relax." Angel leaned comfortably between the window and the booth. "I'll be very good to her. I promise."

Skata risked a quick glance around the diner. The only other people there were at the other end, engrossed in a conversation over an onion basket. He grabbed the back of Angel's neck and slammed his face into the table.

CHAPTER SEVEN

When Easton came back with their drinks and plates of food on a plastic tray, Skata was sitting with his hands folded on the table and Angel's smile was a little too wide.

Easton set their meals down. "There you go," she said and turned to Skata. "I get off work in half an hour. You can stay, right?"

"'Course," said Skata, with a grin he couldn't help.

"Awesome!" She gave them both a bright smile and walked away to another table.

Angel watched her with a dreamy smile. "She's so…perky."

"Do you *want* a stake in your heart?"

Angel subconsciously brushed the bridge of his recently punched nose with a thumb and straightened. "How exactly did you end up babysitting her?"

"Her family went to the same church I did," said Skata, watching Easton speak to other customers. He had always known she would grow up well, and she hadn't disappointed him. It was surreal, seeing her all grown up.

"Wow," said Angel, dipping a French fry in ketchup and biting off the end. "You went to church."

"It was a long time ago." Skata took a drink of his water. "I must have been about sixteen, and she was six or seven. I watched her for a few years and then the family moved away, and that was that."

"Well, you two seem to have really hit it off."

"She's like my sister."

"Yeah." Angel pointed to his nose. "I got the memo."

They ate their meal in practical silence until Skata said, "So, the Montgomery brothers." Angel glanced up at him and took a long, noisy slurp of his milkshake. "I need to meet them."

"So ring their doorbell. Pretend you're the…" He waved a hand around in the air. "Pizza delivery guy."

"Thanks."

"I don't know about you," said Angel, leaning forward, "but if I want to meet someone, I either walk up and introduce myself, or I compel them to throw me a party." He smiled and paused for a second before adding, "Or both."

Skata shook his head. "You may have noticed, I'm not you."

"Oh, I noticed." Angel shrugged. "I'm *much* more fun to be around."

"Could you *be* any more unhelpful?" Skata asked, ready to

take Easton and the car and make the vampire walk back to the house.

"On a scale of one to ten, I'd say I'm at a five right now. But," he held up a finger, "I think I know how I can help you out."

Skata leaned back, incredulous. "Really."

Angel took another long sip of his milkshake. "Ask me nicely."

Skata blinked and looked around the restaurant. "You're kidding."

The vampire's eyebrows rose. "I am not."

"No," said Skata.

Angel sighed loudly. "Fine, then. I'll make it easy for you. Say please."

Grinding the word through his back teeth, Skata replied, "Please."

"Hmm," said Angel, as if judging Skata's sincerity. "You said you need Jackson, right?"

"I need something Jackson took from Rukiel."

"Right. Whatever. I'll throw a bash so big Jackson couldn't refuse even if he wanted to. It's a perfect opportunity for you two to hit it off."

"I don't want to 'hit it off,'" said Skata. "I just want to steal what he stole from Rukiel."

"So meet him, say hi, and then am-scray to his house," said Angel, with a squinty smile that said he thought Skata was being very obtuse about the whole plan. "Get your doodad and get out while he's away from home."

"What about the other brother?"

"Gideon? It's a big house." Angel shrugged. "Take a stake and try not to get killed."

"Why do I get the feeling this is just something you cooked up to get rid of me without getting in trouble with Cassis?"

"I would never. I like Cassis."

"I'm surprised, given the fact he isn't evil."

"I'm not *evil*." Angel took another fry. "I'm…ethically unfettered."

The idea of breaking into someone's house and hunting for a stolen object was in no way appealing, but doing it while one of them was away would make it easier. "How old are they?"

"Who?"

"The Montgomery brothers."

Angel pushed his empty milkshake cup away. "I don't know. I'm pretty sure they have some medals from the War of 1812, though."

Skata slammed his glass of water down. "They're vampires, too?"

Angel looked genuinely startled. "Moroi. You didn't—wait, Rukiel didn't *tell* you?"

"He sure did not," Skata snapped, his dislike for the lounge owner rising rapidly.

"Jeepers," said Angel, winking. "This'll be fun."

"Man, vampires that old can compel *other vampires,* and I'm supposed to just waltz into their nest and steal from them?"

Angel studied Skata's expression. "I wouldn't worry too much," he said, patting the air over Skata's hand. "You're *lousy* with vervain, so he can't bite you without getting a mouthful and he probably can't compel you. And they're not *that* old in the grand scheme of things." He paused for dramatic effect and added, "Maybe you'd better take some in a spray bottle, just in case."

"I'm done!" Easton appeared and sat down next to Skata. "You two eat fast." She looked at Angel's basket of French fries before taking one.

"Help yourself," he said.

Skata asked, "Don't you get tired of those things, working here all the time?"

She stopped mid-chew and rolled her eyes at him. "They're *fries.* You don't just 'get tired' of them."

"Point taken."

"Hey, where are you staying?" she asked, taking another fry.

Skata let out a slow breath. "I'm…"

"With me," said Angel, helpfully adding, "he's boarding at my place."

"You two must be pretty good friends, then," said Easton.

"I'm working on matching friendship bracelets," said Angel.

"You live in that mansion just outside of town, right?" she asked him, ignoring the sarcasm. "The Tudor?"

"Bingo. Hey, you should come over!" Angel clasped his

hands together, as if the idea had just struck him. "Take a look around; spend some more time with your big bro here."

"I don't think that's a good—" Skata began.

Angel interrupted. "Why, of *course* it's a good idea."

"I'd love to! I've always adored that house," she admitted. "And now that Leslie's staying there, I like it even more."

"What about me?" asked Angel, widening his eyes.

She leaned against Skata's arm and said, "I'll have to wait and see. Do you mind if we stop by my house first?" she added, looking down at her waitressing outfit. "I need to change."

****

"You didn't tell me her last name was Cleaver," said Angel as they pulled into the driveway of Easton's quiet suburban home.

"Everett," said Easton, climbing out of the back seat. "You can both come inside; you don't need to wait out here. I'll be a few minutes."

Skata and Angel followed. The house was painted white with dark trim, and several trees along the front and side yards clung to the last of their summer green. The porch light was on, attracting moths that fluttered against the glass.

Easton fished a key from her purse and opened the door, calling, "Graham, get down here!"

Skata followed her into the foyer but turned around at a grunt from Angel.

The vampire looked like a mime pretending to be trapped behind an invisible wall of glass. "Something wrong?" asked Skata, knowing very well that Angel could not get inside unless someone who lived there specifically invited him. Easton's 'you can come inside' had been too general for the vampire.

Angel's mouth curled as his blue eyes narrowed. "Let's be adults about this."

Easton hung her purse around the banister and looked back at Angel. "Aren't you coming in?"

"He's waiting outside," said Skata.

"Don't be rude," said Easton. "Come on in, I don't bite."

"That's *such* a relief," said Angel, stepping over the threshold. He gave Skata a cheeky grin, and Skata's stomach twisted. Easton had no idea that the vampire could now enter her house any time he wanted, and the thought was enough to make him sick.

"Where is Graham?" Easton muttered, crossing over to the staircase. "Gra—there you are."

A teenager shuffled out of the kitchen with an earbud in one ear, the other hanging over his shoulder. "What do you want? Who are these guys?"

"You remember Leslie, right? He used to babysit us back in Montana? You were only a toddler, though, so…"

"Nah, I remember him." Graham pulled his other earbud out and shook Skata's hand. "Cool to see you again, man."

"You got older," said Skata, blinking. The kid was nearly as tall as him.

Graham blinked sleepy eyes and said, "Yeah, that's what happens."

"I'll be right back," said Easton, jogging up the stairs and out of sight.

Skata folded his arms and watched Angel, who was eyeing the potted tree growing in the corner by the door. To Graham, he said, "So you must be what, sixteen now?"

"Seventeen." Graham leaned against the banister. "So what are you doing here, anyway?"

"Passing through," said Skata.

"Is this thing real?" asked Angel.

Graham peered around Skata and saw Angel still squinting at the tree. "Yeah, that's real. Mom loves it."

"Plants grow outdoors for a reason, if you ask me," said Angel. "Your mom has sucky taste in decorating."

Graham's sleepy expression was broken by his sudden grin. "What was your name again?"

"Gandhi," said Angel.

"Angel," said Skata.

"Who?" said Graham.

Easton came down the stairs in skinny jeans and a long sweater, her hair unpinned from its voluminous pompadour. "I'm ready; sorry about that." She unhooked her purse from around the bannister and looked at Graham. "You've had dinner, right?"

"Yeah, leftovers," he said. "I'm good."

"Okay, Mom and Dad should be back from their date sometime before ten."

"Easton," said Graham. "I'm seventeen. I can take care of myself."

For a moment, she looked as if she would say something more but changed her mind. "Right. I'll be back in an hour or two, okay?" She briefly rubbed the side of his head, in spite of the fact he was at least six inches taller. "Love you."

He lifted one hand, his gaze already on the phone in his other one. "Yeah, sure, whatever."

****

"Wow, this place really is gorgeous." Easton's enthusiasm fairly echoed in the cavernous foyer as soon as they entered Angel's home. "You actually live here?"

"Yep, just me and the bats," said Angel, closing the heavy front door. He grinned at his own joke and shrugged at the look Skata gave him.

Skata shrugged off his coat and hung it next to Angel's leather jacket on the coat rack before following the others into the kitchen. Letting Easton out of his sight with the vampire wasn't going to happen, even if he was a moroi.

Easton hopped onto the island while Angel put a pot on the burner and took a jug of milk out of the fridge. "Skata," he began, but shook his head and continued, "'Scuse me, *Leslie*—do you want some hot chocolate?" He shook the jug of milk for emphasis.

Easton's eyebrows rose. "You're calling yourself Skata?"

Angel finished pouring milk into the pot. "I'm just going to…grab something real quick." He made a hasty and graceful exit from the room at a fast walk.

Easton gave Skata a playful pout. "Did you get tired of Leslie?"

"I would have," Angel shouted from the opposite side of the wide, adjoining living room.

Easton stared through the curved cutout and lowered her voice. "Can he hear us?"

"Don't be ridiculous," was the loud whisper from the other room.

"That," said Easton, "is some seriously good hearing."

"I know," said Angel, walking back into the kitchen.

Skata crossed his arms. "I thought you said you were getting something."

Angel pursed his lips in thought. "I *was*. I was getting out of the way while you discussed the frankly embarrassing birth name you were given."

Easton faced Skata and mouthed, "Sorry."

He ran a hand through his crew cut hair and told Angel in

a low voice, "If you ever use that name again. I *will* break your legs."

"I'll keep that in mind, Rocky." Angel stirred the hot chocolate and gave him a thumbs-up with his free hand.

"Wow." Easton pulled her hair around her shoulder. "How long have you two known each other, anyway?"

"About ten hours," said Angel.

"Long time," said Skata simultaneously.

Angel quickly added, "What he means is that ten hours can feel like a lifetime."

"That's an understatement," muttered Skata.

"I'm confused," said Easton.

"I'll explain later," he told her, with a warning glance at Angel. That would hopefully give him enough time to come up with a convincing lie, one that did not involve vampires or vampire hunting or anything else world-changing. "It's...complicated."

"Which reminds me, I should update our Facebook status," said Angel, pulling two mugs out of the cabinet.

"You might want to say good-bye to him, Easton," said Skata, curling both hands into fists and hiding them behind the island. "He probably won't be alive tomorrow."

"I don't care whether you guys have known each other for ten hours or ten years," Easton declared, slinging an arm around Skata's neck. "You are so good for each other."

"See?" Angel stretched out an arm and pointed at Easton. "She likes me."

"I didn't say that," she said, tilting her head toward him with a knowing look. "Oh, wait, don't put marshmallows on mine!"

Angel stopped just before putting any in her cup. "You don't like marshmallows?" His lip curled in disbelief. "What hell did you crawl out of?" He popped one in his mouth and handed her the mug, sans marshmallows.

"One where marshmallows are disgusting," she replied, taking the mug.

He held up one between his thumb and forefinger. "They're like little pillows you can eat."

She gazed at it. "Mmhmm, not really a selling point."

He shrugged and ate that one, too.

Skata watched Easton sip her hot chocolate. "Where's mine?"

"Oh, sorry." Angel motioned toward the empty pot. "You didn't ask for any. I'll make a note next time."

Easton lifted her mug to hide her face and laughed. "Do you want mine, Les—sorry, Skata?"

"Don't be so selfless," Angel reprimanded her. "Drink up." He raised his mug in Skata's direction. "Yo ho ho. By the way, Easton, are you free on Friday night?"

She squinted. "After eight I am, why?"

Angel's smile twisted into a smirk. Looking at Skata, he said, "Because that gives you two hours after work to get ready for the year's most epic throwdown."

CHAPTER EIGHT

When Skata came back from dropping Easton off at her house, Angel was stretched out on the couch reading *The Bell Jar* by Sylvia Plath.

"This chick had some serious issues," announced Angel, turning a page.

Skata pushed the book forward toward Angel's face and scanned the back. "Probably why she killed herself."

"Oh, well."

Skata let go of the book, and Angel gave him a sideways look. "What?"

"You invited her to the party."

"I did not," said Angel, looking mortified. "She committed suicide. Even if I invited her, odds are she wouldn't be able to att—"

"Easton, you moron, not Sylvia Plath."

Angel grinned briefly. "So I invited her. Your point?"

"My point is you invited her to a party with a bunch of glorified zombies."

Angel squinted, as if he couldn't see the point Skata was making. "Pretty sure any party she's ever gone to has included at least one non-human, trust me. There are vampires and werewolves the council doesn't even know exist, me being one of them. Also, I resent your use of the word 'zombies.'"

"This council." Skata sat down on the arm of the couch. "You said the preacher was on it?"

"And the sheriff," said Angel. "*And* a bunch of the deputies. *And* the founding families. *And* they want all vampires and werewolves dead. I'm sure they'd love your input. You can join their merry little band of self-righteous killers and lead them on a crusade against bloodthirsty monsters like myself."

"Don't flatter yourself. I don't care enough about you to lead a crusade."

"Whew," said Angel, turning another page.

Skata ignored his sarcasm and cracked his knuckles. "I'm only after one vampire, and trust me, he deserves all the enemies he gets."

Angel lowered the book onto his chest. "What's got you so hot and bothered about this Samuel guy, anyway?"

Samuel.

How he hated him, more than Angel could ever understand. "Practical reasons, such as, he turns anyone he feels like and they all end up as strigoi."

"Aha." A faint smile lifted one corner of Angel's mouth. "Uncle Sam wants *you*."

"Something like that," said Skata. "Back to the party."

"Easton will be *fine*. I'll watch her like she was...whatever normal people watch. And if Jackson so much as turns in her direction, I'll be there with a stake and a smile."

"Incredibly, I'm still worried," said Skata.

"Oh, relax." Angel stood up and stretched his arms over his head. "See you in the morning. Sleep tight and don't let the were-wolves bite." He winked and left the room whistling.

* * * * * * *

Skata quickly found out that when Angel threw a party, there were no half-measures. Conversations over the next five days all tended to sound similar.

"You got a DJ? Seriously?"

"I know it's not exactly the LSO, but I've heard good things." And,

"You do realize that if anything even vaguely vampiric happens to Easton, I'll drown you in a vat of vervain, right?"

"Threat acknowledged and overruled, although if I ever start a band I'm calling it 'Vaguely Vampiric.'"

And,

"I find it kind of hard to believe that you're going to all this trouble to throw a party just as a distraction."

"Don't cramp my style, brother."

Now, at nine o'clock on Friday night, Skata was ready for the party to be over and done with. He just wanted Easton to be safe and to get the stake from Jackson without a hitch.

He was going to leave out the back door once he had been introduced to Jackson. The plan was to make sure the younger Montgomery brother saw him, and then Skata would get out, get the stake, and be back before Jackson knew anything was wrong. With any luck, Skata would have an airtight alibi and Jackson would be short one stolen item.

"So I'm supposed to break in through the window by the tree on the second story," Skata repeated, running though the plan for the last time. "Right?"

"So I hear."

"And if you're wrong, Gideon catches me."

"Probably not. There's a council meeting tonight, which means Gideon will probably be spying on it."

"Good," said Skata. "Because when I die, it won't be at the hands of an irate three-hundred-year-old vampire."

Angel folded his arms and shrugged. "Well, you know what they say. Go big or go home. And as much as I hate to point it out, you are literally homeless—"

The doorbell rang, interrupting the conversation. "I thought the party didn't start for an hour," said Skata, watching Angel cross over to the door.

"It doesn't," said Angel. He pulled open the door, and Easton walked in, her navy-blue sweater toning down the shimmery gold tank she wore.

"Hey!" she said, grinning. "Am I on time?"

"Absolutely," said Angel, taking her purse and hanging it on the coat rack.

Skata pointed. "Why is she here?"

"Finishing touches!" Angel patted Skata's arm as he walked past. "She's giving me a hand."

"We all know *you* can't decorate worth a dime." Easton mimicked Angel's gesture and patted Skata's arm. "I can tell by looking at you."

Angel stepped into the kitchen and called, "Easton, might I borrow a minute of your time?"

"Coming," she replied. To Skata she added, "Don't worry, it's just some decorating." She kissed his cheek and followed Angel.

Skata rubbed his hands over his face and groaned.

* * * * * * *

As soon as Easton entered the kitchen, Angel grabbed her

arm, a finger raised to his lips. Easton's eyes widened, but she remained quiet, casting a quick glance back out toward the foyer.

"What?" she hissed.

He whispered, "I need your help."

"With what?"

Angel peered over the top of her head, making sure Skata wasn't lingering around the doorway. "How do you feel about being a distraction?"

She folded her arms. "Whom are we distracting?" she asked suspiciously.

"Jackson Montgomery."

"Oh, but—*why*? He can get pretty much anyone he wants."

"Be-*cause*—" He looked over her head one more time and lowered his voice. "If he realizes Skata's not at the party tonight, things are going to go down. Not good things."

"What on earth is that supposed to mean?"

"Just trust me."

"I don't know you well enough."

Angel frowned and whispered, "This is for Skata. Your former babysitter, your older-brother-figure, whatever you want to call him. Purely unselfish reasons."

She cast a worried glance at the doorway. "Is he in trouble?"

Angel smiled. "Not if you help me out here."

"I don't…I was planning on bringing Macon," she began reluctantly.

He interrupted. "Macon who?"

"My *boyfriend.* Macon."

"Well, darn," said Angel. He bent down and looked unblinkingly into Easton's eyes. "You're going to distract Jackson until the party is over, and then you're going to forget we had this little conversation. Okay?"

She nodded slowly. "Okay."

"Good!" He brought his hands together, the compulsion over, and a brief flash of bewilderment overtook her face before she smiled.

"So!" She turned around. "What do we have left to do?"

* * * * * * *

An hour later, guests were arriving in groups of three and four. Electronic music pumped through the air in time to the flashing lights that burned spots onto the back of Skata's eyelids. Angel stood by the living room fireplace where he could survey everything, occasionally bumping fists with someone or kissing pretty girls on the cheek.

Skata made his way through the crowd. "Hey," he barked. "Where's Jackson?"

"Beats me," Angel said, raising his voice to be heard over the noise.

"If he doesn't come, this whole thing was a bust."

"No party's a bust unless I bust it. You should go get a beer," the vampire suggested, raising a red plastic cup. "Have a dance, bump and grind a little."

"No, thanks."

"Party pooper," said Angel, taking a long drink.

Skata turned to scan the crowd and saw Easton, colorful lights sweeping across her face as she approached.

"Hey!" She reached them. "Has he shown up yet?"

"Oh, yes," said Angel, nodding conspiratorially to Skata. "I told her about Jackson."

"You *told* her?" It was hard for Skata to keep his voice low when everything in him wanted to yell over the music, but he couldn't risk Easton finding out more than she already knew. "I told you to shut up about it."

"Don't worry," said Angel, waving a hand. "I compelled her. She'll forget what little she *does* know after she leaves tonight."

"You did *what?*" Skata exploded.

Angel nodded to the beat of the music. "Think about it—if she can keep him distracted while you bounce over to his house, he won't notice you're gone. Problem solved," he finished, taking another drink. "You can thank me later."

Skata was about to punch the vampire in the stomach—it was close range, no one would have noticed—when Easton said, "Oh, there he is!" and walked away from them toward the door.

Skata turned, temporarily distracted. "*That's* Jackson?"

Angel swallowed the last of his drink and tossed the cup

across the room into a trash can. "Just don't get him on your bad side," he said, patting Skata's shoulder before striding over to meet Jackson Montgomery.

There was nothing threatening about the appearance of the new vampire. Rakish auburn hair, large gray eyes too keen for their age, and a smirk didn't equal the most dangerous of first impressions, but as Skata frequently had to remind himself, you couldn't judge a vampire by appearance. The harmless, mid-twenties exterior was a disguise for a monstrosity with centuries of accumulated speed, strength, and cunning.

How he hated it.

He took his time joining Angel and Easton, but Jackson noticed him immediately and held out a hand, leaning forward to say over the music, "Jackson Montgomery. And you are?"

"Skata," said Skata.

"Oh, yes." The vampire smiled. It was a friendly smile with no animosity behind it, and Skata knew he couldn't trust that, either. "The new guy. Not a bad party, is it?"

"Sure," said Skata, folding his arms to keep himself from snatching Easton away from Jackson when she tucked her arm around his and said, "Let's get a drink, huh?"

"Why, Miss Everett," said Jackson in a teasing voice. "I thought you despised me."

"Uck, that was then." She nudged him. "This is tonight, and tonight we're supposed to have fun."

"I do believe you're right. Let's do that."

As soon as they left, Skata turned a simmering glare on Angel. "Don't you dare let them out of your sight."

"Wouldn't dream of it," said Angel, then added a surprised, "Well, well, well."

The night had barely started, but already Skata was done with it. "What?"

"It's just a wild guess, but I'm going to assume that's Macon."

Skata followed the vampire's gaze to a young man who was watching Easton and Jackson at the refreshment table, his glare fairly jumping off his face.

"Who the hell is Macon?" demanded Skata.

"Easton's boyfriend," he responded. "Mm. He doesn't look happy."

"Whoa." Skata held up a hand. "Easton has a *boyfriend*?"

"Oops," said Angel.

"You little—"

"Okay, first of all, don't say anything you might regret later." Angel put a finger to his lips before adding, "Secondly, lots of girls have boyfriends. I'll explain it to you later, but right now you have to skedaddle."

It was too much to deal with right now. Skata had to get to the Montgomerys' house before Gideon came back from spying on the council meeting. In Angel's ear he hissed, "Make sure this doesn't go south."

"Will do." Angel's made a shooing motion with his hands. "Run along! Go steal the thing!"

"Stake."

"Whatever. Go fetch." Angel clapped his hands together as Skata walked away.

CHAPTER NINE

The Montgomerys' sprawling Plantation-style mansion sat three miles away, surrounded by several acres of well-manicured land. Skata parked a quarter of a mile down the street and crossed through the yard on foot, keeping to the shadows cast by the trees.

He saw the giant, twisted oak stretching up to the second and third floors on the left side of the house and made his way toward it. He paused before sprinting out across the open gravel path that wound around the house.

He reached the oak and pulled himself up on the lowest branch. They were all thick and sturdy, an easy climb. One branch led out to the window which, according to Angel's questionable information, should lead directly into the younger Montgomery's bedroom.

Straddling the branch, he gripped the bottom of the window and attempted to push it open. It was locked, but the locks were old-fashioned and simple. The screen was easy to remove, but the window was a different story. He drew a knife from inside his coat and worked it between the window and the frame. It took several minutes before it finally gave.

Skata pulled himself in headfirst through the window, easing himself over the sill. The large room would have been confusing to someone who did not know the owner's species, for it seemed to be a combination of a professor's study and a dorm room. Three shelves lined the far wall on the other side of the four-poster bed, and while two of the shelves were lined with books, the middle one was entirely dedicated to music. Vinyl records, 8-tracks, cassette tapes, and CDs surrounded a charging iPod.

A stack of mint-condition National Geographics from 1888 sat on a vintage steamer trunk near the door, and on top of them was a thin wooden box, maybe a foot long.

"If you're the stake," Skata whispered, "this was way too easy." He crossed the room, wincing every time his step ushered a creak from the floor.

The box had no lock. He opened the lid and there, nestled inside the velvet lining, was nothing.

Not that he had expected to find the stake so easily. He grunted and set the box back down and began a search of the large room, careful to place everything back exactly as he found it.

He knew he had exhausted every possible hiding place in the room, but he stood in the center of it and slowly turned, double-checking himself. There was only one conclusion: Jackson had hidden the stake too well for Skata to find it.

Unless it was hidden somewhere other than his room.

He pulled out his cell phone and called Angel. It rang four times before Angel answered, speaking loudly over the background noise.

"What?"

"It's not here."

"Come again?"

"The *stake*. It's not here."

"Bummer," said Angel. The noise muted, and he heard the vampire yell, "Do that in the bathroom! Ew!" Then to Skata he continued, "So where is it?"

"How should I know?"

"Look around. I'm sure it's somewhere. Maybe he uses it to pick his teeth."

"How late does the council meeting run?" Skata pulled his sleeve back and looked at his watch. The hands pointed to ten twenty-three.

Angel said, "Ten-thirty. Which means you'd better get out of there, unless you want to be caught trespassing by a moroi who could eat you for dinner."

Skata pulled the phone away from his ear but put it back to ask, "How's the situation with Easton?"

"Judging by the look on Macon's face, she's doing her job to perfection. I should probably compel him to forget this."

"No," hissed Skata. "You can't just waltz around compelling people."

"Sorry," said Angel, a tone of exaggerated apology in his voice. "I seem to have gotten my lines crossed with the Morality Police. Please hold; we'll try to reconnect you."

The phone went silent.

"Son of a bitch." Skata jammed the phone back into his pocket. And then he realized the most obvious flaw in this plan—he could not lock Jackson's window from the outside. He was going to have to close it, lock it, and find another way out.

* * * * * * *

Angel looked at the phone in his hand for a few seconds before putting it back in his pocket. Skata wasn't his problem anyway, not technically. Besides, he could take care of himself. There were more pressing matters at hand, like the horde of dancing young people trashing his house.

He crossed over to Macon. "You, my friend, look like you could use a drink," he remarked, leaning against the wall several feet from the young man.

Macon snorted and glanced at Angel. His eyes landed on the bottle of beer the host was offering, and after only a second of hesitation, he took it.

Angel watched him pop the lid off with one twist and down several large swallows. "You're Easton Everett's boyfriend, right?"

Macon released a long breath through his nose. "That's right."

"So go cut in."

"I'd only get a lecture on what a control freak I was." Macon shook his head and took another swallow.

"You look much more…muscly than he is," said the vampire, nodding toward Jackson. "What could he do to you?" Macon was no taller than Jackson, but his muscles were thicker and wider—and anyway, Macon didn't know Jackson was stronger by far.

"Nah. I think I'll just talk to her later, catch her outside, maybe."

Angel eyed the bottle of beer in Macon's hand. "I forgot to check your I.D."

Macon looked at him. "I'm twenty-three."

The vampire shrugged and lifted his own bottle to his mouth. "You never know. Young people and their underage drinking. What *is* the world coming to?"

If Macon replied, Angel didn't hear him. His attention was caught by the sound of Easton's voice across the room.

"What's wrong?" she was asking.

Angel lowered his beer and watched, maintaining an air of nonchalance, as Jackson smiled at Easton.

"So tell me, honey," he said, "how much have you had to drink?"

"I had some punch," said Easton with a breezy laugh. "I have to drive home later, you know. Why?"

"Because," said Jackson, and a hint of over-niceness snuck into his syrupy Southern accent, "you've never liked me nearly this much. I'll admit I bought the whole 'let's have fun' thing for a while, but it's been over half an hour and you're still here."

"So?"

Jackson lifted Easton's chin, his eyes narrowing as his lips curled in a suspicious smile. "What are you up to?"

Fortunately for Easton, she was genuinely bewildered. Angel gave himself a mental pat on the back—compelling people had always been one of his better talents. "I don't understand what you're talking abou—"

"Where did Skata go?"

Angel handed his beer to Macon with a brief "Take that" before he made his way through the crowd toward Easton and Jackson. He lost sight of them for a brief moment as a girl climbed onto a guy's shoulders and began waving her arms in the air like they were at a mosh pit.

He pushed around them, and suddenly, he was face to face with Jackson.

The vampire was still smiling, but there was no humor in it, and he gripped Easton's upper arm tightly with one hand. "Where is he?"

Angel pointed at himself. "Are you talking to me?"

Jackson's expression turned to disgust. "The game is over.

You know the funny thing about compulsions? An older, stronger vampire can override the previous compulsion most of the time. One command, and she may just get the sudden urge to lie down in the middle of the street. Where did the hunter go?"

"I hate to break it to you, but I am not my housemate's keeper," said Angel, with a flippant smile.

"Excuse me," said Easton politely, "what's going on?"

Jackson put a finger to the side of her face, turning it toward him. "You run along and forget all this." He kissed her cheek and gave her a gentle nudge. "Go talk to your boyfriend."

Her face still a portrait of confusion, Easton walked away toward Macon.

Jackson turned back to Angel, folding his arms. "Don't make me compel you, too."

* * * * * * *

Skata's watch read ten thirty-five p.m., and the stake was nowhere to be found. He was out of time. The house was old and there were no alarms, so he could leave through the front door and get away before anyone saw him.

Still, his sense of caution made him go around through a less-obvious way; he saw the kitchen and moved quietly through it, into what had probably been a parlor in the eighteen hundreds.

To his surprise, it still seemed to *be* a parlor, furnished with antique chairs and some kind of fancy mahogany table near the center of the room.

One of the chairs was occupied by a man who gave off the aura of a black-and-white movie star, his casual suit spotless, his hair impeccable. He held a cup and saucer in one hand.

He rose to his feet as Skata entered the room, setting the cup and saucer on the table. "Good evening," he said, as if he had been expecting a visitor. "I am Gideon Montgomery. You must be Skata." He held out his hand.

It took Skata a moment to realize that the vampire wanted a handshake.

Refusing the handshake would probably be a bad idea, so he stepped forward and clasped it briefly before letting it go.

Gideon smiled and gestured to the other side of the small table, where a second cup and saucer sat steaming. "I took the liberty of making you a cup of tea."

"Tea," Skata repeated.

"Yes." The vampire gestured congenially once more toward the tea. He might as well have said 'at ease,' for Skata felt obliged to lower himself into the other chair.

Gideon sat down again and leaned back while he watched Skata with unwavering intensity. His eyes were an ordinary chestnut brown, nothing special to look at, but something else to be watched by. Skata had the feeling that they missed very little. He rubbed his palms across his thighs and cleared his throat. "So," he began.

"Why are you here?"

"I got bit by a werewolf and was too busted up to travel," Skata replied obtusely. "Still am."

"Yet you seem to have no trouble sneaking into people's homes," Gideon remarked. "What were you looking for in my house?"

Skata shifted in his chair, his cup of tea untouched. He wasn't a tea person on the best of days, especially not when he was being politely interrogated by a vampire who could snap his neck as easily as flex his fingers.

"It's kind of a long story," he said doggedly.

Gideon folded his hands. "How very fortunate. I happen to have an entire night at my disposal."

CHAPTER TEN

G ideon was just finishing his cup of tea when the front door burst open and Jackson's voice was heard snarling, "Where is he?"

Skata pushed back his chair to stand, but Gideon held up a hand.

"In the parlor," Gideon called, barely bothering to raise his voice above speaking level.

Jackson appeared in the room with a rush of blurry movement. He looked significantly less polished than the last time Skata had seen him. "I don't know you, but I've had enough."

"Calm down, Jackson," said Gideon. "We are simply sharing a drink."

"Actually, I broke in," said Skata. "Your brother made me tea."

"Yes, well, you seemed fairly harmless," said Gideon.

Skata's smile slipped at the nonchalant insult.

Jackson sauntered over to the table and leaned his fingertips against it. Then he grinned, his fangs appearing as he said, "I don't take kindly to people sneaking into my house."

"Jackson," said Gideon, clearing his throat, "this gentleman tells me you took something from Rukiel. Is this true?"

"Sure. What of it?" he asked easily.

"I have specifically instructed you to avoid prodding the hornet's nest."

"One of his goons came at me with it." Jackson shrugged both shoulders. How he could seem so relaxed and yet so on the verge of attacking him, Skata had no idea. It was almost impressive. "He's not getting it back without an apology."

"Not going to happen," said Skata.

"Then I guess he's never getting it back."

Gideon stood up and faced his brother, his face impassive. "Please return the item to this man and let him return it to Rukiel."

Jackson straightened, and Skata could already tell the gist of what he would say. "Sorry. You and I get along because we don't interfere with one another. This counts as interference."

Clearly and firmly, Gideon repeated his order. "Give the item back."

Jackson shrugged. "Go to hell."

For a moment, Skata thought the older moroi would give in and tell Skata he was sorry, but it couldn't be done.

"Please," said Gideon.

For a long moment, Jackson only stood there, his eyes cold,

his chest heaving with quiet, enraged breaths. Then he reached inside his jacket and pulled out a slender piece of wood, which he twirled in his hand like a drumstick before throwing it at Skata like a knife.

The stake grazed the side of his head and struck the wall behind him. Skata stared at the stake, firmly embedded in the thick wood.

With only a look somewhere between a grimace and another snarl, Jackson turned and sauntered from the room.

As soon as he left the room and his footsteps could be heard retreating up to his room, Gideon strode over to the stake and pulled it out of the wall. It looked easy when he did it; a simple grasp and tug.

Skata knew he would have spent fifteen minutes trying to yank it free.

"Here is the misappropriated item." The moroi glanced over the stake before handing it to Skata. "I apologize for my brother's actions. He can be stubborn."

"I noticed." Skata tucked the stake into his belt, still dumbfounded at the vampire's cooperation. "Thanks."

"Are you Rukiel's new retriever, then?"

"No, we're making a trade."

Gideon put one hand in the pocket of his jacket. "What is your end of the bargain?"

"Information," said Skata. "That's all I'm telling you."

Gideon smiled. The expression was almost tolerant, as if he

was humoring Skata. It was annoying, but he knew better than to pick a fight over it. "Have a pleasant evening, Skata."

Skata's phone rang. He lifted a hand to Gideon and walked out the front door, his heart racing. That had been much too close. It was a good thing the older brother was so agreeable—otherwise, Skata knew he would have left the house in several pieces, if at all.

His phone was on its last ring when he put it to his ear. "Yeah? What is it?"

"Please tell me you got the thing," said Angel.

Skata looked down at the stake in his hand. "I got it."

"Fantastic! Now I feel like I should inform you of a tiny problem we might have."

Skata unlocked the car door and climbed in, tossing the stake onto the passenger seat. "What?"

"I'm pretty sure Easton's boyfriend is a werewolf."

* * * * * * *

Skata was at the house in less than three minutes. He stormed in through the back door and found Angel waiting for him.

"Pretty sure you broke some traffic laws there," said the vampire.

"Shut up and tell me about Macon," said Skata. "Where's Easton?"

"Back with Macon," said Angel. "I'm kind of curious as to how you got out of the house alive, given you were caught stealing from the Montgomery brothers."

Skata turned around and shoved the vampire in the chest. "You were supposed to keep Jackson off my back."

"Hey," snapped Angel, "I did as much as I could."

"Did you tell him where I was?"

Angel narrowed his eyes. "He figured it out pretty quickly on his own. But, hey, you're in one piece. Take the win."

"That's thanks to Gideon, not Jackson," said Skata, folding his arms. "Tell me about Macon. Are you sure?" The thought of Easton entangled with a werewolf, particularly against her knowledge, was vinegar on an open wound.

"Pretty sure."

"How can you tell?"

Angel held up a finger. "A, he smells weird. B, he's way more jacked than any twenty-year-old I've ever seen. C, he was scanning the room like people were after him the whole time, and D, I made a remark about his needing to act like an alpha and he got all twitchy."

Skata moved toward the crowd. "She needs to get away from that guy."

"Whoa, whoa, whoa!" Angel grabbed his arm.

Skata lifted a fist, ready to break the vampire's nose for the second time in a week, but Angel caught the swing with his open palm.

"That was pathetic," said Angel.

Skata let out a breath through his nose. "Let go before I stab you."

"With what?"

With his left hand, he withdrew Rukiel's stake from his belt. "With this."

Angel gazed at the stake, then gave Skata a withering look. "You go out there and drag her away from Macon and she might never forgive you."

"I'll live," said Skata, turning and striding toward the living room.

He heard a faint sound, like rushing wind, and Angel was in front of him, blocking his way. "Hold up, cowboy."

Skata shoved the stake into Angel's thigh. The vampire grunted in pain, and Skata pushed around him into the throng of strangers. The music was already beginning to vibrate inside his skull.

He scanned the crowd for a familiar head of long, brown hair. It was impossible to see amid the swirl of flashing lights and dancing shadows, so he turned and headed for the only logical option: the DJ booth.

"Hey, what's the matter with you, man?" the DJ demanded, his voice high-pitched and indignant.

"I just need to borrow your microphone," Skata assured him, picking up the microphone. He smacked it against his fist. "Hey."

The sound screeched through the house and put an immediate stop to the party. Dozens of faces turned toward him, blinking and confused.

"Party's over," said Skata. "Get out."

A complaining murmur rose as people protested at the abrupt ending. Skata saw Angel leaning against the kitchen door, his lips twisted to one side as he spun the stake in his fingers in a painfully conspicuous manner. At least he wasn't interfering.

The partygoers looked reluctant to leave. They were milling around like penned horses in a storm, and he was through.

He lifted the microphone again and said, "Now."

People funneled toward the front door, muttering complaints and shooting glares at him and his ruination of their fun. He stood with his arms folded until he saw Easton. They met in the corner, and she gave him a confused look. "Why did you stop the party?"

"It was giving me a headache."

She put her hands on her hips. "It doesn't have anything to do with the fact that my boyfriend was here, does it?"

"Don't be stupid."

Easton tossed her head. "That was rude of you, by the way. Did Angel tell you to do that?"

"No, Angel did not," said Angel, appearing behind Easton and giving Skata a wide, *we-will-have-a-talk-later* smile.

Easton gasped and crouched down to look at his leg. "What happened to you?"

Angel glanced down at the bloody hole punched through his jeans. "Oh, that was a minor accident."

"A minor accident," she repeated in disbelief.

"Mmm-hmm." Angel cocked his head and looked at Skata. "Just a scratch, really. I hardly felt a thing."

"You should get it looked at, though," said Easton, rising to her feet.

"You just did," the vampire pointed out. "Voila."

She gave him a pointed look. "I mean a professional look. Like at the hospital?"

"Nah." He waved a hand. "It looks worse than it was."

"Yeah," said Skata. "Let's hope it doesn't happen to you again."

The vampire's smugness faded into a narrow-eyed frown.

"You two have some issues to work out," said Easton. She rose up on her toes to look over Skata's shoulder. Macon was waiting by the door, impatience written across his face. "Right, well, I should go before he bursts a vessel." She kissed Skata on the cheek, patted Angel's arm, and jogged across the room to meet her boyfriend.

He gestured wildly with his arms before they left, closing the doors behind them and leaving the house empty and silent.

Skata was slammed into the far wall before he realized Angel had even moved. "A word to the stupid," said Angel in a low voice, "don't *ever* think about doing that again. It hurt."

"It was supposed to," said Skata, pushing Angel away and striding toward the door.

"Oh, sure, just walk away. What about this?" Angel called, spreading his arms to indicate the mess of plastic cups, paper plates and unidentifiable items that the partygoers had left behind.

"Not my problem," said Skata, and slammed the door behind him.

CHAPTER ELEVEN

The *Diamond Straight* was lit up, and the line, while not terribly long, was still too long for Skata. He glanced at the back of the line, shook his head, and walked around it. "Hey," he said to the bouncer, "remember me?"

The bouncer narrowed his eyes. "What do you want?"

"Relax. Your boss is expecting me this time."

The bouncer frowned and stepped inside to shout, "Hey, boss!"

A moment later, Rukiel appeared, the golden light from the doorway seeming to light his hair on fire like an unearthly halo. "Ah, Skata." He gestured with two fingers. "Come in."

The bouncer scowled at Skata as he stepped past, ignoring the indignant exclamations from everyone waiting in line.

He followed Rukiel through to his office, where the proprietor wasted no time. "Where is it?" he asked, shutting the door.

Skata reached into his jacket and pulled out the stake. "Right here. Tell me where Samuel is first."

Rukiel seemed ready to get the transaction over with. "He was last seen in Elloree three days ago."

"That's, what, forty miles from here?"

"It is. Stake, please."

Skata handed it over, silent in thought. Then he asked, "Why would he settle in Elloree?"

"That, I do not know. Also, it was not part of our deal."

"Fine." Skata put his hands in his pockets, but before he turned to go, he asked, "What's so special about that stake anyway?"

"It can kill moroi."

"Ah," said Skata, attempting to mask his confusion. And to think, he'd stabbed Angel in the leg with that thing. The night could have been very different.

Rukiel folded his arms and arched an eyebrow. "I get the impression you weren't aware of the fact that your average wooden stake will only wound a moroi, not kill them."

He hated to admit it, but he found himself saying, "Maybe."

"You seem distressingly ignorant for a hunter."

"I'm only hunting one guy," Skata answered, crossing his arms over his own chest. "I'm not exactly Van Helsing."

"Obviously," said Rukiel. He seemed to take pity on Skata, because he continued. "A moroi can only be killed by fire, or a stake specially cured."

"How's that?"

Rukiel *tsk*'d his tongue. "So many questions." He waved a hand airily, the dim light catching the rings that decorated his fingers. "You got the stake—an impressive feat, I might add—and returned it to me. I gave you your information. You paid the price and purchased the product, and this interview is over."

Skata shook his head. "Fine."

"I cannot, in all good conscience, let you go out that door without a name."

"A name?"

"You are simply too inept," said Rukiel. "Stop by the church and have a word with Lucas Colton."

"Who's that?"

"Someone who can help you."

"Thanks, but I don't think a devout pew-sitter is going to help me much."

"He's no pew-sitter." Rukiel tilted his head back and grinned, exposing the small, sharp points of his teeth. "He's the preacher. You should go talk to him—he stays late at the church most nights."

CHAPTER TWELVE

Skata wasn't sure whether it was because of Rukiel's urging or his own curiosity, but fifteen minutes later, he found himself standing just outside the doors of Salvation Church. A bell hung in the steeple of the little white building. It looked old enough to tear down—everything except the thick oak doors.

Skata gave them a nudge. Unlocked. But then, who would break into a church?

He stepped inside the darkened building and strode slowly down the aisle between dozens of wooden pews. He cleared his throat. "Hello? Anybody here?"

"I'm here," called a disembodied voice. Skata turned in a circle, looking for the source. "Just give me a second," the voice added.

Skata stood in front of the pulpit, a solid wood affair with an infinity knot carved across the front. "Take your time."

A moment later, a man around Skata's age emerged from a side room. "Hey," he greeted in a husky voice, holding out his hand with a friendly smile. "What can I do for you?"

Skata squinted, taking in the man in front of him as he gave his hand a few solid shakes and let it go. Curly hair, a soul patch, and faded jeans didn't look terribly standard-issue for church staff. "You Father Colton?"

"Nah, just a preacher. Call me Colton." He was several inches shorter than Skata but a few years older, he guessed; although he looked more suited to a herd on a ranch than a flock in a church. "You must be the newcomer."

"Skata," said Skata.

Colton grinned. "I know that look. You get used to the way news travels around a small town, trust me."

"Apparently," said Skata.

"So what can I do for you?" the preacher asked again, folding his arms.

Skata rubbed the back of his neck and reconsidered his visit—but he was already here, and if he was going up against Samuel, he needed to up his odds of survival as best he could. "Rukiel said you know things."

"Sure, I know things." Colton shrugged. "You after something in particular?"

Skata glanced at the pulpit. No one stood behind it, but he couldn't help the feeling that he was on trial and as soon as he told the preacher he was hunting a vampire, he would be kicked out. "It's like this," he began.

"You're a hunter," said Colton.

Skata stopped abruptly. "How'd you figure that?"

"Doesn't take much to figure it out."

"I hate small towns," Skata muttered.

"You get used to 'em. I'm from Dallas myself." He pointed at Skata and said, "You ain't from the Bible Belt either, are you?"

"Montana," said Skata.

Colton whistled. "You come all this way just to chase someone down?"

"You got a problem with that?"

The other man smiled faintly and shook his head. "You want my help tracking down a...what? Werewolf? Vampire?"

"Vampire," said Skata.

Colton grunted. "Which kind?"

"Moroi."

"Huh. Moroi don't usually cause too many problems." He narrowed his eyes in thought. "You looking to kill him?"

"I am."

Colton nodded and scratched his chin. "If Rukiel sent you to me, there must be a good reason. How bad is this fella?"

"Crazy murderer," Skata supplied.

"Let me guess," said Colton. "You've never hunted a vampire before and you're screwing it up?"

"Let's just say it's still kind of new," Skata replied, crossing his arms over his chest defensively.

Colton nodded again and seemed to reach a decision. "Well, I'm in the business of saving people, not killing 'em. Which I guess includes helping you not die, huh?" He clapped Skata on the back and strode back in the way he'd come with a vaguely bowlegged swagger.

Skata followed him through the side door and down a short flight of wooden stairs. "How do I kill a moroi?"

"Just hold your horses." The preacher flicked on a light switch. The room lit up, showing an unfinished basement cluttered with shelves, tables, chairs, and cardboard boxes.

"What is all this?" asked Skata.

"Oh, you know." Colton rolled his sleeves up to his elbows and bent over a tattered cardboard box. "Extra hymnals, stuff like that. So how long have you been in the hunting business?"

"Depends."

"On what?"

"On what you mean by that."

"How long have you wanted to kill this guy?" asked Colton, pulling a heavy-duty flashlight out of the box and setting it on the nearby card table.

"About a year."

Colton glanced up. "He turn someone?"

"Yeah."

"Someone close?"

"None of your damn business."

"Uh-huh," said the preacher, unconvinced. "You wouldn't be so set on revenge otherwise, right?"

"What are you looking for?" Skata asked impatiently, making no effort to mask the abrupt subject change.

"Here it is." Colton straightened, holding a dark cherry-colored stake in his hand. "This should help."

"That's no hymnal," said Skata. "Hey." He stepped closer. "Rukiel has one of those. He said they kill moroi. How'd you get one?"

"Eh, long story." Colton waved his hand, dismissing the question. "Rukiel tell you anything about these stakes?"

"He said it was specially cured. Something like that."

"Not quite. It's made from special wood, sure, but there's nothing special about the cure."

"What's so special about the wood, then?" asked Skata, jerking his chin toward the stake.

The preacher touched the tip of the stake. "This stake is over nine hundred years old," he said. "It was carved in the Dark Ages, from the wood of a tree known as the Blood Oak."

Skata snorted. "Sounds like a myth to me."

"Come on, man." Colton spread his arms and gave Skata a pointed look. "You're looking to get revenge on a vampire and you get all skeptical now?"

Skata lifted a hand, conceding the point.

Colton tossed the stake to Skata, who caught it before it struck his face. "There was only one Blood Oak tree, and a few overzealous Catholic knights carved up the tree and made stakes.

'Course that was back when people thought anything non-human was either a demon or an angel."

"Don't know if I believe in demons, but vampires seem pretty close," said Skata, inspecting the smooth stake. It was surprisingly heavy.

"Vampires are no demons," said Colton. "They've just got more problems than most."

"Doesn't the Bible say something negative about blood-drinkers?"

Colton smiled, as if pleased at Skata's sketchy Biblical knowledge. "In Deuteronomy, God's people are commanded not to drink the blood of any creature."

"Seems like a weird thing to have to tell people."

"Well, blood is life." Colton shrugged. "God would eventually give us His blood to drink, as a symbol of His death on the cross. Drinking it from an animal would be kinda like sacrilege, you know?"

"So at least strigoi vampires are what—abominations, then?" Skata asked, pushing the subject. "They crave blood, and so they kill for it."

"You ever committed a sin?" asked Colton suddenly.

Skata frowned. "Hasn't everyone?"

"You ever committed a real bad one?"

"Aren't they all bad?"

Colton pointed at Skata, who cursed. He'd put his foot right in that one.

"Exactly. All sins are bad," said Colton. "Everyone has their own demons, their own sins they struggle with more'n the others. One guy might have an issue with porn, while vampires have issues with drinking blood."

"Well, looks like we're all going to hell, then," said Skata flippantly.

"Everyone can be forgiven," said Colton, "even vampires."

"Then let 'em." Skata hefted the stake in his hand one more time and tossed it at the preacher, who caught it deftly and set it on the desk, where it rolled to the edge and stayed there. "Don't think forgiveness would do much good. 'Bless me Father, for I have sinned' and then they'd go right back out and use someone's neck like a soda fountain."

"There's a cure for strigoi, you know."

This caught Skata's interest. "What, so they can un-vampire themselves?"

"Far as I know, that's impossible. But moroi don't crave blood the way strigoi do, and a strigoi can get kind of an 'upgrade' to moroi. Fixes a lot of problems."

This was news to Skata. "How do they do that?"

"According to what I've heard, the moroi who turned 'em just needs to inject all their current venom into the strigoi. That's usually enough to do it, or so I hear."

"Sounds risky," said Skata.

"Yeah," said Colton, scratching his cheek. "Good chance of dying."

"Too bad," said Skata and turned toward the stairs.

Colton chuckled. "You have some real issues, don't you?"

"Sure do," said Skata. "Thanks for the info."

"Glad to help," said the preacher. "I keep pretty late hours here, so if you need anything else, feel free to drop by. Hey," he added.

Skata paused at the top of the stairs and looked back down at the preacher, who was rubbing the back of his head with one hand. He looked like he might be having misgivings. "What?"

"There's a saying," said Colton, resting his hands on his hips. "Before you set out to get revenge, dig two graves."

The preacher's words struck deeper than Skata found comfortable. "Thanks," he said sharply, walking through the door, "but I don't need you to tell me what's right or wrong, Father."

"It's *preacher*," Colton called.

Skata ignored him and shut the door behind him, striding back down the aisle.

CHAPTER THIRTEEN

A sound blasted Easton out of sleep. She rolled over in bed and felt around on the stool by the window for her phone. She sat up, pushing her hair out of her face, and answered with a groggy, "Hello?"

"Don't tell me you were asleep."

Her mind moved sluggishly through her list of contacts, trying to match the voice to a name. It resurfaced, empty. "Sorry, who is this?"

"Ouch."

"Angel?"

"Bingo!"

"Why are you—wait." She pulled the phone away from her ear and looked at the time. "It's one thirty-seven in the morning."

"Your point?"

"How did you even get my number?"

"You may have given it to me earlier."

"I don't remember that."

"Well, I'm not surprised, what with the music and the booze, etcetera."

Easton rubbed her forehead. "I wasn't drink—what do you want?"

"Are you awake?"

"I am now."

"Great."

Something clattered against the window. Easton threw the sheets off and sat up straight. Another rock bounced off window. "Are you throwing rocks at my window?"

"I'm not really throwing them so much as lightly tossing."

Easton stood up and peered out the window. A figure stood on the lawn below it, just visible under the slope of the roof. "You're insane."

"It's a distinct possibility," said Angel.

Easton hung up. She tossed the phone onto her bed, unlocked the window, and heaved it upward. It was sticky with humidity, but after several hard tugs, it gave way. She pressed her palms against the windowsill, leaned out into the muggy night air, and demanded, "What do you want?"

"Can I come up, pretty please?"

"No!"

"Fine. I just want to talk."

"Go talk to Skata, who happens to live *in the same house as you*."

"He came home an hour ago and went to sleep without even telling me goodnight. My feelings were hurt."

"Right. I think it would take a lot more than that to hurt your feelings."

"Don't make me come up there," he called in wheedling tones.

Easton rolled her eyes. "Do I look stupid enough to let a practical stranger into my room at night?"

He disappeared from view, but before she had time even to lean farther out the window, he appeared over the edge of the roof, as confident as a cat burglar and three times as fast.

Easton gaped at him. "And just what do you think you're doing?"

"You're right," he said, crouching outside the window. "You're not that stupid, so I figured I'd have to invite myself." He stuck two fingers through the window. "You really should invest in a screen."

"I should invest in a guard dog," she replied with a sigh. "One second." She opened the top drawer of her dresser and removed a handgun before saying, "Come in."

"I'm impressed." He crawled through the window and jumped down into the bedroom. He gave each corner a sweeping glance before crossing over to the bed and flopping down on his back. He frowned and rolled over, reaching behind him. He tugged a once-pink stuffed rabbit out from between the pillows and narrowed his eyes at it.

"That's Bunnicula," said Easton, by way of explanation. "She was my favorite doll when I was a kid."

"Bunnicula?"

"The stitches around the mouth were weird, and I thought they made it look kind of like Dracula." She leaned against the wall and rubbed her arms. "Bunny plus Dracula equals Bunnicula."

Angel looked intensely at the doll before turning it around to face Easton. Moving the arms to mime his words, he said, "So, Macon seems like an interesting guy."

Easton groaned. "You woke me up in the middle of the night to ask me about my boyfriend?"

"We could always talk about something else," said Angel, and the stuffed rabbit rubbed its chin with one stubby paw. "But I really like this Macon subject."

"For heaven's sake, why?"

"Because I don't like him," stated Angel abruptly.

"Is that supposed to affect me in some way?"

"Maybe."

"Don't be childish."

He widened his startlingly blue eyes. "Me, childish? Perish the thought."

"You're holding a stuffed bunny," she pointed out.

He looked down. "It's *your* stuffed bunny." He rolled off the bed and tossed the doll back against the pillows. "Nice picture," he said, motioning toward a framed photograph of her with two other girls from her junior year. They wore blue-and-yellow tank tops and pleated skirts. "Cheerleader?"

"Junior and senior years."

"I *highly* approve."

"Look, if you have nothing important to say, get out and let me go back to sleep."

He turned around. "That's a little mean, after you invited me in."

She held up her gun and let him see her turning the safety off.

He smiled down at her, and a warm feeling flooded her—suddenly, she really wanted him to stay, as long as he liked.

"Macon," said Angel. "How long have you been dating him?"

Easton shrugged. "About a year," she said, surprised at how much she trusted Angel. How could she ever have doubted him? "Since we graduated high school."

"Does he ever call off dates last-minute? Disappear on conspicuous nights?"

"Conspicuous nights?" She drew her eyebrows together. "What do you mean?"

"Oh, I don't know…say—full moons?" His smile was narrower now, more reptilian, but she didn't notice. The only thing she could think about was giving him anything he wanted, and if that meant answering questions about Macon, then fine.

"I don't…" she began slowly. Bewildered, she finally said, "Actually…" Angel lifted his eyebrows. "A few nights every month he goes camping with some friends."

"What friends would these be?"

She shrugged. "Just…his friends. You know. I've never met them."

"Hmm."

"Why? What's going on?" She looked up at him, searching his face. "Is Macon in trouble?"

Angel looked past her head at the wall and said grimly, "Trouble. I think you could say that." He gripped Easton's shoulders and looked down directly into her eyes. "You're going to forget we had this conversation," he said, a kind, lilting tone in his voice. "You're going to climb back into bed and go to sleep, and you're going to dream about rainbows and kittens."

"Okay," she said.

He patted her cheek. "Good girl." He strode back over to the window. "Lock this behind me."

She followed him over and was so busy locking the window as instructed that she didn't notice his spectacular leap from the roof to the ground.

* * * * * * *

In his dream, he was jogging up the stairs to the bedroom. "Em, darlin', are you home?"

The Honda was still parked in the driveway, but she might have gone for a walk down to the park or maybe out to the pasture for a quick ride. That gave him enough time before they left to shower and change his clothes into something more appropriate for a fancy dinner. He'd never been one for dress-up affairs, but Em loved them.

He turned the knob and walked into his room, in the middle of shrugging off his Carhartt jacket, when he paused. "Em?"

His wife sat on the edge of the bed, her shoulders angled toward the window, away from him. Her dark hair tangled in undone waves around her face, obscuring her head and shoulders and making it impossible to see any expression. Her fingers curled in fists, clenching and unclenching in her lap. She dropped them to her sides.

He crossed quietly over to the bed, concerned. "Em, is everything okay?"

She lifted her head and turned her face toward him, the movement slow and doll-like; something out of a dream. Only then did he notice the open window—no, not open. Broken, cracked, splinters of glass spilled across the floor and the edge of the bed. The chill that shivered through his bones had nothing to do with the winter air.

"Baby." Her voice was soft and inviting. You could almost miss the fangs set between her lips. "You're home early."

Skata rolled over and opened his eyes. It took him a moment to remember to breathe. Weren't nightmares supposed to stop after the first few months? It was closing in on a year since her death. This couldn't be normal…

There was an unhappy yowl from the other side of the bedroom door.

Cat.

Evil cat.

Skata rubbed his hands over his face and stood up. The clock on top of the shelf claimed that it was seven twenty-five in the morning. He felt as though he'd hardly had any sleep at all.

A quick, cold shower jump-started his blood flow, and by the time he was dressed and headed down the stairs, he felt more like himself. Not that being himself was any kind of pinnacle of achievement.

Morticia bounded down the stairs behind him with a series of sharp, whiny sounds that sounded like fingernails on a blackboard. The cat reached the bottom of the stairs before he did and turned to watch him with large, unblinking eyes.

"What do you want?" he demanded. He opened the front door, and the animal shot outside like she'd been fired from a cannon.

"Finally," he grunted. He made his way to the kitchen where he found Angel expertly flipping pancakes in a nonstick skillet.

"Look at you," said Angel, without turning around, "all bright-eyed and bushy-tailed. Pancake?"

"Is it poisoned?" asked Skata, sitting down on one of the barstools with a groan.

"For shame. Breakfast is the most important meal of the day. Poison is reserved for dinner."

Skata grunted. "What are you so happy about anyway?"

"Nothing. Oh, by the way—" Angel scooped the pancake

out of the skillet and onto a waiting plate "—I paid Easton a little visit last night."

Skata accepted the proffered cup of coffee with a narrow look at Angel. "What did you go there for?" he demanded, taking a small brandy tin out of his pocket and pouring a teaspoon of vervain into the cup.

"Well, the good news is that I know Macon is definitely a werewolf. The better news is that he probably has a pack somewhere close by, too."

Skata set the coffee down. "What makes you so sure?"

"Just the fact that Macon goes camping on a monthly basis, with a group of friends Easton's never met. Oh, and that happens to be on full moon nights."

"The next full moon is in three days," said Skata, making a split-second decision.

"Think we should follow him?"

"Not 'we'. I'm going to follow him. You can stay here."

"I feel like Batman," said Angel grandly, flipping another pancake with an expert twist. "Sending Robin into the big, bad world all by himself."

"If anyone's Batman, it's me."

"Whatever you say." Angel set a plate with two pancakes, plenty of butter, and a generous puddle of syrup in front of Skata. "Eat up, sidekick."

The doorbell rang just as Skata took his first bite. Angel

moved the skillet onto a cold burner and tossed the towel over his shoulder. As he passed Skata, he said aloud, "No, no, don't worry—I'll get it. It's not like I'm doing anything at the moment, anyway."

Skata ignored him and listened as he ate his pancakes. Angel answered the door, and Skata heard him say, "I didn't know you made house calls."

There was a quiet response, and then Angel shouted, "Whoever let the cat out is going to regret it if he ever does it again, Skata!"

A moment later, the vampire strode into the kitchen with Morticia close on his heels, rubbing up against his legs like she hadn't seen him in weeks. Cassis followed close behind him.

"You look much better," he remarked.

"It's all the late nights and Dick Tracy stuff," said Angel, clicking his tongue once. "Does wonders."

Cassis blinked. "That doesn't sound like resting."

"I'm fine," said Skata.

If the dhampir had been going to make a big deal out of Skata's state, he decided against it. Instead, he pulled out another bar stool and sat down. "Any leads on your vampire?"

"Yeah," said Skata vaguely. "He's somewhere in these parts."

Angel turned around. "That's good news."

Cassis shook his head once and said, "I don't know if I'd call that 'good news.'"

"Sure it is," said Angel. "The sooner this guy—" here he

jerked his thumb in Skata's direction "—catches his vampire, the sooner he'll stop terrorizing my cat."

"I'm surprised you haven't tried to leave already," Cassis told Skata.

"Would it do any good?" asked Skata darkly.

"No," said Angel. "My word is my bond. James Bond." He set another plate of breakfast down in front of Cassis. "Dig in."

"I saw Colton at the café this morning," said Cassis, changing the subject. "He says you stopped by the church building last night."

"I was getting some help," muttered Skata, finishing the last pancake.

"You asked for help?" Angel looked impressed.

Skata gave Angel a dark look. "Shut up now, or the next stake'll be in your heart."

"Wouldn't kill me," said Angel airily.

"I know." Skata set down his fork and sighed. "That's one of the things Colton cleared up last night. You could have told me I was returning something I might actually need," he added pointedly to the vampire.

"Why would I want you walking around with something that could kill me?"

"He liked you," interrupted Cassis, apparently trying to smooth over the conversation before it became an argument.

"He was all right." Skata rubbed the back of his neck. He must have slept wrong; his muscles were tense and knotted.

"Well." Cassis stood up and moved the stool back into place. "I just came by to check on you, so." He nodded at Skata. "Remember, nothing strenuous for a few more days, at least."

"You're moving my time down?"

"You moved it down. I'm just trying to help you not die."

"Noble of you," said Skata without any real annoyance.

The dhampir grinned and lifted a hand in Angel's direction. "It was nice seeing you, Angel."

"Oh, always a pleasure," said Angel with exaggerated politeness.

"Take care of him," said Cassis as he walked out.

"I will," said Angel and Skata at the same time.

CHAPTER FOURTEEN

I have a great idea."

Skata stiffened as Angel leaned down over the back of his chair. "Don't want to know," he said shortly.

Angel stepped around the chair, ignoring Skata's protest. "We should go scope out the wolves together and turn it into a camping trip."

Skata leaned his head back and eyed the obviously insane vampire. "Let me just think of the two million other people I would rather do something with this weekend."

"There are roughly six billion people on this good earth of ours," said Angel, bending over and picking up a discarded issue of *Guns & Gardens*. "I'm flattered you'd pick me out of two million."

"I didn't say that."

"Yes, you did."

Skata slapped his magazine down across his thigh. "You're

not coming. Can I be any clearer, or do you need me to switch to baby talk?"

Angel held up his hands. "Fine. It was just a thought." He tossed the magazine back onto the couch.

"Stop thinking and find something you're good at."

"Someone's in fine sarcastic fiddle today." Angel lifted his eyebrows. "Are you coming down with something?"

"Yeah," Skata grunted. "A bad case of house arrest."

"Think of this as a hospital, but with more freedom."

"In a hospital, there would be attractive nurses and less snark."

"Attractive nurses I can get for you," said Angel, "but I'm afraid I can't help you with the snark."

"Then go away."

"I'm going, I'm going. If you need anything, get it yourself." Angel opened the front door. "Oh, and don't eat the cat while I'm gone."

Skata lifted his head and scanned the room for any sign of the feline, but she was probably somewhere upstairs, hiding from the tip of his shoe. "Don't bet on it," he said, lowering his gaze back to the page.

* * * * * * *

It was an exceptionally warm day. The air wrapped everything in a sweltering blanket, and the few sparse clouds did nothing to block the sun.

Angel pulled into the town square and parked next to the fountain and statue of Hezekiah Hammond, the town's founder. It was a presumptuous statue and Hezekiah was standing like he'd just climbed Kilimanjaro, but whatever. Salvation wasn't his town anyway.

Angel stopped to appreciate the sight of three pretty college girls standing outside the general store before he walked past them inside.

Sheriff Amory nearly ran into him on his way out.

"I'm so sorry," Angel apologized, sidestepping the man.

"Don't sweat the small stuff," said the sheriff cheerfully. He tilted his hat up and glanced through the doors. "Some day, ain't it? Saw some kids frying an egg on the hood of a car."

"And I bet you gave them a ticket," said Angel, winking.

The sheriff chortled. "It was my car," he said. "No harm done." The walkie-talkie on his belt crackled with a voice, and Angel watched, intrigued, as the sheriff answered.

"Yeah, Steve, what is it?"

"Sir, we've got another one of those animal attacks out near North Bend."

A deep furrow cut between the sheriff's eyebrows. "How bad?"

"Just one, sir. DOA."

"Right. Just sit tight now, I'll be there in a jiffy."

"Yes, sir."

The walkie-talkie went silent, and the sheriff lowered it with a deep sigh. His eyes met Angel's and he blinked a few times, as if remembering that he wasn't alone. "Guess you heard," he said.

Angel folded his arms and sounded as concerned as possible. "Animal attack, huh?"

"Yeah," said the sheriff, with forced nonchalance. "We've had a few of 'em over the past week."

"What kind of animal?" asked Angel.

"Mountain lion, probably," said the sheriff immediately.

Angel was careful not to smile. *Nailed it.* He let a small look of understanding dawn across his face. "Ah," he said, with meaning. He stepped closer, lowered his voice conspiratorially, and said, "Do you think it was vampires?"

The sheriff blinked. "Now how does a fella like you know about that?"

Angel smiled as though the sheriff had cracked a joke. "Just because I'm not on the council doesn't mean I'm stupid, now, Sheriff. I've always been…ah, privy to these things. In fact," he continued, as if taken by a sudden thought, "I'd like to help, if I could."

He could see the sheriff's brain slowly turning, taking in the rich young man who was offering to lend a hand. Angel knew everyone on the council drank, ate, or wore vervain to keep from being compelled, so he had to be sneaky.

"After all, this is my town, too," he added seriously.

"Might be," said the sheriff, stroking his goatee. "I think we could use someone like you on the council. New demographic."

"Just let me know if there is *anything* I can do," said Angel, patting the sheriff's arm.

"I'll tell you what you can do," said the sheriff, pushing open the door and letting in a wave of late-summer heat. "There's a council meeting on Friday, at seven o'clock. Be there, and I'll introduce you to the rest of the folks."

"Absolutely. Thank you for your trust," he added. "It means a lot to me."

"See you then, son."

When the sheriff's back was turned, Angel's smile dropped and he stood in thoughtful silence. He considered calling Skata, but changed his mind. He would keep this to himself for now.

* * * * * *

As soon as the vampire left, Skata tucked his revolver into the back of his jeans and headed out. It was roughly two miles to the church building, but he didn't mind the walk. At the very least, it was a form of exercise that wouldn't reopen his stitches or give Cassis a heart attack.

South Carolina was a far cry from Montana, Skata thought

as he walked along the side of the road, weeds reaching for his boots and cicadas humming from the shadows. Everything was draped with Spanish moss—which he knew was neither Spanish nor moss and therefore completely ridiculous—and the humidity was almost suffocating. Sweat trickled down the back of his neck and down his forehead into his eyes.

As soon as he killed Samuel Lemeck, he was going back to the mountains. Not Montana. Maybe Colorado or Wyoming.

He turned into the churchyard and went inside the building. It was a little cooler thanks to the vaulted roof, if not much. Didn't these people know about air conditioning? "Hey," he called. "Colton, you in here?"

The preacher's head appeared around the same doorway as the last time. "Oh, hey," he said, lifting a hand. He stepped around, wiping his palms on the thighs of his jeans and leaving gray smudges. "Dusty down there," he remarked. "What can I do for you?"

"I noticed your dirt bike out in the parking lot," said Skata. "I need to borrow it."

Colton's eyebrows rose, and he looked past Skata out the doors as if making sure the bike was still there. "What for?"

"Off-roading."

Colton indicated the bandages visible under Skata's shirt. "Aren't you supposed to be taking it easy?"

"Yeah," said Skata. "Hence the bike."

After a moment, the preacher nodded. "Yeah," he said, nodding slowly, "you can borrow it, on one condition."

"Name it."

"You gotta tell me where you're going. I'll know if you lie to me," he added in a bluntly threatening manner.

Well, the preacher already knew most of his situation. The truth could only hurt so much, and at the most he'd be short one dirt bike. "Rukiel said the vampire I'm after was seen in a town forty miles from here. That was a few days ago."

"Huh. Weird," said Colton, drawing his eyebrows together. "If someone was after me, I'd book it a lot farther than that."

"That's right. I have a hunch he knows where I am and is…I don't know, 'circling.' I want to have a look around the woods and see if I can find anything."

Colton pushed his hair behind his ears. "Okay," he said finally, "but I have a second condition."

Skata blew out an annoyed breath. "What is it?"

"I'm coming with you."

Skata stared at the preacher. "Why does everyone in this blasted town think I need babysat? Trust me, I don't need you."

"Trust *me*," said Colton with a warning look that said Skata was close to losing use of the dirt bike. "You need me. That's my final offer, take it or leave it."

Skata swore under his breath. "I'll take it."

"Good. Just so happens I've got another bike in the storage

shed." He looked over his shoulder as he exited the building. "I'm taking the Yamaha."

* * * * * * *

There was no sure way to know where to begin looking for Lemeck. Skata knew his *modus operandi* was to hang around the outskirts of towns, occasionally venturing into the fringe for an energy fix. There were plenty of woods and marshlands around Salvation where a vampire could stay near civilization and remain hidden.

They decided to take off from the parking lot and make a wide circle around the town.

They rode for half an hour, until they came to a place where the trees and underbrush grew too dense for the dirt bikes.

Colton leaned his elbows on his handlebars and shook his head. "Can't ride through that. Turn back or walk?"

"Walk," said Skata, dismounting.

"You bring any weapons in case this goes pear-shaped?"

Skata held up his revolver. "Enough to deter him for a while."

Colton chuckled and unzipped one of his saddlebags and took out a crossbow. "Barnett Ghost 400." He patted it with fondness. "You used to crossbows?"

"I've used them a time or two."

"Heads up." He tossed it to Skata, who caught the crossbow and the following pack of bolts.

"What are you going to use?" asked Skata, eyeing the preacher's saddlebags.

Colton unzipped the leather gun case from the other side of his dirt bike and held up a bulky black shotgun. "I've got this baby right here."

They set off into the underbrush. It was difficult to be quiet while dry grass crunched underfoot and thorny vines snagged your jeans every other step, but they did their best to keep the noise down.

"Hey," said Colton, glancing back at Skata. "What are you gonna do if you find this guy?"

"Shoot him," said Skata.

"Won't kill him. You don't have the right equipment."

"I didn't say kill him, I said shoot him."

"You ever thought of maybe getting his side of the story?"

Skata turned around, fighting to keep from pointing the tip of the crossbow at the preacher. "Let's get something straight," he growled. "His story doesn't have a *side*. You don't know it, and I do, so shut up."

Colton eyed the crossbow with something like anger, but he said nothing else. They had hiked at least another mile before the preacher spoke again. "So what did he do?"

Skata eyed the sprawling roots of the enormous banyan tree ahead. "Mind your own business."

"Hey," Colton whispered quickly, lifting a hand. He crept forward several yards and crouched down. Skata followed to see what the fuss was about.

"There was a fire here," said Colton, touching the ashes mingled with dry kudzu leaves on the ground.

"In this weather?"

"Maybe it was for cooking, not heat. Either way, it's cold." He ran a hand through his hair and rose to his feet.

"No more than a day or so old, I'd say." Skata slapped at a mosquito that buzzed around his neck. "He was definitely here."

"How do you know it was him?"

"Shoes." Skata pointed toward an imprint in the ground, barely visible in the dirt. "Been tracking those footprints for months."

"Sounds like fun."

"Sam, what are you doing?" Skata mused aloud quietly, turning in a circle, scanning the ground for more prints. The vampire had been careful. There was not another print to be seen.

"It's gonna be dark in less than an hour." Colton squinted at the sky. "We should head back. Don't want to be stuck in these woods. Might end up as another mountain lion attack," he added wryly.

He had been so *close*. Skata ground his back teeth together and, before he quite realized what he was doing, let his fist fly. His knuckles split open against the splintered bark of the banyan root.

"Hey." Colton reached out, his hand nearly touching Skata's arm, but not quite. "Calm down, man, we ain't done. We'll find him."

"Damn straight." Skata spat on the ground and turned around, just in time to see a mass of gray fur and muscle slam Colton to the ground.

CHAPTER FIFTEEN

Skata aimed the crossbow and fired a bolt without a second thought.

The wolf moved just in time, the arrow piercing its shoulder and not its back. The wolf's high-pitched howl became a snarl, angrier than before. Bared teeth flashed above Colton's exposed neck when a gunshot rang out and the snarling fell silent.

Colton shoved the body off him with a grunt of effort and stood up, breathing hard. He bent over and lifted his shotgun from the ground. "That was close," he said with a grin that disappeared as quickly as it showed up.

Skata kicked the limp wolf in the ribs. The close-range shotgun blast had torn a softball-sized hole through its side. "Doesn't get much deader than that."

"Just wait," said Colton.

"For what?"

The preacher gestured toward the wolf. "When a werewolf

is killed in wolf form, it returns back to the original form as the body cools."

There was nothing but the sound of Colton's heavy breathing and the din of cicadas for several minutes.

Slowly, fur gave way to skin, claws to fingers, and they were looking at the bleeding, naked corpse of a boy no more than nineteen or twenty.

Colton crouched down and locked his fingers behind his head. After a moment, he said, "Beta. Probably just doing whatever he was told." He reached out and closed the boy's eyelids with his fingertips. "He was just a kid."

"Yeah, a kid trying to kill us," Skata pointed out. "And don't even think about giving me that 'thou shalt not kill' crap, because I don't buy it."

"Nah, man, I get it. This was self-defense. It's just…" Colton rose to his feet and kicked the ground, the action too small for how upset he looked. "We need to take him back."

"Back where?"

"His home. He deserves to be buried."

"He's a werewolf."

"He's a *person*," snapped Colton, a fierce glint in his eyes. He rubbed his mouth and stepped toward the body. "We're taking him back."

"How? Ride back to town with a corpse over the bike? Say 'hey, does he belong to anyone? We shot him twice in the woods.'"

"In self-defense," Colton reiterated.

Skata shook his head. "The kid's naked and doesn't look like he could hurt a fly, not in this body."

Colton dragged his hands over the back of his head and down across his face. After a moment of heavy silence, he said, "Good point. I have a better idea."

* * * * * * *

It wasn't easy to ride with a corpse across the back of your bike, but Colton seemed to manage. The weapons were all placed on Skata's bike, and they made their way through the back roads to Salvation Church.

"Good thing nobody saw us," said Skata, watching Colton heft the body over his shoulders. "This would be hard to explain."

Colton grunted in response. "I'll put him downstairs. Then we'll go see the mayor."

Skata settled back on the bike and waited several minutes as the preacher disappeared and came back, minus the body.

"Covered him with a tarp," he said, mounting his Yamaha. "Still, we better hurry. Lock on the door's busted, so it won't keep anyone from getting in."

They rode across town to the mayor's mansion.

"Hope he won't mind us busting in," said Skata, climbing off the bike and standing at the bottom of the staircase that led up to the double front doors. It was all very southern-style ostentatious, and he half-expected to see a parade of tuxedos and hoop skirts swoop down the stairs.

"If he does, too bad."

They walked up the stairs and knocked. The door was quickly opened by an attractive woman in her mid-forties. Her blond hair was straight out of an expensive bottle, and her face spoke of more than one Botox injection.

"Hello, Honoria," said Colton with a brief smile. He stuck one hand in his pocket and with the other he gestured to Skata. "This is Skata. He's a—friend."

"Hi," said Skata.

"Yes, of course." She swept a critical gaze over him, but smiled again at the preacher. "It's always so nice to see you, Lucas. Won't y'all come in?"

"Don't mind if we do." Skata stepped inside and let out a deep breath of relief as cool air enveloped him.

As she shut the door behind them, Honoria asked Lucas in a low voice, "Now, what is this all about?"

"We—well," Colton faltered.

Skata stepped in. "Werewolf attacked us in the woods, and we had to put it down."

Honoria put a hand to her throat. "I see." She drew in a deep breath and asked, "Do you have any idea who it was?"

"No, ma'am," said Colton. "He ain't from around here."

She let out the breath and nodded. "I'll get Harold to call an emergency council meeting. First the animal attacks, now this? It's too much to be coincidence."

Skata frowned. "What animal attacks?"

"We'll go over everything at the meeting," Honoria assured him. "Meanwhile, I think there are some scones in the kitchen and drinks in the refrigerator—you boys can help yourselves. Please excuse me." She turned on her heel and crossed the grand foyer, hurrying up the stairs as fast as her pencil skirt would let her.

Skata looked at Colton. "I'm in a council meeting?"

"Yeah." Colton gave him a slight shake of his head. "Not really your kind of folks."

"Didn't figure so."

They walked into the vast kitchen. It dwarfed Angel's and made Skata question why people needed four ovens.

Colton crossed over to the cut-glass bowl of scones sitting on the island and took two, offering one to Skata. "She makes good scones."

Skata took the scone, and they stood eating in silence. He hadn't realized how hungry he was until now—hiking for hours through miles of wild terrain and oppressive heat had a way of stretching the stomach. He had eaten three scones and was on his fourth when Colton spoke again.

"So you're staying with Angel, huh?"

"Unfortunately."

"Weird," said Colton. "He doesn't strike me as the kinda guy to keep house guests."

"Beats me," said Skata.

Colton gave Skata a piercing look before changing the subject. "This is the second werewolf to try and kill you in a couple days."

"I noticed."

"Both times you were looking for this Lemeck guy, right? That doesn't seem weird to you?"

Skata leaned his good elbow against the island. Pieces began to float together in his mind, turning, trying to fit. "Why would werewolves want to keep me from finding a vampire?"

Colton shook his head. "I don't know, but if one is happenstance and two is a coincidence, then this sure ain't happenstance."

"I need a beer," said Skata. He opened the stainless-steel fridge and crouched down. "What the heck is Tsingtao?"

Colton shrugged. "I don't know."

"Huh." Skata took a bottle from the fridge and studied the label. "Well, it's beer." He looked over at the preacher. "Can I get you a drink, Father?"

"I already told you—it's preacher, not Father." He held up two fingers. "Twice."

"Do you want one or not?"

"Fine."

"Good for you." Skata gave him a beer, and they leaned against the island. "I thought preachers didn't drink alcohol.

Some Bible rule."

"Nah. There's rules against getting drunk." Colton popped the cap off the bottle. "So I don't get drunk."

"Takes the fun out of things, doesn't it?"

Colton's lip curled in disgust. "Yeah," he said. "Sure. I really miss hangovers and vomiting."

Honoria walked into the kitchen with clicking heels and stopped short when she saw the depleted amount of scones in the bowl.

"My goodness," she commented. "Don't y'all eat at home?"

Colton grinned. "You're a fine cook, ma'am."

"Well, thank you, Lucas." She squeezed his arm. "Everyone will convene in the den, so would you mind showing your friend here where it is while I see to the guests?"

"Sure thing." Colton's smile was uneasy as Honoria left the kitchen. "Man," he told Skata in a low voice, "this can't go well."

* * * * * * *

The small, gathered crowd only half-filled the spacious den, although there was only one chair and so everyone stood, waiting for the mayor.

Skata scanned the new faces—half a dozen people who looked both wealthy and concerned, plus the uniformed sheriff and several deputies, and—

Angel waved his fingertips at him across the room.

Skata leaned down to Colton and asked in a low voice, "What the hell is Angel doing here?"

"Beats me," was the hushed reply. "He's never been to one of these before."

"I thought there weren't any unnaturals allowed."

"Yeah, 'cause they *aren't.*"

The mayor stepped into the room and pulled the doors closed behind him. "All right, everyone, settle down." He smiled and gave a sweeping, panoramic wave. "Long time, no see."

Everyone except Skata and Colton chuckled at the joke.

"Why are we here, Harold?" asked the sheriff, nudging his hat back on his forehead.

The mayor gestured toward Colton. "Unfortunately, we are gathered here because Mr. Colton and this man were attacked by a werewolf earlier today. Mr. Colton, would you tell everyone exactly what happened?"

Colton scratched his jaw. "Uh…right." He put his hands in his pockets and gave a slight shrug. "Don't know who he was— there was no I.D. on him. He was a beta. Don't think he's from around here, though."

"Was the attack random or planned?" asked a man who looked uncomfortably warm in a camouflage jacket.

Colton shook his head. "Can't tell, but Skata here was attacked by a werewolf just outside of town less than a week ago, so."

"Two werewolf attacks in a week?" The woman next to Honoria covered her mouth.

"That isn't all." The mayor motioned to the sheriff, who walked into the center of the room.

"Thank you, Mayor," said the sheriff with a nod. "Folks, we have a problem. The department has reason to believe that a strigoi vampire has been killing on the outskirts of our town."

There were several repetitions of "How many?"

"Three," said the sheriff, holding up the same amount of fingers. "Hitchhikers and campers from out of town, so far, but they're getting closer to town, and we need to start taking precautions."

The room took in a collective gasp and began to buzz with quiet speculations and exclamations of distress.

"What can we do?" demanded Angel.

Skata stared at him and mouthed, "What do you think you're doing?"

The vampire ignored him as the sheriff said, "Carry a stake with you at all times, or at least a gun with wooden bullets. If you need any, just come by the station and we'll take care of you. Also, make sure you and all your loved ones are on vervain."

Wooden bullets were a new idea to Skata, who was impressed in spite of himself. Colton, however, looked distinctly unhappy.

The sheriff continued. "Also, don't go anywhere alone, if you can help it. I'm doubling patrols temporarily, and me and my boys will give you any help you need."

"Sheriff," said a new voice, and a woman stepped forward who Skata recognized as Easton's mother Phoebe. He vaguely recalled Easton's father being from Oregon, which meant Easton's mother must come from a Salvation founding family.

It's a small world.

"What about the non-humans living among us?" asked Mrs. Everett. "Are we safe from the Montgomery brothers? From Rukiel?"

"That's a good question, Phoebe," said the sheriff, "but don't worry. We're keeping a good eye on them."

Colton folded his arms over his chest. "They've never given us a reason not to trust them."

All eyes turned to him.

The preacher glanced up, obviously uncomfortable with the attention but firm in his stance. "I get we should take precautions, but spying on good people, it just…" he shrugged. "It doesn't seem right."

"Desperate times call for desperate measures," said the mayor. There was a warning edge to the smile he gave Colton before he continued. "That's not up for discussion."

"All right," said Colton. He added, "I'm leaving," under his breath as he pushed past Skata and left the room.

Skata cast a glance at Angel. The vampire's lips were pursed in thought, but he kept any obvious thoughts off his face. Skata figured he could interrogate Angel later. He followed Colton out into the thick night air and down the steps of the white mansion.

Colton turned and jabbed a finger toward the house. "They're a bunch of frickin' morons."

"That doesn't sound very loving of you," jibed Skata.

"You agree with 'em?"

"I'm no vampire-hugger," said Skata, "but I doubt spying on anyone's going to do much good for non-human relations. I don't think the law in this town's going to be very sneaky about it, either."

Colton pushed his hands back over his hair. "You going after Samuel?"

Skata noticed the subject change but decided not to chase it. In this state, Colton looked capable of punching a hole through a brick wall. "Probably Sunday. Saturday's a full moon."

"So? Don't think many werewolves chase cars."

"I think there's a werewolf pack in the mountains near here. I want to make sure."

"Why? What's it to you?"

"One of the werewolves is the boyfriend of a girl I know. Easton Everett."

Colton's eyebrows rose, and Skata explained his unusual relationship with the family. When he was finished, all Colton said was, "You going alone?"

Skata walked across the lawn toward the dirt bikes, and Colton followed suit. "I was," he said, mounting up.

Colton smiled.

CHAPTER SIXTEEN

Skata was sitting in the living room watching a superhero show when Angel strode through the front door.

"Aww," he said, pressing a hand to his heart. "You waited up for me."

"What do you think you were doing at the council meeting?"

"Hi to you, too."

"Answer the question, vamp."

"Oh. We're back on a species-name basis, I see." Angel sauntered into the living room. "Well, human, I was invited. Much like you, I gather."

"Who invited you?"

Angel fluttered his eyelashes. "Sheriff Amory himself. You see, I'm now a very helpful Salvation citizen, and I want to do my part to help, just like everybody else." Here, he clutched his chest with enthusiasm.

Skata snorted and lifted the remote, turning the show off. He hadn't been paying attention anyway.

"Turnabout's fair play," said Angel, "so why exactly were you there?"

"I was there with Colton."

"A cowboy team-up. That's adorable."

"We were attacked by a werewolf."

"Yeah, I caught that part. Such an exciting little life you have. I guess I should ask what were you *doing* that sparked said attack?"

"Hiking," said Skata.

"I see. Is this code for 'looking for a vampire so I can kill him?' I'm surprised the preacher went with you."

Skata was surprised by the preacher period, but he only said, "That's close enough."

"Maybe you should, I don't know—actually lie low while you're supposed to be lying low."

"I'm going up to see if Macon's part of a pack," said Skata calmly, focusing on the blank screen in front of him. "That's that."

Angel clicked his tongue. "Don't blame me if you get a wolfy kick in the butt."

"I've already survived a werewolf bite. I don't think a kick would hurt that much."

"So willful," Angel reprimanded. "I bet your mom had gray hair by the time you escaped the ovarian Bastille."

"Shut up," said Skata.

* * * * * *

Saturday evening came quickly. Skata made an effort to try and salvage part of his healing process by resting on Friday, and by the time Colton showed up on Saturday afternoon, he was beyond ready.

Colton grinned as he stood in the doorway and watched Skata double-check his weapons. "What's the matter, feeling a little stir-crazy?"

"You have no idea."

"Easy now, cowboy," said Angel, leaning against the wall. "Remember, you don't have the best track record with were-wolves."

Skata slung his pack over his good shoulder. "I don't have the best track record with vampires, either." He nodded at Colton, who turned and strode outside to the '67 Chevy pickup idling in the drive.

"Bye now," called Angel sweetly, waving.

Skata glared at him over his shoulder and didn't respond. He tossed the pack into the truck bed and climbed into the passenger seat.

Colton turned the radio on to a country station and pulled out, his arm out the open window.

They took the winding road that led away from Salvation up into the mountains. It was a long drive, and after an hour of endless trees, he dozed off. What felt like minutes later, Skata opened his eyes and grunted, "What?"

"I've been trying to wake you up for a while, man." Colton

gave him a concerned look. "You okay?"

"I'm fine." Skata rubbed the sleep from his eyes and focused through the windshield. They were parked underneath the draping roots of a banyan—these trees were never-ending and a little bit creepy, like something out of an illustrated horror book.

"You sure this is the place?" asked Colton, exiting the truck.

"According to Angel," said Skata. "So we can only hope he passed on the right information."

Skata lifted his pack out of the truck bed and watched as Colton opened the metal box beside it. The box was filled with weapons, including the Barnett Ghost and a Winchester rifle that looked as if it had been well-used.

"Need anything?" asked Colton, removing the crossbow and a hefty revolver. He spun the revolver around like a Wild West deputy before sticking it in the back of his jeans.

Skata held up his sawed-off Remington 870. "I'm good. Let's go."

* * * * * * *

Angel stared at the basement door, his arms folded. He dug his fingers into his skin hard enough to draw blood before saying, "Nope."

He rushed out of the house, moving so fast that a human

would have seen only a blur. Why couldn't someone invent a patch for this kind of craving?

Angel halted in the middle of the street, where he proceeded to put his hands in his pockets and stroll down the street. The pavement was badly in need of repair, the curb completely overtaken by unruly kudzu vines. He walked until he reached town—maybe he just needed some fast food.

He was crossing the town square when he saw a familiar figure walk out of the general store, her long brown hair blowing in the hot summer breeze. She held a paper bag full of what appeared to be junk food and soda.

"Easton!" He jogged over to where her VW Beetle was parked.

She looked up at the sound of his voice. "Hey!" she said in surprise. "What are you doing here?"

"Looking for a bite to eat," he replied, smiling. He indicated the paper bag. "Girl's night in?"

"Girl's night out, actually. I'm going to surprise Macon."

Angel chuckled and glanced around, wondering how many people would notice if he snatched her in public. "Yeah, you probably don't want to do that."

Her smile took a suspicious turn. "Oh yeah? Why's that?"

"Just trust me," said Angel, with a brief smile. "You don't."

She unlocked the car, hefting the bag under her free arm. "I already told you," she said, "I like you, but I don't trust you."

He had to be smoother about this—having her eye him with

suspicion was the last thing he wanted, but it was happening anyway. "He probably doesn't invite you for a reason. You don't want to embarrass yourself."

She opened the car door. Angel pushed it shut, his palm resting against the glass. "Seriously," he said, his smile narrowing. "Don't."

Anger and something close to fear flashed across Easton's face. "Back off."

He looked directly into her eyes, feeling the slight shift in his mind as he compelled her. "You aren't going up to the mountains to see Macon. You're going to go home, and you're going to watch a movie and text him that you miss him."

Easton backed up a step. "No," she said, looking Angel up and down, like he had turned into a homeless stranger harassing her for spare change. "I'm not. Get away from me."

His eyebrows rose. "Oops," he said aloud. "That should have worked."

"What should have worked? Your lame attempt at hypnotism?" She flung her car door open again and slid into the driver's seat. "Don't talk to me again."

Of course. Her mom was on the council; she would have put Easton on vervain.

He gripped the car door before she could pull it shut. "So sorry about this," he said with a sigh, "but I did warn you."

* * * * * * *

The binoculars were army surplus, and the night vision was blindingly green. Skata passed them to Colton. "You seeing what I'm seeing?"

Colton squinted through the binoculars. "If what you mean is a bunch of kids smashing beer cans on their foreheads, then yup."

Macon's friends had only put up one tent, where they had stashed their backpacks and then proceeded to break out enough snacks to feed an army. As Colton passed the binoculars back to Skata, one of the campers threw back his head and unleashed a very human howl.

Skata exchanged a look with Colton, and the preacher looked up at the sky. It was dark, and clouds obscured everything but the faintest glow. A breeze kicked up, scurrying the cloud cover along faster.

"Aaaany minute now," said Colton softly.

As if on cue, a ragged hole in the clouds let a bright shaft of moonlight through. The light filtered down to the forest floor.

Macon was the first to shift.

He fell to his knees with a cry that reached the knoll where Skata and Colton were watching. The transformation was quick, but it wasn't smooth. Skata watched in morbid fascination as muscles and bone shifted, rearranging the body into a different form. Clothing split and fell to the ground, joints stretched.

Eyes looked toward the binoculars, two shining orbs of reflection.

"Oh, shoot," said Skata.

"Yep," said Colton. "Time to go."

The men jumped to their feet and took off running amid the baying of werewolves below. The howls grew closer as they raced through the trees, back toward the truck.

"This was your idea," shouted Colton, leaping across a fallen log.

"I didn't twist your arm!" He saw a break in the trees ahead. "Get the keys out!"

"Didn't lock it," said Colton. He yanked the driver's door open and climbed in just as Macon hit the window, claws screeching across the glass.

The engine rattled to life, and Colton slammed his foot down on the accelerator. Tires screeched against the dirt road, and the truck swerved before straightening out and racing down the mountain, away from the pack.

Skata twisted around. "They're not following us."

"'Cause they're smart," said Colton. "Either that or they were just chasing us away."

"From what?"

"You tell me, man. It's your quest. I'm just the sidekick."

* * * * * * *

It was late when they arrived at Angel's house. Skata climbed out of the truck and lifted his pack from the bed. "You coming in?"

"Nah, I'll head home and crash. See you in church."

"Don't hold your breath," said Skata, lifting a hand in farewell.

Colton returned the gesture with a "Take it easy" and pulled out of the driveway, disappearing down the long tree-lined stretch of gravel.

The front door opened just as Skata lifted his hand to knock. "So," said Angel in a conspiratorial tone, "how did it go?"

"Macon's in a werewolf pack."

"Bummer," said Angel. He still hadn't opened the door more than a few inches.

Skata kicked the base of the door with his foot. "Is this payback for Easton's house, or what?"

"About Easton," began Angel, "I should probably explain—"

Skata's face darkened, and he pressed against the door with his hand. "Let me in."

Angel lifted his hands in surrender and stepped aside as Skata pushed past him.

"Living room," said Angel.

Skata crossed the foyer and stopped short at the sight of Easton sitting in the center of the living room, her wrists and ankles tied to a heavy chair. A strip of duct tape was pressed over her mouth, but when she saw Skata, she unleashed a muffled scream, her eyes wide and furious.

Slowly Skata turned back to face Angel.

The vampire opened his mouth, then closed it before Skata grabbed a fistful of Angel's shirt and shouted, "What the hell have you done?"

"It was for her own good," he said, gripping Skata's wrist and twisting it away from his shirt. "Trust me."

"You freaking *abducted* her—"

"Well, she had her car all loaded up for a little road trip." A sarcastic smile stretched across Angel's mouth. "To meet up with her boyfriend. Basically, I saved the day."

Skata raked his hands through his hair and lowered his voice. "Did she see anything?"

"You mean like my scary vampire face? Nah. There was, however, another slight fiasco wherein I tried to compel her not to go."

"And?"

"And Mama Everett apparently has her kids on vervain after the meeting last night."

Skata stared at him, attempting to process the enormity of this problem.

"So," said Angel, clapping his hands together faintly. "That happened."

"Are you incapable of doing anything right?" snapped Skata, furious.

"Next time, I'll just let her get herself killed!" Angel snapped in return. "I know it looks sketchy, but this was actually pretty magnanimous of me, you know."

Skata crossed the living room, pulled a knife from his boot and cut away the duct tape binding Easton to the chair.

Immediately, she tore the strip of tape off her mouth and snarled, "Someone had better tell me what's going on before I call the sheriff."

CHAPTER SEVENTEEN

Angel sauntered into the room and held up a finger. "You can't call the sheriff because I have your cell phone. Besides, what would you tell him? That your former babysitter and his roomie are chatting with you in the living room?"

Easton grabbed a book from the coffee table and threw it at him. He turned his head as it smacked into his chest and fell to the ground. His smile stretched thin, but all he said was, "Ow."

Easton's face was flushed, and her skin was red where the tape had stuck, but she looked ready to tackle Angel to the floor.

"You deserved that," Skata told Angel.

Angel tilted his head in concession and picked the book up off the floor.

"You kidnapped me!"

"Well," drawled Angel, "you're over eighteen, so technically, I borrowed you."

"You're not helping," said Skata.

"Somebody start talking right *now,*" said Easton. "I mean it."

Skata rubbed his face. "It's—"

A tinny pop song began playing out of nowhere. Angel reached into his pocket and withdrew a cell phone.

"Give me that," exclaimed Easton.

He wagged a finger and answered the phone. "Easton's cell phone, this is Angel speaking. How can I help you?"

Easton drew a finger across her throat and hissed, "You're *dead.*"

Angel smiled and mouthed back, "I know." Aloud he said, "Mmhmm, she's here. No, no, everything's fine, she's just—busy. Of course I'll tell her you called. Absolutely. Bye now." He hung up and slid the phone back into his pocket.

"Who was that?" Easton demanded.

"Calm down, it was only Graham."

"Is everything okay? Is he okay?"

"*He's* fine. But apparently you were supposed to call when you reached the campsite or something like that."

"I hate you," stated Easton flatly.

"Oh no!" Angel pressed a hand to his chest. "I can't take it!"

Skata took hold of Easton's arm and suggested, "Why don't you sit down?"

"I don't want to sit down."

"You really should."

She stood for a long second and then crossed the room and seated herself on the couch, her legs crossed and her arms folded.

"I'm sitting. Now talk."

"A-ah." Skata rubbed his hands together and shot a glance at Angel. The vampire adopted a look of intent concentration, as if hanging on every word as yet unspoken. "Well—this...you really...it's like—"

Angel rolled his head and his eyes at the same time. "Let me." He lowered his gaze to meet Easton's. The veins around his eyes began to pulse black as his eyes turned a bloody red and he bared his fangs in a macabre smile.

It took less than ten seconds for the transformation to take place and leave the vampire's face. The angry blush faded from Easton's face, leaving her pale and frozen in place.

"I don't get it." The whispered words punched through her lips. "What—what is that?" She asked Skata, "What is he?"

"I'm your friendly neighborhood vampire," said Angel with tight-lipped smile. "And not the only one, but let's start small."

Easton stood up, gripping the arm of the couch for support. With a kind of quiet solemnity, she said, "Don't you dare come near me again. Ever."

For once, Angel made no sarcastic remark. He kept his mouth closed and only swayed a little from side to side, his arms crossed over his chest.

"Skata, we have to talk," said Easton.

"Yes, we do," Skata agreed, with a pointed look at Angel. "Out."

The vampire unfolded his arms and rotated his neck. "You

have a lot to talk over." He left the room with so little protest that, for a moment, Skata watched the doorway, waiting for him to return and take it all back. Maybe he was listening from the kitchen, but it didn't matter.

"Right," he said, clearing his throat again. The atmosphere was so uncomfortable he wanted nothing more than to hurry back out the front door, but he stayed where he was. "So, uh... you must have questions."

Easton snorted. "Questions? Yeah, I guess you could say that. You're living with a vampire? Or was that some kind of horrible practical joke, because it wasn't funny."

"It's not a joke." Skata breathed out through his nose. This would take a while.

****

The green digital numbers on the kitchen clock read 4:00. Skata shuffled into the kitchen, stifling a yawn that threatened to unhinge his jaw.

Angel stepped into the kitchen from the opposite entrance. "How'd it go?"

Skata blinked at him. "You're still up?"

The vampire smiled and took a sip of coffee from the mug in his hand. "Points for observation skills. I take it she's okay, then."

"You do, huh?"

"You let her leave when she wasn't?"

Skata spread his arms. "What was I supposed to do, huh? Keep her duct taped to a *chair*?"

Silence settled for a moment, the only sound a faint, electronic hum from the refrigerator. Then Angel asked, "So what's she going to do now? Go home and tell everyone they're being overrun by vampires? Did you tell her about Macon?"

"I had to."

"And?"

"I think she's...still processing."

Angel leaned back and widened his eyes. "You just gave her information that could potentially crucify not only me but every non-human in town and let her waltz out the door having an existential crisis. Thanks a lot."

"She's not the killing type," Skata muttered.

"That's what most people say before they find out—oh, wait! Yes, they *are*."

Skata looked at the vampire, his mouth drawn in a grim line. "She's not that kind of person."

Angel just lifted his eyebrows and drank the last swallow of coffee. He set the mug on one end of the counter and gave it a shove, sliding it across to the sink. "Wonderful. Now I can sleep easily knowing Easton isn't 'that kind of person.'"

Skata hardly noticed when the vampire left the kitchen. He leaned against the island and rubbed his face with both hands, pushing his fingers into his hair until it stood on end. Tomorrow was Sunday, which meant Easton would be at church in the morning, if she wasn't too shaken.

He could always call and—wait, Angel still had her cell. He was probably upstairs prank-calling all her contacts.

"Angel!" He took the stairs two at a time, gripping the curving bannister, and pounded on the vampire's door. "Angel!" When there was no response, he decided he was probably being ignored. He tried to open the door, but it was locked.

Muttering every unflattering name he could think of in Angel's direction, he took out his Swiss Army knife and fiddled with the lock until the door opened. The king-sized four-poster was empty, the sheets still smooth. Angel was nowhere to be seen.

Skata cautiously stepped in, half-expecting Angel to jump out from somewhere and yell "Boo." Wind blew in from the open window, twisting the curtains into a dance. Skata looked down at the desk. It was surprisingly cheap, something temporary from Ikea. He looked around the rest of the room and realized how odd it was—everything besides the bed was cheap, not made to last. It was like Angel had wanted the luxury of a large, old, secluded house, but was ready to bolt at any moment.

Tucking the nagging question into the back of his mind, Skata once more focused his attention on the desk. There was a cup for a set of pens—at least those were expensive—and in the side drawer, underneath a few issues of the town newspaper, was a box.

He looked over his shoulder, making sure the vampire wasn't hanging from the ceiling or watching from outside the window. When he was sure he was alone, Skata took the box from the drawer and set it on the desk. He lifted the lid off and set it next to the box. There was not much inside, only a few pieces of paper and some envelopes.

The first envelope was thick, heavy paper with a gold-embossed stamp on the flap. It was a circle, and inside the circle nestled a V-shape. There was one sheet of ivory stationary inside. He saw the date on the header—*February 4, 1966*. It read *From the desk of Mr. Wesley Phillips*, and began with the words *Dear Ms. Taylor.*

Skata slid the paper back into the envelope and set it on top of the lid. He didn't have time to read everything. There were three sheets of paper, faded and yellowing. They seemed to be charts of some kind. He figured out that it was the months of the year, and at the top was the number #139. Interesting, but not enlightening. There was something else—a list, with seemingly random classifications and numbered letters.

He sighed and shuffled the papers together, but as he did, a smaller piece fell out onto the floor. He bent down and picked up. It was a Polaroid photograph, the colors distorted from age. It was a shot of a crowd at some concert, the mingled bodies making it hard to see. There were only a few blurry spots recognizable as faces, but he knew one. It was Angel, his arm around the waist of a pretty young woman in cropped shorts and a bra. So the picture was from the late sixties or early seventies.

He turned the picture over to see if anything was written on the back. There was only the date, written in smeared blue pen—*1966*. The same date as on the letter from Wesley Phillips.

"You're reading someone else's mail. That's illegal."

Skata set the paper back inside the box and set the lid on top, settling it down over the edges. "Where's Easton's phone?"

Angel remained standing on the ledge just outside the large, open window. "You have no idea how to ask for something, do you? Hint—snooping through someone's stuff isn't the way to get on their good side."

Skata almost made a remark about the lack of a 'good side' to work with, but he was pretty sure he had already said that earlier in the week. "You have weird decorating tastes," he said, looking around the room, particularly at the Ikea dresser and the four-poster bed. "What is it—antique nomad?"

Angel's wide, closed-lip smile was not pleasant. "That's none of your business. Just like nothing in this room is your business."

"Just give me the phone."

In a blur of motion, Angel was no more than three inches away from Skata. "Say please." His eyes were bloody red, the veins around them pulsing darkly under his skin.

For the first time, the vampire alarmed Skata. "Fine. Please." He folded his arms, staring the vampire down. Angel's eyes searched Skata's, and then he grinned, a faint look that brushed his mouth and gave Skata a glimpse of both fangs. Then the an-imalistic vampirism melted from his face and his eyes were once more clear blue-gray.

He reached into his pocket and held up the phone. "Here you go."

"You didn't mess around with it, did you?" Skata asked, taking the phone before the vampire could change his mind about giving it.

"I resisted that temptation."

Skata stalked back to the door, but hesitated. "Hey, Angel?"

"What?"

"Angel's not..." His lips twitched, in spite of the seriousness he felt asking the question. "Your real name, is it?"

"Are you kidding? What kind of nineteenth-century Southern parent would name their kid Angel?"

"Good," said Skata and left the room.

CHAPTER EIGHTEEN

Skata found the Everetts' house number in the phone book and called three times before giving up. He would have to drive over there himself, and if Easton wasn't home, then he was going to do something he hadn't done in a long time.

He was going to church.

He found the car keys in the bowl on the foyer table and took Angel's convertible without bothering to leave a note.

The town was small, and the route to Easton's home was easy to recall. Skata turned into the driveway and considered leaving the engine running, just in case Easton greeted him with a shotgun. He decided against the idea and braced himself before knocking on the front door.

For several long moments, nothing happened. He scratched his cheek and looked down at his boots, then punched the front door and shouted, "I'm sorry, all right?"

There was a sigh from the other side of the door. Easton's muffled voice asked, "For what?"

What kind of question was that? "For, uh...I don't know."

There was the sound of the door unlocking and Easton opened it. "Angel's the one who kidnapped me. You didn't do anything to be sorry about. I just...I need some time to process."

"That's a better answer than I expected," he admitted, relieved.

She raised an eyebrow. "What did you expect me to do, throw a fit?"

"No," he said, unconvincingly. He reached into his pocket and handed her cell phone back. "Here."

"Thank you," she said, accepting it. "Now scram. I need to think."

"Right." He returned to the car and climbed in. That had been uncomfortable, but at least it wasn't disastrous. She was a tough, strong-minded girl; she always had been. She'd be fine.

He blew out a breath and backed out of the driveway, trying to convince himself that cursing Easton with the truth had been the right thing to do.

After all, he couldn't take it back.

* * * * * *

Skata pulled up at the general store with a mind to buy a six-pack or four. He was no closer to finding Samuel than he had been a week ago, and he was already more involved in Salvation than he wanted to be. It was as though the town had him trapped between its teeth and couldn't decide whether to spit him out or chew him up and swallow him.

He locked the car and had just crossed to the sidewalk when a voice behind him said, "Mr. Skata?"

He turned around, frowning. "Just Sk—whoa."

The man facing him was enormous: six-five if he was an inch and at least three hundred pounds that seemed to have been filtered entirely into muscle. A weirdly delicate earring dangled from his left ear. "Are you or are you not Skata?" he demanded in a voice like a bass drum.

"Yeah, I'm Skata," he replied cautiously. "Who are you?"

"Rukiel wants to talk to you."

"Thought he said our transaction was over," said Skata.

"I don't know any details. I'm just here to bring you in."

Skata glanced around for an escape route if he needed one. "Do I have a choice?"

The man's forehead seemed to protrude even further, and he bared his teeth in a ferocious grin.

"Guess not," said Skata. "Lead the way."

* * * * * * *

Skata was driven to the Diamond Straight in a car with darkened windows. He was then ushered through the empty bar and lounge into Rukiel's study and told to sit down.

Skata sat down in the larger of the two chairs and drummed his fingers on the arm.

"Thank you for coming." Rukiel stepped into the room, closing the door behind him. The gold-tipped swagger cane under his hand winked in the light from the window, and he was once again oddly dressed in an ivory-and-gold suit.

"Didn't have much of a choice," said Skata.

Rukiel leaned both hands on the cane and cocked his head to one side. It was obvious that he did not have exact approval for Skata's choice of seating, but he made no remark on it. "I only have a moment."

"Imagine that," said Skata. "I have all day."

Rukiel smiled politely. "I will overlook your attitude."

"Shucks. Thank you."

"I will only overlook it once," said Rukiel. "Pertinent information has reached me, and I thought you may be interested. I know where Samuel Lemeck is currently residing."

Skata stood up. "Where is he?"

"Beulah. It's a small town thirty miles west of here. He seems to be circling Salvation, no doubt waiting for you to appear."

"Beulah," Skata repeated. He shook his head. "How did you find him? And more importantly, how do you know he's still there?"

Rukiel's polite smile grew sharp. "He's leaving quite a trail behind him."

"A 'dead bodies' kind of trail?"

"Not quite. Strigoi. It seems he is incapable of turning a human into a moroi."

Skata scratched absently at the itching wound under his shirt. It was beginning to heal—the most annoying stage of any injury. "What do you want in return?"

"I only want you to stop him."

Skata's eyebrows rose. "You want me to kill him?"

"That is your intention, isn't it?" Rukiel inspected the gold ring on his right thumb. "Non-humans like myself remain hidden from most humans because we keep it that way. Mr. Lemeck is being rather…untactful about his existence. He must be stopped before he exposes us further. He was in Beulah this morning, but I cannot guarantee he will remain there."

"Any idea where I can find him?" asked Skata, already starting for the door.

"I suggest bars. Drunk humans are easy prey."

* * * * * * *

He ran into the house. There was no time to waste; he had to grab his bag, swing by the church building to see Colton, and go.

"I really need my jeep back," he muttered, picking his bag off the floor of his room and heading back down the stairs.

Angel appeared from the direction of the basement, his eyes on the bag over Skata's shoulder. "Road trip?"

"Lemeck's in Beulah," said Skata briefly, unwilling to give Angel the unabridged version. "I'm going to make it there before nightfall and kill him before he has a chance to turn anyone else."

"What does that mean?"

"Rukiel claims that Lemeck can't turn a human into moroi. They're all turning into bloodthirsty strigoi."

Angel adopted a theatrical voice and asked the middle distance, "Are *you* living with fang dysfunction?"

Skata grunted. "I'm already late."

"Have fun," said Angel. "Take my car."

Skata held up the keys. "Sure thing."

"Hey," Angel began, but Skata was out the door and climbing into the car. As he pulled out of the driveway, he held his arm out the window with his hand in a rock n' roll gesture.

He saw Angel flip him off in the rearview mirror.

* * * * * * *

Skata arrived at the church building and saw Colton's truck parked across the small gravel parking lot.

171

Skata stood a dozen yards from the front doors, watching as Colton—looking very informal in his usual faded button-down and dusty boots—shook hands with Honoria Campbell and the mayor.

Realizing that small-town churchgoers were inordinately chatty and this would take too long, Skata cupped his hands over his mouth and shouted, "Hey, Father!"

Colton glanced around until his gaze landed on Skata. A brief look of frustration crossed his face, and he shouted back, "I'm kind of busy—"

"Yeah, uh—can't you just pay someone else to stand there and shake hands? This is important."

The preacher turned a smile on Honoria and said something that seemed to smooth over any possible friction. Colton jogged down the steps and strode toward Skata—whether to talk or punch him was up for debate.

Skata recognized the Everett family, sans Easton, standing not far away. Colton noticed them as well and raised a hand with, "I'll be with you in a minute! Hey, Graham!"

With clenched teeth and a smile, he told Skata, "Sundays are kind of busy for me, in case you hadn't noticed."

"I need to borrow that stake of yours," said Skata, without preamble.

Colton's eyebrows drew together. "The moroi stake?"

"That's the one."

Colton crossed his arms. "What for?"

"Rukiel told me where to find Samuel. He's in Beulah, turning everyone he feels like into a strigoi."

"Strigoi, huh?" Colton rubbed his chin. "Follow me."

They walked around the small building to the door on the side. Colton disappeared inside and reappeared seconds later, holding the stake. "Here." He tossed it to Skata, who caught it and slid it inside his jacket. It was far too hot and humid to be comfortable, but when dealing with vampires, the more clothes the better.

"You sure you don't need help?" Colton asked.

"Positive," said Skata. "Thanks anyway."

Colton looked as if he was about to press the issue, but he only followed Skata back into the parking lot. "When will you be back?"

"Tomorrow, if everything goes well." Skata opened the door of Angel's convertible.

Colton blew out a deep breath. "Hey, look—be careful, man."

"Sure." Skata climbed into the car but looked up before he closed the door. "By the way, I had to tell Easton about non-humans last night."

"Why?"

"She was going to meet up with Macon in the mountains, and Angel kidnapped her."

Colton's look of concern deepened. "She okay?"

"She will be."

"Right." He nodded and knocked his fist against the top of the door. "Take care of yourself."

Skata only nodded before pulling out onto the street, headed for Beulah.

CHAPTER NINETEEN

elcome to Beulah!

W Skata glanced at the sign as it whipped past in a blur. "Thank you very much." He turned the music off and rolled the windows down. The sun was still up, just starting to sink behind the trees. He would have gotten there sooner, but one of the roads was closed off due to the water rising from the last rainstorm, and he had to take a detour that added two hours to his driving time.

From the looks of it, Beulah was the kind of small town that made it into episodes of *The X-Files*. He half-expected to see the streets lined with crumbling houses full of ax-wielding, cannibalistic hillbillies. It took less than two minutes of driving to reach the center of town, making Salvation look like a teeming metropolis in comparison.

He parked across the street from the post office and climbed out of the car that now felt severely out of place. Double-checking that he still carried the stake and his revolver, he tugged his jacket forward to make sure they couldn't be seen before starting down the sidewalk.

A handful of teenagers stood outside smoking, and the thick scent in the air definitely wasn't tobacco. The nearest was a girl who looked about as small-town as a high rise, her eyes ringed with thick black eyeliner and black lipstick to match.

"Hey, Wednesday," said Skata, snapping to get her attention as he walked up. "Where's the bar?"

She looked him over, blowing a plume of smoke from between pursed lips. "It's Sophia. And who's asking?"

"Me."

The two boys with her laughed.

She rolled her eyes. "Come on. I'll show you."

He glanced behind him out of habit, scanning for Samuel, before following her down the sidewalk, away from her companions. "Nice town."

"If by 'nice' you mean 'crap,' then sure."

"Better than some."

"It's a dead end, just like everywhere else." She sighed and pushed open a door. Loud country music spilled out. "Here you go. Bar."

"It'd be nice if they'd put a sign on it," said Skata, walking past her.

She snorted. "Yeah, right."

The moment Skata was inside, he stopped short. It was like all of his nerves had been lit with a match, and for the first time, he almost wished he had brought Angel with him.

"Counter's over there," said the girl. "Or are you looking for someone in particular?"

He looked down at her. "What's your name?"

"Sophia."

"Right, Sophia. Do you know a guy named Samuel Lemeck? He'd be new in town."

"Sure," was the response that jarred Skata more than he anticipated. "This way." She gestured for him to follow and made her way across the room to a table in the corner. A man slouched comfortably back in the chair, a beer in his hand.

"Hey, Sam," said Sophia. "This guy's looking for you."

"Well, *finally*," the moroi exclaimed. "Skata, isn't it?" He nodded at the chair across the table. "Why don't you sit down? Sophia, would you mind getting another beer?"

"Sure." She flashed Skata a wicked smile and walked away.

Skata felt unnaturally calm as he took a seat opposite the vampire. His pulse pounded in his wrist, but his breathing was even, his hands steady.

"So, Skata." Sam settled back in his chair. He was an unassuming-looking man in his late forties, with sandy hair and friendly green eyes. "May I say it's nice to finally meet you? I mean, face-to-face."

Skata felt a muscle in his face twitch. Lynyrd Skynyrd's *Down South Jukin'* came on the radio. "Can't say the same."

"No, I didn't think you would. So, tell me." He set his beer on the table and asked, in a voice that most people used for exchanging good news, "are you here to kill me?"

"That's right."

"Mmm." Sam twisted his mouth in thought, nodding slowly. Then slowly, he smiled with sympathy in his eyes. "Well, Skata, I wish you the best of luck, I really do. Sophia?"

Searing pain ripped into Skata as sudden pressure clamped down on his neck. He reached back and his fingers found hair; he tore, felt breath snarl hot against his skin. Fingers dug into his shoulders, and the pain grew sharper.

Sam lifted his beer and took another drink.

Skata reached into his jacket. He found the stake and stabbed it back into Sophia's chest. Her mouth came away from his burning neck, and he stood up, kicking the chair aside, and pulled the stake out of her. Without a sound, she dropped to the floor and lay still.

Sam clapped, slow and approving. "Nicely done, I like it."

Skata started toward him, but Sam lifted a hand. "It's all right now," he called.

Everyone in the bar stood up, straightened, and turned around. One look at their faces, and Skata knew he was in deeper trouble than he had thought.

"By the way," said Samuel, propping his feet up on the table, "I've turned everyone here, which means you're the only fresh blood in the bar." He pointed two fingers at Skata and shouted, "Drinks on him!"

Skata sprinted toward the window. A vampire slammed into him halfway there, sinking its teeth into his arm. He shoved the stake through the vampire's ribs and shook him free. As the body hit the floor, he knew the brief action had wasted too much time. He was surrounded by hungry strigoi, drawn by the smell of blood, sharks in a feeding frenzy.

If I'm gonna die, he thought, *I'm taking them with me.*

He switched the stake to his right hand and crouched. "Come and get me, you sorry sons of—"

Screams ripped the air apart as fangs came at him from every side. Using the stake was cumbersome and took too long, but he had nothing else to kill a vampire with—he shoved and tugged, not thinking, reacting on instinct alone.

A vampire climbed onto a table in front of him and jumped. Skata punched him in the face and turned, ducking and stabbing. He saw the table Samuel had been sitting at. The moroi was gone, but had left a room full of hungry, newborn strigoi.

The stake was ripped from his hand. He jumped back and picked up a chair—he swung, smashed it against the wall, and picked up a splintered leg as another vampire shoved him against the wall.

He stabbed her with the wood and shoved her off—the vampires weren't thinking, acting purely on their desire for his blood, but they were alert enough to realize he wasn't going down as easily as they had assumed he would.

Breathing hard and fighting the exhaustion that leaked out

of his open wounds, Skata looked along the walls for another exit. The window to the left was blocked, the window to the right was too far away, and there was no use even thinking about the door—

There was one more exit, behind the bar. Skata sprinted around a table and shoved it behind him. The vampires swarmed over it; a hand grabbed his leg, he kicked it away and made it behind the bar, where he kicked hard at the tall shelf.

It tottered; he kicked it one more time and it came down, bottles crashing and bursting open, an explosion of glass and alcohol. He slammed the exit door closed behind him and raced for the car. Pounding feet followed him, the air filled with shouts and howls.

He pulled the gun from his holster and turned, firing all six bullets from his revolver. They slowed down the vampires in front; he twisted into the driver's seat and slammed the door behind him, pressing down on the locking mechanism.

They were furious, bodies slamming against the walls of the car, climbing on the roof, scratching at the glass like animals. Skata turned the key in the ignition and put the car in drive. Spitting blood through his teeth, he pushed the accelerator to the floor. Rubber screamed against the pavement as he took off, bodies peeling away from the car and rolling heavily behind him.

He knew he was veering too far to the left of the empty road, but it was all he could do not to drive off the side. He rubbed his face, and his hand came away red and wet with blood. He had no idea how badly he was injured, he only knew he was bleeding, exhausted, angry, frustrated, and should definitely check into a hospital.

He decided to drive straight back to Salvation. He hated hospitals.

* * * * * * *

By the time he turned into the driveway that led up to Angel's front door, black was crowding the edges of his vision and he was so lightheaded he thought he might pass out. He stumbled up to the front door and fumbled to insert the key in the lock.

The door swung open at his touch.

He swayed on his feet and gripped the side of the door frame. Angel didn't leave the door unlocked, did he? He stumbled into the kitchen—the light was on, and an intruder probably wouldn't have left the light on—he fell heavily to the floor.

He pushed himself up into a sitting position and leaned against the cabinet behind him, closing his eyes briefly.

"Don't do it," he said aloud, his voice heavy and quiet. "Come on, man, don't fall asleep."

"Em, darlin', are you home?"

The Honda was still parked in the driveway, but she might have gone for a walk down to the park or maybe out to the pasture for a quick ride.

That gave him enough time before they left to shower and change his clothes into something more appropriate for a fancy dinner, maybe her favorite button-down. He'd never been one for dress-up affairs, but Em loved them. She even managed to wrestle him into a tie or a suit on occasion, tying the tie for him because he never could remember the right technique.

He turned the knob and walked into his room, in the middle of shrugging off his Carhartt jacket, when he paused. The air was charged with a warning. "Em?"

His wife sat on the edge of the bed, her shoulders angled toward the window, away from him. Her sleeve was torn, and her dark hair tangled in undone waves around her face, obscuring her head and shoulders and making it impossible to see any expression. Her fingers curled in fists, clenching and unclenching in her lap. When he came in, she dropped them to her sides.

Something was very, very wrong. He crossed quietly over to the bed, concerned. "Em," he asked gently, "is everything okay? Are you hurt?" He put a hand on her shoulder, near the tear in her sleeve.

She lifted her head and turned her face toward him, the movement slow and doll-like, something out of a dream. Only then did he notice the open window—no, not open. Broken, cracked splinters of glass spilled across the floor and the edge of the bed. The chill that shivered through his bones had nothing to do with the winter air blowing in.

"Baby." Her voice was soft and inviting, some horrible parody of seduction. You could almost miss the fangs set between her lips and the dripping wound on her neck. "You're home early."

He stepped back as though her touch had burned him. "No." The word was as cracked and broken as the window, but the pain inside him had nothing to do with the glass. It was immediate, a horror that it was real and a plea that it might not be.

Don't let it be real, he prayed. Please. Please. God, please. Please, no.

Em stood up and walked toward him, her bare feet soft and silent on the cold floor. Her eyes were surrounded by black, throbbing veins, her eyes red with blood lust.

He couldn't move. His bones turned to iron, surrounding his heart and squeezing his lungs, killing him. Not Em. Never Em.

There was a rush of movement, and she was no more than a few inches away. She pressed a hand against his chest and rose onto her toes. Her lips were warm and soft against his neck.

It was a twisted nightmare.

It wasn't real.

God, it wasn't real. It couldn't be.

She whispered, husky and hushed, "Just one taste."

"Em." His words were nothing, a strangled prayer, a sob, begging, threatening. "No."

"It's okay." She curled her fingers against the back of his neck. He felt the scrape of her teeth. "I just need one bite."

Skata pulled himself to his feet, using the counter as leverage. His skin felt like paper, and his heart was a chain holding him underwater, suffocating him. Stiffly, he turned on the sink and filled his palms with cold water, letting it pour onto his head, down his neck, and across his closed eyelids.

The front door opened, and he shut the faucet off. "That you, vamp?"

"Skata?"

Colton's voice.

He turned around and saw Colton and Angel both standing there, staring at him like he was some kind of evil spirit. "Yeah?"

"Hey, man." Colton held out his hands, his voice cautious, like he was talking to a stray dog. "Just—take it easy, okay?"

Skata peered at him through the water trickling from his hair. "What's wrong with you?"

Angel moved so fast it might as well have been teleportation. He gripped Skata's throat with iron fingers and hissed, "You'd better explain yourself before I break your neck." His fingers tightened, cutting off Skata's air.

Was this another step of the dream? Had he only thought he was awake? "What—the hell," he gasped.

Colton walked up, still cautious, his eyes intense with an emotion that Skata couldn't place. "Let him go."

Angel snarled and shoved Skata hard against the sink before stepping back.

"What's the matter with you?" Skata demanded, his voice raw and his heart hammering. "What the hell did I do?"

"Don't make me rip your heart out," spat Angel, folding his arms as if to physically restrain himself from attacking Skata again.

"What—"

"Why'd you do it, man?" Colton asked, searching Skata's face.

"Do *what?*" Skata exploded. He felt like he'd been cut into a dozen pieces and thrown into a strong wind.

Colton looked at the floor. "Cassis."

"What's the matter with him?"

"You should know," said Angel, his eyes turning a bloody red. "You're the one who murdered him."

CHAPTER TWENTY

I s this some kind of joke?"

Angel's smile curved mockingly. "Do we look like we're joking?"

Skata looked to the preacher. "Colton?"

Colton shook his head. "I'm sorry, man, but we know you did it."

"Kill Cassis? Why would I want to kill Cassis?" Skata's brain reeled, trying to think past pain and exhaustion and make sense of what was happening to him. "He's one of the only people I never had a bone to pick with."

"They caught you on tape," said Angel, tilting his head and baring his fangs. "So you can stop any time now. It's pathetic." He reached into his pocket and withdrew his cell phone.

Colton glanced at the phone. "What are you doing?"

"I'm calling the authorities."

"Wait!" Skata pressed his hands to his temples. "I didn't kill Cassis—I was in freaking Beulah all day."

"They have it on tape, man!" Colton pinched the bridge of his nose and let out a long breath. When he finally met Skata's gaze, his eyes were sad. "I just...don't get it."

"I didn't…" Skata stopped and closed his eyes as dizziness swarmed inside his skull. He didn't realize he was falling until he heard Colton say, "Whoa, easy, there," and he felt the preacher's arms lifting him up.

"He's hurt bad." Colton's voice.

"Looks like Cassis fought back," said Angel. His voice was hazy.

Skata felt himself being lifted, then lowered onto the couch.

"Get a first aid kit," said Colton. Skata could barely hear anything now; he felt like he was sinking under deepening water, all voices muffled and fading. "What did this?"

He's talking to me. "Vampires," Skata managed, his eyes still closed. "Sam."

"Sam? Samuel Lemeck did this to you?"

Unable to explain the long and short of it, Skata grunted an affirmative.

There was a "here" from Angel. First-aid kit, probably. He felt Colton removing his jacket and shirt with the confidence of a paramedic and none of the gentleness.

"Looks like you really have a way with people," Colton remarked.

"And half-breeds," said Angel. His voice dripped with acid.

"Let it go for a minute, okay?" Colton opened one of Skata's eyes, and Skata found the strength to shove his hand away before drifting out of consciousness.

* * * * * * *

When Skata awoke, he was still on the couch, covered in bandages and gauze patches. Colton was asleep in a nearby chair, but he opened his eyes as Skata attempted to sit up.

"Hey, hey, easy." Colton stood up and helped Skata up, leaning his back against the arm of the couch. "You're in bad shape."

"No shit," said Skata vehemently. "Where's Angel?"

Colton shrugged. "Avoiding you. He's pretty angry at you, man."

"I didn't know he was so attached to the dhampir," said Skata.

"Cassis was a good guy. Everybody liked him."

Skata gripped his head. "Tell me what happened."

Angel appeared back in the room with a faint sound, like rushing wind, following his speed. "Please, allow me," he said, and before Colton could protest, he crouched down too close for Skata's comfort and said, "Roughly an hour and a half ago, you took a knife into Cassis's home and stabbed him to death. Thirteen times, to be exact."

Skata narrowed his eyes. "What makes you think I did it?"

Colton cleared his throat. "The house across the street has a security camera outside. Mrs. Fleming's a little paranoid."

Angel straightened. "Sucks for you."

"It wasn't me," growled Skata.

"It…" Colton rubbed a hand over his face. His eyes were tired and disappointed, but he only shrugged and said, "It was you, man. I saw it."

"I need to see the footage," said Skata.

"Seriously?" Angel sneered. "Just because you're the dumbest felon in history doesn't mean you're innocent."

Colton held up a hand, frowning suddenly. "No, wait." He looked at Angel. "You're right."

"Thank you," said Angel, at the same time Skata barked, "Excuse me?"

"Whoever it was," said Colton, "walked right in front of the security camera like they knew it was there." He gave Skata a probing expression. "You're stupid, but you ain't that kind of stupid."

"Thanks," said Skata.

Colton hit Angel's chest. "Get the footage."

"Why would I do that?"

"Look—the guy's covered in bite marks, okay? You really think that looks like Cassis did it? Besides, you know Skata. He's been tracking the same person for a year, and you think he'd ruin all that work for a random murder?"

"It might have been planned," said Angel, but after a moment, he said, "Fine. I'll see what I can do." He faced Colton and hissed, "Don't even *think* about letting him go."

"Oh, he ain't going anywhere."

The vampire was gone.

After a long moment, Skata said, "He saved my life." His voice broke; he cleared his throat and said, "I had no reason to kill him."

"Where were you?"

"I was in Beulah."

"What happened?"

"Rukiel told me where Sam was, and when I got there, I walked right into a bar of newborn strigoi."

"Where did Samuel go?"

"I have no idea. I was a little busy trying not to die."

"Who found him? Cassis?"

Colton sat down again and leaned back in the chair. "I did."

"What were you doing there?"

"Shannon Amory's car broke down, so I picked her up from school. We were swinging by Cassis's place to pick up Maylee."

Skata recalled Maylee's round face, her feather-soft *'Skafa.'* "She see anything?"

"We don't know. Shannon didn't, at least." After a moment, he said, "It…it doesn't make sense, you know?"

"Trust me," said Skata grimly. "I know."

"Who'd want to hurt a guy like Cassis? He didn't owe

anybody money, didn't make enemies. The council didn't know he was a non-human."

"What about the stabbing?"

A few seconds passed, and Skata was about to clarify his question when Colton said, "I'd say it was an eight-inch Bowie knife with partially serrated steel blade. Carotid artery was cut first, then the body was stabbed, like they were making some kind of statement."

Skata had no time to reply, because Angel appeared holding a CD-ROM. "A little old-fashioned, but it works."

"Have any trouble getting it?" asked Colton, standing.

"I got it from a cute little deputy—Amy, I think her name was." Angel winked knowingly, but there was no humor in his face when he looked at Skata. To Colton, he said, "There's a laptop in the kitchen."

Colton got to his feet but grabbed the vampire's arm. "I'm leaving for five seconds," he said. "He better be alive when I get back."

"I'm not the murderer," said Angel.

The preacher gave him a warning look and left the room at a jog.

Angel said nothing to Skata, and Colton hurried back, a laptop balanced on his arm as he typed something on the keyboard with his right hand. "Got it." He sat down on the sofa next to Skata while Angel moved to stand behind them. Colton put the CD-ROM in the drive and pushed 'play.'

The film was black and white, a cheap security camera bought by someone afraid of being burgled. The seconds counted rapidly in the upper left-hand corner, but it was almost a full minute before any sign of action took place.

"There." Colton tapped his finger against the screen.

A figure sauntered down the street toward Cassis's small brick house. Skata felt as if a sinkhole had opened inside his chest. From the boots to the jacket to the haircut, he was looking at himself.

"Just wait," said Angel, catching Skata's dismayed expression. "It gets better."

The figure paused in the middle of the street, and slowly, he turned his head to look directly into the camera.

Skata's blood ran cold. There was no doubt now—it was his face smiling wickedly at the camera.

The figure turned, the camera cutting him off as he walked up the front steps of Cassis's home.

"Hey, wait." He tapped Colton's shoulder. "Go back."

"To where?" Colton moved the video back several seconds until Skata said, "Stop. There."

He watched intently as the culprit smiled at the camera.

"Yeah, you're right," said Colton, rubbing his chin. "That is weird."

"Skata smiling?" asked Angel.

"No, the eyes." Colton rewound the video again and tapped the screen. "Look. That's *tapetum lucidum*. Human eyes don't reflect like that except in photographs."

Again, Skata watched as the figure crossed the street until only the lower half of him could be seen, stepping onto Cassis's front porch. There was a moment where nothing seemed to happen; Skata guessed he was picking the lock. Then the door opened, the culprit stepped inside, and the door closed.

Colton stopped the video.

"If it wasn't Skata, then who was it?" asked Angel, his voice still full of suspicion.

"It. Wasn't. Me," said Skata through clenched teeth.

"Maybe..." Colton clasped both hands together in a praying position and tapped his index fingers against his nose. "Could be a shifter of some kind."

Skata fell silent, trying to put the scattered pieces together. Surprisingly, it was Angel who broke the silence. "Looking at the camera *was* weird, even by my standards."

"Thank you," exclaimed Skata, lifting a hand in exasperation. "Why would I have done that, huh? You think I wanted to get caught?"

"Looks like someone wanted you to get caught, whether you committed the murder or not," said Colton.

"Why, though?" Angel rested against the back of the sofa. "Just to get you in trouble?"

"This is Samuel's doing. It has to be." Skata pushed his hands through his hair, hating the existence of his nemesis so strongly that it threatened to make him dizzy. He stood up, adrenaline overriding the pain of his injuries, and picked up his shredded shirt and jacket from the floor.

"Hey, where do you think you're going?" asked Colton.

"I'm going to find the son of a bitch trying to frame me, and I'm going to kill him."

Colton shook his head. "The sheriff and his men'll be out looking for you. Other people too, probably. Sooner or later, they'll figure out where you're staying."

"That's why I need to find the real culprit before I'm lynched."

Colton stood up with a look of resignation. "If we're going to do this, you have to change into better clothes so you don't look like you got into a fight with Cassis."

Angel raced up the stairs and was back in less than a second. He tossed Skata a fresh pair of jeans and a shirt Skata recognized as his own, from his pack. "Hurry up."

Skata dressed in record time and realized with a flash of irritation that he'd lost the moroi-killing stake during the bar fight. He shook his head and told Colton, "I think I owe you a Blood Oak stake."

"You—what, are you telling me you lost it?" Colton demanded. When Skata hesitated, Colton curled his hand into a fist. Instead of punching Skata, he flexed the fist and moved past Skata muttering, "Unbelievable."

* * * * * * *

"Right, so," said Colton, slowing down as they reached the block where Cassis had lived just hours before. "We don't want to get too close. There are still squad cars at the house."

"Right," said Skata.

Colton turned around. "Use the Luger under the seat. It's already loaded. And don't lose this one," he added darkly.

"So it's a shape-shifter of some kind," said Angel, squinting out the windshield. He tapped the glass. "You really need to clean this."

"Yeah," said Colton, turning his glare on the vampire and ignoring the last remark, "it's a shifter."

Skata knew very little about shape-shifters. He'd never run into one before, and the more time he spent in Salvation, the more he realized just how much he didn't know.

"What if it tries to mimic one of us?" asked Skata. "How do we identify it?"

"We could always shine a flashlight in its face," suggested Angel. "I'm sure it would love that."

Skata searched for an option. "I guess we should come up with some kind of code."

Colton nodded. "Good idea. Let's see..."

"Got it," said Skata. "Earlier today, one of the vampires who attacked me was named Sophia. When we meet back up, we're the only ones who will know the answer."

"Fantastic," said Angel, climbing out of the car.

Skata and Colton shut their doors quietly, while Angel

slammed his with carefree abandon and drew sharp looks from the other two.

"My bad," Angel whispered. He pointed left. "I'll go this way."

"I'll poke around where the police are," said Colton, gesturing toward sheriff cars parked in front of the house. "That won't raise any questions."

"Then I'll take the next street over," said Skata.

"Hey, wait," said Angel, watching Skata with narrowed eyes. "Why exactly are we letting him go off by himself? What if another body mysteriously shows up?"

"It wasn't him," said Colton, double-checking the revolver in his hands.

"We don't know that."

Colton lowered the revolver, obviously irritated at the vampire's attitude. "You want to stay in the car?"

Angel lowered his head. In a penitent voice, he said, "No."

"Then shut up and go search." Colton pointed at Skata. "If we find out it was you, you're dead."

"Fine." Skata walked away from the others in the direction he had chosen. His day had gone from bad to horrid to hellish, and he wasn't about to let it get any worse. The air was filled with the hum of cicadas and crickets and the occasional far-off rattling of wheels on train tracks.

He moved away from the rows of houses into the park. It wasn't a large park, maybe ten acres at the most, but densely crowded with trees. A small playground sat in the center, and a faint breeze pushed the swing, the chains creaking with each gust.

Skata's finger brushed the trigger as he moved as quietly as possible, placing his feet carefully on the grass.

He saw a gleam in the shadows, gone before he had time to blink. He moved in that direction, keeping as much to the darkness as he could. The playground was empty as far as he could see.

There it was again, that wink of light—no, two.

He lifted his gun and whispered, "Got you."

* * * * * * *

Angel leaned against the truck and checked the time again. It had been fifty-four minutes since they split up, and he hadn't seen a thing. He called Colton.

Colton answered with a hushed, "Yeah?"

"Nil on my end," said Angel. "What about yours?"

"I've got nothing. Skata back with you yet?"

"Not yet. Listen, another squad car drove by a few minutes ago," said Angel, craning his neck to see to the end of the street. "I like Skata as much as I like anyone, but I refuse to go to jail for him."

"On my way," said Colton and hung up.

Angel slid his phone back into his pocket, frowning. The evidence pointed to Skata, but it pointed almost too clearly. Although he refused to let on, he leaned more toward the shape-shifter theory than any other, but damn…he'd liked Cassis.

"Stranger things have happened," he mused aloud and let out a deep breath. He wasn't just angry, he realized, and the thought unsettled him. He was hungry.

"Hey!"

He straightened as Skata jogged up, glancing both ways before crossing the street. He kept his head down until he reached the shadow of the car. "Where's Colton?"

"He'll be here in a few minutes," said Angel. "I'm almost disappointed to see you."

Skata ignored the remark. "I saw him."

"Him? Him who?"

"The shape-shifter." Skata swore under his breath and hugged his bruised ribs. "I almost had him."

Angel blinked once and said lazily, "I am unconvinced."

"Yeah, well, screw you."

Angel heard Colton approaching down the street. "Preacher-man's coming back," he said, relieved. Colton's presence would keep him from ripping off Skata's head.

"Ten bucks says he didn't find anything either," said Skata.

"I know he didn't," said the vampire easily. "I talked to him just before you showed up."

Colton emerged from the shadows, frustration on his face.

When he saw Skata, he asked, "Did you see anything?"

"Saw," said Skata. "Didn't catch."

Colton made a guttural sound and scratched the side of his head. "That ain't good."

"Before we continue," said Angel, holding up a hand, "what was the name of the vampire, Skata? Sarah?"

"Sophia."

"Right, right." Angel nodded. "Sophia. Well!" He climbed into the passenger seat. "Let's go."

Colton shook his head at Skata. "Sorry, man."

Skata's face was drawn as he climbed into the back of the truck. "Don't worry about it."

CHAPTER TWENTY-ONE

Colton drove them back to the house in silence. Angel rubbed his right thumb across the knuckles of his left hand and looked at the window, eying Skata's reflection.

"I *will* punch you in the fangs," said Skata finally.

"You'd be able to smell it, right?" Colton glanced at Angel. "If there was a change?"

"Yes," said Angel. "He's clean; I just like making him uncomfortable."

"I've had a bad day," said Skata, setting the Luger back on the floor. "Don't push me."

Angel frowned. "I'm old enough to be your great-grandfather. Possibly even your great-great-grandfather. Respect your elders."

"Oh, good," said Colton, turning onto Angel's winding drive. "We're here." He parked and said, "I'm not going to turn you in yet. *Yet*, you hear me?"

"Loud and clear," sighed Skata, looking too tired to argue.

"Angel, keep an eye on him until we get this straightened out."

"I charge five bucks an hour for babysitting," said Angel, climbing out of the truck.

"I'd put you down for free," Skata grunted, also exiting the truck.

"Beats me how either of you survived this long," said Colton.

"I got by on my good looks and charm," said Angel. He peered at Skata. "What did you get by on?"

"Maybe I just killed people I didn't like," said Skata.

"Both of you better be alive when I swing around tomorrow," said Colton, driving away before he could become embroiled in another argument.

Angel took the keys from his pocket and unlocked the front door. Skata stepped in past him, and Angel said, "All righty, stay inside until further notice."

"Right, because going outside alone would be a great idea with half the town after me."

"Wouldn't that be sad," said Angel with a snide smile. "Go…I don't know. Shower or go to bed or something."

Skata rubbed a hand over his face. "I'm too tired to argue."

Angel smiled thinly. "That's the spirit."

"Watch your back tomorrow, vamp." Skata walked up the stairs, his steps as slow and pained as an old man's.

Angel watched with a glimmer of amusement. "Need a stair lift there, grandpa?"

"Says the guy who's old enough to be my great-great-great-great-grandfather or whatever the heck you said. I don't think I ever caught your age, by the way."

"I never threw it," said Angel, "but I'm a hundred and forty-six."

"You're a creepy old man, you know that?"

"Shut up and stop bothering me."

"You need to get a real lawn so you can tell kids to get off it."

Angel threw up his hands and headed into the kitchen, calling, "I'm going to check in on you later, so you'd better be in your room!"

Skata did not reply, but Angel listened as the hunter crossed the hall upstairs, into his room.

The vampire shook his head and sat down at the dining room table. He dug his fingernail into the wood and scratched a long, thin line. More scratches joined the first, digging the scar deeper. He continued to scratch the line, over and over again, keeping busy with the mindless occupation.

Hungry.

He heard the water shut off upstairs; Skata was done with his shower. Angel pushed back from the table and jogged up the stairs to grab a pair of pajama pants from his room. A cold shower wouldn't help, but he could pretend it would.

There were two other showers in the house, both badly in need of repair. He hadn't planned on staying in Salvation long enough to bother fixing them, but now he wished he had.

Sharing a bathroom wasn't something he had ever envisioned doing.

He knocked the back of his fist against the wood. "Hurry up in there."

The door opened, and Skata pushed past him. "Sleep tight, vamp."

Angel shut the door behind him and twisted the lock in irritation. As he pushed the shower curtain aside and leaned over to turn the faucet to cold, he paused.

Reaching down, he picked up something from the drain and held it up between his thumb and forefinger.

A tooth.

"What in the..." He crouched by the side of the shower and studied the contents of the drain. There were two more teeth. His fingers came up coated with thick, gelatinous slime, transparent and downright...

"Gross." He shook the stuff off his hand and studied the teeth nestled in his palm as he called Colton. As soon as the preacher answered, Angel skipped over any hellos and said, "So Skata just got out of the shower."

There was dead silence.

Then Colton said, "I'll just be honest and say I don't know what to say to that."

"I was hoping you could explain why exactly there were slime and teeth in the drain?"

"Slime and *teeth*? What color is the slime? What consistency?"

"I don't know, it's *slime*. Clearish, kinda thick, kinda drippy."

"Okay, just don't say 'drippy' again. What about the teeth?"

"Looks like three back molars."

"What's the ratio of slime to teeth?"

"What — seriously? A palmful of slime. Three teeth. Is this really relevant?"

"Oh boy."

"'Oh boy' isn't the answer I was hoping for," said Angel.

"It's not good."

"Is it ever?" Angel snorted. "What are we up against?"

"Skata didn't come back with us."

Angel snapped his teeth together. "I was afraid of that. So who *did* come back with us?"

"I'm pretty sure it's a Skin-Changer. It's an older, rarer kind of shape-shifter. The Germans called them doppelgangers, literally translated as 'double walker.' They don't change into animals or anything like that; they mimic another person so closely they can actually *become* a real copy of them: same memories, same smells, same everything. That's why you didn't catch it. They're pretty dang rare—this is actually kind of exciting."

"Yaaaaaay. So what do I do about it?"

"Well, they're pretty dangerous and there isn't much on them—at least not that's been translated from German. As far as

I know, they live for a few hundred years and are generally stronger than an average person."

"As strong as a vampire?"

"Well, a strigoi. Being a moroi, you can probably beat him."

Angel pinched the bridge of his nose. "How does this explain the teeth and slime?"

"When a doppelganger becomes another person, they literally *shed* the old one. It's honestl—"

"If you say 'pretty exciting' again, you're going to regret it."

Colton cleared his throat. "So doppelgangers shed the old person, or—well, more like they shed the *excess*. Say the previous form was fatter or taller or whatever, they'd shed what they didn't need, and the rest just physiologically changes to match the current form. It's incredible."

Angel rolled his eyes. "Here's what I don't get—if he's looked like Skata for hours, why the mouth transformation now?"

"Did you punch him in the face? Knock some teeth loose?"

"No." Angel turned to the door. "But if he's got the real Skata somewhere—"

"The real Skata wouldn't have gone down without a fight," finished Colton. "Okay—just —don't let the double-walker know you know he isn't Skata, all right? I'll be there as soon as I can."

"Oh, no rush," said Angel, hanging up the phone. He couldn't afford to shower now—he had to watch and make sure the shapeshifter in his house didn't sneak out and murder somebody else.

He unlocked the bathroom door and opened it.

The doppelganger smiled at him. "Sorry," he drawled, "I forgot my teeth."

* * * * * * *

When Angel came to, his first thought was *I'm on fire.* He tried to move, but nothing gave. Opening his eyes, he looked down and saw his hands and ankles chained to the chair in the living room. The pain was searing, liquid lava sizzling under his skin; he barely registered that the double-walker would have gone into the basement for the chains.

The syringe from the first aid kit lay on the floor a few yards away, empty. The sharp smell of vervain hung in the air, filling his lungs, choking him. He leaned forward, straining against the chains. After several minutes of struggle, he sat back, breathing heavily. There was no point in doing anything but waiting for Colton—he was too weak, he hadn't fed, and the vervain was probably killing him.

Breathing was almost impossible. His vision swam, plagued by swarms of black-and-white clouds, and his blood ran loud in his ears.

Someone pounded on the front door, and he just made out Colton's voice calling, "Hey, you in there?"

Angel's attempt at a shout came out a strangled groan.

"Angel? Angel! Hang on, I'm coming in!"

Angel fully expected Colton to knock the door down with brute force. Instead, there was a small scratching sound, and a moment later, the preacher ran in, folding a Swiss Army knife back in on itself. "Seriously? I leave for ten minutes, and you get chained to a chair?"

Angel gave him a withering look.

Colton didn't bother to look for a key to the chains; he unfolded the knife again and picked the lock like it was second nature. "You okay?" He unwound the chains and tossed them to the floor, helping Angel out of the chair.

Angel gathered up the rest of his strength and gasped, "The twit injected me with vervain." He sucked in a dry breath, watching as Colton ran into the kitchen and ran out again moments later, a glass of water in his hand.

Colton tilted Angel's head back with a "Here, drink this," and Angel was able to take a single swallow before the water slammed into his stomach like a sledgehammer.

He rolled over onto his side, coughing so hard he wouldn't have been shocked to see his liver hacked up. "Water," he spluttered. "Who knew?"

"You looked like you had the worst case of the flu I've ever seen, so I figured you wouldn't be able to keep anything down. Just needed a little help," said Colton, thumping Angel's shoulder.

Angel managed to sit up, leaning against the legs of the chair.

He could breathe a little easier now and the heat inside him had cooled a degree or two, allowing him to think. "He could have killed me."

"Yeah, but he didn't." Colton regarded him thoughtfully.

"Right." The vampire leaned his head against the arm of the chair for a moment before grabbing it and using it to haul himself to his feet. "I don't know why."

"Beats me." Colton stepped forward, as if afraid the vampire would collapse again.

Angel waved him off. "I'm fine."

"Yeah, sure you are."

Angel stood up straight to prove his point and immediately wished he hadn't. He leaned over again, pressing his palms against his knees, and groaned. "Oh—yeah." He squeezed his eyes shut. "I'll kill him. He's dead. I'll bury him just so I can vandalize his tombstone."

Colton put his hands on his hips, a deep furrow between his eyebrows. "If you're sure you're good, I need to get back out there and look for Skata."

Angel stood up straight again, refusing to let the fading pain and dizziness bowl him over a second time. "What are we waiting for?"

Colton looked skeptical. "I don't think it's such a good idea—"

"If I fall over, I fall over." Angel sighed noisily. "I'm not exactly the president of Skata's fan club, but he didn't kill Cassis and this doppelganger did."

"Right," said Colton. "Well, I guess like you said, if you fall over, you fall over." He crossed over to the door and stepped out without bothering to see if Angel was behind him.

The cool night air was welcome relief against Angel's flaming skin. He held up a hand, and under the moonlight, he could see the blistered red already fading. He climbed into Colton's truck, and as they drove, Angel said, "I don't suppose you have any more nuggets of information concerning Fake Skata."

"A little, maybe. Doppelgangers can completely mimic anybody they want, but if my intel is right, then the change takes a few minutes and it ain't pretty. Bones breaking, teeth falling out, skin growing and old skin needing ripped off."

"It makes the term 'shifter' seem so blasé," remarked Angel. "How do we kill one?"

"You can shoot 'em." Colton shrugged. "The trouble isn't that they can't be killed, just that it's hard given they're fast and strong. Stronger than I thought, I guess," he added, with an apologetic glance at Angel.

"I noticed."

"Yeah, sorry about that."

"So a bullet in the head should take care of this guy?"

"Well," Colton hesitated, then shrugged again. "I mean, in a worst-case scenario, I guess…"

"You don't think we should kill the murderous evil double-walker man, why am I not surprised?"

"No," said Colton, a defensive edge in his voice. "I don't. Least not right away, not until we find out what he's up to."

"Wait until he chains *you* up and injects *you* with poison," Angel huffed. "Then we'll talk."

They parked in the center of town by the statue of Hezekiah. He stood proud and oblivious, his arms outstretched.

"I'll go that way," said Colton, pointing to the row of shops past the general store. "Be back here in twenty minutes."

"Keep your fingers crossed that we're both ourselves when we get back," said Angel.

"Guess we'll have to use your original idea." Colton removed a flashlight from his back pocket and shone it in Angel's eyes. "Foolproof, even if it was your idea."

"If you think of something better, let me know," said Angel dryly. He walked away from the preacher, his senses on full alert, his body nearly recovered from the effects of vervain.

He left the square, running for the suburbs. It took less than five seconds to reach Easton's house, and he pushed the doorbell and waited.

He heard footsteps, and a moment later, Easton opened the door. Her eyes widened when she saw who it was.

"Angel?" She stared past him, bewildered. "What are you doing here? Is anyone with you?"

"Can I come in?" he asked, batting his eyes. She looked about to say 'no,' and he interrupted. "Oh wait, I forgot. You invited me."

He stepped past her into the foyer, but she grabbed his arm. "I told you to stay away from me. What do you want?"

"I was just wondering if you've seen Skata," he said nonchalantly.

She frowned. "Sure. He's out on the back porch with Mom right now."

Angel raced past Easton down the hall. She followed, shouting, "What's wrong?" as Angel pushed open the French doors leading out to the back porch.

He came to an abrupt halt and spun around, blocking her view. "Don't look."

She gave him an exasperated look, but before she could step around him, he grabbed her, pulling her away from the door as she struggled against him, her scream expected but nonetheless loud.

He couldn't let her see the sight of her mother's corpse slouched against the red Adirondack.

CHAPTER TWENTY-TWO

The first thing Skata noticed was the smell. Dank and metallic, the bitter scent of rust filled his lungs, and he jerked his head up, sucking in air like a drowning man. *Where am I?*

That freak of nature wearing his face had taken his shirt and jacket to complete the ensemble, no doubt to trick Angel and Colton. Good thing it had its own jeans.

He shook his head, trying to clear it. His hands were tied around some kind of pole. Another rope was around his neck to keep him from moving more than a few inches. He tried to move, to get a look at his surroundings, but all he could see was a blackened concrete wall and mottled pipes. Somewhere, water dripped in a steady, maddening rhythm.

"Hey!" he shouted, lifting his head as far as he could. The black cloud on the wall spread to the ceiling. Looking down, he saw the floor was coated with the stuff, too; it had rubbed off on his jeans and his hands where they had touched the floor. "Where are you?"

"Right here." The shape-shifter stepped in front of him, out of a door Skata couldn't see.

Seething with rage, Skata couldn't even think of the right words to fling at the creature.

The shifter's eyebrows rose. "What do you think you're looking at?"

"Your neck," said Skata. "Come over here. I want to break it."

The shifter laughed. It sent shivers up Skata's spine, hearing his laugh come from a mouth that looked just like his, in a face that would have fooled his own mother. The thing even walked like him, moved his arms like him, and intoned his words the same way.

The shape-shifter crouched down in front of Skata, and deep, shiny black flooded the corners of his eyes, filling in the iris, the pupils, the white, leaving them empty and soulless. "Your sense of humor needs a little work."

The shifter lifted his hand, his fingers curled in a fist, but he never struck a blow. Instead, he lowered it, a small smile playing around his mouth. "Do you know what I had for dinner tonight?"

"The soul of a helpless victim?"

The shifter chuckled. "A slice of warm apple pie—there was something unique about it. Cardamom, I think."

Skata froze. There was only one person he knew who put cardamom in their apple pie, and that was Olivia Everett.

"You son of a bitch."

"Guilty."

"If you hurt anyone in that family, I swear——"

"You'll what?" The shifter turned his expression into one of deep interest. "Kill me?"

"Slowly."

"It's too late for that, cowboy; guess you'll just have to make good on your threat."

"What did you do?" Skata's voice tore from his throat, and he lashed out, unable to make it far before the rope around his neck strangled him.

"Easy there, Leslie," said the shifter, "you can't get back at me if you decapitate yourself. And, no, before you ask, I didn't hurt Easton."

"You know I'm going to kill you," said Skata, trying to keep his temper in check. An outburst would do him no good here. "So why haven't you gotten me out of the way yet?"

He grinned and patted Skata's cheek once before rising to his feet. "Sorry, but it's just not your time yet. You'll have to hold out a little longer."

"What's the matter?" spat Skata. "Can't kill somebody unless you're hiding behind someone else's face?"

"Why would I use mine if I can borrow yours?" The shifter shrugged his shoulders. "Besides, you're easy to copy. Same height, a little more on the beefy side, but I've been worse."

"You sick bastard."

The shifter paused and narrowed his eyes. "Interesting observation," he said slowly, "coming from you." There was no obvious animosity in his voice or expression, but somehow it was conveyed in the slowness of his movements—his blink, the way he turned his head.

"I'm nothing like you."

"I *am* you." The shifter got on his knees in front of Skata, gripping the rope around his neck and pulling it tighter. "I'm in your head. I know everything in here—" he touched Skata's forehead "—and here." He pressed a finger against Skata's chest. "Trust me. We have more in common than you think."

"You killed an innocent woman—"

"Shhh." The shifter pressed a finger to his lips. "You don't want to embarrass yourself."

"I don't know what you're talking about."

The shifter gave him a narrow-eyed, strangely condescending smile. "Your denial is endearing, but it'll get you exactly nowhere."

Skata felt his pulse pounding against the side of his neck, throbbing against the rope.

"Now…" The shifter pointed in the direction he'd come, to an entrance Skata couldn't turn far enough to see. "I have to leave. Be a good boy, Skata."

"Go to hell."

"Already been," said the shifter. "Got out on good behavior." He took a stride, then paused and said, "There is *one* thing I just don't quite get. Angel. Explain *that* one to me."

"He's not worth explaining," Skata grunted, leaning the back of his head against the pole so he could breathe a little more easily.

"Hm. See, if I were you, I'd have staked him a long time ago."

"He's a moroi, staking only pisses him off."

The shifter smiled again—that condescending look just shy of a smirk. "Then try explaining his freezer full of stolen blood bags. He keeps it in the basement. Now correct me if I'm wrong, of course, but I thought moroi don't really crave blood. It's one of the perks of their kind."

"You're a liar." Skata's mind raced, trying to remember any evidence of Angel being something other than moroi. He had never shown any signs—he could walk in the sun, he had no desire for blood…

The shifter said, "I would be offended, but I'd hate to be a hypocrite. Still, the next time you see your vampiric friend, you might want to bring up the subject, just for kicks."

* * * * * * *

Lights flashed red and blue outside the Everetts' home. Angel stood on the lawn, watching as what seemed like the entirety of the sheriff's department milled in and out of the house. Colton stood on the driveway with Mr. Everett, his arms folded tightly as he helped the man speak to the deputy in charge.

Two paramedics appeared at the front door, lifting a stretcher across the stoop. Dark stains already blossomed across the white sheet over Olivia Everett as they pushed the stretcher to the idling ambulance.

Angel saw Graham step outside, his face passive with shock, and shuffle over to stand by his father.

He turned around, searching for Easton. She was nowhere to be seen. A brief search of the kitchen, the dining room, the living room, and even the back deck revealed nothing but yellow tape.

He jogged up the stairs and down the hall. Easton's bedroom door was shut. He did not hesitate before knocking his knuckles twice against the wood. "Easton? It's Angel."

She didn't respond, and he tried the doorknob, surprised when it opened. Cautiously, he stepped into the room, looking behind the door at the closet, then at the empty bed. A warm breeze blew the curtains, calling his attention to the open window.

He could just make out the silhouette beyond the curtains.

Easton did not turn around when he climbed out the window. Fractured moonlight caught the brown strands of her hair. Her arms were wrapped around her knees, and her tear-stained gaze stared out at the trees that lined the yard and beckoned beyond.

"Nice view," said Angel.

Easton did not look over at him. Instead, her head turned from side to side, like something confused her and she couldn't make it out. "This doesn't make any sense." Her voice was thick and strained with tears. A breathy sob rattled her, and she seemed suddenly so fragile that he wanted to put his arms around her and keep her together, stop her from shattering to pieces.

He did. Softly, he stroked her hair, resting his chin on the top of her head. "Shhh."

Immediately, she turned her head into his shoulder, her slender shoulders shaking. "Why would he want to kill Mom?" Her mangled words were barely intelligible.

Angel leaned his cheek against her hair and rocked gently, as if Easton were a small child troubled with nightmares. It was the only thing he could think to do. "I don't know," he said in a hushed voice, "but Skata didn't do it. It wasn't him."

"I just don't unders-stand," she stuttered, trying to breathe, fighting to fill her lungs with night air.

Angel closed his eyes and held her, let her cry her tears until his shirt was soaked with saltwater and she felt a little less fragile, a little emptier.

Eventually, she was able to sniff back more tears, but instead of pushing him away she just leaned against him, and he looked down, surprised. Her swollen eyes were shut, tears drying on her cracked lips. Her breathing was even now, and she was blessedly unconscious.

How long he remained on the roof, holding the wrecked, sleeping girl in his arms, he didn't know. It must have been an hour, maybe two, before Colton leaned out the window and whispered, "Hey."

Angel lifted his head and looked over his shoulder at the preacher. "She's asleep."

"Good." Colton cleared his throat softly and said, "We should get outta here. Let them...you know."

The vampire nodded. "Hang on." He maneuvered Easton so he could lift her without waking her and then passed her to Colton. The preacher set her on her bed as gently as if she was made of fine-blown glass.

Then he straightened, and the silver light filled the crevices under his eyes and around his mouth with shadows. "We need to find Skata, and we need to find that *thing* before it does this to someone else."

Colton left the room as if unable to wait even a second, but Angel stayed for a moment, gazing down at Easton. If only his willpower could make someone be all right.

If only.

He exited the room, leaving her bedroom door open a few inches, just in case. Colton was already waiting in his truck, the engine running, yellow headlights illuminating the street ahead.

"What took you so long?"

Angel got settled in his seat. "I was just—checking on Graham. Poor kid. Where do you think the doppelganger went?"

"Hard to tell. Technically, he could be anywhere, but my best guess is somewhere private and out of the way. He's smart; he wouldn't be somewhere people could accidentally trip over him."

"I'm guessing doppelgangers aren't the kind to hole up in sewers?"

"They're like you and me, man."

"That is supremely unhelpful. Where do we start looking?"

"I don't know." Colton stretched his arms, gripping the steering wheel. Angel noticed his knuckles were white with tension. "There are a few older buildings on the far edge of town, from before the renovation. We could check there."

"Yay!" said Angel. "Let's go."

"Buckle up."

"Do you mean that literally or figuratively?"

The preacher did not look amused. Angel sighed and tugged the seat belt across his torso, latching it firmly, and said, "There. I'm all safe. Because it's not like I wouldn't heal if we got in a car wreck."

"Can we just—for once—lighten up on the attitude?" Colton asked, and it sounded like a genuine request. "I have enough to process tonight without dealing with your sarcasm on top of it."

Angel shifted and watched the road ahead. "Okay, okay. I'll try. Let's go catch Skata's evil twin."

CHAPTER TWENTY-THREE

Could you drive any slower, gramps?" Angel looked over at Colton.

"I'm driving five miles over the speed limit."

"By the time we get to your ghost town, the shifter will probably have killed half of the *living* town."

In response, Colton pressed the pedal down, and the car sped forward, turning a sharp left. Angel's shoulder slammed into the door. When he straightened, he gave Colton a wide, insincere smile and looked back out the windshield.

"We better hope this doppelganger is willing to reason with us," muttered Colton.

"Wait, wait, wait." Angel held up both hands. "Time out. So we're *seriously* not going to kill it? It's been *murdering* people!"

"Oh, really? Wh—you think I hadn't noticed?" Colton shot him a black glare. "You're what, a hundred and fifty, with sketchy morals at best. You trying to tell me you've never murdered anyone?"

The vampire felt himself begin to sulk. He hated when the preacher made a point. "All right then, so how do we capture it? It's strong, it's fast, and a good mimic. A *really* good mimic."

"Shoot it in the leg."

Angel blinked and leaned to the left. "I'm sorry, what?"

"Shoot it in the leg," Colton repeated. He gave Angel a look that said *what?* "It ain't a vampire."

"Won't it—I don't know, heal itself into another body that *isn't shot in the leg?*"

"I'm not going to shoot it with bullets." Colton reached down and lifted a shotgun from between the seats. "A bullet will just heal and fall out if we shoot a doppelganger."

"So what do we use? Pixie dust?"

"Rock salt."

"Rock salt." Angel blinked. "You sure that'll do it?"

"It should put him out of business for a few minutes, which will be enough to tie him up. If he tries to shift out of the ropes, we'll be there with real bullets."

"I'm assuming you brought rope?"

"In the trunk."

Angel leaned back. "You're the *man.*"

"We're here." Colton switched the headlights off and slowed down, pulling into a wide, open lot. Three or four buildings, gnawed by time and weather, loomed in the darkness.

"It's nice," said Angel, stepping out of the car and making sure to close the door quietly. "Let's get a condo here."

The preacher did not answer. He walked across the ground, a mixture of gravel and overgrown weeds. Moonlight glinted off the barrel of his shotgun.

Angel looked uneasily over his shoulder. Colton saw him stop and whispered, "What is it?"

The vampire shook his head, still scanning the silhouetted buildings. "My spidey senses are tingling."

"Why?"

"I don't know. I'll keep an eye out." Angel waved a hand. "You move. I'll...'cover you'."

The preacher nodded and kept walking toward the structure farthest to the left. Angel felt fangs push through his gums and the faint, I-just-licked-a-penny taste that came with it. There was no sound, and the shifter couldn't possibly be that stealthy. Nothing was stealthy enough to escape his hearing.

He followed close behind Colton as the preacher pushed against the nearest door, the rotting wood giving way under his hand.

Angel looked down at the crumbled pieces. "They don't make them like they used to."

"Shut up." Colton held up his free hand, pausing before he moved farther into the dilapidated building.

Something rustled through the air. Angel turned, scanning. "Did you hear that?"

"I heard it," said Colton grimly. "Any idea where it came from?"

"Somewhere up ahead." The building was a wreck, full of places where the roof had caved in, plants struggling through walls, and nests where animals had lived and died. Angel reached down and knocked a piece of plaster aside.

A piece of gray fur shot out like he'd kicked it, scrambling for the door. They watched as it darted out into the night.

"Rats," said Colton, managing to make the word sound like a curse.

"Rats," Angel agreed. He moved ahead, across the demolished room toward the door set in the far wall. He turned the handle and pushed it open. "Well, I think we can cancel this place out."

Colton looked over his shoulder. The roof was completely gone, a mound of junk piled in the center. "What was this place?"

"Beats me." Angel shrugged. "Haunted house?"

"Yeah, but what was it *before* it was a haunted house?"

"Pre-haunted."

Colton turned away, letting the butt of the shotgun hit Angel's shoulder. They strode back outside and headed to the next building.

The sign above the door was faded, almost unreadable. After a second, Colton said, "Library."

"You think our homicidal double-walker is an avid reader?"

"You never know." Colton stepped inside, shotgun at the ready.

Shelves leaned everywhere, stacked like fallen dominoes.

Moth-eaten books were strewn all over, and the air smelled like mildew and dust.

"Hey." Angel took a book off one of the shelves. It crumbled away in his hand, and he pulled it away and held his hand up for inspection. "Looks burned."

"The whole place does," Colton agreed, lowering the shotgun a few inches to study the side of a shelf, blackened and burnt. "Maybe there was a fire."

"No kidding." Angel paused—he heard something, somewhere below. He looked at the floor then at Colton. "Basement," he whispered, touching a finger to his lips.

There was another door behind the remains of the front desk, and a rusted metal shelf leaned against it.

"Keeping something out?" Angel suggested.

"Or in," said Colton.

Angel pushed his shoulder against the door while Colton kept a lookout. The shelf slid across the floor, nearly toppling before Colton whirled around and caught it before the crash.

"Come on," he said, exasperated.

Angel tugged on the doorknob, and it slid against the warped door frame with a screech that made them both wince.

A set of blackened metal stairs led down until the light was gone, sucked away.

"If we don't come out alive?" said Angel, pointing a finger at the preacher even as he peered into the darkness, "I'm blaming you."

Colton ignored him and went first, stepping cautiously on each stair, testing each one before putting his full weight on it. The stairs groaned each time, but they held firm.

Angel noticed a flashlight sticking out of the preacher's back pocket and pulled it out. He switched it on. "Honey," he sang quietly, pointing the beam toward the bottom of the stairs, "I'm home."

"What do you think you're doing?" hissed Colton.

"The shelf was in front of the door," said Angel, "which means the doppelganger isn't here."

A groan from below caught their attention. Angel and Colton hurried down the rest of the stairs. The basement was as blackened as the rest of the structure, but the concrete walls and floor had preserved it better. A cement support pillar stretched from floor to ceiling, and as Angel rounded it, he saw Skata, his face bruised and his eyes shut.

Angel crouched down and shook Skata's shoulder. "Hey, anybody home?"

Skata jerked awake, fury flashing automatically across his face before confusion replaced it. With no preamble, Angel shone the beam of light into the man's eyes—one was swollen nearly shut and smudged with purple, but the other was fine.

"Get that thing out of my face," snapped Skata, but his voice lacked its usual feeling.

"It's the original." Angel set the flashlight on the ground and went to work on the ropes knotted around Skata's neck and wrists.

"Hey, man," said Colton, watching Skata as Angel helped him to his feet. "You don't look so good."

Skata leaned against the pillar, his face haggard with pain. "What tipped you off, Sherlock?"

Angel folded his arms and leaned against the other side of the pillar. "Where is he?"

Skata bowed his head. "I don't know."

When Skata looked up, there was something in his eyes that Angel recognized and feared. It was hard, set, as if the connection between heart and head had been severed.

He had become more dangerous than either of them.

"Give me the gun," said Skata.

"I don't think so," said Colton. "We need to get you taken care of."

"I said," Skata repeated, stepping forward, "give me the gun."

"No," snapped Colton.

Angel hadn't seen the chunk of concrete in Skata's hand, and he didn't notice it until Skata cracked it against Colton's head. Skata grabbed the barrel of the gun and wrenched it from the preacher's grasp, pumping the barrel and turning to face Angel in the same motion.

"Back off," he growled.

"You don't even know where the doppelganger is," said Angel. It felt bizarre to be the one attempting to talk sense. *But here I am.*

"I'll find him."

The vampire motioned toward the gun. "It's loaded with rock salt—"

"Works for me," Skata spat. "Knock him down long enough to cut off his head. Even he can't survive that."

Angel glanced at Colton as the preacher shifted, waking up. "I hate to be the voice of reason, but the last time we tried to catch this thing solo, it didn't exactly go north, if you know what I mean."

"You shut up." Skata pumped the shotgun, as if they needed further proof he was serious. His eyes were a little too wide, his jaw a little too set. "It told me about you."

"What are you talking about?" Angel demanded, taking a step forward.

Skata fired, the shell clattering to the ground as salt blasted the pillar by Angel's head.

The vampire jumped, staring incredulously at Skata. "Watch it!"

"The freezer in your basement, vamp. What's it full of?" Skata's voice was raised, as raw as an open wound.

Angel froze. It was a nightmare come to life, a dark room with the curtains suddenly flung open, revealing the one thing he had tried so desperately to hide.

"Fine," he heard himself say. He felt like a child on trial, humiliated and unprepared. "So what?"

Skata laughed, a sharp and broken sound. "You know the

funniest thing about this? I was starting to think you were different. Shame on me, right?"

Colton staggered to his feet, one hand pressed against a bloody wound on the side of his head. He lifted a finger to his lips and indicated Skata.

Angel held Skata's gaze. "If you get yourself killed now, you'll never get your revenge. Wouldn't that be a shame?"

"Keys," said Skata.

"What?"

"Car keys. Give them to me."

"I don't—"

"I'm not talking to you." Skata backed up and gestured toward Colton, who scowled at Angel like the situation was his fault. He took the keys from his pocket. "Listen, Skata—"

"Shut up and toss them."

Colton groaned and tossed the keys to Skata, who snatched them out of the air.

"Don't come looking for me," said Skata.

"You have no idea what you're doing," Colton began.

"That's the trouble, preacher," said Skata, backing up the stairs. "I know exactly what I'm doing."

The door slammed closed. Darkness swallowed them, and Angel pressed both fists against the pillar. "Idiot," he muttered with vehemence. "Knuckleheaded, dimwitted, knuckle-dragging *dipstick.*"

"You or Skata?" asked Colton.

"Both."

"What's in the freezer, Angel?"

Angel punched the pillar, blowing out a chunk of concrete the size of his fist. "Blood bags! Feel better? You want me to say it again? You think I'm proud of it?"

"Why didn't you tell anyone?"

"Because Blood Drinkers Anonymous was closed, and I forgot to check myself into rehab."

Something swelled in his throat and threatened to choke his voice, but his eyes remained locked on Colton's even after he realized his vision was blurred. "I'm shocked that you have no immediate comeback."

Colton scratched his cheek. "A man once said 'the flesh is willing, but the spirit's weak.'" He shrugged and shook his head, staring at the floor. "I'm not angry with you."

"You should be. I know what I am, and I've known since the second I was turned. There's something evil in me, right? I have to be invited over a damn doorstep."

"You're a good man, Angel." Colton looked up, and Angel was surprised to see there was no trace of accusation in his face.

"Don't give me that," Angel scoffed, taking an unsteady step backward. He felt off-balance, as if the floor had been replaced with the rolling deck of a ship at sea. "I've tried to go without drinking. I've tried, and I can't do it. I never can."

"Angel…" Colton rubbed the back of his neck.

"Go ahead," snapped Angel. "Say something preacher-like.

Tell me I'm worth saving, just like anyone else."

Colton took a moment to answer, and Angel felt his heart clench like a fist. "I'm damned, aren't I?" he asked bitterly. "Figures. Hey, here's another fun fact for you—the only reason I let Skata stay with me was because I was using him to get to Samuel. He's the one who turned me. Call me a good man one more time—except you can't, right?"

"You know what grace is, right?"

Angel braced himself. "Sure."

Colton sounded almost nonplussed as he continued, like he was trying to teach a grown man the alphabet. "The one thing I know about grace is that it ain't for people who don't need it."

Angel suddenly felt threadbare, like the evening had cut a thread and unraveled him until there was nothing left but string and empty space. The wall met his shoulder, and he did not quite know whether he had leaned or fallen against it.

Colton put a hand on his shoulder. The gesture was reassuring somehow as Colton said, "Let's go find Skata."

CHAPTER TWENTY-FOUR

It took them just under an hour to get back to Salvation. Angel could have made it there in several seconds, but with dangers on the loose, he didn't want to leave Colton. As they arrived back in town, the first thing they noticed was the abundance of patrol cars, cruising slowly down every street.

"They're looking for Skata," said Colton, watching as one of the vehicles slowly turned down the next street over.

"Technically they're looking for the doppelganger," said Angel.

"Yeah, and we don't know where either of 'em *are.*"

"No ideas?"

"First Cassis, then Olivia. There's no pattern to try and follow yet."

Angel took a deep breath and rotated his neck and shoulders to loosen up his tense muscles. "Then let's look around. He's got to be here. Split up again?"

Colton did not look happy about it. "I guess we have to, but we only have one flashlight."

"Your point?"

"We'll check each other when we see each other again," said the preacher after a moment, waiting for Angel to approve.

The vampire nodded. "Sounds good."

"We should meet somewhere near the center of town."

Angel spread his arms. "How about...*the center of town?*"

The preacher gave him an unamused look. "If we haven't found either of them yet, we'll expand our search."

"That's...what, the mayor's house?"

"The mayor's house, the Montgomery mansion, and your place."

"Got it." Angel saluted with two fingers and jogged away from the preacher, every sense on full alert. He combed three blocks, jumping fences and narrowly avoiding an angry Rottweiler. He slowed to an easy walk when he reached the next street.

A patrol car drove up behind him and slowed to keep his pace. Angel looked over and saw the sheriff rolling the window down. "Howdy."

"Howdy," said Angel.

"What are you doing out so late?"

"Just getting a little fresh air," said Angel, taking a deep, illustrative breath. "Yourself?"

"What do you think?" The sheriff's frown was a deep line carved in his face. "Looking for Skata. Someone said he's been staying with you, is that right?"

"I know, right? That's what you get for taking in a stranger. He runs off and starts killing people—that's why I recommend background checks, Sheriff."

"You never can tell," said the sheriff with a deep sigh. "If I ever see him, I swear it'll take everything I have not to kill him myself. Cassis was all but a surrogate father to my granddaughter. I can't hardly stand it, seeing Shannon all broken up like this."

"It must be hard," said Angel, surprised to feel genuine sympathy.

"It is. It is."

For a minute, nothing happened. The sheriff stared vacantly through the windshield, the car engine thrummed, and Angel wondered whether he was supposed to leave or not. He broke the awkward moment by saying, "Well, I'm about to head home."

The sheriff straightened and looked at him as if he couldn't remember having seen him there before. "Yeah, the streets aren't safe. I could put a deputy on watch at your house, if it'd make you feel more comfortable.

"Oh, that's all right." Angel waved a hand. "I'll lock all the doors and windows and give you boys a call if I see any sign of him."

"Right. Don't engage him if you do see him," said the sheriff, pulling away from the curb.

"I wouldn't dream of it," said Angel, waving. "Good luck with the manhunt!"

He watched the car drive away, and only when it was out

of sight did he roll his eyes and give a small bounce. That had been closer than he was exactly comfortable with. He turned and continued his walk.

He felt as if he was pushing through thick fog, the aftereffects of the vervain and his own hunger reminding him of the one fact he could stand by: being a vampire really sucked sometimes.

* * * * * * *

By the time he reached Hezekiah's statue, he had combed every shadow and tree, been through every yard and down every alley he saw.

Colton approached, his face drawn. "Anything?"

"Nope." Angel snapped his fingers. "Light me up, brother."

Colton shone the flashlight in his face and he stood, unblinking, until the preacher was satisfied. "You're clean." Colton flashed the light in his own eyes with a grimace.

"Genuine article," said Angel. "And no sign of the counterfeit."

Colton leaned against the foundation of Hezekiah's statue and looked like he was having a hard time standing on his own two feet.

Angel knew the feeling. "Looks like it's time to peek under the outskirts."

Colton nodded. "We'll circle the mayor's house first."

It didn't take long to reach the mayor's mansion, but they paused outside the ring of light from the windows. For a moment, the only sound was the water splashing in the white stone fountain in the center of the front lawn.

Colton lowered his flashlight, cupping a hand over the beam to dim it.

"Prowler," snorted Angel, scanning the ground.

"Hey." Colton moved toward the fountain and crouched, shining the flashlight at the base of it. "Looky here."

Angel frowned at the sight of the gelatinous, flesh-colored pile. "That's disgusting," he said, looking away from it and scanning the rest of the yard. "Who on earth did he turn into this time?"

Colton let out a heavy groan. "It's like looking for a needle in a haystack, except the needle can actually turn into hay. I didn't sign up for this crap."

Angel patted the preacher's shoulder. "Now, now. Remember your blood pressure."

Muttering something about 'frickin' blood pressure,' Colton stood and shrugged Angel's hand off his shoulder. He looked ready to football tackle the next person he saw to the ground.

"Any idea who he might have shifted into?" Angel asked, putting his hands on his hips and squinting at the mansion.

"I don't know." Colton started off toward the mansion with new purpose.

"What are we doing?" asked Angel, following.

"We have to let them know they're in danger. We know the double-walker shifted into someone else, so they won't be looking for Skata."

"Which maybe they should be, now," said Angel, frustrated.

They strode up to the front door, and Colton knocked. They stood, waiting uneasily, until Honoria opened the door.

"Lucas!" Honoria kissed him on both cheeks and extended a bewildered smile to Angel. "You were at the last council meeting. Angel, isn't it?"

"Name," he said, with an indifferent smile. "Not occupation."

"What are y'all doing out here with a criminal on the loose?" She stepped back inside, gesturing for them to come inside. "Don't tell me this is a social visit."

"No, ma'am," said Colton. "It's about Skata."

Her face lost all semblance of charm. "That man can go to hell for what he did. Olivia Everett was one of my dearest friends."

Colton's eyebrows rose a little at the sudden vehemence from the soft-spoken woman. "Is your husband here?"

"He's in his study. He's been a little out of sorts since he got home."

"I think everyone's a little out of sorts right now," said Colton soothingly, in spite of his obvious frustration.

She nodded, pushing a hand through her hair. "I'll go let

him know y'all are here—there's fresh coffee in the kitchen, help yourselves."

"Thank you," said Colton, as Honoria walked away toward the study.

Angel followed Colton into the kitchen and leaned against the island. "Who keeps paper cups by the coffee maker?" he asked, tilting his head. The cups were stacked neatly upside-down next to a basket that held small packets of sugar, brown sugar, cane sugar, and Sweet'n Low.

"The Prescotts, apparently. Coffee's not too bad, though. Want some?"

"Thanks, but no thanks." Angel watched Colton stir a packet of brown sugar into his cup. "Why does a guy like you take up the cross?"

"Why is a guy like you so curious?"

"Oh, you know." Angel shrugged. "You seem more like the kind of guy to have a job at a rodeo. Heck, if not for the bitterness factor, I'd peg *you* as the vampire hunter, not Skata."

Colton smiled tiredly and took a sip of the coffee. "Guess you can't judge a book by its cover, huh?"

"I guess you can't," said Angel.

"I'd have pegged you for the kind of guy who hangs out at strip joints and ends up in jail for disorderly conduct all the time, but here you are."

"In a kitchen," said Angel.

Colton's grin faded suddenly as he looked past Angel. "She

should be back by now." He set the coffee cup down and pulled out several drawers until he found the knife drawer, from which he pulled a large stainless-steel boning affair.

Angel was beginning to feel jumpy and high-strung as he followed Colton out of the kitchen. His fangs were trying to reappear, and he had to concentrate hard to force them back into hiding.

"Honoria?" Colton walked across the foyer, holding the knife with the blade angled down, away from his forearm. There was no reply, and he looked back at Angel, who pushed ahead of the preacher and opened the study door with a kick. It slammed against the wood paneling behind the door, leaving a dent.

"Mayor?" Colton stepped across the dark-red-and-brown rug, toward the desk.

Angel lifted his head and took a deep breath, and as he did, he felt his fangs push through in defiance. Man, it felt good. "Blood," he said, sniffing the air.

Colton ran around the desk and paused abruptly. "Oh, man."

Angel jumped on top of the desk and looked down at the bodies. Honoria was slumped on top of her husband, blood soaking the floor beneath them. Angel reached down and touched the blood leaking from a stab wound by Honoria's shoulder. "She's cooled off."

"She didn't have time to cool off," snapped Colton.

They stared at each other.

"She was already dead," said Colton, kicking the nearest chair. It flew into the shelf, knocking several hardcover books from their cases. "I can't believe this."

"Shhh." Angel pressed a finger to his lips and pointed toward the study door.

Colton switched his hold on the knife back to his right hand and nodded at Angel, who raced to the door. He stopped short as the barrel of a gun came around the corner, followed by Skata.

"What are you doing here?" asked Colton, surprised.

Angel took the flashlight from Colton's pocket again and shone it into Skata's eyes. "He's clean. Can't say I'm not disappointed, though."

"I traced the shifter here," said Skata, glancing at Colton.

"Oh, it's actually a double-walker," said Colton, once again looking inordinately excited about the fact. "Also called a doppelganger."

"It's dead when I find it," said Skata flatly. "That's what it is."

Angel tilted his head back and looked at the ceiling. A faint sound drifted through the layers of thick floors and walls. "He's upstairs."

Colton glanced up. "Did you hear him?"

Angel nodded. "Follow me."

"Hey." Skata grabbed his arm, and the grip was hard, even for a human. "I'm going in first."

"Go right ahead." Angel patted his shoulder. "I'll stand behind you."

"Skata," said Colton in a hard voice, "if we kill this guy on sight then we might never know what he was after, or if there are more. We have to catch him alive."

Skata turned his back on the preacher. "Speak for yourself."

They hurried up the stairs, moving as quietly as they could, not knowing how good the shifter's sense of hearing was. Skata walked ahead of them, placing his steps carefully on the old wood. It groaned softly under their weight.

Skata looked back at Angel and jerked his head questioningly toward the bedroom door in front of him. Angel nodded, and that was all the affirmation Skata needed. He turned and slammed into the door with his shoulder.

The doppelganger was crouched on the floor, and he lifted his head as they came in, his teeth bared, black eyes flashing. He convulsed and shuddered, falling to his hands and knees as the splintering sound of bones shifting under his skin threatened to make even Angel's veteran stomach turn.

The doppelganger didn't cry out once; he groaned through his teeth, a low sound of pain and possibly anger. He reached over his shoulder and tore away the last of his peeling flesh, and as he dropped it on the floor, he spat blood and teeth out of his mouth.

The shotgun blast exploded in the air. Salt struck new flesh and bone, and the shifter howled as the force of the shot knocked him over. Skata pumped and fired again, stepping closer with each shell that hit the floor.

Angel heard Colton shouting at Skata over the noise and raced forward, pinning Skata's arms to his chest before the man realized why his shotgun had clattered to the floor.

"Let go of me before I add you to my hit list, strigoi," Skata hissed.

"Let him go, Angel." Colton picked up Skata's gun and crouched next to the unconscious double-walker. The creature had taken Skata's form again.

Angel pushed Skata away and ran his tongue across the tip of his fangs. Maybe now that Skata knew his true nature, he might at least appreciate the effort it took not to eat him.

Colton nudged the doppelganger, who remained immobile. "We need to take him somewhere fast."

"Apparently Angel has a solid basement," said Skata.

Angel reached down and hefted the limp double-walker over his shoulder. "It's better than solid," he said with a wink. "It even has a cell."

* * * * * * *

Skata almost wished Angel had been lying, but there really was a room in the basement: large, with bars and a hefty lock on the door. Either the house had been built on top of an old jail, or it had once belonged to smugglers. When they dragged the doppelganger into the cell, Skata tried not to pay attention to the large, white freezer shoved into the opposite corner. He'd noticed Angel watching it as though it was alive, but the vampire had only tossed Colton the key and gone back upstairs.

It had been nearly an hour since then, but Skata had not moved. He stood inside the cell a yard from the chained doppelganger, waiting to see signs of life. The creature hung by his hands, chained to a bar that ran across the ceiling.

"Hey." Skata glanced over at the sound of Colton's permanently hoarse voice. "How's he doing?"

"It," said Skata pointedly, "is out cold. I thought you said this wouldn't take long."

"Not if you shot him normally, but he was in the middle of a transition." Colton shot Skata an irritated look. "That's a doppelganger's weakest point."

"Answer me this, Father," said Skata, nodding toward the unconscious creature. "Why does he keep using my body?"

"Could be trying to psych you out." Colton folded his arms across his chest and watched the doppelganger. "Either that or you're convenient. A stranger in town makes an easy scapegoat. It's a good move."

"Or maybe you're just comfy," said Angel, walking down the stairs and leaning against the door of the cell. "I mean, just look at you, all those cushy muscles. Although, I think he looks better with the whole long Ivy League crew cut hair than you do."

Skata ignored him. Just suffering under the knowledge he was staying his hand from the vampire when he had pushed a piece of wood through his own wife's heart—he took a deep breath.

Chains clinked softly as the doppelganger stirred and lifted his head. Black eyes stared at Skata, stared into him.

"Hey there," said Angel, waggling his fingers in the shifter's direction. "You know, we really need to think of a name for this guy. 'Skata Two-Point-Oh' just doesn't sing."

Colton lifted his chin in the doppelganger's direction. "You got a name?"

The creature did not respond; he just continued to watch them all, like he was taking mental pictures and storing them for later.

"It doesn't matter," said Skata.

"I'll call him…Skinner," said Angel, shrugging. "It seems appropriate."

"You look hungry, vamp." The doppelganger's voice was a perfect imitation of Skata's, but instead of the seething anger Skata felt, the doppelganger's face held a sharp kind of mischief.

"You could just compliment my personality," said Angel, with a deep sigh.

"He's just pushing buttons," said Colton. "Figuring us out."

"I imagine that's the last thing you want," said Skinner, turning his head to look at Colton.

Skata crossed over to the doppelganger and gripped a fistful of his hair, pulling his head back. Looking into those black, empty eyes that seemed to laugh and scream at him, he wanted nothing more than to sever Skinner's head from his neck with a serrated knife. "Why the murders?"

"I hate to break it to you," said Skinner, "but you have a lot to learn about interrogations."

Skata let go of the doppelganger's hair and walked over beside Colton. In his ear, he whispered, "I need you to leave me alone with this guy for a few minutes."

Colton's laugh was one syllable. "What, so you can beat him to death?"

Skata glanced at the doppelganger. "He's murdered three people, maybe more."

"Torture is inhumane," began Colton, but Skata patted his shoulder.

"Have a little faith, Father."

"Fine," said Colton. "Five minutes. That's it."

Angel straightened as Colton stepped out of the cell. Immediately, Skata slammed the cell door shut. "I might need more than five minutes."

He saw the look of surprise, then suspicion flash across Colton's face as the preacher reached into his pocket. Colton looked at Angel. "He took the key."

Skata held the key up. He might regret this, but he had to do it; the need was too strong to restrain. Neither Angel nor Colton would give the creature what he deserved.

"I must say," said Angel, pursing his lips, "I didn't expect 'pickpocket' to be one of your talents."

Skata stopped listening then. He knew Colton was shouting at him; he heard the cell door rattling. Skata tuned the sounds out as he picked up an extra length of chain and looped it around the door and the bars, dodging Colton and Angel's attempts to grab him. He locked the chains—they might be able to pick the lock on the cell door, but getting past the chains would take longer.

Skata turned to face the doppelganger. "You're going to talk."

"Or what?" asked Skinner, turning a bored expression on Skata. "You'll kill me?"

From his boot, Skata drew his favorite hunting knife and pressed it into the center of the creature's breastbone. "You're smarter than that. Figure it out for yourself," he said, and tore the knife down the doppelganger's chest.

CHAPTER TWENTY-FIVE

Y ou know," said Skinner, "I'm all for torturing the bad guy, I just wish you'd do it with a little more finesse. Respect for the craft."

"You don't need finesse to cause pain," Skata retorted, flicking excess blood off his knife.

"Be that as it may." Blood from healing wounds dripped down his face, his shoulders, neck, and chest, and had he been human, he would have been dead half an hour before. "You haven't looked me in the eye once this entire time, which strikes me as odd given the intimacy of our…current situation."

Skata grunted.

"You're not *scared*, are you?"

"I'm a lot of things," said Skata, wiping the rest of the blood off on the thigh of his jeans, "but scared isn't one of them."

"Oh, sure it is," said Skinner, leaning his head back. "Everyone's got a little kryptonite buried somewhere. I just didn't think yours would be eye contact."

Skata stabbed the doppelganger in the thigh and tore the knife out. "Shut up."

Skinner lifted his head and blinked once, slowly. "Must be irritating, trying to cause pain and getting no response. Kind of anticlimactic, I would think."

"And yet, it's not going to make me stop," said Skata. "Not until you tell me why you killed those people."

Skinner hesitated before asking with a curling smile, "Would you believe I have somnambulism?"

"It takes you a while to get hints, doesn't it?" Skata stepped back. The stone floor under the doppelganger was slick with blood, and he stared at it for a moment, surprised by the amount. *Then again, when you can magically heal yourself as soon as you're injured, I guess it doesn't matter much.* "Just because you don't react much doesn't mean you don't feel pain. Tell me what I want to know and I'll stop."

"You don't really *get* pain, do you?" mused Skinner. His narrow gaze and seeming imperviousness to torture made Skata feel like he was the prisoner, not the other way around. "See pain has classifications, just like everything else. This isn't pain. This is you stabbing me with a knife over and over and *over* in a mind-numbing attempt to make me talk, but this isn't pain. This is hurt, and they are very different things."

"Well, until you talk, I'm going to hurt you as much as I want to," retorted Skata, switching the knife to his left hand and flexing his right hand for a punch.

"Ahhh," breathed Skinner. "There we go. You're not really doing this to make me talk; you're doing this because you want to. Now you're just being honest about it."

Skata slugged the doppelganger in the face, splitting Skinner's lip open and leaving a dark bruise that began to fade as soon as it appeared. "You don't know anything about me."

Skinner shook his head like there was a fly buzzing around it. "You said it yourself," he replied, shrugging. Over his head, the chains rattled against the bar. "And I hate to bring it up again, but I know everything about you. I get trying to pretend it's not true, but the fact is that I have the advantage over you, plain and simple."

Skata gripped a fistful of the double-walker's dark hair and pulled his head back before placing the tip of his knife underneath Skinner's eye. "It doesn't look that way to me."

"Then you're not looking very closely, are you?" asked Skinner. "You think I'm the bad guy because I killed those people, but what puts you in a different position?"

"Don't give me that 'we're the same' crap," spat Skata.

"Oh, but we aren't," said Skinner quietly. "You're much worse than I am. See, I've done a lot of bad things in my lifetime, but I've never killed a pregnant woman before. That's all you."

Skata had never stabbed a man in the eye before, and he was almost surprised at how soft it was, like spearing an olive with a toothpick at Thanksgiving dinner. Skinner still did not scream—his breathing took on a high, panicked sound, and he wrenched in Skata's grip, but the doppelganger remained quiet. It was like a match to gasoline; Skata's anger raged as he dropped the knife and punched Skinner in the face, the pain in his knuckles the only thing that felt quite solid, quite real. He wanted to tear the doppelganger to pieces—he *needed* to tear him—

"Skata, *stop!*"

The voice barely broke through, reaching inside him and turning everything backwards.

He lowered his hand and stepped back, blinking rapidly as the cell came back to life around him. He glanced down at his hand—his fingers were black and bloodied. He could feel his pulse in every vein with each heaving breath he took, and he tried to breathe, to remember how.

Skinner hung forward, limp and dripping blood into the pool on the floor. Suddenly, there was something so human and helpless about the way he looked that Skata turned around, unable to look at him just then.

Easton stood outside the cell, her mouth open. Colton stood behind her, a pair of bolt cutters in his hand. Angel stood on Easton's other side.

Dazed, Skata pointed at Easton. "What is she doing here?"

"Sorry, man," said Colton. "You went way too far. We had to *do* somethin—"

"What have you—what are you doing?" Easton interrupted Colton, her gaze unwavering as she stepped forward and gripped the bars, staring at Skata.

Skata blew out a deep breath, struggling to hold himself together. "You shouldn't be here." To Angel, he shouted, "You shouldn't have brought her here!"

Easton whirled to face Colton. "Somebody tell me what's going on."

Colton tucked his thumbs into his belt loops—for a preacher, Skata couldn't help but notice that personal situations did not seem to be his element.

Angel seemed to notice, too, because he said, "Fun fact: what looks like Skata, talks like Skata, and walks like Skata, but is not, in fact, Skata? A doppelganger!"

"That—that's the thing that killed Mom?"

"Yeah," said Colton, lifting his gaze to meet Easton's. "It is."

Easton turned back to face Skata, her thoughts flying across her face like a film reel. Shock, hurt, and confusion were displayed there, and she didn't seem to care. "So what is Skata trying to do?"

Angel opened his mouth to reply, but Colton gave him a warning shake of his head, and Angel only cleared his throat, bowing out of the conversation.

"He was supposed to be questioning him," said Colton in a hard voice as he gave Skata a flinty stare, "until fifteen minutes ago when he started doing this."

How has it only been fifteen minutes? Skata would have sworn he'd been in the cell closer to an hour.

"You couldn't break in?" asked Easton. Her eyes were still

bloodshot and streaks of mascara still smudged under her eyes, but she was clearly pushing her current anguish to the side and trying to deal with the situation in front of her.

"I picked the lock open, but he chained it," said Colton, nodding toward it. He hefted the bolt cutters. "If you didn't work, these were next, although the chain's too thick. It would've taken longer."

"He could have just put a 'do not disturb' sign on the door," said Angel, "but no."

Easton's brown eyes narrowed. "Let me in."

Skata didn't move. "I can't do that."

"Let. Me. In," she repeated.

"No."

"He killed my *mother*." Easton's voice was quiet, but somehow that only sharpened her words. "I doubt you have more cause to hate him than I do. Unlock the door before I call the sheriff." She held up her cell phone. Skata hadn't even noticed her dial the number.

"Mmm, bad idea," said Angel.

"It's gonna be a good idea if Skata doesn't make a move," Colton disagreed.

"Open the *door*, Skata," snapped Easton, her voice raised nearly to a shout.

Skata clenched his jaw, and for a moment, he said nothing. Then he swore under his breath and unlocked the chain, yanking it off the door and throwing it into a pile on the stone floor.

Easton walked inside without looking at Skata. "You should go clean yourself up."

"Leaving you alone with that thing is—"

"He's chained to the ceiling," snapped Easton, "and Angel will stay here. Colton, would you mind keeping an eye on Skata, please?"

"Yes, ma'am," said Colton, stepping forward. He nodded his head at Skata, who wasn't sure whether he was furious or relieved.

"Don't worry," said Angel, tapping his fingers against the cell bars. "I won't let him touch a hair on her head."

Skata hesitated for a moment, torn. Then he shook his head. "Damn it, Easton, he's *dangerous.*"

Without saying a word, Easton spun around and grabbed Skata's wrist, holding his bruised, bloodied hand in front of his face. Neither of them spoke, and after a moment, she let go, her point made.

Skata shot Angel a warning look as he left the cell and headed up the stairs with Colton close behind.

* * * * * *

Easton reached into her pocket and withdrew a hair elastic. As she twisted her hair into a ponytail, she said, "Stop looking at me."

"You're handling this all very well, given recent events," Angel remarked.

Easton snapped the elastic on the final twist and turned to face him. "Thank you. It's called compartmentalization."

"Skata said you were a tough cookie," Angel replied.

Easton rubbed her arms, feeling the sudden chill of the stone basement. "I actually wanted to thank you. For yesterday. You were really sweet."

"No need to sound so surprised," he said airily, but his voice grew more serious as he added, "You're welcome."

Easton glanced back at the doppelganger.

"We're calling him Skinner," said Angel. "I felt it fairly apropos. Go ahead and chat; just pretend I'm not here."

Easton took another step toward Skinner. She curled her hands into fists, trying to stop them from shaking.

There were no visible signs of injury on him, not anymore, but there was plenty of blood. She looked down at the sticky substance beneath the soles of her tennis shoes. There was so much of it…more blood here than her back deck. It wasn't coming out, she would have to try something different—bleach, a wood stain, something so Graham wouldn't have to…

Snap out of it.

She looked up and was suddenly paralyzed by black eyes.

"Shouldn't you be in mourning?" he asked immediately, as if he had been waiting, even subconsciously.

Easton slapped him as hard as she could before she even realized her hand was moving. The force of the slap shoved his head to the right, and he looked calmly taken aback as he re-focused on her. This time he said nothing, but there was a new interest in his demeanor.

"You killed my mother."

"Oh, I did more than that, sweetheart."

"I know you did. You also killed Cassis and the mayor and his wife."

His smile held a dimension of curiosity. It was more than strange, seeing Skata's face used like this. It was clearly a mask—if she had paid more attention when Skinner came by, if she hadn't been so preoccupied with worrying about Macon, she would have noticed.

He had Skata's body, but everything was 'off,' everything belonged to someone else. The way he tilted his head, his small, constant smile, the way he often narrowed his eyes to a near-squint. Even the way he spoke—he didn't speak in a straightforward way like Skata; he drawled, dragging out each word with sharp affectation. He seemed bizarrely genuine in his insincerity.

"I can't believe I didn't see it."

"See what?" he asked.

Easton blinked, realizing she had spoken out loud. "You're nothing like him. You may look like Skata, but it doesn't even suit you. It doesn't fit."

"Agreed," he said. "Yet isn't it funny how nobody ever seems to look closely enough to notice." He didn't phrase it like a question.

Easton swallowed hard, her heart burning against the vile replica in front of her. She promised herself the slap was the only way she would hurt him. From the look of it, Skata had already done the rest, with plans for more. "Why did you kill them?" She tried to read any feeling in his eyes, but there was nothing to read. It was like looking into the wrong end of a telescope—he was clearly observing her, but she couldn't see him. "Why would you want to?"

"Strictly business," he replied readily. "Nothing personal."

The rein on Easton's rage snapped, and she stared, unable to register the callousness of his words. He must have noticed the way she stiffened, because he added, "What did you expect? A sob story? Something to justify a heinous crime or two?"

"Fine," Easton snapped. There was no real way she could have this conversation without playing into his hands some way—the trick was to remain distant and let any remark he made slide over her, no matter how deep the wound. "Why frame Skata for the murders?"

"Figure that out for yourself, why don't you?" His mouth curled.

"Because he's new in town?"

"I knew you could do it."

It was a valid reason. Skata hadn't been in town very long, and barely anybody knew him. Still, something gnawed at her. "So what, you just planned your random murder spree to happen the first time a stranger showed up?"

His smile didn't widen, but it seemed to deepen somehow. It was just shy of menacing. "What's the matter? Don't believe me?"

"No," said Easton.

"Smart move."

Easton felt suddenly as though she were viewing the scene from an outsider's perspective, from a third invisible person who could see them both at the same time. She saw herself—pulsating with anger, with confusion, and the need to shove her feelings aside to keep her heart from crumbling into dust. Opposite herself, she saw Skinner—a cheap imitation of the real Skata, hanging by his arms, soaked in blood and completely defenseless, just like her.

Just like her, the only real armor he had was the armor he could build himself out of nothing, and if that meant insulting her, deflecting her, or simply trying to get under her skin, so be it. To her, he was the enemy—the demon who had brutally stolen her mother not twenty-four hours ago.

But to Skinner, she was the unchained enemy. And as she looked into Skinner's blank, black, empty eyes, she didn't feel hatred or the desire to hurt him the way he hurt her. Those desires faded into a threadbare, exhausted sense of reality.

"I'm going to forgive you," she said softly. His eyes narrowed. "Not today," she continued, pushing her hands back through her bangs. "One day. But I want you to know that right now, I want nothing more than to go home and watch some stupid cooking show with my mom, but I can't. I want to give her the longest hug in the world, but I can't. I'll never be able to make her laugh or cry or anything ever again, and that is *your* fault." She shoved him in the chest with both hands, just hard enough to make him swing. "Your fault."

She turned and hurried from the cell.

CHAPTER TWENTY-SIX

S kata popped the lid off a bottle of beer as Easton walked into the room. "Any luck?"

"Not really." She leaned her elbows on the island. "He's very tight-lipped."

Skata nodded and spun the bottle cap on the counter, watching it spin like a coin. "You okay?"

"I'm actually really not okay," she said, her voice thick as she glared at the counter. "My mom was murdered yesterday. Graham won't come out of his room, and Dad—do you know what it's like to see your dad sobbing? It's like..." She shook her head. "And the preacher and a *vampire* have to come get me because you've gone berserk torturing somebody—"

"Hey," Skata interrupted harshly, "he deserved everything he got and a lot more. I don't know why you aren't agreeing with me."

"I *do* agree with you!" she snapped, tears glinting sharply in her eyes. "When I saw him, when he spoke, do you think I didn't want to hurt him more than you did? He murdered my *mom*. But he's caught now—he's chained up in the *basement*. He's not going to kill anybody else, and hurting him won't save anybody."

"It might if he'd tell us why the hell he did it."

"You don't know that," she shot back.

"And the doppelganger is snug as a bug in a…" Angel paused mid-stride and did a half-turn when he entered the kitchen. "Bad time?"

"Don't worry about it," said Skata, draining the contents of the bottle and throwing it in the trash.

Angel tilted his head and said, "That's supposed to recycle."

Skata cracked his knuckles and moved around the island, ready to try and slam the vampire into the floor, but Angel dodged the situation by asking breezily, "Where's the preacher-man?"

The question was enough to remind Skata that Angel could break his spine with a finger, and he shrugged. "He went back to the church building. He's trying to come up with something to break the doppelganger's ability to mimic."

"Hallelujah," said Angel. "One of you is bad enough."

"Angel," said Easton suddenly, sniffing and giving herself a slight shake, "can I have a minute with Skata, please?"

"Sure thing." He winked at her and was gone in a rush, disappearing somewhere upstairs.

Skata eyed Easton warily. "What?"

She slouched on the bar stool, her gaze tired but steady. "What happened to you?"

He frowned and crossed over to the fridge, pulling out another bottle of cold beer. "What's that supposed to mean?"

"I don't remember ever seeing you like this."

"That's because I never drank around little kids," he retorted.

"You know that's not what I meant. You used to be…warm, and—and funny, and I thought you were the most amazing person I'd ever met."

"Kids are stupid that way," he said roughly, taking a quick gulp of the beverage. It wasn't helping, but it was cold. "And people change."

"Not this much. Not without something happening to them."

"I'm doing just fine, so stay out of it."

"I bet that sounded more convincing in your head," she said acidly.

"My life is none of your business, Easton, just like yours is none of mine." He took a deep breath, trying to keep his temper under control. This was the little girl he used to give piggyback rides to, the girl who had once made him a tea party out of toilet water—a fact he hadn't known until after the fact. And she was grilling him about his personal life, his motivations? It felt like some kind of universal joke. Someone, somewhere, was laughing at him. "Leave me alone."

"That's the way you like it, huh?" Her teeth were half-bared, her eyes as hard as the granite countertop. "Alone, because that way you don't have to answer to anybody."

"Yes!" He threw the bottle into the sink, where it shattered, chipping the white porcelain. *Breathe.* "So what? So what?"

She took a deep breath and slid off the stool, shoving it in against the island. "I can't make you change," she said stiffly. "Nobody can. But you know what? Fine. If you like it like this, go right ahead and keep doing what you're doing. I don't care. ANGEL."

Angel appeared in the kitchen not a yard from her. "You rang?"

"Drive me home," she said and hurried out the door.

As she slammed it behind her, Angel turned to Skata. "Nice," was all he said, before following Easton out to his car.

* * * * * * *

When Angel returned, Colton was standing over the dining room table with a toolbox and a leather tool belt spread out before him.

"Where's Skata the First?" asked Angel, sauntering up and peering at the items in front of Colton.

"Beats me. I guess he got out of here for a while." Colton held up a plastic bag of ground herbs, something from the bulk section of a health food store.

Angel nodded and tapped the tabletop until Colton demanded, "What?"

Angel took a deep breath and let it out. "There's no nice way to say this, so I'm just going to go all Gossip Girl and ask if you knew about Skata."

"What about him?" Colton unscrewed a whiskey flask and took a whiff. He made a face and poured a small amount into the glass mixing bowl in front of him.

"His wife?"

Colton blinked. "He has a wife?"

"Correction: he *had* a wife."

Colton frowned. "What happened to her?"

"If what Skinner says is true, apparently Samuel Lemeck turned her into a strigoi, so he killed her."

Colton shifted his jaw, understanding clouding his eyes. "If it's true, it makes a whole lotta sense."

"Yep," said Angel. "There's one more trivia fact for you."

Colton tipped a small jar of silver powder into the bowl and stirred it. "What's that?"

"Apparently, Mrs. Skata was with child at the time."

Colton stopped stirring. "She was pregnant?"

"Yep."

"So he killed them both?"

"Yep."

Colton paused. "Did he know?"

"About the baby? Nah."

263

The preacher rubbed his chin thoughtfully. "Why did Skinner tell you all this?"

Angel shrugged, his hands in his pockets. "He probably thought I'd use it against Skata somehow, maybe rub his nose in it."

Colton nodded. "You won't, though," he said. "Right, man?"

"Just because I'm a vampire doesn't mean I'm a terrible person." Angel took his right hand out of his pocket and crossed his heart. "I'll be good."

"Right." Colton went back to stirring, eyeing the mixture closely, occasionally pulling something new out of the wooden toolbox on the table.

"Are you about done with that?" asked Angel. "And by the way, it smells disgusting."

Colton grinned. "Silver shavings, some dried coriander, and pure alcohol. Can't imagine it'd smell *good*."

"What are you going to do, spray him with it?"

Colton reached into the toolbox and held up a tranquilizer dart the length of his index finger. "Nah. Half a dozen or so of these should do the trick."

Angel picked up the small bottle of silver shavings. "I thought this was for werewolves."

"Shape-shifters."

"Ah. How long will the effects last?"

"Maybe twelve hours, he won't be able to change into anybody. He'll have to return to his original form and stay that way."

Angel nodded. "It's too bad there's still one thing missing."

"What's that?"

"Motivation. Specifically, Skinner's motivation for wanting to frame Skata."

"He's working for Samuel."

"Who's on the run and probably not rich enough to hire an assassin," Angel pointed out. "And it doesn't get much more as-sassin-y than a doppelganger. I'd be charging a lot of money for my services if I were him, which probably means—"

"It's personal," Colton finished, his eyes narrowing in thought. "This means something to him."

"I wonder what Skata ever did to him."

"Maybe he didn't do anything," said Colton suddenly. "May-be Skata was just collateral damage."

"Come again?"

"Skinner's working with Samuel, but that doesn't have to mean he's working *against* Skata."

"That's a lot of 'S' names," said Angel. "Call Samuel 'Le-meck' instead, it'll help keep things straight."

Colton rolled his eyes and continued. "Maybe Skinner's in this for personal reasons that have nothing to do with Skata."

"Maybe we should ask him," said Angel.

Colton held up the tranquilizer dart, now filled with the new concoction. "Maybe we should."

* * * * * * *

"See? Right where I left him." Angel smiled as he unlocked the cell door. "He's already on such good behavior."

"It's not like he can go anywhere," said Colton, loading the last dart into the long, handheld tranquilizer gun.

"Maybe he thinks it'll get his sentence reduced," Angel suggested.

"Nah, with what he did? He's doing fifty to life."

"Ooh, but how long do doppelgangers live, anyway? We might need to adjust the sentence."

"Good point. Doppelgangers usually live to about a hundred and thirty, on average. All the shape-changing helps keep 'em young."

"So what do you think, eighty years in here?"

"I think that's going easy on him."

"You two are adorable," said Skinner, interrupting their pointed banter. He did not seem particularly perturbed by their presence or their conversation. "Especially if you really believe this place can hold me."

"I bet I know what he's thinking," said Colton, looking at Angel. To Skinner, he repeated, "I bet I know what you're thinking. As soon as you're all done healing yourself, you'll just change into somebody smaller and skedaddle, right?"

"Something like that," said Skinner, "although the word 'skedaddle' hadn't really entered the picture."

"You're having way too much fun," said Angel, with a bemused look over at Colton.

"Am I?"

"I'm pretty sure your eyes are twinkling," Angel affirmed. "Should I be worried?"

"Nah. I got this."

Angel folded his arms, vaguely confused by the firm belief that Colton did, in fact, have the situation well in hand. Bizarrely well in hand. In fact, he seemed to have *every* situation bizarrely well in hand. "I feel so safe with you," he confided sweetly.

Colton's lip curled. "Don't ruin the moment, man."

"Sorry." Angel cracked his knuckles. "So how do you want to do this?"

"Shoot first," said Colton. "Ask questions after."

Skinner frowned. "What——"

Colton shot him with four darts: two in the neck, one in the leg, the other in the arm. When Angel gave him a wide-eyed look, he shrugged and said, "Covering the bases."

Skinner's face twisted into a scowl. "Ow. What the hell were those?"

"Darts," said Colton, tucking the gun into the back of his jeans and looking through the bars.

"What are you trying to do," asked Skinner incredulously, "put me to sleep?"

"Not exactly," said Colton.

There was a loud crack, like someone stepping on a dry branch, and Skinner's head snapped back with a grunt of pain and surprise. Angel grimaced——watching the transformation was not only painful, but disgusting. Flesh loosened and dripped off Skinner's bones, which broke audibly and put themselves back together, shifting under his skin.

"I may throw up," stated Angel.

Colton, his arms folded, only watched with a keen expression on his face. "So don't watch."

"I'd love to stop, but I can't look away. Morbid fascination," said Angel, pressing a hand against his stomach. "I'd do the whole body-switch thing once, then zip. Never again."

"You're telling me," Colton agreed. "Lots of doppelgangers pick one person to mimic as long as they can because the transformation's so painful."

"So Skinner's a freak *and* a masochist. What a multitasker."

Skinner's new form hung, exhausted, from the chains. He had shed the darts along with everything else; they were on the floor now, mixed up with the excess Skinner had shed.

"He has different hair," Angel remarked. The doppelganger's true form sported steel-colored hair shaved close to his skull. "All 'prison inmate' as opposed to Skata's Ivy League thing."

"Bet more's different than that," said Colton, unlocking the door. He stepped in past Angel, who stood a yard away from Skinner. "Hey." He snapped his fingers in front of Skinner, who did not respond.

"Be right back," said Angel. Almost before the last word left his mouth, he returned, holding a plastic bottle of water. "Back." He tossed it to Colton, who twisted the lid off and splashed the water on Skinner's head and face.

Skinner lifted his head then, and Angel saw hard eyes and a soft mouth in the face of a man who could have been anywhere between thirty and forty.

"I'm up, I'm up," drawled Skinner.

Colton crunched the water bottle into a ball of plastic and tossed it by Angel's feet. Angel frowned and picked it up. "Littering is bad," he told Colton. "Especially in my house."

Colton ignored him. "So this is what you look like," he mused, studying Skinner. "How old are you?"

"Didn't anyone ever tell you it's impolite to ask a person their age?" The doppelganger's gray eyes were sharp as he watched Colton.

"I'm gonna guess…what, forty?"

"Cold," said Skinner.

"Thirty-five," Angel chipped in.

"Too young," said Colton.

"Thirty-six."

"Even colder."

"Forty-five," said Angel.

"Bingo," said Skinner.

"Dang, you look good for your age," said Angel, lifting his eyebrows.

"Says the vampire," snorted Colton.

Angel pushed his fingers through his thick black hair. "That's what makes me an expert."

"Less adorable now," said Skinner, "and I'm not hanging around for the *view*, so whatever kind of interview you two have in mind, let's get to it, shall we?"

"We want to know why you're so okay with killing people you've never met," said Colton.

Angel wrinkled his nose. "I thought we were going to be more diplomatic about it."

"That *was* diplomatic."

"No, that was direct. Diplomacy is never direct. It's like the cardinal rule of diplomacy. Diplomacy one-oh-one, if you will."

Skinner closed his eyes and smiled briefly. "You two put Laurel and Hardy to shame."

"Thank you," said Angel. "Answer the question."

"Nah."

"Why not?"

"Don't want to. What I *can* tell you is the reason Samuel's working so hard to wipe this town off the map."

Angel looked at Colton, who shrugged and said, "Let's hear it."

"Picture the late eighteen hundreds," said Skinner. "Hezekiah Hammond and his followers move to the Carolina backwaters and think 'why not settle down right here?' The only problem being the town already there."

Angel frowned and glanced at Colton, who shrugged. "First I've heard of it."

"It wasn't a town for people, so to speak," said Skinner. "It was a town for vampires, werewolves, shape-shifters, etcetera. But Hammond didn't think that was much of a problem, so he burned the place down and built a quaint little town on top of the old one."

Angel widened his eyes and glanced at Colton, who shrugged and said, "Nice guy."

"I didn't really take Samuel as the group justice type," said Angel.

"Don't start," said Colton. "So what, Samuel lived here then?"

"From what I've gathered," said Skinner.

Angel rubbed his chin. "You weren't even a twinkle in your father's eye at that point, so why do you care?"

With an impatient sigh, Skinner replied, "Let's just say I have my own reasons for doing what I do and leave it at that."

"No can do, compadre," said Angel.

"He's right," said Colton. "We don't have a reason to trust a thing you've said so far."

"If it's proof you want, you can find it in the city planning records at the sheriff's office," said Skinner. "Town's too small for a municipal building, apparently."

"A ferry station and no municipal building," muttered Skata. "Go figure."

"How do you know the plans are there?" asked Lucas.

Skinner let out a short sigh and said, "Because I used to know the former sheriff. That enough for you?"

"For now," said Colton.

Angel blinked. "It is?"

"Ain't much else we can do till we see if he's telling the truth or not."

"They're not going to let us into the sheriff's office to look at their records, especially if those records include a deep, dark secret," Angel pointed out. He folded his arms and looked at Skinner. "Unless we had the sheriff with us, that is."

"No," said Colton.

"What?" Angel spread his hands. "He has us! It's not like he could *do* anything."

Through his teeth, Colton said, "Don't make me list everything that could go wrong if we let this guy loose."

"It's hardly letting him loose," said Angel, rolling his eyes. "It's more like supervised parole."

"He's stronger than you," Colton pointed out.

Angel grimaced. "True. But," he added, pointing, "you have your bizarrely encyclopedic knowledge of us non-person-people. I'm sure you could think of something."

"Nah," said Colton firmly. "Ain't happening. Besides, he won't be able to shift again for a couple hours."

"We can wait," said Angel.

"Does the shifter get a say?" asked Skinner.

"Shut up," said Angel and Colton together.

"It's a good idea," said Angel.

"It's a very, very bad idea," said Colton.

"Buuuuuut…." Angel grinned coaxingly. "Come on. It'll be fun."

Colton folded his arms tightly across his chest and frowned. "Fine. But if either of you does anything stupid—"

"You'll say a prayer for us?"

"Sever your spines," said Colton.

Angel blinked. "You might have just convinced me to join your congregation, preacher. The sermons must be fascinating."

"Just remember that communion is grape juice."

Angel smiled nicely. "I'm sure I can improvise."

Colton's return smile lacked all humor. "Don't even think about it."

"Spoilsport."

CHAPTER TWENTY-SEVEN

A re all your ideas this bad, or is this all to impress me?"
Angel turned to look at Skinner, who was peering
at the three squad cars parked outside the station. "I'll
have you know most of my ideas are brilliant."

"This isn't one of them," said Colton, drumming his fingers
on the steering wheel. "He doesn't even have the right clothes."

"They're Skata's," said Angel, eyeing Skinner's casual outfit
of worn jeans, a button-down shirt, and a jean jacket. "So they're
pretty generic. I think he'll pass."

Colton eyed Skinner in the rearview mirror. "You do anything to screw this up, and I'll gut you with a screwdriver, you got
that?"

"That," said Angel, "is not a very heavenly attitude."

"Boys," said Skinner, "relax. This isn't my first rodeo. I've
seen the sheriff, and he's not here, come on." He climbed out of
the car and walked toward the front door, where two deputies
stood talking.

Angel and Colton quickly exited the car and followed, unwilling to let Skinner take the lead. "If this goes south," Colton began, but Angel interrupted.

"Guts," he said. "Screwdriver." He tapped the side of his head. "Got it."

"Yeah," growled Colton.

They came up behind Skinner, who was talking easily with the deputies. "—pull in some temporary help," he said, then turned and nodded to Angel. "Howdy."

"Hey, Sheriff," said Angel, putting his hands in his pockets. He nodded toward the doors. "Can we have a word with you in your office?"

"Sure thing." Skinner patted the nearest deputy on the shoulder as he walked past, pushing the doors open and striding through the lobby. Once inside, Colton took the lead and moved into the sheriff's office. Skinner and Angel followed him inside, and Colton told Angel to watch the door.

"What for? The sheriff being in the sheriff's office isn't exactly unheard of," Angel pointed out, keeping an ear to the door.

"The real sheriff discovering a fake sheriff in the sheriff's office *is*," snapped Colton. To Skinner, he said, "All right, now where's all this incriminating evidence?"

"Don't know," said Skinner. "Getting you in here was my job description; the treasure hunt wasn't."

Colton bared his teeth, but all he said was, "Fine. Five minutes, in and out. Angel, stay by the door. Skinner, job description's been updated. Start looking."

Skinner frowned but opened a cabinet near the window and began to search. Angel remained listening, watching the others work. After a moment, Colton said, "Think I got something."

He set a cardboard box on the desk and lifted off the lid. It was full of thick, yellowed folders. "It certainly looks old enough," said Angel. He crossed over to the desk and pulled one of the folders out, then sniffed it. "Iron gall ink. These have to be the right ones."

"I guess I'll watch the door, then," said Skinner.

Colton whistled low through his teeth as if commanding a dog. "Don't even think about it. Angel, go watch the door."

Skinner hooked his thumbs through his belt loops. His appearance was older and portlier than his true form, but the lazy scowl was genuine. "Just trying to help."

Colton looked up. "Here's something." He held up an unsealed manila envelope and tossed it to Angel.

When the vampire gave him a *why do I have to open it* expression, Colton held up his gun and nodded toward Skinner. "Free hands."

Angel gave a long-suffering sigh but opened the envelope. Inside were twelve fading black-and-white photographs. They could have been shots from a war correspondent for the destruction they showed. Burned-out buildings, destroyed and blackened. Bodies, impossible to tell what species, melted and reduced to twisted skeletons. The last photograph showed Hezekiah in the flesh, standing in front of a brick building, half-reduced to rubble. He was smiling, his arms held out as if at a festival.

Colton walked over to look at them.

"Well," said Angel after a moment, "he was creepy. Congratulations," he added to Skinner. "You've been vindicated."

"Fantastic," said Skinner. "So I can leave."

"No," said Colton, pointing the gun at Skinner's kneecap. "You can't."

"We need to get out of here," said Angel, flicking the envelope. "We need to put this back."

Someone knocked. "Daddy?"

All three of them froze at the female voice outside the door.

"You were supposed to be listening," hissed Colton.

"Oh, sure, blame me!"

Shannon's voice held suspicion as she asked again, "Daddy?"

Angel and Colton both turned to look at Skinner, who noticed their expressions and straightened as if he'd been startled awake. He breathed out through his nose, sighed loudly, and called, "I'm having a private conversation, dear."

The door flew open, revealing Shannon holding a handgun. "Funny," she said. "I just hung up with him."

* * * * * * *

277

Wolfsbane and vervain made a bitter mixture, but Skata was used to it. He stirred them into his coffee and set the spoon on the counter, watching steam rise from the surface of the beverage. He had thought he was prepared for anything—life never handed him a damn thing, and he lived ready to dodge or swing. But the last couple days…

He blew out a breath. And here he'd been living with the thought all vampires could be killed with a wooden stake.

"Awesome," he muttered into his coffee as he took a long swallow, regardless of the heat.

The sound of shattering glass spun him around. He set the coffee down and took a knife from his belt. It wasn't silver, but it was Damascus steel and that counted for something. He moved around the kitchen island and looked around the corner, into the foyer and the living room beyond.

A cold draft blew in from somewhere. That meant a broken window, and if Angel thought his tenant was going to pay for it, he was sadly mistaken. Skata crossed the foyer and stayed in the doorway of the living room, crouched at an angle where he could see most of the room while remaining hidden.

A figure moved across the other side of the room, prowling between the sofa and the bookshelves.

Skata rolled his eyes and got to his feet. "Hey, kid."

The figure rose to its full height and spun, startled.

"What do you think you're doing?" Skata demanded, keeping his knife in full view. If the kid attacked, at least he'd know he had it coming.

The boy couldn't have been more than twenty-one or twenty-two, but the agility with which he jumped over the sofa and coffee table wasn't that of an average college athlete. "You Skata?"

"That's me," said Skata, "but I think you've got the wrong house."

"Nah," said the boy. "I don't." He lunged at Skata with an animal growl.

Skata ducked, letting the werewolf smash into the wall behind him before turning and grabbing a fistful of the boy's hoodie. He pushed his blade against the side of the kid's neck and said, "Who's your boss, moron?"

The boy bared a mouth full of sharp teeth, panting and snarling.

"I don't like asking twice." Skata pushed deeper, drawing blood.

"Screw you," the boy spat.

"Fine." Skata grabbed a fistful of the boy's fauxhawk and cracked the boy's head into the wall. The werewolf sank down without a sound.

"Idiot," said Skata. He reached down and grabbed the hood of the kid's sweatshirt so he could drag him somewhere out of the way. He had only dragged the unconscious werewolf a few feet when the sound of tinkling glass snapped his attention back to the window.

Two more figures jumped in and stood, watching him.

"Oh, great," he said, and stood up.

The werewolves launched themselves at him, mouths open. It didn't matter how much wolfsbane was in his blood, it wouldn't do a thing if they tore his throat out.

He braced himself as the first werewolf slammed into Skata. He felt the knife punch through the werewolf's stomach as they fell backwards, felt warm blood leak through his shirt. Skata rolled over, shoving the body off just as the other werewolf tackled him, teeth sinking into his back.

Hot pain flooded Skata's injuries, and anger flooded the rest of him. Skata reached back and grabbed a handful of fur—the werewolf had completed its transformation, and Skata didn't even have a knife.

The werewolf released Skata momentarily, positioning to get a better grip, and Skata rolled over, grasping at the wolf's face. He dug his thumbs into the creature's eye sockets, pushing as hard as he could and feeling very sure that the snapping teeth would bite off his face any second.

The werewolf shook its head violently, trying to free itself, and as it pulled, Skata released it. The werewolf slipped back, off-balance, and Skata gripped the knife from the stomach of the other werewolf. As the werewolf came for him again, Skata crouched low and drove the knife into the side of the creature's neck, pulling on the hilt to rip the gash open as far as he could.

A whimpering howl tore from the werewolf's throat, and he staggered limply to the side. Skata kicked it in the ribs and pulled the knife free, only to grab the wolf by an ear and stab it through a damaged eye.

A loud, angry snarl came from behind him. Skata turned, wiping an arm across his blood-spattered vision. The first werewolf had woken up, and now he hung back, waiting.

"Come on," Skata invited angrily, his pulse throbbing in his neck. "Come *on!*"

"Well. Your housekeeping certainly leaves something to be desired."

Skata recognized the posh Southern accent, but knew better than to turn his back on the werewolf.

"Would you like a hand?" the voice inquired. Glass slid across the floor by Skata's foot, kicked by someone, and the shadow striding across the floor became a man.

Not a man—a vampire. Gideon Montgomery let out a sigh, his shoulder straight, and met the gaze of the werewolf who began to back away.

Gideon undid the button of his dress jacket.

The last werewolf turned and ran for the kitchen, propelling himself on his hands and feet despite not having fully shifted. Before Skata could blink, Gideon was in front of the werewolf, blocking its way, and he saw the vampire put a hand on the werewolf's chest.

No, not on. *Through.*

The werewolf collapsed like a puppet with the strings cut, and Gideon dropped a bloody heart from his hand.

Gingerly, the vampire reached into his breast pocket and withdrew a handkerchief. He stepped over the three bodies littering the foyer and approached Skata, wiping blood off his hands like it was dirt or syrup or something else ordinary.

His casual attitude bothered even Skata. "Thanks."

"Yes." Gideon shifted his jaw thoughtfully to the side and looked at the wreckage. "I presume you have an explanation."

The front door opened, and in spilled four people, bringing a heated argument with them. Colton's voice shouted above the rest, "Shut your faces! Now! Before I shut 'em with a staple gun!"

Skata and Gideon faced the group as they shut the front door behind them, and suddenly there was silence.

"House rule number one," said Angel, shutting his eyes and pointing toward the nearest dead werewolf. "Don't make a mess. I told you that. First thing."

"Howdy, Gideon," said Colton.

"What," said Shannon, "the *heck*—"

"Oh, don't act so surprised." Skata blinked as the sheriff leaned against the wall and continued, "it's always like this, or so I gather."

"There's no logical reason for you to bring the sheriff with you," said Skata. "That being said, that better not be who I think it is."

"It is," said Angel. "I can explain."

"Don't," interrupted Colton, lifting a hand to silence the vampire. "You'll make it worse."

"Okay," said Angel, "I can change the subject. Like—oh, here's a good one—hey, Skata? Why is Easton's boyfriend dead on the floor of my foyer?"

CHAPTER TWENTY-EIGHT

Any of that blood yours?" asked Colton, before Skata could answer the first question.

"A fair amount," said Skata. "As for Easton's boyfriend—I didn't…it was—fast. He attacked me, so I killed him. Fair and square."

"Men," said Shannon.

"I know, right?" said Skinner.

Skata pointed at the doppelganger. "Can someone explain why he's walking around instead of chained up in the basement?"

"I was forced," said Skinner.

"It had to do with Samuel," said Colton. "We'll explain in a minute. Why are you here?"

The question was directed toward Gideon, who smiled politely. "I came by to have a word with an apparent killer and found him in a predicament, so I lent a hand. The allegations against him piqued my curiosity."

"For the record, I didn't do it," said Skata.

"So I gathered from the presence of our good sheriff behaving very unlike himself," said Gideon, with a brief glance at Skinner.

"Sue me," sneered Skinner. "I dropped out of acting school. Now if you ladies will excuse me, I'm going to the bathroom to return what I borrowed. Be right back."

Colton shook his head and followed Skinner. "I don't trust you."

"Suit yourself."

Shannon watched them leave before looking from Angel to Skata to Gideon, then back. "Anyone going to tell me what's going on?"

"Oh, that might have to wait," said Gideon, adjusting his cuffs. "Someone is turning down your driveway."

Angel turned to stare at the door. "He's right. They're trying to be sneaky."

Skata groaned. "This has been a really long day."

"And getting longer," said Angel, peering through the peephole. "It's the sheriff."

* * * * * * *

"So, how's it feel to get busted by an anonymous tip?" Angel leaned against a wall and gazed sympathetically through the cell bars.

Skata gave him the darkest glare he could dredge up. "How would it feel to get stabbed in the heart with a toothpick?"

Angel stretched his mouth in an exaggerated frown and shrugged. "You tell me, jail boy."

"'Jail boy'?" Skata lifted his eyebrows. "That's the best you've got?"

"Yes, well." Angel sniffed. "I'm not the one sitting in jail for *homicides*. Of varying degrees, I might add."

Skata leaned his shoulder against the bars. "Great job of covering for me there, by the way. I loved the look of shock on your face. The stammering was stellar."

"Well, unlike our doppelganger acquaintance, I completed my tour in acting school," said Angel. "Besides, what else could I have done? 'Ohh, I'm sorry, Sheriff, I forgot aiding and abetting were crimes.' My playacting saved us all from the frying pan. Except you, anyway."

"This isn't the frying pan," said Skata. "This is the fire. Speaking of which…" He turned to look fully at the vampire. "You're a strigoi, so why don't you fry every time a little sunbeam touches you? I keep forgetting to ask."

Angel's smile was uncharacteristically humorless. "There's your business, and there's none of your business." He made a gun with his fingers and pretended to shoot it at Skata. "That's none of your business."

Skata made a noncommittal sound. "Do you keep some kind of talisman in your pocket?"

Angel tapped the bars with each word. "None. Of. Your. Business."

Angel smiled, but for once there was no humor. It was a caricature that suited his face like an ill-made mask.

Skata sat on the floor and pressed his back against the opposite wall. "Forget it."

"Already forgotten."

"—get off my back, all right?"

Skata and Angel both turned to look as Colton strode around the corner, his face wearing a dark scowl. Skata dropped his search for any sign of good news on the preacher's face. "What now?"

"What's there to tell, man? Three dead teenagers, a crime scene out of a B-grade horror movie? You with weird injuries *and* the murder weapon?"

"And Gideon didn't exactly stick around to bail you out," said Angel.

Skata raked both of his hands over his head.

"Oh," said Colton, "and Angel and I are both under suspicion as accomplices, although Shannon's vouching for us, so that should clear up. She told the sheriff that a doppelganger was involved, so there's a shot you might be exonerated."

"Yay," said Angel.

Skata leaned his head back against the wall and shut his eyes. "She okay?"

"Shannon? Yeah, she's fine. She's used to all this crazy."

That was one good thing about the day. "Where's Skinner?" Silence answered his question, and Skata opened his eyes. He didn't say anything—he only trusted the sinking feeling in his chest as Colton and Angel traded uncomfortable glances.

Finally, Colton said, "He got away."

"You just left him alone?"

"I locked him in the bathroom, man. The window was yea big." He made a small box-shape with his thumbs and forefingers. "I underestimated him."

"Yeah," said Angel. "He's like an octopus."

"I guess he probably didn't leave any evidence behind, either," said Skata tiredly.

"You guess correctly."

"Some exoneration." Skata half-heartedly knocked his fist against the wall. "Hey, did Gideon mention why he dropped by in the first place?"

"Ye-es," said Angel slowly.

"I get it," said Skata. "It's all bad news."

"He was there to kill you," the vampire finished helpfully.

Skata blinked. "Oh, that's great. Don't know why I expected anything else."

Colton folded his arms across his chest with the look of a man who wanted to take both sides and found himself getting cornered into picking one or the other. "He thought you were the one murdering people, so I mean…the guy was trying to help."

Skata rested his hands on his knees and looked evenly at the preacher. He could feel himself pulling, stretching thin, a hair's breadth away from snapping. "Shut up."

"He did change his mind when he saw the werewolf problem," said Colton, grimacing.

"I said shut up." Skata straightened his back, trying to relieve the sharp pain of the werewolf bite. He had given up trying to ease the pain in his shoulder—he was failing Cassis in every way possible, and the thought disgusted him, even though he'd barely known the man.

Colton walked away, out of sight, and Angel watched him. "As much as I'd love to stay here and hang out, I have a mess to clean up back at the house. If they let me clean up the yellow tape, that is."

Skata shut his eyes again. He didn't feel like talking—not with Angel, not with anyone. He wanted to slip into unconsciousness and wake up in a different reality.

He heard Angel click his tongue and say, "Don't go anywhere, now," before walking away.

As the vampire's footsteps faded, another set approached. Skata looked up as Colton reappeared with a white box tucked under his arm and a deputy following close behind.

"House call," said Colton as the deputy unlocked the cell, his hand planted firmly on the gun protruding from his holster.

Skata let out an exhausted breath. "Nice."

Colton crouched on the floor next to Skata and opened the box. "Shirt off."

Skata tugged his shirt over his head and down around his forearms, as far as the handcuffs would let him. Colton eyed the bloody gashes in Skata's back with a critical eye before saying, "Ah, you'll live. These ain't that bad."

Skata begged to differ as Colton got to work patching him up with all the tenderness of an army medic. "Preacher, doctor, gunslinger. Nice skillset."

"You should see my day jobs," said Colton.

"Hurry up," said the deputy, his hand twitching nervously. He looked like a gawky twelve-year-old, thought Skata sourly.

"Right. Last step," said Colton, positioning himself on one knee.

"A proposal?" said Skata.

"Your shoulder's dislocated," said Colton, ignoring Skata's joke. "On three."

Skata took a deep breath and nodded.

"One," said Colton, and shoved.

For exactly three seconds, the pain was excruciating. It was over just as suddenly, reduced to a powerful ache. Skata tried to unclench his muscles and breathe, glaring at the preacher through half-closed eyes. "All those night jobs and you can't even count to three."

"Eh, that'd take all the fun out of it." Colton taped one more square of gauze over the tear in Skata's back before shutting the first aid kit and standing up. "I'll be back tomorrow, see if I can do anything to…" He shrugged helplessly.

"Yeah," said Skata. "Thanks." He chuckled bleakly. "Can't believe I'm in here and Samuel's out there doing God knows what."

Colton gave Skata's good shoulder a brief bump with his fist. "Can't be in two places at once, man."

Skata straightened, and they stared at each other with a sudden glint.

"If," hissed Colton, holding up a finger, "even if we could find Skinner, he's still a killer with sketchy motives, and I don't think he'd want to help."

"But he could," said Skata, "if he wanted to."

Colton glanced at the deputy, who was gazing back down the hall. "I'll see what I can do, but no promises."

"Don't worry about me. I'll just stay here and get some shut-eye." Skata gingerly pulled his shirt back into place and stretched his legs out. He closed his eyes and listened as Colton and the deputy left the cell. The door creaked shut, and he heard the key turn in the lock, sealing him in.

* * * * * * *

Easton was curled up on her bed, trying to finish the last chapter of *Les Miserables* while studiously ignoring the black funeral dress hanging on her closet door when someone knocked on her window. She knew who it was before she rolled over to look and was not surprised to see Angel perched outside.

She sighed and unlocked the window. "What do you want?" she asked, lifting the book. "I'm reading."

He tilted his head to study the upside-down cover. "Ah, *Les Mis*. Never liked it. The musical isn't bad, though."

She put a hand on her hip. "What do you want?"

He smiled disarmingly. "Can I come in?"

"You've been invited, so yes. Isn't that how the vampire thing works?"

"I was being polite."

"Whatever. Come in. If you try anything, I have a wooden stake." She reached into her nightstand drawer and held it up for confirmation.

"So I see." He hopped nimbly through the window, but eyed the stake with an expression that was difficult to read.

"Don't get all offended, now," she warned. "I'm basically a walking cheeseburger to you. It's self-defense."

"You're not a walking cheeseburger, Easton."

"Really. What am I, then?"

"You're a person." He sighed and straddled her desk chair backwards, folding his elbows across the back.

"Which you eat."

"No, I don't."

"What do you do, then?" She set her book down on the bed, gripping the stake firmly in her right hand. She could never imagine herself really using it, but she was prepared. "Is it true you can hear someone's blood pumping from a block away?"

"Gracious, no."

She sized up the distance between them—six feet, maybe seven. "Can you hear mine from here?"

He nodded.

Easton sighed and tapped the blunt end of the stake against her thigh. "I don't believe things are made evil," she said finally. "Even vampires."

"We were human once," he pointed out. "I know for a fact that negative changes happen."

"You try, though. I know plenty of people who don't even do that."

"Yeah, well." He shrugged, but his cocky demeanor hung around him like a ragged cloak. "Trying only counts for so much. Still gotta have blood."

"And if you didn't have it?"

"That's called starvation," said Angel. "Or so rumor has it."

"So what do you do? Blood bags from hospitals? Coconut milk?"

"Coconut milk actually curbs the craving sometimes," he said quickly.

"Well, it would," said Easton, "I read it has a bunch of the same components as...." She shook her head. "Why did you come here?"

His crystal eyes met her gaze for a moment before he looked down. He took a deep breath, pressed his lips together. When he finally did speak, his voice was strained and quiet. "Macon's dead."

The stake slipped through her hands and fell to the floor with a clatter.

"He attacked Skata, tried to kill him. Skata had to kill him first."

"He can't...he wouldn't—" Thick, hot words tangled and choked her into silence.

Angel stood up and crossed over, stopping a foot in front of her. "I'm sorry," he said, and somehow, she knew he meant it. He picked the stake off the floor and pressed it gently into her hands. "I'm so sorry."

Easton realized she was crying as her vision blurred and her throat swelled, and she wrapped her arms around herself, trying not to break. "People need to stop dying," she spat, wishing she could turn the words into something hard and throw them. She wanted to shatter something, to hurt something.

She felt Angel's hand on the side of her head, and she wanted to lean into him, wanted to see if he could keep her from falling apart, but she couldn't move. She shut her eyes, hating herself for crying in front of him, and she said so, clearing her throat and managing, "I don't usually cry like this."

"I know."

She felt arms under her, lifting her up and setting her back down, and she realized she was being held like a small child. It was too much effort to care—she let herself curl into Angel, clutching the stake tightly and letting angry tears burn tracks down her face as she sobbed herself into a black, exhausted sleep.

* * * * * * *

Sunlight streamed onto Easton's face and woke her up. She yawned and pushed herself onto her elbow, barely stopping herself from shrieking at the sight of Angel stretched out next to her, his hands folded on his stomach.

Easton shook her head and flexed her fingers, stiff from gripping the wooden stake all night. She set it on the foot of the bed and looked back at Angel, taking the opportunity to study him while his guard was down.

His youthful attitude and confident demeanor made him seem younger than he looked, but now she could see the faint lines dug around the corners of his eyes. His skin was smooth and healthy, but he somehow looked vaguely haggard despite it.

"I thought the creepy vampire was supposed to watch the girl sleep," Angel murmured. He opened his eye and blinked a few times before pushing himself up into a sitting position, his back resting against the pillows.

"I'm smashing stereotypes," said Easton, raking her hands through her tangled hair. "How old are you?"

"So forward." He stretched his arms over his head and said, "I was born in eighteen sixty-nine. Lucky me, I skipped out on the Civil War."

"How old were you when you were bitten?"

"Thirty-four."

"Were you a cowboy?"

He drew his eyebrows together. "Do I *look* like a cowboy?"

"Nah. You look like a mercantile owner or something."

"Ouch."

"Have you fought in any wars?"

He held up a hand, counting on his fingers. "World War One, World War Two, and the Korean War."

"Vietnam?"

A shade passed over his face, but was gone as quickly as it came. "I was busy."

Easton sensed he wanted her to change the subject, so she stood up and stretched. "How's Skata holding up?"

"How'd you find out?"

"Colton called me and filled me in."

"Well, you know Skata; he's a born felon. Jail suits him."

Easton rolled her eyes. "I'm going to grab a shower. What are you going to do?"

"Help preacher-man look for Skinner, probably."

Easton raised her eyebrows. "Why?"

"A hare-brained idea that probably won't work," said Angel, standing.

Easton opened her closet and pulled out a tee shirt and a pair of cutoffs. "None of this makes sense. Why is everything happening—I mean, why now?"

"I guess it makes sense to somebody." Angel stood up and spun the stake in his hand. "We just need to figure out who and find them."

"Easier said than done."

Angel grunted in response and looked thoughtfully at the stake.

Easton paused, thinking. "There would have to be a pattern, right? If we stepped back and looked at the big picture, we might be able to see that pattern. At the very least, we might see something we missed."

"I'll get out the corkboard and red string," said Angel dryly. "What did you have in mind?"

"I know someone who's good at that kind of thing. He might be able to help."

"Bring this person by my house later, then," said Angel. "I'll get Colton."

"Sure thing."

Angel tossed the stake back onto the bed and climbed out the window.

CHAPTER TWENTY-NINE

The doorbell rang at eleven thirty-seven.

Angel groaned. "I'll get it."

"I've got it," said Colton, walking out of the living room with a trash can full of glass shards in his hand. "You're the one who looks like an extra from *Carrie.*"

Angel looked at the bloody rag in his hand and the half-cleaned mess surrounding him. "Right. You get it."

Colton set the can down and opened the door.

"Hey," said Easton, her hands in her back pockets.

"You're earlier than I expected," Angel called, looking over his shoulder. "Texting was invented for a reason!"

Easton grinned. "Sorry. Can I come in?"

"'Course," said Colton, stepping back to let her in. "Who's this?"

Angel stood up and eyed the person standing on the front steps behind Easton. He wasn't terribly remarkable to look at—Caucasian, mid-twenties, dark hair, average build—but the way he looked at the bloody foyer with total unconcern struck Angel as unique.

"Hi," he said. "Easton said you need me to think for you, or something…?"

"This is Spencer," said Easton.

"He-ey, Spence," said Angel, raising an eyebrow.

Spencer gave him a withering look. "Spencer. What did you do in here, have a ritual sacrifice?"

Easton went a little pale, and Colton quickly said, "That your gear?" and gestured to the bag slung over Spencer's shoulder.

For a moment, Spencer looked like he was about to correct Colton, but he settled on, "Yes. This is my gear."

Angel wrung out the towel over the bucket. "So is Spencer aware?"

Easton blinked. "Aware?"

"In the cosmic sense. Of things beyond the usual."

"A chupacabra ate my aunt," said Spencer, "so yeah, I'm aware."

Everyone turned to look at him with stunned expressions.

"Kidding," said Spencer. "It was a joke. Unbelievable."

Colton and Angel traded uncertain glances, and Angel got the feeling Colton was ready to drag Spencer into the kitchen by his hair and have a serious talk with him.

"I mean, if you guys don't actually need me, I could always be doing something else. Elsewhere," said Spencer.

"No," said Easton quickly. To Angel, she said, "Trust me, he'll help."

Spencer walked around the mess in the foyer and into the kitchen. "This'll do," he said, setting his laptop on the island.

Everyone stood around Spencer as he opened his laptop. "Okay, so you need to find a vampire or something, right? What I'm going to do is create an algorithm using data to narrow down the most likely locations for this guy to be."

Angel smacked his hand against his forehead. "Why didn't I think of that?"

Spencer twisted to look at him. "Do you really want an answer?"

Angel blinked at Easton. "Does he have a sense of humor?"

Ignoring the others completely, Colton said, "I thought you needed a supercomputer for this kinda stuff."

"My brain," said Spencer, pulling up a program that looked more science-fiction than reality. "That's the supercomputer here."

"Oh yeah," said Angel. "He'll fit right in."

"I don't think…never mind," said Colton, shaking his head and crossing over to the fridge. "Do your thing, buddy."

"Spencer," said Spencer. "Now tell me everything you know to find this Samuel guy."

* * * * * * *

Three hours later Spencer was engrossed in three screens—his computer, his tablet, and his phone. The computer screen displayed a green graph with various sections filled with text, and Angel had no idea what was happening on the other two screens. It looked very CIA.

Easton had made a run to the General Store for Red Bulls, and there were three discarded cans around the workstation, and Spencer was drinking another, when he wasn't drumming his fingers on the table.

"Geez," said Angel. "He's like an energy-drink alcoholic. An energolic."

"Coulda fooled me," said Easton dryly, leaning against the counter. She had remained in the kitchen while Angel answered Spencer's questions as well as he could. Colton had a counseling session with a parishioner, so he had excused himself and promised to be back as soon as possible.

"You don't need to stay, you know," said Angel, stretching his arms over his head. "You could go watch a rerun of Gilmore Girls or something while I watch this idiot."

"Heard that," said Spencer, without looking up.

"Oh no. Better break out the sleeping pills or I'll be up all night."

"He's helping," yawned Easton, repeating herself for at least the dozenth time.

"He doesn't have to be such a little—" Easton caught Angel's eye, so he finished, "—genius about it."

Spencer set the drink down and clapped his hands together. "Okay," he said. "I really only want to explain this once, so I think we better wait for the angry guy."

"Colton," said Angel. "I can't wait to tell him you called him that."

"Whatever." Spencer stood up and rotated his neck and shoulders.

Angel scrubbed his hands through his hair. "Not to be pedantic," he said, yawning, "but how did you guys meet?"

Spencer groaned and dug the heels of his hands into his eyes. Without bothering to explain himself, he walked out of the kitchen and through the foyer. Angel and Easton watched as he collapsed on the couch, one arm flung over his face. "Wake me up whenever," he called.

"We were hiking the same trail, and we both got lost," said Easton, shaking her head. "It was about a year ago, and it was so hot. I think I had like nine ticks on me at the end of the day. Anyway, we ran into each other and decided to stick together until we found our way back to the trail."

"He sounds like a real keeper," Angel grinned.

"Oh yeah."

"How did the whole 'vampires are real!' conversation come up?"

"That was easy," said Easton with a snort. "When he first ran into me, he thought I was a werewolf, and he started asking me questions like 'so what do you think of full moons?' and I just thought he was weird."

"So you decided to be friends? That makes sense."

"Oh, he's fun. And kind of likable in an unlikable sort of way."

Angel took out his phone and looked at the time. "All right, come with me."

"Where?" She didn't look overly concerned, but properly wary.

"I'm both injured and proud that you ask," he said. "Stay here then, I'll be right back." Angel jogged out of the room and up the stairs, where he took a wooden stake off a top shelf in his bedroom, then returned to the kitchen.

Easton was leaning over Spencer's laptop, squinting at the running program. "I'm not a computer science major, but this doesn't look great."

"It probably isn't," said Angel. "Our luck is waaaay too bad for that." He motioned with two fingers. "Come here."

She crossed over to him and stood with her hands in her back pockets. "What?"

He held up the stake by the sharp end and waited. After a moment, she cautiously held her hand out and he smacked it lightly into her palm. "Hold that."

"Okay," she said slowly. "Want to tell me why?"

"Hit me."

Easton rolled her eyes. "Come on—"

He smacked his chest. "I'm serious, hit me. You won't hurt

me," he added. "I have complete confidence in myself."

"Be that as it may," she said, with the voice of someone speaking to a stubborn toddler, "I'm not going to stab you with a wooden stake."

"You can do it."

Easton frowned. "Is this a sick way of committing suicide or what?"

"Easton, dear, please. I'm five times stronger and faster than you, at least. You won't kill me."

"I meant for myself."

"Please?"

She groaned and made a half-hearted stab toward his heart. He swatted her hand easily away and gave her a pointed look. "That," he said, "was pretty pathetic."

"I don't want to hurt you!"

"You could stab me literally anywhere but the heart and it would hurt, but it wouldn't kill me. Besides, stabbing people in the heart isn't as easy as it sounds. Would you please have a little faith?"

Easton bounced on the balls of her feet. "Okay. Fine. I'll do it." Without further warning, she lunged at him, swinging the stake toward his chest. He stepped out of the way, grabbing her wrist and pushing it back toward her shoulder. "A for effort," he commended. "Do you exercise?"

"I jog. And hike. I'm outside a lot," she said with a mock glare.

"Ohhhhh." She jabbed at him again; he dropped his shoulder, moving out of the way. "Better."

She rolled her eyes and struck at his chest again, and again he stepped sideways, grabbing her wrist and easily prying the stake from her hand. "Tell me," he said, "just what exactly are we trying to accomplish? And by 'we', I mean 'you.'"

"Thirty seconds ago, you wanted me to stab you through the heart," she said, folding her arms. "So that's what I'm trying to do."

"Well, it looks like you're trying to get yourself killed." He handed her back the stake and flicked her just below the collarbone with two fingers.

She winced. "What was that for?"

"That's bone," he said. "A puny little human isn't going to be able to drive a stake through that."

"Dolph Lundgren probably could," she remarked.

Angel gasped. "I'm going to tell Dolph you called him puny."

Easton snatched the stake back from Angel. "So you want me to try and injure you or *what?*"

"The way to a vampire's heart is through his ribcage," he said, pointing toward the exact place. "If you're ever in a fight with a vampire, you probably only have one shot, so remember that."

"Or," said Easton, "I could just stake the vampire in the face and slow him down while I got the heck out of there."

Angel paused. "There is also that option. Yes."

Easton's grin faded, and she sighed. "I think I'll probably just actively avoid fighting with vampires."

The front door slammed, and Colton strode into the kitchen with a nod. "Hey."

"Why the long face?" asked Angel, noticing the man's dark expression.

"Shannon wanted to talk, but all it boils down to is that clearing Skata's gonna take a miracle."

Angel leaned his elbows on the counter and frowned. "No evidence to say he didn't do it."

"Right."

"Aren't they taking Skinner's…leftovers to forensics?" asked Easton.

"Yeah, but they aren't a big priority, apparently."

"An innocent man is locked up while the guilty man does Lord-knows-what, and forensics aren't a 'big priority'?" Easton's mouth formed an O as she stared at Colton.

Angel squinted. "I don't know, 'innocent' is getting pretty blurry around here. Skata's killed people out of revenge, too."

"Skata babysat me, for heaven's sake."

"Ted Bundy probably babysat, too," said Angel. "Spencer!"

Colton glanced over his shoulder into the living room. "Find anything out?"

"He'll have to tell you," said Angel, making his way over to the sleeping man. "Said he didn't want to explain it twice." Without ceremony, he dug underneath Spencer and shoved him off the couch onto the floor.

Spencer sat up with several slurred, intelligible words.

"Three nickels for the swear jar," said Angel.

From the kitchen, Easton called, "You have a swear jar?"

"For him, I'm making one," Angel shouted, "as soon as we're done here." To Spencer, he added, "The preacher's back. It's lecture time."

"Lecture? It's not a *lecture*." Spencer climbed to his feet and strode into the kitchen, muttering, "I should have charged for this."

Colton folded his arms as if to keep from punching Spencer, although he'd only been back for a minute. "What's the deal, man?"

"It's not pretty," said Spencer. "The attacks you told me about—the werewolf attacks in the woods—they've all happened while you're searching for Samuel, right?"

Colton glanced at Angel, who said, "Bingo."

"So they're systematic. The werewolves are protecting Samuel; they even retaliated the one time you found him."

"Skata found him," said Angel, "but your point stands."

"Yeah, of course it does." Spencer cracked his knuckles. "And that was at the same time the doppelganger or whatever framed Skata, so that guy's obviously in on it, too."

"Okay," said Easton, frowning.

Spencer looked at her face, then at Angel's. "Okay," he said, turning finally to Colton, "at least tell me *you* see where I'm going with this."

Colton's lips were pressed in a tight line, but he glanced at Angel and said, "War. They're acts of war."

Easton held up a hand. "Hang on—war? What do you mean *war?*"

"I mean people dying," said Spencer blankly. "To death. These are battles going on, not just random attacks. I'd say they're building up to a full-scale attack, and it should happen soon, if my graph is right. They can't just keep escalating—shit's going down, and it's going down soon."

Colton shook his head. "Salvation used to be a haven for non-humans. Maybe Samuel wants to take it back."

"That makes sense," said Easton with a groan. "Darn it."

"I can't believe I'm saying it," said Angel, "but Skata would be useful right about now."

"Yeah, well," said Colton. "I might be able to help you with that."

CHAPTER THIRTY

A ngel held up a finger. "Skinner mentioned a boathouse, and you—"

"Ferry station," said Colton. "Not boathouse."

"Right," said Angel. "So Skinner mentioned a boathouse, and you think he's going to be there because...why?"

"Because there's only one ferry station in the whole dang town," said Colton, glaring, "and it was owned by Oliver Rayborne."

"Who's Oliver Rayborne?" asked Easton.

"According to Shannon, the Raybornes were one of the founding families. Oliver Rayborne was a model citizen to the public, but there were rumors about what happened behind closed doors."

"So what happened to them?"

"Well, the kid disappeared, and the wife overdosed on some sleeping pills, and Oliver packed up and moved away once speculation set in."

Angel blinked. "That's…happy."

Easton cocked her head. "So how does Skinner fit into all of this?"

"I think the kid, Hazard Rayborne, is actually Skinner," said Colton.

"Wow." Angel rubbed the back of his head. "This feels like playing telephone except nobody remembers the original phrase."

Easton lifted both her eyebrows. "You've played telephone?"

"We had variations back in the day, you know."

"And which day was that?" asked Spencer.

"Focus," said Easton quickly.

"Right." Spencer shut his laptop and slid it back into its case. "You guys go have fun. I'd like to survive the week."

Easton frowned at him. "Spencer."

"Hey, I'm just the tech guy. It's up to you to save the world and stuff."

"Good riddance," said Angel. He cracked his knuckles and made a shooing motion at Easton and Colton. "Come on, Avengers. Assemble."

"Actually, you guys are more like the young Justice League," said Spencer. "Before they picked up speed."

"Get out," said Angel.

* * * * * * *

The preacher drove them to an empty stretch of road and pulled over to the side. "Here we are."

Angel opened the door and stepped out. "Well, I certainly love what nobody did with the place."

Colton locked the car. "That's the idea. It's mostly over-grown, so keep your eyes peeled for the markers."

"What kind of markers?" asked Easton, twisting her hair into a ponytail.

"Shannon said the trees are marked," said Colton. "With spray paint."

"Boy, I hope Skinner's here," Easton sighed and stepped into the tangle of greenery. The shade was thick and heavy, and in-sects created an insistent hum.

"If he ain't here, we're back to square one, so he'd better be," said Colton.

Thunder rumbled. Where the leaves parted above, patches of gray clouds could be seen, growing darker with the passing minutes.

Colton scowled at the sky. "Great."

"Come on, buddy," said Angel. "Where's your *esprit de corps*?"

"I left it back with my French classes."

"Hey." Angel turned and saw Easton pointing at a tree bear-ing a faded yellow arrow against the bark.

"Forsooth!" said Angel. "A sign!"

Easton gave him a dark look and followed Colton in the di-rection of the arrow, while Angel shrugged and did the same.

They found seven arrows leading them over two miles into the woods, and then the arrows stopped.

"Think we missed one?" Angel turned in a circle, scanning the trees.

Colton rubbed his forehead. "I don't think so. It should be somewhere around here."

"We should have brought Shannon."

"She's with Maylee," said the preacher. "I asked."

Easton sighed. "Okay, so...maybe we split up?"

"Oh, good idea!" Angel clasped his hands together. "That always turns out so well!"

She glared at him. "Do you have a better idea?"

A drop of rain fell on Angel's collarbone. He looked down, then up at the sky as it unleashed a soft, warm rain.

"Come *on*." Colton looked close to punching the nearest tree.

Angel took a deep breath, then pointed right. "It's that way."

"How can you tell?" asked Easton.

"I can smell it."

"You're telling me you can smell him in the *rain*?"

"Not the doppelganger," said Angel. "The boat house. It took me a minute to recognize the delightful scents of mildew and algae."

Colton tucked Skata's sawed-off shotgun inside his jacket, and they headed toward the ferry station.

"What I want to know," said Easton, just loud enough to be

heard over the rain, "is who would want to take a ferry anywhere around here."

"Maybe they really liked alligators," suggested Angel.

"Shut up." Colton put a finger to his lips and indicated the clearing ahead. The once-white ferry station was overgrown with kudzu, but a cracked window and the empty, rotting dock were visible.

"I shall have a word with the management," said Angel.

"I'll go have a quick look," said Colton. "Stay here." Without waiting for a response, he bent low and jogged toward the shack.

"Can you still smell it?" asked Easton curiously.

"Nope. Too much rain."

"Your sense of smell must be murder sometimes."

"That's why, contrary to pop culture, we vampires tend to avoid living in big cities," whispered Angel. "The smell is practically medieval."

They were soaked to the skin now; the rain had made the air steamy and difficult to see through. They watched, wiping rain from their eyes, as Colton snuck up to the window and slowly rose to look in. After a second, he ducked down and hurried back.

"Problem," he said. "Graham's inside."

Angel blinked. "Graham?"

Easton said, "My brother Graham?"

"He's on the floor. He's breathing, but it looks like he's unconscious."

"We have to get him out!" Easton's voice rose. "What does Skinner want with him?"

"What if he *is* Skinner?" Angel pointed out. "Don't get me wrong, Skinner's annoying, but he's not stupid."

Easton removed her phone out of her back pocket. "I'll try calling him." They waited, tense, as she called her brother. "He's not answering," she said, putting the phone back in her pocket.

"I hope your cell is waterproof," said Angel.

"It is."

Colton said, "I'll go get him."

"Hey, we didn't come along to be your entourage," Angel pointed out.

"Think I don't know that?" Colton snorted. "The less people who go barging into enemy territory, the better. Anything goes wrong, y'all can come in after me."

"We will," said Angel and Easton simultaneously.

Colton took off toward the ferry house again, and Angel and Easton crouched deep in the foliage, waiting. The preacher moved around the corner of the shack, out of sight. They heard the faint sound of glass shattering.

There was a muffled shout, followed by a gunshot.

Easton stiffened. "Angel?"

"I'm going to check it out." He straightened. "Stay here."

"Is there anything I can do?"

"If I don't come back, go get help."

She nodded. "Go."

He turned and ran to the shack, moving so quickly it took less time than a breath. It was difficult to see through the cracked, fogged window, but he could just make out Colton on the floor in front of the back door, a few feet from Graham.

Angel moved around to the back door, squinting for a clearer view. The back door looked as if it had been rigged with a trip wire; Colton must have fallen, and the gun had gone off. The shell was on the floor, and fresh blood spattered the wood, mingled with crystals of rock salt.

Angel licked his lips, trying to ignore the scent of blood permeating the rain. He could see Colton's chest rising and falling—at least he wasn't dead. He had to get Colton and the kid out of there before Skinner came back. He wasn't at all sure he could handle the doppelganger, and he hated that uncertainty.

He opened the door and attempted to step inside, but an invisible force blocked his way. He might as well have tried to walk into a brick wall. He cursed and raced back to Easton who jumped, startled by his sudden return.

"What happened?" she demanded. "Is he okay? Are they alive?"

"The door was rigged with a trip wire, and Colton shot himself with rock salt."

"Okay?" She gestured toward the shack. "Why didn't you get them?"

"I can't. I haven't been invited in by the owner." He shook his head.

Easton paused. "I'll drag them outside, and you can carry them back."

Angel hesitated, wanting to say 'no.' The situation was still dangerous, and he had no idea when Skinner might show up. On the other hand, it was their best option. "Okay."

Easton opened her mouth, but whatever she'd been about to say was replaced with, "Turn around!"

Angel spun and came face to face with Skata.

Skata blinked, the green in his eyes swallowed with inky black. "Just can't stay away, can you," he said and grinned.

CHAPTER THIRTY-ONE

Angel ducked just before the double-walker's knife cut through the air where his head had been, and he lunged forward, tackling Skinner to the ground. "Go!" he shouted at Easton.

He had no time to look away and see if she listened; Skinner hooked his leg around Angel's waist and flipped him, reversing their positions. Angel grabbed the doppelganger's throat and squeezed until he felt it giving under his fingers, but Skinner's scrabbling hand grasped his knife again, and he stabbed it into the vampire's chest.

Angel channeled the wave of pain into a growl of rage as he released Skinner's throat and went for his black eyes instead. Skinner pulled the vervain-coated knife from Angel's chest and stabbed him again, this time in the throat.

Angel choked and released Skinner, grabbing for the knife to pull it out of his neck.

Skinner jumped up and raced for the nearest tree, where he

ripped a sharp branch away from the trunk and spun it. "Left alone," panted Skinner, watching Angel as he pulled the knife from his throat and pressed a hand over the burning, healing wound. "All I want to be is left alone."

Angel spat out a mouthful of his own blood and staggered to his feet. "Screw that."

Skinner threw the branch, and Angel darted out of the way, but Skinner had another sharp piece of wood, one coated with faded, peeling paint. As Angel moved out of the way of the first projectile, Skinner threw the second one.

Angel looked down as the stake punched through his stomach so far the end was barely visible.

He really hoped Easton had gotten away.

* * * * * * *

Easton raced through the woods, her cell phone clutched tightly in her hand. The rain stopped abruptly, leaving behind steaming ground and dripping leaves.

"You might as well stop now."

Skinner's voice was too clear—he was too close. "Come on, Easton."

Easton slowed, trying to catch a breath, and turned around. The doppelganger was ten yards behind her, his head tilted to one side. She expected him to smile, but he did not.

"Stay away from me," she snapped.

"And why would I do that? Not to be touchy, but you're the ones who came looking for me."

"Why did you take my brother?"

"A little thing called collateral. Don't worry," he added, walking toward her, slow but without fear. "He's alive."

"You can't take on the whole town."

"As adorable as the thought is, I don't care about taking over your little town." He stepped over a rotting log without bothering to look down, his steps sure. "I'm just a foot soldier, after all."

"You don't seem like the foot soldier type," said Easton, backing up.

"Let's just say it's a means to an end."

Easton stopped walking. "What are you doing?"

He blinked. "What do you mean?"

"You could have killed me at any point in the last minute, so why haven't you?"

He shrugged a shoulder. "Maybe it's because I remember buying you a blue bicycle for your fourth birthday."

"Skata did that. Not you."

"Same difference."

"No, it isn't. Wearing a Skata suit doesn't make you him."

"They do say the clothes make the man," said Skinner, grinning, "but don't worry. I'm hardly having an identity crisis. I'm wondering how it would feel to kill someone my current form cares about. I've never done that."

"You could just go away."

"Don't want to." He sprang into a full-on run toward her, and Easton spun, sprinting away as fast as she could. The forest flew by; she imagined she felt Skinner's breath on the back of her neck, heard his footsteps on her heels.

She was so focused on running that she didn't realize someone was in front of her until she ran into him.

Jackson caught her as she stumbled. "You do send the most cryptic messages."

Easton pointed behind her, too shaken to be shocked at Jackson's arrival. "Back—there," she panted. "He's chasing me."

"The doppelganger?"

She nodded, gasping for breath.

"Stay here." Jackson blurred past her and was gone.

Easton sagged against a tree and pressed a hand against the stitch in her side. "Thank you," she mouthed at the sky. "Good timing." She only waited a few moments, but it felt like a silent eternity before the sound of rushing wind blew up to her and Jackson appeared, wearing a mischievous smile.

"Look at you, staying put," he said. "He's been taken care of."

She stared at him in disbelief. "Already? What did you do?"

He held out a hand. "I'll show you."

They walked several hundred feet to a stand of half-grown trees. Eaton stared at the doppelganger, who simply stood with his arms folded and his eyes narrowed. "Why isn't he moving?"

"He can't. I compelled him not to move until I told him to." Jackson glanced at the doppelganger, who bared his teeth in response. "Now then." Jackson turned his full attention to Easton. "Don't tell me you were out here alone."

She turned and looked back in the direction of the ferry station. "I wasn't."

* * * * * * *

Jackson could push his hand several inches past the doorframe, but no farther. "Stay here," he told her again before leaving. "I'll be back."

Easton knelt on the ground in front of the prostrate Angel, who had managed to roll onto his side to better ease his bloody coughing.

"I'm going to pull the stick out," said Easton, fighting the tremor in her voice. "You can't bleed out, right? You're a vampire." She wasn't sure how that worked, biologically—he was losing a lot of blood as it was. Maybe he'd have to drink more. She didn't want to think about it.

He spat out another mouthful of blood. "Just—do it—already," he gasped.

Easton took a deep breath, gripped the slat of wood firmly,

and pulled. It came free of his stomach with a meaty sound that threatened to make her vomit. "Are you okay? Angel, are you okay?"

"Ooof." He groaned as Easton helped him sit up. "Wow, that hurt. Don't get me wrong, I've had worse, but man. What a torpedo."

"You're okay," Easton confirmed aloud. "It's a good thing he didn't stab you through the heart or you'd be dead. Deader."

"Where is he?"

"Who, Jackson?"

"Do I care about Jackson?"

As if on cue, Skinner strode into the clearing with Jackson close on his heels.

Angel struggled to his feet. "What's the big idea?"

Jackson patted Skinner's shoulder. "Go on."

The doppelganger gave everyone a crushing look before stalking dutifully into the ferry house and reappearing a moment later with Colton draped across his shoulders like a prize deer.

"And Miss Easton's brother," Jackson reminded him.

"Sure," said Skinner, making it sound like a curse. He dropped Colton to the ground with a thud and collected Graham.

"Hang onto the boy," Jackson instructed. He knelt on the grass and lifted Colton in his arms as if the burly preacher weighed no more than a toddler. "Let's get to the hospital."

CHAPTER THIRTY-TWO

Angel lowered the fitness magazine and drummed his fingers on it. Ten minutes seemed like an eternity. Easton had been allowed back with Graham and Colton since she was a family member, but Angel had kindly been told to take a seat in the waiting room.

Life currently felt like a game of Russian roulette, but there was a bullet in every chamber. Skata was in jail, Colton and Graham were in the hospital, and the doppelganger—well, at least he was currently being held by the Montgomery brothers.

"I know I haven't been a, uh, praying man for a while," he muttered, squinting at the ceiling, "but if you could help us out here, that would be great."

"Was that a prayer?"

He looked over at Easton, who appeared to the right, holding out a small plastic cup of coffee. "No. How are they?"

"Colton's going to be even saltier than usual, and he has a

mild concussion. Same with Graham. They're both going to be fine. It's you I'm worried about."

"Me? I'm fantastic."

"You're talking to the ceiling and reading a women's health magazine."

He glanced down at the magazine on his lap. An actress beamed from the cover, holding a cake that was supposedly a weight-loss miracle. "I like women, so naturally I care about their health."

She smiled. "Take the coffee."

He took the cup and watched as she sat down next to him. "Everything's going to be fine."

"Everything, huh?" he grunted. "Because it looks to me like everything's going to hell in a handbasket and we can't do jack about it."

"We found Skinner," Easton pointed out.

"We sure did." Angel calmly set his cup of coffee down on the wooden arm of the chair and hurled the magazine at the opposite wall. "Hooray."

"Hey! What's your problem?"

Angel rubbed his hands over his face and leaned back, picking up the coffee cup and sipping the hot beverage. It was terrible coffee, but it was better than nothing. "I'm frustrated. Sorry."

She shrugged, twisting her mouth and looking at the green carpet. "I guess everyone's stressed."

"Stressed would be crying into a carton of Rocky Road. This

is not stressed. This is nuts."

"Colton's going to be all right, and Skata's in jail where nobody can hurt him, and Jackson swore he and Gideon would keep a close eye on Skinner. This is the lull in the storm, right?" She touched his arm, and he recognized it as an attempt to comfort him. She drew in a surprised breath and pulled her hand away as if she'd touched a flame. "Are you okay?"

"I am very much not okay, why do you ask?"

"Angel, your arm is *freezing*. And you're way too pale."

"I washed up in the bathroom with cold water."

"That's not what this is." She shifted so she could get a better look at his face. "You're really pale."

"Vampire," he grunted. "Pale is in the resume."

"Will you stop joking for half a second? You're not well."

He sighed deeply and swallowed the rest of the coffee in one gulp. "I'll be all right, okay? Leave me alone." He didn't mean to snap, but he couldn't find it in him to take it back.

"Easton Everett?"

Easton gave Angel a deep frown before standing up and facing the orderly. "Yes?"

"Your brother is awake. You can see him now, if you like. Room 103."

"Thank you." Easton looked down at Angel, her frown deepening.

"Sir?" The nurse crossed the waiting room to get a better

look at Angel, and he smiled politely at her even as he swore inwardly. "Are you all right? Do I need to check you—"

He snarled—whether it was a word or just a growl, he didn't know. Before he quite realized what he was doing, he had shoved the woman against the opposite wall, his fingers digging deeply into her arms. He could hear Easton's voice beyond the rushing of blood under the orderly's skin, but he didn't want to listen. He could feel his fangs swelling in his mouth, pushing down, preparing to pierce the orderly's flesh and find the thick, hot juice inside—

Someone grabbed the hair at the back of his neck and snapped his head away, his teeth nearly grazing the orderly's neck. Easton then slapped him with enough force to jar him halfway back to the present moment. The orderly had not moved; she simply stood, frozen, mouth agape.

Angel stared at Easton, but she didn't look like Easton. She looked like food, and he was hungry. So damn hungry.

"Don't." Easton's voice was thick, and her eyes were red, but he couldn't focus on her words, couldn't concentrate on what she was really saying. "Stop."

He felt his eyes burn with the sting of tears and his body growl with the sharp pangs of starvation. *I'm sorry,* he wanted to say. *Run. Get out fast.*

Instead, he took a fistful of her hair and sank his teeth into the side of her neck. Her scream was faint, a sound from a dream. He felt her punch him repeatedly, the blows not enough to penetrate the relief, the sheer relief, of drinking again.

And then a single thought, in a voice he did not recognize, stabbed through everything else.

You're eating her.

He seized the shock of the realization and used it to shove Easton away. His mouth was hot and slick, and he thought the taste of liquid copper might suffocate him. Easton fell against a chair beside the stunned orderly.

Angel suddenly felt the overwhelming urge to throw up, and he ran from the waiting room and through the front doors. He raced in stops and starts, pausing only to lean against a telephone pole here, a tree there. He felt as if his chest had cracked open and there was nothing left to leak out. He barely made it through his own front door.

It took him almost a full minute to unlock the basement door before he stumbled down the steps, his mind hazy with shades of red. He lifted the lid of the freezer and forgot everything but his hunger. Bag after bag he drained, blood splattered across the floor, his hands, his torso.

He lifted his head as he smelled a new scent, a smell of pine and fur. He turned around to face the red-haired woman standing at the bottom of the basement steps. Her black dress and glossy smile gave the appearance of someone who expected to be picked up and taken out to a fancy dinner, except for the stake in her hand.

"I heard you were a more meticulous housekeeper," she remarked, casting a wry gaze across the blood-bag-littered floor.

Angel crouched, his veins filled with reborn strength, his senses sharper, keener, overwhelming. "Who are you?"

She held up the stake. "Hmm. I thought it was obvious. I guess you aren't terribly smart."

"Someone's already tried that today."

"Well, then. In that case." There was no light to reflect on her eyes, but her irises shone like liquid gold the closer she came, and her smile widened and her teeth sharpened. Four more figures bounded awkwardly down the stairs, filling the basement with more scents—dirt, rain, mildew, moss.

"You'll find the doggie chow down at the General Store," said Angel. "Aisle six."

Her laugh was a throaty purr. "You're very cute, Angel. Unfortunately, you just aren't cute enough."

He anticipated her jump. She launched herself into the air with superhuman strength and knocked him back into the freezer. As he moved backwards, he reached out and grasped the stake in her hand, twisting it out of her grasp with a wrench.

He spun to the right, pulling her around, slamming her neck into the edge of the freezer. He slammed once again and heard a crack; it was all the time he had before the rest of the wolves were on him.

He couldn't keep track of the gray fur or the gaping wounds or the flashing teeth; he fought one and another appeared. He was strong now; he had eaten well for the first time in months, but even a strong vampire could not take on four werewolves at once.

A deafening gunshot blasted through the air, and the wolf snapping at Angel collapsed to the ground. Another shot, and another, and Angel stared at Shannon, who pumped and fired and pumped and fired with a perfectly calm expression. The last werewolf sprang at her, but she shot him down with the others.

"What are you doing here?" asked Angel, as silence resumed.

"I came for an update and stayed to save your hide, you bimbo. Colton wasn't answering his phone, and I thought you might know something about it." She lowered the shotgun and glared at him.

"They weren't my fault!" he protested.

"Where's Colton?"

"He's in the hospital." Angel looked down at the wolves and was surprised to see them still breathing. "What's in the casings?"

"Gunpowder, stupid. I came prepared, not licensed to kill. Get your butt up here. Why is Colton at the hospital?"

"He got Home Aloned by a tripwire and knocked himself out. He probably won't want to talk about it, and I'm not going with you. He's fine."

Shannon frowned and reached the top of the stairs. "Why aren't you coming?"

"I was there like ten minutes ago, and I messed up."

She turned to look down at him. "What did you do, eat all their blood bags?"

He also reached the top of the stairs and stared at her. "Youuuuu're not even fazed," he said slowly.

"By what?" Then she rolled her eyes. "The fact you're not a moroi? I already knew that. Colton told me."

"I tried to hide it so well, too." He shut the basement door and locked it solidly behind him. He'd have to figure out what to do with the werewolves later. Right now, he was too tired to think about it.

"You got pretty well mauled down there," said Shannon. "You should come to the hospital and get stitched up."

He took a limping step toward the living room and winced. "I'll heal up in a jiffy."

"Fine, but you'd better get yourself cleaned up before anyone else bursts in on you and sees your current look."

He gave her a thumbs-up, and she started for the front door. Before she reached it, she paused. "You're forgetting something."

"Thank you, dear lady, for saving my life," he sighed. "Now go. Wait."

She raised an eyebrow. "What?"

"When you get to the hospital can—could you just—see if Easton's all right? And if she's not—do me a favor and don't call me."

Her other eyebrow rose. "Why wouldn't she be all right?"

He looked longingly toward the couch. Part of him wanted to accompany her to the hospital, but the rest of him never wanted to set eyes on Easton again. "There's a nurse, too, I think.

See if she's okay. Oh, and she knows about vampires now, if she didn't before."

"For heaven's sake, Angel."

"I know. Please?"

She sighed. "Okay."

"Thanks."

She left, and Angel trudged up the stairs, gripping the railing tightly to keep himself from falling. Sleep. He needed sleep. If he was lucky, maybe he would never wake up.

Then again, he thought with a deep sigh as he collapsed on the floor halfway to the bed, *luck was never my biggest fan.*

CHAPTER THIRTY-THREE

A slap to the face made Angel sit up.

"Oh, excellent. You're awake."

Angel squinted until the blurry figure became clear. Gideon's face was as unreadable as always, but there was an air of urgency about him that mildly alarmed Angel. "What do you want?"

"Get yourself cleaned up and come along. I'm afraid there's a rather serious problem requiring our immediate attention."

"Serious problem?" Angel sat up and was surprised to find that he was in enormous pain. His very veins felt like paper, as if the blood was going to pump right through them. He caught a groan between his teeth and managed to ask, "How serious is serious? Because I have a few problems of my own right n—"

"Yours," said Gideon, "can wait."

Angel struggled to his feet and stretched. Even that movement hurt. He hadn't felt this bad since he'd caught influenza in 1918. "Okay," he groaned. "I'll bite. What's up?"

"Jackson and Skinner are missing," said Gideon. He held out a clean pair of jeans and a shirt. "I took the liberty of removing these from your closet, as you are…disheveled."

Angel decided to simply roll with Gideon and took the clothes. "Any idea where they went?"

"Not presently, but there were no signs of a struggle."

"Do you think Jackson compelled Skinner somewhere?"

"I can't be certain." Gideon stated for the door. "Get dressed. Oh, and I took the liberty of removing the werewolves from your basement. They won't remember a thing."

"You make me excited to get older," said Angel.

Gideon shut the door.

Angel wondered if it was possible to have a blood hangover as he washed up and put on the fresh clothes. The mirror showed him a reflection he was tired of seeing, but all his wounds appeared to have healed. He turned to look at his back. Nothing. He turned the cold water on and let it fill his cupped hands before he poured it over his head.

As he smoothed his hair back, he felt something at the nape of his neck, underneath his hair. Probing with his fingers, he felt a series of ridges and dents.

A bite.

He had been bitten by a werewolf.

He didn't have a blood hangover; he had been poisoned. The sickness he was feeling now was only a shadow of the pain to come. He had three days at most.

Angel gripped the side of the sink and looked in the mirror. "Don't look at me like that," he told himself. "You deserve this."

He pulled on his shirt and jogged down the stairs past Gideon. "We need to stop by the hospital."

"Why?" asked the older vampire, following him out the front door.

"Because three people I know are laid up there, and I want to see how they're doing."

"One of them you put there, did you not?"

"*How* did you find out?"

"Word travels quickly through the minority in this town."

Angel climbed into the driver's seat of his car and watched Gideon seat himself in the passenger side.

"The Everett girl knew the dangers of becoming involved with a vampire of any sort."

"She trusted me, and I broke it." Angel pulled out of the driveway and wondered why he was bothering to go to the hospital. It felt like a gross falsehood, like putting on a display of humanity to try and erase what he had proved the night before—he was more animal than human. And now he was dying—he shouldn't be bothering to check in on friends, if they were that.

"Your self-loathing is understandable," said Gideon, "but it is in no way helpful."

Angel glanced at the moroi. "Well, we can't all be perfect."

"If you are implying I am perfect, I am flattered and you are mistaken."

"Have you ever done anything that made you hate yourself? I mean really hate yourself."

Gideon smiled in a cold, genteel way. "I have no guilt," he said after a short moment of silence, "but I have a very profound regret."

"Oh yeah?" Angel glanced at Gideon again. "I don't believe it. You're like the annoying version of what most humans think vampires should be like. I've never even seen you wear anything but a suit."

"Jackson," said Gideon coolly.

"What about him?"

Gideon did not take his gaze away from the windshield, and he did not say anything.

Angel was so taken aback that he ran a red light. "You turned Jackson?"

"I did."

Angel focused on the road ahead, unable to think of a flippant retort. "How'd that happen?"

"I had only recently been turned myself." Gideon sighed and twisted the ring on his right hand. It was the only ornament he wore, and, judging by the engraved M on the top, Angel guessed it was a family heirloom. "In a fevered rage, I turned the one companion I had." Another sigh. "Unfortunately, Jackson did not have much self-control."

"He's not a malkavian," said Angel, referring to the breed of vampires who couldn't handle the bite and went insane. "That's something."

"He came close enough for me to wonder. I was in no state to assist him through his transition."

"How old were you guys?"

"Jackson was a mere twenty-five years old. I was thirty-seven. Old enough to know better."

"If you ask me, you shouldn't be responsible for what you do when you're turning," said Angel. Unwittingly, it made him think of Easton, of his attack the night before. "It's what you do after that you should feel bad about." *God, if I turned Easton—I don't think I did—but if I turned Easton, please strike me down with lightning.*

"Actions have consequences," said Gideon. "Whether we take responsibility for them or not."

Angel said nothing until he parked the car in front of the hospital and asked, "You coming in?" as he climbed out.

Gideon responded by exiting the car and glancing at the parking lot like it was a garbage dump. Angel was ninety percent sure the vampire didn't mean to come across as condescending; he wore that condescension like one of his well-tailored suits, and it was hard to imagine him without it.

The inside of the hospital was well air-conditioned, but Angel felt hot. He realized his senses were duller than the day before; the sterile smell was less sharp, and he couldn't hear every snatch of conversation floating from every room.

He should have let the red-headed vixen stake him in the

heart and get it over with quickly. He brushed the thought aside and took a page from Gideon's book—there was no use in wishing things were different. This was his life, and he had wrecked it from beginning to end. The only thing he could do was try and fix some of it now, at the last minute.

He walked up and leaned against the front desk. "Excuse me."

"Just a second," said the orderly, an attractive woman of thirty or thirty-one who sounded like she was having a bad day.

"I'd give you a whole minute if I could see you smile."

She looked up, prepared to tell him off, but the moment he compelled her, a smile grew on her face. "What can I do for you, sir?"

"I'm here to see Easton Everett."

"Are you a family member?" she asked, still smiling.

He winked, although for the first time in a hundred years compelling a person was taking a great deal of effort. "No."

"She's in Room 109," she responded happily.

"Thank you." He turned away from the blushing orderly and gave Gideon a strange expression.

"You don't need to know this, but I also attacked an orderly here last night, and I'm not sure why security isn't tackling me."

"I know you attacked an orderly last night," said Gideon. "I told you news travels fast. I stopped by to clean up your mess."

"You aren't surprised, either, come to think of it."

"I was hardly surprised to notice you've been lying about

your true nature, no."

"I didn't exactly *lie*," muttered Angel, scratching the back of his neck. "I just never said I wasn't."

"I suspected you were a strigoi when I smelled the blood in your basement the first time," said Gideon. "Yet you walk in sunlight without so much as a sunburn. You understand the confusion."

"Sure do." Angel stopped at Room 109. "Do you mind checking on Colton and Graham first?"

"Graham Everett?"

"He's in room 103."

"You *have* been very busy," said Gideon. "I will humor you, but we mustn't waste our time."

"Absolutely not."

Gideon turned and strolled back down the hall. Angel entered Easton's room and swallowed. The heart monitor beeped steadily in the corner, and an IV dripped into her wrist. Her eyes were closed, and she was a little on the pale side, but she wasn't dead and she wasn't turning.

Angel sighed deeply, almost overwhelmed with relief. He approached the bed. "Easton."

She blinked her eyes open, and when they focused on Angel, she drew her eyebrows together. "Get out."

"I understand if you're upset," he began, but she interrupted him.

"I said get out." She pushed herself up, the sheets falling

away and exposing the bandage on her neck. "Leave me alone. Please."

Angel shut his eyes, just for a moment. This was the girl who had cried herself to sleep in his arms, before she knew what he was really like, and it was surprisingly hard. He nodded and left the room without looking back. Shutting the door felt like the most final thing he had ever done.

He leaned against it. There were no thoughts in his mind, no strength to think of more. There was nothing. So much for hope.

Angel walked back down the hall with his hands in his pockets. The orderly at the front desk smiled invitingly but he continued past her, pushing open the front door and taking a deep breath of the thick, syrupy summer air.

Hope sucked.

CHAPTER THIRTY-FOUR

He hadn't gone ten steps when a voice called out, "Hey, man! Where are you going?"

Over his shoulder, he called, "Go back inside, Graham."

"Nah, it's all right; the doctors said I could—"

"I don't mean that. It's just...you should go back inside."

"You don't look so hot yourself."

Angel turned to face Graham and was surprised to realize that the seventeen-year-old was taller than him. "I'm a little tired. You should get back to your sister."

"Yeah. Pretty weird."

Angel realized he didn't know exactly how Gideon had 'cleaned up' the mess. "Do you know what happened to her? Or you, for that matter?"

"Everyone says I passed out from heatstroke. Easton was attacked by a dog."

Angel wrinkled his nose at the weak explanation but said,

"Yep, pretty weird."

"Honestly…" Graham lowered his voice. "I don't believe it. I've never seen a dog run out and bite somebody's neck before. I think something else happened."

Angel widened his eyes. "Like what?"

"I don't know. Maybe the cougar everyone's been talking about."

"Probably," said Angel seriously.

"Probably," repeated Graham, with less certainty. "But hey, the preacher wanted to see you."

Angel sighed and followed Graham back inside. Even jogging up the stairs rendered him breathless. Who knew dying was so much fun? "Which room is he in?"

"He's in here." Graham led him to a room at the end of the hall and ushered him inside. "I'm going to see Easton."

"Right. You do that."

Graham paused, concerned. "Are you two okay?"

"What," asked Angel in a clipped voice, "is that supposed to mean?"

"I just wondered. I thought you were going to ask her out or something. She talks about you."

Angel blinked, taken aback. "She does?"

"Well, not nonstop or anything," Graham amended. "But you come up more often than Macon did."

Angel had practically forgotten about Macon. "Oh. Well, first of all." He gestured widely to an unseen audience. "There's no 'us two.' Secondly, if she even thinks about getting the teeniest, tiniest crush on me, tell her it's a bad idea." Not that there was a real possibility of that happening, thought Angel. *I mean even if you wanted to fix things, you're dead in three days or less, so there goes that.*

Graham looked both nonplussed and concerned. "Why's that?"

"Because," said Angel matter-of-factly, "I'm a jerk."

Graham opened his mouth to say something else, but Angel made shooing motions with both hands. "Go see your sister! Go!"

"Right, okay." Looking even more bewildered, Graham turned and shuffled down the hall, and Angel hurried into Colton's room. He pulled up the extra chair and sat down next to the bed with a sigh.

"Wow," said Colton. "You look like you should be here instead of me."

Angel leaned his head back, folded his hands, and shut his eyes.

"I'm gonna go out on a limb here and say Easton wasn't really attacked by a dog."

"Ting ting ting, give the man a prize."

"I'm gonna go out on another limb and guess it was you."

"Bingo again. You're going to run out of limbs and be permanently hospitalized at this rate." Angel opened his eyes. "I'll send you flowers."

"Why'd you starve yourself?"

"What makes you think I starved myself?"

"Frickin' unbelievable," said Colton. "Would you talk to me like I'm an adult, for once?"

"Of course. You're the one who missed a trip wire and knocked yourself out."

Colton's light eyes narrowed. "I *will* kill you."

"Before you kill yourself?"

Colton lifted a fist, and Angel had the good sense to flinch. Colton lowered it and asked, "I guess Easton's okay, though, right?"

"She's fine. She hates me."

Colton chuckled. "She doesn't hate you, man."

"I *drank* her *blood.* She's smart enough to hate me."

"Nah. She's smart enough to get over it. Just figure yourself out and don't worry about her."

Growing angry with the current line of conversation, Angel changed the subject. "How long until you're up and at 'em?"

"Tomorrow. Dang doctors want to keep an eye on me until tomorrow morning."

"Lucas Colton: Preacher. Badass. Human salt-shaker."

"Look, man, the stuff stings, all right?"

"I can't believe a trip wire actually took you down."

"It had two connectors, okay? I took out the first one. He was good."

"Well, I wouldn't take it too hard," said Angel. "After all, you're a man of God. I hear they're peace-lovers."

"Reckon we could all use some peace about now," said

Colton, scowling.

"I find it ironic, you saying that to a vampire."

"Just because you've got fangs doesn't mean you don't want a little peace."

"Yes. Well." Angel cleared his throat and stood up. "In happy endings, monsters don't get peace."

"I've seen lots of monsters, and you ain't one of 'em."

"Of course I am. I'm a whole genre of monster movie."

Colton snorted. "What's up with Skinner?"

"Montgomery Management had him for a while, and now he's gone, along with Jackson, so Gideon and I are off to track them down."

"Dang it," said Colton with feeling.

* * * * * * *

"Are you quite ready?" Gideon asked. He was standing by the front door with a faint air of impatience that probably masked a much larger amount.

Angel breezed past him. "Waiting on you now."

The moroi followed him through the parking lot. "I hope your time at the hospital was worth the waste."

"You could have headed out before me," Angel pointed out. "Nobody compelled you to stay."

"A hunt for two people is most likely a two-person job," said Gideon stiffly, climbing into the car.

Angel started the engine. "Where do you want to look first?"

"It can be difficult to predict my brother. How predictable is your friend Skata?"

"The guy's pretty private. Likes to keep to himself." Angel glanced both ways and spun the steering wheel. The car moved sharply to the right and spun in a U-turn.

"I do believe that was illegal."

"It was kind of fun."

"Your idea of fun and mine are not necessarily aligned."

"You have an idea of fun?"

Gideon looked at him sharply. "I find your levity in this situation grating."

"I'm only a hundred and twenty-six," said Angel. The sign for the jail flashed by on his right. "Cut me some slack."

"What do you have in mind?"

"I think the best person to predict Skata's next move is Skata," said Angel. "And unless Skinner's changed his shape again, he's still working from Skata's brain. I say let's pick it."

****

There was only one deputy on duty, and he looked fresh out of training school.

"They're sure scraping the bottom of the barrel these days," Angel remarked quietly.

Gideon put a hand out and stopped him from approaching the desk. "Let me handle this."

"Be my guest." Angel put his hands in his pockets and watched Gideon approach the desk and ask to speak to Skata. Compelling the orderly at the hospital had been enough—he felt like it had taken all the compulsion energy out of him. He wondered if Gideon sensed it.

The deputy hesitated. "I don't think I can do that."

Gideon nodded once. "I would consider it a great personal favor."

"Sure thing!" The deputy grabbed the keys and stood up. "I'll just come with y'al—"

"We would very much like to speak to Skata alone." Gideon firmly pushed the deputy back into his chair and took the keys.

"Oh," said the deputy. "Go right on in."

Gideon walked away, and Angel leaned over the desk to look at the deputy's name tag.

"Thanks, Eric."

"You're welcome," said Eric.

As soon as they rounded the corner, Angel said, "I thought all the deputies were jacked up on vervain."

"They are," said Gideon. "I doubt the compulsion will hold

long. We need to make it brief."

Skata sat up as they reached the cell. "Visiting hours are over."

"It's nine in the morning," said Angel.

"Got that," said Skata.

"Oh, wait, was that the wrong reaction? Sorry. Oh, no!" Angel leaned against the bars, arms folded. "I feel terrible!"

Skata nodded at Gideon. "What's he doing here?"

"We have a slight problem," said Angel.

"Please don't tell me it involves a doppelganger wearing my body."

"I could tell you that, however I'd be ly-ing," said Angel in a sing-song voice.

Gideon spoke up. "It would seem he and my brother have disappeared together."

"I hope they're very happy," said Angel.

"As the doppelganger was in your form," Gideon continued, ignoring Angel, "we were hoping you might have an idea regarding their next move."

"Hey," said Skata. "Buddy. He's the one who reads my brain, not the other way around. You should've kept a tighter leash on Jackson."

He looked tired, Angel noticed, tired and pissed off, and like he needed a proper shower. "Come on, just guess." Angel pressed his face against the bars. "If you were Skinner, where would you go?"

"I have no idea."

"Not even the tiniest inkling?"

"Bupkis."

"This is rather important," said Gideon.

Skata stood up. "Look, if I was Skinner, I'd have convinced Jackson to get some kicks turning the town to scrap, and then I would've gotten back at him for the little compelling stunt you said he pulled in the woods."

Angel straightened and opened his mouth to respond, but Skata interrupted him. "But," he said, "if I were Jackson, I would've compelled Skinner to keep that from happening. On the flip side, Skinner's not stupid. He probably found a way out of it. Talked him into something else or offered to trade something for it. There are too many options and not enough ways to narrow them down."

"You have a good point, though," said Angel. "Do you think Jackson's gone to the dark side?"

"Improbable, but possible," said Gideon tightly. "He has… phases, in spite of himself. However, speculation gets us nowhere."

Skata rubbed his chin. Angel could see he was thinking, trying to dredge up something in spite of insisting he couldn't help. He wondered if Skata would be so keen to help if he knew what Angel had done to Easton the night before.

While Skata thought, Angel's phone rang. He walked over to the far wall and answered the unknown number, prepared to hang up on a scammer. "Yellllo?"

"Is this Angel?"

Angel blinked and lowered his voice. "Graham, how did you get my number?"

"Uh...Colton gave it to me?"

Of course he did. "Is everything okay?"

"Sorta," said Graham. "It's just—Dad said he was going to come by at ten, and he never did. He's not answering his cell, either. I was hoping you could check on him? They won't let me out of the hospital until tomorrow since I was unconscious so long. It's like prison in here."

Angel gently banged his forehead against the wall. "Yeah, sure, I'll swing by. He probably just forgot."

"Yeah. He's been really distracted. You know. With Mom and...everything."

Angel grimaced. "Hey, don't start crying on me, buddy, okay? That makes things awkward really quick."

"I'm not crying. Geez."

"Good. Keep an eye on your sister."

"Right," said Graham, and just before he hung up, Angel heard the teenager mutter, "Because you're so not dating."

Angel hung up and walked back over to the others. "Anything?"

Skata shook his head. "Nope."

"I might know where they are," said Angel, "but we have to hurry."

"Where?" asked Skata.

"Easton's house. Pretty sure her dad's dead."

CHAPTER THIRTY-FIVE

They pulled into the Everetts' driveway and hurried up to the front door. Angel turned to Gideon. "I'll go in, and if they're here, I'll chase them out the back."

The moroi, who had not been invited in by a resident of the home, nodded and strode around the back without so much as a 'be careful.'

The door was locked; Angel sighed, made a mental apology to Easton, and rammed his shoulder into the wood. The lock gave way, and the door swung open, slamming into the wall hard enough to leave a dent.

"HELLO THE HOUSE," he bellowed, jogging down the hall, rushing through the living room and kitchen. He heard a sound upstairs—faint, but enough to send him running up the staircase. A door was open, leading into some kind of home office.

He pushed the door open and was met by the sight of Easton's father, bound and gagged to the leather desk chair. He made a series of muffled grunts as Angel appeared, and Skinner straightened from his position bent over a filing cabinet.

"Well." Skinner shut the drawer, a manila envelope in his hand. "If it isn't Salvation's friendly neighborhood strigoi."

"What's up?" Angel replied, pointing at Easton's father. "Why'd you keep him alive?"

"He's not on the council," said Skinner, as if that made everything clear.

"You're not going to kill him…because he's not on the council," said Angel slowly.

"I only needed a file from his dearly departed wife, and as for *his* life, I really don't care."

There was neat handwriting on the envelope tab, spelling out the words *Council Index.* Angel's mind raced, pulling together Skinner's victims, every council member he had killed. The doppelganger hadn't killed him when he could have, more than once. He could have killed Easton. He could have killed Graham.

Whatever Skinner's grudge against the council, Angel was glad the doppelganger didn't seem to realize Angel was part of it.

Skinner proceeded to calmly rifle through the papers in the folder as if a vampire wasn't standing two yards away. Easton's father was still wriggling in the desk chair, trying to articulate words through the duct tape across his mouth.

"I don't get why you kidnapped Graham," said Angel honestly. "That seems weird."

"I got wind that Colton had talked to the Shannon girl, and

it looked suspicious, so when I ran into Graham hiking, I went all carpe diem and thought I could catch a council member."

"Colton might be on the council, but he's a disgustingly good person," said Angel.

"It was overcomplicated, and I'm not proud of it," muttered Skinner. "Besides, the Montgomery guy showed up, so nothing too tragic happened."

Angel took a deep breath before asking the final question pressing down on him. "Why Cassis?"

Skinner closed the folder and looked at him with Skata's face. "That was an order from Samuel," he said, with a hint of distaste. "Nothing more, nothing less."

Angel blinked. "Just like that, you admit you're working for Samuel?"

"There's no real point in denying it," said Skinner breezily. "After all, anyone who might object to the idea won't be around much longer."

"What's that supposed to mean?" snapped Angel, although the sinking feeling in his stomach told him enough.

Black spilled into Skinner's eyes again. "Let's just say you might want take a vacation."

"Thanks, but going to Hawaii while you kill everyone isn't really my style."

"Oh, don't be so dramatic. He doesn't want to kill everyone. My job's almost done."

"And what is your job? Get rid of council members?"

"Is it that obvious?"

Angel rubbed his forehead. There was too much to deal with and too little time, and he could only imagine how hot and bothered Gideon would be at the delay. "By the way, where's Jackson?"

"I left him with some friends." Skinner held up a hand. "Don't worry, they won't hurt him. Unless his brother or some helpful do-gooders decide to butt in."

Angel looked back at Mr. Everett. He had stopped struggling and had resorted to staring. The vampire sighed and looked at Skinner, who was also watching the prisoner with an expression that said, *this might be a problem.*

They looked at each other.

"We should probably do something with him," said Angel.

"Don't look at me."

Angel rubbed his chin for a moment. "Gideon's outside and might be strong enough to compel past the vervain."

Skinner smirked at the mention of Gideon. "Was he waiting to give me a hug?"

"If by 'give you a hug' you mean 'capture you and force you to give him Jackson's location,' then yes. Big hug."

Skinner smiled, but only for a moment. "Listen."

"Listening," said Angel.

The doppelganger tapped his index finger against the envelope. "I said before, I'm almost done with this mess. Once I've had my revenge, I'm out of here."

"You think Samuel's going to let you leave?"

"He won't care what I do once I'm finished. Besides, he hates humans, not non-humans."

"So, what, he wants to give Salvation over to them?" Skinner's glance was sharp, but he said nothing. "Noble," said Angel, "if you leave out all the innocent people who will wind up dead."

"I'd care, but I don't."

"Huh." Angel raised his eyebrows and then shrugged.

"If you've got something to say, say it."

Angel snorted. "I'm the last guy on earth who's going to preach you a sermon."

Skinner looked even more suspicious. Angel continued, "I get it. You want revenge, you want the town back, you had a tragic childhood, and I'm sure you're very misunderstood. But what about the kids who won't have parents? What about people who have nothing to do with this? You're not just going to get revenge for your own personal reasons, you're going to turn a bunch of otherwise happy people into *you*."

Skinner's eyes had narrowed into slits, but he said nothing.

"Personally," said Angel, "I'm a fan of running away from my problems until they get tired of chasing me. If I were you, I'd just ditch this town and forget about it."

Skinner took a deep breath, like he was about to either scream or jump into the deep end of a pool, but all he said was, "I'm going to walk out that door, and if Gideon tries to stop me, his baby brother will be dead before happy hour."

With that, Skinner ran out of the room and leaped over the banner. Angel rushed to the rail, but Skinner was no longer running; he only strode through the foyer, looked back at Angel for a long second, and left out the front door.

Angel raced back to the office, shoved the window open, and shouted, "Calling all moroi! Do not go after Skinner. I repeat! Do not go after Skinner!"

Gideon stepped out of the shadows near the grove of young trees. "I presume you have a good explanation."

Angel grimaced and glanced at the gaping Mr. Everett. "I'll explain while you take care of a little problem."

* * * * * * *

They moved to the front porch, and as Gideon compelled Easton's father to forget everything that had taken place in the last half hour, Angel leaned against the wall and considered his options. Gideon said he would make sure Mr. Everett went to the hospital to visit his kids, and then no doubt he would unleash some sort of tirade on Angel.

But amid the immediate problems, a single thought bumped against Angel's mind again and again. *You have no reason to stay here. Ditch Salvation and go somewhere safer. You're already exposed here.* It was solid advice. It was typical. He was tempted to listen to himself and leave, but a larger part of him knew there was no chance. There were too many variables. Things.

Well, he admitted silently, people. Too many people.

He had committed the cardinal sin and started liking a few of them. Living with himself was hard enough already—the guilt would be too much if he deserted his friends now.

Not that any of it mattered, really, since he was dying.

Eh. Whatever.

He shrugged and focused back on Gideon, who ushered Mr. Everett back over the threshold, sans duct tape and rope. Mr. Everett walked back up the stairs with a dazed look on his face.

Gideon then proceeded to stare Angel down.

"What," said Angel.

"In precisely five minutes, Mr. Everett will get up from his chair, leave the house, get in his car, and drive to the hospital."

"Nifty."

"Now," said Gideon, and Angel knew by his tone—this was Angel's last chance. Gideon was done playing the restrained, polite 'good vampire.' His brother was involved, after all. "Would you care to explain where Jackson is?"

"I don't know where he is. Skinner wouldn't tell me except to say Jackson was 'with friends,' and they'd kill him if we went looking. He did imply that Jackson would be fine if we left Skinner alone, though. He also mentioned that he's only here to finish killing council members and then he's bugging out."

"He has caused enough trouble," said Gideon, straightening

his already even cuffs. "I am done being polite. The next step is to discover where they are hiding my brother, and then capture Skinner for more useful information."

"Oh, is that all there is to it?" Angel smacked his forehead. "And here I thought it would be hard."

Gideon said nothing; he only descended the stairs, leaving Angel to follow and ask, "So what's the plan, professor?"

"The plan is to find a werewolf to question."

* * * * * * *

"Here, doggie, doggie!"

Angel put his hands behind his head, irritated at the distinct lack of werewolf. "This sucks."

Gideon appeared with a whoosh. "I caught the scent of a werewolf farther upwind." He nodded in that direction.

"Ducky," said Angel.

"Follow him and herd him to me," said Gideon.

Angel took off without bothering to respond. He might not be feeling up to snuff, but he could still move. Green and brown blurred past him, and his reaction time was still four or five times quicker and more agile than a human's. He caught the scent— there was a difference between the smell of a wolf and a werewolf. A wolf smelled like a dog, only muskier. A werewolf smelled like a human wearing a mangy fur coat.

He let out a long, ear-splitting whistle, and the scent stopped moving farther away.

Angel came to a halt, cupped his hands around his mouth, and shouted, "Who's a good boy?" Herding the werewolf toward Gideon was too complicated; Angel had a better idea. He'd just get the werewolf to chase him straight into Gideon's open arms.

An abrupt snarl slunk through the air as the wolf prowled into view, low-hanging branches brushing across its thick, gray fur. It sounded like an accusation—*Vampire. How dare you.*

Angel turned and ran, hoping Gideon was ready for them. The wolf let out a howl that sounded much too close, and Angel sped up as fast as he could. He was slower than usual; he could tell his speed was maybe forty-five miles an hour, not sixty-five. He crashed into the clearing and shouted, "Brought it!"

Gideon flashed past him; there was a sharp squeal, and Angel leaned against a tree, his heart pounding painfully between his ribs. He straightened and looked over his shoulder.

The older vampire's fingers clutched the werewolf's throat. His eyes were blood-red and his fangs were perfectly visible below his curled upper lip. The werewolf had not shifted back to human form, but the tang of fear filled the clearing.

Gideon reached into the pocket of his jacket with his free hand and withdrew a slender, knife-thin piece of wood. Without so much as a blink, he drove the point into the muscles above the wolf's front right leg.

The werewolf yelped and thrashed in the vampire's grip, and Gideon let go, but the wolf wasn't going anywhere. It looked exhausted, even after such a short struggle, and fell limp before it made two steps.

"Wolfsbane?" Angel guessed.

"Rather," said Gideon. He looked down at the unconscious wolf, its sides rising and falling just enough to let them know it was alive. Then Gideon looked back at Angel and asked sharply, "Are you unwell?"

"Nope, I'm hunky-dory." Angel gave him a thumbs-up. Hunky-dory was a lie, but 'nope' hadn't been. He didn't feel unwell. Unwell was how he'd been feeling for a while. Now he felt downright miserable. He guessed he had twenty-four hours; maybe a little more if he was lucky.

He thought of Easton and Colton in the hospital, of Skata in jail, of Salvation's brief and violent future.

Gideon hoisted the werewolf onto his shoulders. "We haven't the time to dally. If the wolves have my brother, he is in constant danger of being bitten."

"That's terrible," said Angel without much sympathy. "I'm right behind you."

CHAPTER THIRTY-SIX

The werewolf was a black-haired woman who was probably in her late twenties, but the hardness in her eyes suggested someone much older. Her wrists, ankles, and neck were tied around the bars of Angel's basement cell, and her human teeth were bared as if she'd forgotten she no longer sported wolf teeth.

"I suggest you tell us Jackson's location sooner rather than later," said Gideon. It was his second time asking her for it, and Angel had the feeling there wouldn't be a third.

"Just tell him," he suggested. "Trust me, you do *not* want to see him pissed off."

"Y'all are cute with the good cop, bad cop routine, but—"

Angel cut her off with a snort. "Technically it's more like bad cop, slightly worse cop."

Gideon lifted an eyebrow.

"Sorry. Bad cop, a *lot* worse cop," Angel amended.

"I've got no idea where he is." The werewolf shrugged.

"Of course you do," said Gideon. "And unfortunately, I no longer feel inclined to be polite about asking."

"What do you want him back so bad for, anyhow?" Her accent was just as Southern as Gideon's, but lacked any of his carefully cultured enunciation. "He's a pain in the neck."

Angel rooted for Jackson in that moment, for—he guessed—the first and last time.

"Quite," said Gideon. "My brother can be…difficult. No doubt you could find a better hostage."

"We don't think so," said the woman, her grin widening. "After all, if we have him, we have you."

"I agree with the idea behind your strategy," said Gideon. He pursed his lips, and it looked as if he was thinking. Angel knew he was reining in his temper, and the werewolf should be glad. "In actuality, however, it is quite possibly the stupidest idea you could have conjured. You see," he continued, his hands in his pockets, his shoulders squared, "all you have done is inflame my temper. Something that was none of my business is now very much my business. So tell me, how successful does your plan sound now?"

The werewolf growled. A yellow glint lit her eyes, but Angel could smell the fear on her skin.

Gideon nodded once, negotiations concluded. He unbuttoned his jacket with a hand and shrugged it off, tossing it onto the floor. Angel raised his eyebrows at the gesture. As Gideon rolled his sleeves up to his elbows, he said, "Pass me the bucket."

"You've got it." Angel reached down and lifted the waiting

plastic bucket, handing it to Gideon.

The older vampire wound a thick lock of the werewolf woman's hair around his hand and pulled her head back as Angel stepped forward and gripped her jaw tightly, holding it open as Gideon lifted the bucket and began to pour the wolfsbane-infused water into her mouth.

A scream gurgled from her throat. She thrashed against them, but she had no advantage and there was nowhere to go.

Gideon paused. "Where is Jackson?"

"Seriously," said Angel, releasing her mouth so she could answer. "I'd just tell him."

She spat out a mouthful of steaming water and choked, "Go to hell."

Gideon exhaled through his nose —it was not frustration for himself, however.

Angel swayed from side to side. "I'm closer than you think, doggo."

Her gasping breath became a strained laugh. "That's right," she managed, her voice scraped raw. "You're the one they bit, aren't you?"

Angel felt Gideon's gaze suddenly on him and tried to ignore it. "In the flesh."

"Is this a conversation we need to have?" asked Gideon.

"No, that's pretty much it."

Gideon nodded and lifted the bucket again. "Well, then. Let

us do something worthwhile with the time you have left, shall we?"

"Love to," said Angel, and opened the werewolf's mouth again.

* * * * * * *

"It's okay. I just need one bite."

Skata opened his eyes and squinted at the gray, blurry ceiling over his head. Once. Just once, he would appreciate a solid night's sleep. Or afternoon's sleep.

Any sleep.

"Rise and shine." Knuckles rapped against his cell bars.

Skata looked over at the door. "What?"

The deputy said, "Time to let you out for a walk."

"Thanks." Skata rested his head on his arms again. "Ran a few hundred laps in here earlier, so I'm good."

"Look who forgot their happy juice this morning. Honestly, would it kill you to cooperate?"

Skata swung his legs over the side of the cot and sat up abruptly. "What are you doing here?"

Skinner's black eyes glittered at him. The keys dangled from his fingers, a pile of skin and tissue at his feet. "A favor."

Skata barked a one-syllable laugh. "Sorry if I don't throw all my trust at you."

"I don't want it. Trust isn't really my thing." Skinner turned the key in the lock and opened the door.

Skata had a hard time believing his eyes. "All right. What do you want?"

"Sorry, no Q-and-A allowed." He tossed the keys to Skata, who caught them. "What…" He stared, glancing from the keys to the black-eyed copy of himself standing in the cell. "You want me to lock you in?"

"Now you're getting it." Skinner pulled his jacket off.

He even has all my scars, thought Skata, unsure why he was surprised. They switched clothes and boots, and Skata backed out of the cell, still unsure as to whether he was dreaming.

Skinner sat down comfortably on the sagging cot. "Don't stay on my account."

Skata kicked the door shut with his foot.

"By the way," said the doppelganger, raising a finger, "you might want to go find Angel and Gideon."

Skata didn't ask why. He crouched down by the remains of Skinner's shift and scraped the pile into the jacket.

"You're easier to change into than most people," said Skinner. "I must be getting used to you." He laid down, his hands behind his head just like Skata's had been.

For a second, Skata wondered if this was how an out-of-body experience felt. "Uh…right. I'm going."

"You do that. Try not to get caught on the way out." Skinner closed his eyes.

Confused, but filled with adrenaline, Skata hurried down the hall, watching for any real deputies. There was one in the foyer, his feet up on the front desk and his hands folded in his lap. His eyes were closed. Skata had no doubt Skinner had knocked him out, but he was as quick and silent as possible as he jogged out the front door. As soon as it shut behind him, he tossed the jacket in the trash can out front and ran.

* * * * * * *

Gideon removed the clean white square from his pocket and wiped his hands with it, leaving red streaks behind. "I notice you had no objections before I did the deed."

He turned to Angel, who was looking at the werewolf and tapping his lip thoughtfully. Her head hung down, her dead eyes staring at her heart, which was on the ground in front of her.

"Welllllll, I just think killing her might have been…over-kill. And besides, you didn't give me a warning before you did it, which kind of negates the whole 'objection' thing."

Gideon looked at Angel with the face of a man trying to decide whether the other was trustworthy. "We are in the middle of a war, Angel, that much has been made clear. And I'm sorry to say wars are not won with mercy."

Angel frowned, but shrugged. There was no point in arguing; it wasn't like they could put her heart back.

Loud pounding on the front door jerked Angel's attention toward the stairs. "I'll get it."

"I'll clean up," said Gideon, with vague distaste.

Angel gave him a two-fingered salute and jogged up the stairs, but even that felt like an effort. He remembered having the flu once, before he'd been turned, and it had felt an awful lot like this. He'd been optimistic about his remaining time—half a day was more accurate. "Are you a miracle cure?" he asked the door as he opened it. "No! What are you doing here?"

Skinner pushed his way past Angel, panting like he'd just run a two-minute mile.

Angel closed the door and slowly turned to face the doppelganger. "Did I miss a memo?" he asked, squinting. "Why are you back?"

Skinner straightened. "It's Skata."

"Wh…" Angel blinked. "Really?"

"Skinner took my place, and don't ask me why, because I have no earthly idea. Is Gideon here?"

"Hi to you, too. He's in the basement." Angel picked a flashlight off the entryway table and switched it on. "Say cheese," he said, flashing the light in Skata's eyes. "Well, I'll be damned," he said, amazed, then winced internally. *Too soon.*

Skata made a beeline for the kitchen, and Angel followed,

watching bemusedly as Skata twisted the cap off a beer and drank half the bottle before saying, "He told me to look for you and Gideon."

"Why?"

"Beats me."

Gideon appeared in the doorway. He must have overheard the conversation because he did not ask why Skata was there, or if he really was Skata, or how he got out. "How soon can you be ready to leave?"

"Depends on where I'm going," said Skata, draining the rest of the bottle.

"Eight miles south to a werewolf encampment near Klinger swamp," said Gideon.

"So what?"

"You're going to assist us in retrieving my brother by masquerading as Skinner."

Skata didn't look thrilled at the idea. "Why would I do that?" He glanced at Angel, looked away, and did a double-take. "You look like crap."

"Werewolf bite," said Angel, leaning against the island. Might as well let him know; it didn't matter much either way. "It'll do that to you."

Skata's eyes widened, just a fraction. Just enough. "How long have you got?"

"Judging by his pallor and the fact he could barely jog up the stairs, I say perhaps twelve hours," said Gideon.

"Nobody asked you," snapped Skata, with force that surprised Angel.

"In Gideon's defense, he did nail it," said Angel. "Although I was kind of holding out for thirteen or fourteen hours. Oh, by the way, Easton, Colton, and Graham are in the hospital."

Skata set the empty bottle down on the counter. "Explain everything," he said. "Now."

CHAPTER THIRTY-SEVEN

Skata pushed open the door of Colton's hospital room. A teddy bear sat on the shelf, surrounded by get-well cards, and vases full of flowers filled the room. Some had been relegated to the floor for lack of another surface.

Colton was standing by the side of his bed, belting his jeans.

"I'm going to go out on a limb and guess you're not supposed to be up," said Skata.

"I ain't staying here." The preacher pulled a blue tee shirt on, gingerly avoiding his head. "How'd you get out of jail?"

"How do you know I'm me?"

"Lucky guess." Colton glanced at him but only asked, "You seen Easton and Graham yet?"

"Not yet. I...uh, do you know—"

"They're fine, man."

"I wouldn't be so sure."

Colton's eyebrows drew together. "Why not?"

"Well, for starters, we don't know if Angel infected Easton

with vamp venom or not."

"Right." Colton frowned. "Go see the kids, fill them in on whatever they don't know. Their dad's been by, right?"

"He might still be here," said Skata.

"Right. Hey, when you see Easton, try not to freak her out. She thinks you're in jail, so she sees you, she's gonna think you're Skinner. And don't let anyone else see you."

"Like I don't know that," muttered Skata. "Where are you going?"

"Jail," said Colton. "I want to see our doppelganger."

"Good luck," said Skata, only half-joking.

Colton blew out a breath. "You too, buddy."

Skata waited a few beats after Colton left before he opened the door and leaned out to scan the hall. As soon as the way was clear, he jogged out, glancing into each open door, hoping to get a glimpse of Easton.

He finally saw her, backtracked, and hurried into the room, shutting the door behind him. Easton pushed herself up and stared at him with mingled suspicion and surprise. "What—"

He bent down and hugged her, smothering the rest of her words against his shirt. "You're okay, kid. You're okay."

She pushed him away. "Hang on a second."

He lifted both hands. "What?"

"You're not Skinner?"

"No, do you have a flashlight?"

"In a hospital?"

He rubbed his chin and glanced at the door. "I—well…"

Her grin was tired, but her eyes twinkled nonetheless. "I'm kidding. I can tell it's you."

Relieved, Skata frowned to hide a smile and glanced at the door. "Yeah, so could Colton."

"I guess people are getting used to the two of you. Like learning to tell identical twins apart."

He didn't want to get to the uncomfortable part of the conversation, but it was necessary, and he didn't have much time. "Angel bit you?"

She looked at the wall, and Skata stared. "I know that look."

"What look?" she asked, too quickly.

"You're trying to come up with a way to make it sound less bad than it was. Remember when you dug up a piece of glass in the backyard and cut yourself, and I asked what had happened, and you told me it was a paper cut?"

She blinked. "I honestly have no memory of that."

"Well, it happened. This isn't a paper cut, Easton."

"No, but look—I haven't turned. I don't feel weird, and you and I both know he wouldn't have done it on purpose."

"And drunk drivers don't hit people on purpose, either," he snapped.

"Hey!"

"I should have snapped his neck, not punched him in the face."

"You punched a vampire in the face?"

Skata paused. It all sounded different in that light. "Yes."

She snorted before covering her mouth with both hands. "Sorry."

"He's like a damn pit bull, making a great family pet until he turns on you."

Easton narrowed her eyes. "Don't hate on pit bulls."

"Okay, fine, pick another animal, whatever makes you happy. But he can't be handled like a normal guy. He's not even human, he just looks like it."

"He feels like a human," said Easton, but she looked tired now, her eyes threatening to close.

"I'm sorry, what?"

"Feelings," she said hastily, forcing her eyes to open wider. "His feelings. He has them like a normal person."

"It's funny you should feel that way, since apparently, he came by to apologize, and you kicked him out."

She lowered her gaze to her lap. "I feel like crap about that. I just wasn't...ready to see him. I hadn't thought it over."

Skata glanced back at the door. Every fiber of his being was on edge, waiting for an orderly to walk in and see him out of jail. "If you're feeling good about it, I think you should—uh, call him."

She squinted. "Why? I'll see him eventually."

Skata pinched the bridge of his nose and let out a deep breath. "Geez, you've been through enough," he mumbled under his breath before saying louder, "Because he's dying."

Easton sat bolt upright, reaching for the IV drip in her arm. "How? What happened?"

"It's a long story, but he got bit by a werewolf. He's got maybe half a day left, probably less."

Easton pulled the tape away from her arm and withdrew the needle. "Right. I need to go see him."

Skata hesitated, torn between helping her and telling her to get back in bed.

"Skata," she growled, "I'm going to him. He came by to apologize, and he was dying. I'm not living with that, and I—he's—we're practically friends. I am *going* to see him."

"You aren't technically allowed out yet, and I can't be seen. And your dad'll be by—"

"He already came. We're leaving now."

He opened his mouth, but his protest died in his throat when he saw the light burning behind her eyes, the way she stood half-leaning but with clenched fists. "Okay. Where are your clothes?"

* * * * * * *

"Why did you bring the girl?" Gideon Montgomery asked, smiling politely at Easton as if she couldn't hear him.

"Hi to you," said Easton, with groggy sarcasm.

Skata ignored him, helping Easton inside. She was still weak, but was handling herself admirably. "Where's Angel?"

"Ah. He took a turn for the worse twenty minutes ago and went to lie down."

"Jackson?"

"Still no word; all seems to be very quiet, which can mean nothing good."

Skata came to the realization he felt downright optimistic around Gideon. "Right." He and Easton came to the bottom of the staircase. "You going to make it?"

"Nope," she said positively.

He scooped her up and carried her to the top of the stairs.

"So chivalrous," she teased.

He snorted in response and set her on her feet outside Angel's room. "If this wasn't a life-or-death situation, I'd have carried you straight to your own bed."

She didn't seem to hear him; her gaze was focused on the door, and she put her hand on the wood, like she could sense whatever she would see on the other side.

"I don't think you should go in there unarmed," said Skata. "Just in case."

"If he's dying and took a turn for the worse, I'm not sure he'll be up to attacking anyone. Besides, you're in the house." She smiled weakly at him. "Give me five minutes before you go all Papa Bear, okay?"

"Sure. Not a second more."

She nodded and opened the door.

* * * * * * *

Angel's dark hair was a stark contrast to his gray skin. Even his eyelashes looked out of place. Every rattling breath he took seemed to produce more sweat; she could see the pillow under his head was already soaked.

"Angel?" She spoke the word quietly into the dead air, her heart clenching like a fist inside her chest.

His eyes moved under his eyelids before they opened, squinting against the dim light filtering through the drawn curtains. His words dragged out of him, tired and painful. "You're supposed to be in the hospital."

"That's funny, coming from you."

The ghost of a smile flickered across his face. "Been there, done that. It's a bad idea."

Easton pulled her hair over her shoulder, hiding the bandage on her neck as she sat down on the edge of the bed. "They don't have a cure for werewolf venom in those crash carts?"

"Guess not."

She reached over and lifted his hand. It was cold and heavy, and he looked at it like it was a foreign thing, not attached to him.

"Why are you here?" He lifted his eyes to her face, and she

swallowed as she noticed even their impossible blueness had grown as dull and gray as the rest of him.

"Skata told me you were…" She almost said 'sick,' but changed her mind. He knew what he was. "He told me you were dying."

"Question…" He took a deep breath, and Easton ground her teeth against the horrible sound it made. "Still stands."

She squeezed his hand. "You're my friend, you ninnyhammer."

"I bit you."

She shrugged away the flash of horror at the recent memory. "What's a bite between friends?"

"And what about Macon?"

Easton swallowed again. "Don't you have better things to be worried about?"

His pale eyes searched her face, the only thing even half-alive about him. "I should be the last person you want to see right now."

"Well, maybe not the *last*." He almost smiled, but this time it couldn't quite finish. She squeezed his hand again, and his limp grip mustered enough strength to squeeze hers back, just barely. "I wish I could trade places with you."

It was his gaping stare that let her know she'd spoken out loud.

"It's too far," he groaned, shutting his eyes. "It's too much.

I'm hallucinating. The heat has gotten to your brain. Or the humidity. There's mildew in there."

She opened her mouth, but it took several seconds for her to say, "I'm—yeah. Sorry."

"Take it back."

She rolled her eyes at the childish demand. "Sorry, I can't."

He opened his eyes again, and she saw the questions, all of them, spilling over themselves, but he was unable to ask all of them. He didn't have the energy. Instead, he sighed and asked, "Why would you say something that stupid?"

She looked down at his hand, shaking with the effort of squeezing hers but still not letting go. "I'm not scared of it. Dying. I was when Mom died. I was when I thought Graham was dead. I thought I would be afraid of it when you bit me in the hospital, but I wasn't."

His derisive snort lacked the emphasis he probably wanted, but he muttered, "Piffle."

"I'm serious."

"I'm not afraid of dying."

"Piffle," said Easton softly, tossing the word back at him.

"Do I look like I'm scared?" he asked, but the question sounded desperate, as if he needed to hear her say *no*.

The conversation felt wrong to Easton—she was supposed to comfort the dying, not give them existential crises—but she couldn't simply change subjects, so all she said was, "I think you're unsure of what comes after."

He looked the other way, and the gesture seemed to symbolize him drifting away from her. Easton covered her mouth with her free hand, one hot tear slipping down her face, then another, and another. She squeezed her eyes shut, her mind overtaken by the repeated prayer wrenching from deep inside her. *Don't let him die. Please don't let him die. Please. Please keep him alive.*

"Nice thought," said Angel's voice, with only a shade of his usual feeling, "but don't bother."

Easton opened her eyes. He was looking at her again, but he glanced down as soon as she returned it. "I'll pray if I want to."

"Praying over a vampire's a little sacrilegious, isn't it?"

"I don't think so."

"Really."

"I think there'd be some 'thou shalt not pray over a vampire' commandment if we weren't supposed to," said Easton, half-teasing and half-serious. "As it happens, vampires are never mentioned."

"We drink blood. It says something about not doing that."

"It also says not to lie or steal or covet."

He rolled his eyes, and it looked like it took the rest of his energy. "Pretty sure blood drinking's worse."

"Still sin. He can forgive it."

Angel's eyelids dropped, and Easton felt his hand fall away from hers, onto the mattress. "Too…late," he murmured, almost inaudible. "Tragic."

She took his hand with both of hers, lifting it up since he

couldn't, trying to feel some warmth. There was only cold. "I forgive you. I forgive you for everything you've done to me or think you've done. I came here to tell you that." She drew a deep, shuddering breath, strangely devoid of tears, as if her body had suddenly decided to accept what was happening. She bent down and pressed a kiss against his frigid forehead. "I forgive you. I forgive you, Angel."

His lips parted enough to let another breath slip through, along with something Easton could not understand. She leaned down closer. "What?"

"Zacharia." His face hardly moved as his voice pushed through parted lips. "Travalis. My name."

She found it hard to lift her head away from his, even as she smiled. "You have a few hours left, Zach. There's still hope."

"Hold…onto it," said the vampire. He did not speak again.

CHAPTER THIRTY-EIGHT

M y, my, my. Come to see me?"

Colton folded his arms and leveled a humorless gaze through the cell bars. "Why'd you do it?"

Skinner sat up. "Do what?"

"Get yourself thrown in here for a guy you seem to hate."

"It must be eating you alive." Skinner smiled his slow, sharp smile. "It's fun to see you at a loss. Although I admit, it was more fun to see you get knocked out with a booby trap. You must be getting slow in your old age."

Colton smiled at the floor to mask his irritation. "Funny you should mention old age, for a guy who must be in his—what, eighties? Nineties?"

Skinner's gaze narrowed, and his smile widened—never a good combination, in Colton's experience. "Come again?"

"Hazard Rayborne, right? You're doing a heck of a job living up to your first name, man, I gotta say."

The stretched smile slipped into something less amused.

"Where did you come up with that little guess?"

"I might just be a Texas country boy, but I know how to ask around. Didn't take long to put the pieces together. Your daddy'd be real proud of you."

"If I were you, I'd watch my mouth," said Skinner, and now there was real danger in his voice.

"Or what?" Colton raised a skeptical eyebrow and knocked his knuckles against vertical iron bars. "I know a thing or two about doppelgangers, man. You can't shift into somebody with mass that different from yours. Ain't no way you're turning into someone who can squeeze out of here."

"Don't plan on it," Skinner retorted, apparently done playing games. "Why are you really here?"

"I'm here to lend you a hand."

"Why do I feel all tingly with suspicion?"

"You helped Skata, and I want to know why. You tell me, and maybe I can bust you out."

Skinner smiled narrowly. "A man of God busting a murderer out of jail, is that it? It's a good story, if not exactly a surprising one."

"What's that supposed to mean?"

"Oh," said Skinner, his black eyes glittering, "I think you know." His smile twisted—not cruelly, but with the air of someone who knew a secret and found it amusing.

Colton folded his arms over his chest. He knew it was a defensive stance, but the thought came too late, and all he could do was press his lips together and scowl at the smirking doppelganger. "Why'd you help Skata out?"

Skinner crossed the cell, running his fingers across the bars. "Call it a change of heart."

"I told you I'd help you if you gave me a good reason. What do you want?"

"World peace," said Skinner with a smarmy smile. "And one of those big plastic hamster balls. Human-sized."

This had been a bad idea. "Have fun behind bars, buddy," said Colton, turning to leave.

"Not so fast."

Colton paused and let out a deep breath. "What?" he growled.

"I know why you came here, and I know the goodness of your heart had nothing to do with it."

"Really."

"Really." Skinner lifted a finger and drawled, "You wanted to see how much I knew about you."

"I came here out of curiosity, but looks to me like you do everything on a whim. 'Sides, I don't care what you know about me." Colton walked down the short hallway, but before he opened the door, Skinner's voice said in a voice half-teasing, half-warning, "You should."

"Thanks, man," sneered Colton. "Anything else?"

"Just one thing," said Skinner.

* * * * * * *

It took Easton several seconds to realize her phone was ringing. She dug it out of her pocket without looking away from Angel's—Zacharia's—face. "Hello?"

"Remember me?" The voice on the other end was casual but annoyed.

Easton rubbed her forehead. "Spencer?"

"Yeah, Spencer's not available right now. This is the guy who was supposed to be taking care of hot dogs and burgers but is now taking care of hot dogs, burgers, lemonade, coke, diet coke, sprite, water, and ice cream. So…thanks for that."

Easton frowned, trying her hardest to remember what she'd forgotten. "Uh…for…"

"Wow. The town barbecue? Remember? It's only been in the works for two months."

Easton muffled a groan. "I'm so sorry. Oh my gosh. I literally forgot."

"Figures, since the only reason I got roped into doing this was you saying you couldn't handle it by yourself, and now here I am—handling it by myself. Wait—should I take that as a compliment?"

Easton reached forward to feel Angel's—no, Zacharia's—ugh, this was too much to think about—forehead, her stomach twisting at how cold it was. "Spencer, I hate to say this, but I can't talk right now."

"Oh, a bad time. Really? Because I'm—hey, don't touch that!" His sudden shout made Easton quickly pull the phone away from her ear. After a moment, Spencer spoke again in a calmer voice. "Fricking savages."

"Who?"

"Junior-highers who think they can raid the coolers just because the tailgate's open. So are you going to be here in two hours or not?"

This was it, thought Easton, this was how their friendship crashed. "I really can't. Something huge came up, and I'll explain it to you when I can."

She heard the sound of a chip bag opening. "Awesome. Remind me to unfriend you on Facebook."

"Look—I'll make it up to you, okay? I promise."

"Uh-huh. Maybe I'll kidnap someone and force them to help me after the memorial."

Easton had been about to hang up, but she stopped. "What memorial?"

"The one for the..." Spencer paused and continued hesitantly, "people who were on the council." After a moment, he continued. "Apparently, most people didn't think it was a good idea to hold a town barbecue without a moment of silence."

Easton blinked, too surprised at the information to feel sad at the thought. "When is this? Where? Who's going to be there?"

"It's at six tonight at the town hall, and everyone's going to be there. Everyone left on the council, the sheriff's department, anyone feeling guilty or lucky or patriotic or whatever. Where have you been, hiding under a rock?"

"Spencer," said Easton firmly, her pulse beginning to pick up speed, "you cannot let them hold this memorial."

"I hear you. Let me just go find a flamethrower so I can torch the place."

"I'm not kidding, okay? I'm going to tell Colton."

"Yeah, tell the preacher that almost every human in town will be stepping into a red brick, ivy-covered death-trap."

Easton gripped her phone so tightly she was surprised the case didn't crack. "Spencer—"

"Don't worry, I'll get on it! As soon as I finish unwrapping one hundred packs of hot dog buns."

Spencer hung up, and Easton jumped off the bed and raced to the door, nearly running into Skata. He was leaning against the wall with his arms folded and his eyes shut, as if he'd fallen asleep standing up.

"Skata!" Easton shoved him.

He jerked awake. "Where is he?"

"We have a huge problem."

"Why? Is Angel dead?"

"No. His name's Zacharia."

"Who?"

"Angel."

"Angel's name is Zacharia?"

"Zacharia Travalis. Now shut up and listen." She took a deep breath, her mind scattering in a dozen different, terrible directions. "Spencer called. He's getting ready for the town barbecue but they're holding a memorial service for Samuel's victims first, at six."

Skata tensed. "Where?"

"The town hall."

The sleep fell away from Skata's eyes, and he raced toward the stairs. "Gideon!" He glanced at his watch. "That gives us three hours."

"Two hours and fifty-six minutes," said Gideon, walking up the stairs. "This could quite possibly be a trap. However, we may be able to stop his army of werewolves if we can surprise them before they attack."

"I'm not sure we have enough time for 'before,'" Skata began, but the front door opened and Colton strode inside.

The preacher wore an expression of equal parts bewilderment and focus. "I know where Samuel is."

Gideon arched an eyebrow. "The doppelganger told you?"

"That's got 'trap' written all over it," said Skata.

"I know," said Colton, frowning. "But I don't think he was lying. He said they're at the old Huron place."

Skata blinked. "Which is?"

"It's an abandoned campground and RV park," Easton supplied, glancing back at Angel's room. "It's only, like, five miles outside of town."

Skata clenched his hands into fists. "Great, so we can get to them before the attack."

"What attack?" asked Colton.

Skata gave him the details rapid-fire, and Colton took the news by folding his arms tightly over his chest and clenching his teeth. "Great."

"We have an upper hand now," said Gideon pragmatically. "Skata will go to the campground posing as Skinner and release Jackson. Then—"

"Uh, Skata will not," said Skata.

Gideon continued, unperturbed. "I will accompany Colton to the town square and assess the situation. Once Skata and Jackson return, they can go to the Diamond Straight and see if Rukiel is willing to lend us some muscle."

"I don't have that kind of cash," said Skata sharply.

"I have," said Gideon.

"What about Angel?" asked Easton, rubbing her arms tensely.

"You stay here," said Skata, "and keep an eye on Angel. Or Zacharia, or whoever's dying in there."

"But—"

"I'll ask Samuel about a cure if I can." Skata's expression softened slightly as he looked at Easton and then the room behind her. "We'll need someone here in case he says anything useful."

She nodded, torn between feeling glad to stay with the dying vampire and useless at doing nothing else. "Be careful."

Skata nodded and gave her a brief, forced smile. "Take care." He jogged down the stairs, and she heard him say to Colton, "I need a few things out of your trunk."

Without a word Gideon was there and gone, shutting the door like an angry ghost.

CHAPTER THIRTY-NINE

I don't like this," Skata muttered, taking his sawed-off out of Colton's trunk.

"Me neither. Here." Colton held out a plastic bag of shotgun shells.

Skata took it and asked, "Wolfsbane?"

"Yep. Watch your back out there."

"I can handle myself."

Colton snorted.

Aggravated and tired, Skata said, "I drink enough wolfsbane, Father; I've already proven that."

Colton snorted again. "I'm not talking about their ability to turn you, idiot. Even the little ones've got teeth two inches long."

"No worries. I can handle it."

Colton's lip threatened to curl as he glanced at Skata, but all he said was, "Better hope so. You good to go?"

"Hell yeah. Always wanted to go down in a shootout."

Colton's grin was fierce. "Ah, you'll be fine."

"It's not just me I have to worry about. If I make it out without Jackson, Gideon's going to kill me himself."

Colton glanced over his shoulder in the direction the moroi had gone. "Didn't hear him leave."

"Yeah. Vampires'd be a lot less creepy if they didn't move at the speed of sound."

Colton tossed Skata the keys to his car. "Be fast."

"What, no 'be careful'?"

"I got a townful of innocent people to worry about; I don't need to worry about your hide, too."

Skata rolled the window down and hung his arm out. "Yeah," he said through his teeth as he pulled out of the driveway, "I'm starting to think nobody around here's actually innocent."

* * * * * * *

The woods were no place for a vintage Chevy. Skata parked alongside the empty stretch of road and began the hike into the woods toward the campground. After twenty minutes, he saw a rotting wooden sign with an arrow pointing ahead. The faded red paint read *Huron Campground .5 Mi.*

Skata tucked the gun inside his jacket. He was good at concealing weapons, but the sawed-off was larger than the weapons he usually tried to hide. He pushed it up against his arm in the least-conspicuous way and continued ahead.

The hike felt unusually quick, and he heard the wolves before he saw them.

The campground was obviously no longer abandoned—the overgrown clearings were crowded with tents and fire pits. Werewolves in their human forms milled around, talking and barking orders. Two were crouched by a fire pit, roasting a wild pig. Skata glanced up at the sky—in a few hours, they'd be happy to eat it raw.

Skata shook his head and placed a cocky half-grin on his face before striding into view. "I need to talk to Samuel."

The nearest wolf, a goateed man in his late forties, stood up. "He's out."

"Of course he is." Skata rubbed the back of his neck.

A woman in a sweatshirt stood up, winding her hair into a ponytail. "What do you want with him?"

Skata thought her long, sparkly fingernails looked more intimidating than any wolf's claws.

For half a moment, Skata's brain froze. He didn't know Skinner well enough to mimic him, and then he remembered— the doppelganger was mimicking *him*. He gave himself a brief inward shake before saying the first thing that came to mind. "Sorry, I don't speak dog."

"What did you just say?" A brawny young werewolf jumped to his feet, his fingers flexed as if he expected claws to push through his fingertips any second.

"Relax, Fido," said Skata, hoping he wasn't going overboard. "I'm not here to pick a fight."

"Sounds like you are to me, doppelganger."

"Get your ears examined," Skata retorted. "I hear there's a good vet in town."

The man snarled in a decidedly non-human way. "Beat it, copycat."

Skata took a deep breath. There was no way he could afford to get into a fight with a werewolf—they would expect him to have a doppelganger's strength. "Look, pal, it's been a long day. I just need to talk to Samuel."

"You ain't talking to nobody," spat the younger wolf.

Skata raised his eyebrows, but before he could respond, a female voice rang out. "Sit down, Nick."

Everyone turned to look at the newcomer who had entered the clearing. She was a sharp-looking woman, with pale, spiked hair and the fashion sense of a lumberjack. Judging by the way Nick sat down, Skata guessed she was the alpha.

"Doppelganger," she said, jerking her head in the other direction. "Come with me."

Doppelganger. Skata wondered if Skinner had called himself by a name and hoped nearly to the point of prayer he hadn't. "Yes, ma'am." He strode after her, her long legs keeping a good pace ahead of him. "Where are we going?"

"Samuel's office."

Office? She didn't seem surprised by his question—Skata

wondered if Skinner had never been taken there before. His mind raced, trying to put the pieces together—Skinner had taken base assassination orders like a grunt, and he hadn't seemed to mind. A true zealot for Samuel's cause, or a true zealot for his own?

Skata remained behind the alpha until they reached a small building dripping with Spanish moss. He guessed it had been a camp ranger's office or something similar, once upon a time.

"Nice digs," said Skata.

She pushed the front door open and gestured inside. "Samuel will be along."

Skata wanted to ask her name—he assumed everyone, including Skinner, would be aware of it—but he had to be inconspicuous. "Thanks, Moneypenny."

"Christine," she said. "Don't forget it again."

I must be good at this whole Skinner thing. "Right. Sorry."

"I doubt it." Her face held no humor as she shut the door behind him. He listened to her retreating footsteps. Only when he was sure she was gone did he step farther into the small, stuffy building. There was a desk with two chairs on either side, and pinned to the wall was a wrinkled, torn map of Salvation.

He looked over his shoulder once before stepping around the desk and trying the tarnished knob of the door behind it. It was probably just a storage room, but there was always the slim chance that Jackson was there. It was locked, of course, although he tried pounding his shoulder against it for good measure.

The last time he slammed against it, a sound caught his

attention. The faint clattering was difficult to place, but it was enough. Someone was inside.

Skata stepped back to study the door. It was just his luck—the entire building was in shambles, except the door he wanted to go through. He took the shotgun out of his jacket and slammed the butt of it down against the lock. On the third try, the lock broke and the door swung open with force; he caught it just before it slammed against the wall.

He paused, listening. He'd made enough noise already—if any of the wolves had been paying attention, they would have heard him. He waited, listening for the sound of a descending wolf pack. Something small skittered across the roof; a squirrel, maybe. Skata stepped back, pumping the shotgun and stepping into the dark room.

As his foot landed on the other side of the threshold, a syrupy Southern voice said, "Watch your step."

"Jackson?" He reached into his pocket for Colton's keys and switched on the tiny keychain flashlight. "Where are you?"

"Down."

Skata pointed the tiny beam toward his feet and blinked at the sight of the uneven hole dug in the middle of the dirt floor. It had to be at least ten feet deep, and Jackson was inside, a chain around his neck linked to something that disappeared into the black water.

Skata crouched down for a better look. The water around the vampire was fizzing like the head on a good glass of beer, and a sharp, bitter scent filled Skata's nose as he took in a breath. Jackson looked up, and Skata saw the redness around his sunken eyes, veins pulsing black beneath his skin. "Took your sweet time," said Jackson, his fangs flashing in the dim light.

"What's in the water?" asked Skata.

Jackson's smile managed to look condescending despite his situation. "Get bored playin' fetch for your master?"

Skata held up a hand. "Hold on. I'm not Skinner, I'm Skata."

"Nice try." The fangs created a lisp in Jackson's accent that did a little to diminish his ferocity. "No cigar."

"Look." Skata shone the keychain flashlight into his eyes. "No yellow, no black, no weird lens flare."

"Huh." Jackson sagged against the dirt wall behind him. Every breath rasped like sandpaper. "What's a girl like you doing in a place like this?"

"Getting you out of here."

"That's nice of you."

"Gideon's idea, not mine."

"Taking commands from the Commodore now, are we?" Jackson's smirking grin widened, but it did nothing to lessen the panicked glaze in his eyes.

"Shut your pie hole and let me think. You're chained to the bottom?"

"Sure am."

"And why haven't you just hopped out of there yet?"

"Because the water isn't exactly full of chlorine." Jackson spat out a mouthful of something too dark to be saliva.

Skata rubbed his mouth. The vampire had been soaking in a well of vervain for...what, a day? The poison would have entered his bloodstream a long time ago. He was practically marinated in the stuff. "How long have you been in there?"

"Can't say for sure. I lost track of time." He shifted in the water, which hissed and seethed where it came into fresh contact with his skin.

Skata knew there was a good chance the vampire was already dead, but he couldn't give up. "Do you think you can break the chain?"

"If I could, I'd have done it already. I'm too weak."

Skata got to his feet. "Give me a minute."

"The place is crawling with werewolves, in case you hadn't noticed." Jackson's voice broke with a pained shudder. "Good luck getting back in one piece, let alone a minute."

"Thanks," said Skata. "Don't go anywhere."

Jackson responded with a violent cough and spat out another mouthful of blood, panting harshly. When he called up, his voice was weaker than before. "If you see Gideon...before I do—tell him it's all right."

Skata opened his mouth to say something flippant, but there was a sound outside the front door that made him jump to his feet and run into the adjacent room. He shut the door and slid down behind the desk just as the door opened. Skata peered up from underneath the desk as two people strode in.

The first one was Christine, but Skata would have recognized the second in a sea of thousands.

"Well," said Samuel, "where is he?"

"He was in here a few minutes ago."

Skata silently slid his finger to the trigger. Samuel walked around the desk at a leisurely pace, followed by Christine. This was his only chance to get away. They would hear him, or realize his scent was fresh and not lingering. He slid out from under the desk and blasted the shotgun at the vampire and the werewolf.

Christine screamed and collapsed to the floor as the wolfsbane exploded into her flesh. Samuel whirled around, jumping over the desk where Skata dropped him with another blast to the chest. Knowing the vampire would be up and running momentarily, Skata raced out the door and into the woods as fast as he could.

He ran and ran, waiting for the sounds of the wolves baying behind him, hot for his blood. He ran until he heard footsteps over the sound of his own breathing. Veering to the right, he pushed his back against a tree, the shotgun already primed. He drew a knife from his belt, a weapon in each hand. It wouldn't save his life, but it would do enough damage to make him happy.

No more footsteps joined the first. Skata shut his eyes and listened. They were light, too light to be Samuel. Cautious, too cautious to be Nick. He leaned slowly around the other side of the tree, searching for a glimpse of the lone follower.

He didn't expect to see a teenaged girl in a plaid headband and skirt standing ten feet away. She looked like some kind of storybook princess with no idea what she was doing in the middle of the South Carolina woods.

Still. Skata stepped out from behind the tree, his shotgun pointed at her midsection. "Who are you?"

She took several startled steps back, her green eyes wide. "Are you Skata?"

Skata frowned. "No. I look like him but I ain't him."

She narrowed her eyes. "The doppelganger told me to call him Skinner. He said you'd be coming."

"Is that right," said Skata, his mind racing. What was Skinner playing at?

"You're him, aren't you?"

"Listen, lady—" He paused, because 'lady' sounded far too old for the girl, "this is a pretty old trick. You should update your repertoire."

"It's not a trick!" She smoothed her hair angrily. Skata wasn't quite sure how it remained smooth in the humid air, but there were larger questions to ask—like whether she was telling the truth. "Skinner said you were a hunter."

"That would mean I kill werewolves if they piss me off, so coming after me was a pretty stupid thing to do."

"He said you want to kill Samuel."

Skata groaned incredulously. "Was there anything he didn't tell you?"

"I'm here to help you." She took a deep breath, obviously steeling herself for what must be a terrifying encounter with a hunter. "To help you get Jackson out."

Skata blinked. "Why the heck would you want to do that?"

She blushed pink. "I don't want them to kill him."

Good grief. Skata lowered his gun, although he didn't lower the knife. "You can't be willing to risk your neck for a day-old crush."

"No!" She blushed harder and glared. "He—I—it would be wrong, whoever he was."

So the crush was there, but maybe she was against murder. Well, he could work with that. "Look, miss…"

"Bonnie," she said. "Bonnie Havilland."

"Bonnie," he corrected, "two things. One, your wolf buddies aren't going to like you helping their prisoner escape, if you hadn't figured that out. Two, you realize Jackson's like three hundred years old, right? How old are you?"

"Twenty," she said, glaring. "I'm taking a gap year. And I'm a werewolf, you know. I can handle myself."

Skata realized those were the words he'd said to Colton earlier. He hoped he hadn't sounded quite that ridiculous. "Listen," he began, but she cut him off.

"They won't suspect me."

"You seem pretty transparent."

"Skinner said I was 'unlikely.'"

"That, too."

"If you give me something to break his chain with, I can free him and meet you somewhere."

He laughed quietly and shook his head. "I must really look like an idiot."

"I'm sorry?"

"Your idea of a trap couldn't be more obvious." He couldn't help the chuckle that escaped him, and he rubbed his face with the back of his hand, careful not to stab himself in the eye. He needed three years of sleep. Maybe a dirt nap.

"For the second and last time," she said, flushing from anger this time, "it is *not* a trap."

He hesitated. In truth, he was almost inclined to believe her. Everything about her looked too out of place, too innocent for the situation—but that's what made it a good trap, if it was one. "Sorry, Bonnie. The answer's no."

Her glossed lip curled, and her eyes narrowed. "Fine," she snapped. "I'll get him out myself."

Suddenly, Skata was afraid she would go through with it and get killed as a result. She was a werewolf, sure, but she was even younger than Easton. She was just a kid. "That's a bad idea."

"Do you have a better one, then?"

"Okay!" He lowered his weapons halfway. "All right, you can help." He mentally cursed Skinner for dragging someone like Bonnie Havilland into this—if she was telling the truth. Always 'if.'

She didn't even blink. "Then what do we do?"

Skata cast a suspicious glance around, but he didn't see or hear anything. "I've got a pair of bolt-cutters that should do the trick," he said. "Where's the rest of the pack?"

"They're still at camp."

He drew his eyebrows together. "Why's that?"

"Samuel told them to. He said to wait."

Skata took a step toward her. "This have anything to do with the town hall tonight?"

Her eyes widened. "How——"

Skata sheathed his knife and called Colton. The phone rang six times before going to voicemail.

"Come on, man, answer your freaking phone." Skata ground his teeth and glanced at Bonnie, who was staring warily at him. He decided to leave a message in case Colton saw it. "Easton was right; Samuel's pulling something at the memorial tonight. I'll be there as soon as I can."

He tucked the phone back into his pocket. "All right," he said to Bonnie, "come with me."

She began to follow him, but he stopped walking and waved the barrel of the gun once. "Ahead of me, sister."

She set her jaw and jogged ahead of him. Skata wondered how she'd gotten herself entangled in this mess—probably dragged in along with her pack. If the alpha chose to do something, the pack had to follow or challenge, and the thought of Bonnie battling Christine was ridiculous.

Skata took them to the truck. He took the bolt-cutters out of the back. "These should do it."

"Hand them over."

Skata glanced at the tool, then at the werewolf girl.

"I can go faster than you can," she said simply. "I'll get him out and meet you back here. You can have the engine running."

"I should come with you," he said.

"That's a horrible idea," she exclaimed. "Nick and a few of the others have your scent, and you killed Christine. Nothing Samuel said would keep them from killing you if they saw you."

Skata reluctantly handed the bolt-cutters over. "You sure you can do this?"

"Absolutely," she said nervously.

Skata groaned and found himself hoping—ridiculous as it was—that Skinner had chosen the right ally. "Just hurry up, all right?"

"Yes." She stepped back, clutching the bolt-cutters. "If I'm not back in fifteen minutes…I guess I'm dead." With an uncertain glance back at him, she turned and rushed into the woods.

Skata leaned against the back of the truck. Everything was going to hell, and even the preacher wasn't picking up. He called Colton again, swearing under his breath.

It was answered on the fifth ring, and Skata didn't give Colton time to speak. "Where the heck have you been?"

"Manners, Skata, if you please."

Skata froze for half a second. "Rukiel?"

Rukiel didn't answer but Skata knew it was him. "Not to be

cliché or anything," said Skata, bracing himself, "but I've got a bad feeling about this."

"As well you should."

"Where's Colton?"

"Safe in my custody."

"Custody?" Skata spat. "You mangy son of a bitch, what's that supposed to mean?"

"Let's not foul up the line, please. Both Gideon Montgomery and Lucas Colton are perfectly unharmed and will remain that way."

"That sounds like a condition," growled Skata.

"It is. I gather you aren't in town; good. Stay away."

"I was afraid of that," said Skata flatly.

"I don't really believe you are afraid," said Rukiel. "I believe you charge recklessly into whatever situation you please. I do, however, believe you wouldn't like to see Lucas Colton damaged. I cannot honestly say anything about the Montgomery."

Skata smiled. "If you hurt either of them, I'll rip your spine out your mouth. How long were you in on Samuel's plan?"

"Not until recently."

"Did he come over and twist your tiny arm?"

"Your luck is very thin," said Rukiel, his tone still polite. "Please don't tear through it. My term is simple and easy enough for you to grasp. Keep away tonight, and I will release your friends in the morning. You have my word."

"You can take your word and shove it," said Skata, ending

the call. He threw his phone against the car, which proved unsatisfying when the phone didn't break. He picked it up off the ground and opened the passenger door just so he could slam it shut again.

Angel was dying, and Easton was there to witness it. The entire town was at immediate risk. Colton and Gideon were prisoners. Jackson was most likely dead, and his only hope was a schoolgirl with a crush who may or may not be the enemy. He had only started out to get Samuel, to make the bastard pay, to try and put to rest the gnawing, crushing beast inside him.

But here he was, whether by a trick of fate or some divine move.

Divine move. Colton would have given him a pointed look, and standing there in the middle of nowhere, surrounded by impossible odds, Skata was willing to reach for the idea, no matter how stupid.

He rubbed his eyes and leaned against the side of the truck before glancing up at the cloudy sky. "Look," he began and almost stopped there. He felt like a kid. An idiotic kid, no less. Still, he had no other options. It was his only shot. "Look," he repeated, "I'm not Superman. Hell, I'm not even a good guy, but I'm here and that's…" He was surprised by how difficult it was to say the next few words, even to thin air. "I'm not sure what I'm doing. Or what I'm supposed to do. So if you've got any big ideas, just… lay them on me. Give me a sign or something."

He almost said 'amen' but thought against it. Instead, he

climbed into driver's seat and started the engine. He wanted to be ready to move out as soon as Bonnie returned, if she ever did.

Right as he leaned back, his phone rang. He picked it up and felt his heart sink. He hadn't thought it possible.

He put the phone to his ear. "He dead?"

"Not yet; I think I have an idea."

Skata straightened. "Like what?"

"I've been doing research on cures for werewolf bites, and I think I might have found one."

Skata shut his eyes. "Come on, Easton, you can't Wikipedia this stuff."

"Please. I called Spencer, and he was able to find a pretty old idea that says if a vampire is bitten by a werewolf, a high dose of wolfsbane might act as a counter-poison. Like taking belladonna for mushroom poisoning."

"What's the downside?"

"It could kill him, but he's already dying."

Skata rubbed his forehead. "There's wolfsbane in the top dresser drawer in my room."

"I'm in your top drawer and there are like five flasks in here."

"It's copper."

"Got it."

He listened as she rummaged around in his things. "There should be a syringe in there."

"You keep a syringe in your dresser?"

"You never know when you'll need to inject yourself with an antidote."

"How convenient." Easton let out a deep breath. "I'm going to do this. I'll call you back. Pray for him."

Skata opened his mouth, but she hung up before he could reply. He leaned back. A kind of profound silence settled around him. It was impossible. There was no such thing as a last-minute cure, particularly one after a crappy prayer. He felt hoaxed.

But if it worked...

He looked out the windshield. "We'll have an understanding."

A roll of thunder replied.

CHAPTER FORTY

Pain stabbed his head as Colton opened his eyes, struggling to focus on his surroundings. He was in a large chair in front of a larger fireplace. *A fire in a southern summer?* Rukiel was trying to boil them alive. Across from him sat Gideon in an identical chair, his head bowed over his chest and a dart in the side of his neck.

They were both tied firmly with silvery ropes. Colton clenched his teeth and tried to move his wrists, but the ropes were surprisingly well-knotted. He frowned, and the door opened behind him. He waited until Rukiel walked around the chair, standing between his captives, leaning on his swagger-cane.

His black-polished fingernails tapped a steady rhythm, and Colton remembered where he was and why. He also remembered a blow to the back of his head, which explained his nausea. "What'd you do to him?" he asked, his voice slurring in his ears.

Rukiel tilted his head, his narrow eyes glittering gold in the firelight. "A special mixture of my own." He pressed two fingers under Gideon's jaw and waited several seconds. "He's perfectly fine."

"This makes you a murderer," said Colton darkly.

Rukiel brushed imaginary lint off the shoulder of his blue-and-gold suit. "You're both alive," he pointed out.

"Not us, the town. You're going to let a crazy vampire and a pack of werewolves kill God knows how many people, and you just...stand there."

The shifter regarded him with grave amusement. "I have my own people to think about. Also, I have left you unharmed. Were I in your position, I would thank me."

There was a knock on the door, and Rukiel looked over Colton's head. "Come."

A man roughly the size of a sequoia stalked into the room and growled, "Where's the human?"

Rukiel tipped his head toward Colton. "Right here."

"What's going on?" Colton demanded.

Rukiel rested both hands on the head of his cane and gave Colton a look of mild regret. "I am sorry about this. I truly am."

"About what?"

"Consider this your humanity's swan song," said Rukiel. He lifted two fingers and pointed them toward Colton. "Proceed, Tobias."

Colton braced himself as the huge werewolf grinned, displaying a mouthful of too many sharp teeth, and sank them all into the preacher's shoulder. Colton didn't make a sound, and it was over in seconds. Tobias straightened, his mouth bloody, and turned to Rukiel.

"You may go," said the shifter.

Tobias lumbered out of the room, and Colton heard the door shut. Colton shifted his shoulder, trying to assuage the burning pain as much as he could. He blew out a deep breath and smiled blackly at Rukiel. "That the best you got?"

Rukiel was watching him, unblinking. He leaned forward, on the edge of some invisible seat. Colton leaned back as the shifter reached out and placed his hand on Colton's forehead. "Cool," he muttered softly, his face twisted with bewilderment.

Oblivious to personal space, Rukiel lifted Colton's upper lip to inspect his teeth. "I don't understand," he said softly, stepping back while Colton shook his head. "Tobias is my best recruiter."

That caught Colton's attention. He stared in open, angry astonishment at Rukiel. It explained the sudden influx of the non-humans. "You've—you've been turning the werewolves?"

"His bite has never failed." Rukiel ignored Colton's remark but continued to study him. "Not once. What makes you so unique?"

Colton shrugged as well as he could and was arrested by another grimace. Blood was seeping through his clothes and spreading across his shoulder. Most people would have begun to turn by now; their skin would burn, their joints shifting, muscles stretching. The pain would be agonizing, with a good chance of death. "I'm gonna kill you."

Rukiel breathed out through his nose and shrugged. "You have a very unusual sort of angel watching over you, my friend, but I'm afraid his efforts are going to backfire." Rukiel crossed over to the large mahogany desk and pulled a drawer open. Colton could just make out the shifter's movements from the corner of his eye. Firelight glinted off something in Rukiel's hand, and as the shifter closed the drawer, he heard a click.

The shifter stepped back into view with an ivory-handled derringer in his hand. "Did you know I used to run a saloon in Kansas?" he asked, studying the firearm. "Diamond Jack was my name. I looked entirely different then, but I used this piece far more frequently. I haven't fired it since eighteen sixty-one."

"Then don't shoot it," muttered Colton. "Don't want to break a streak."

"I would have preferred not to kill you," said Rukiel, his feminine face folding into something close to actual sorrow.

Colton chuckled, and the chuckle became a laugh. The shifter's sorrowful expression became irritated. "Sorry," said Colton, grinning. "You should turn around."

"There were many idiots brought squalling into the world yesterday," snipped Rukiel, ruffled, "but I was not one of them."

"Somebody say idiot?"

Rukiel spun around, his finger on the trigger, and met Skinner's grin as the doppelganger punched the shifter in the face. The gun fell from Rukiel's hand, but he wasn't easily knocked down; he swung his cane against Skinner's ribs, and Colton heard the crack from across the room.

Skinner hissed, but the pain only seemed to work in his favor. As Rukiel swung the cane again, Skinner twisted and caught it with both hands, wrenching it from the shifter's grasp and spinning it around into Rukiel's skull.

The shifter fell limply to the floor with his arms spread at his sides, blood pooling on the carpet.

"What the heck," Colton began, but Skinner held up a hand.

"No need to thank me," the doppelganger said.

"I wasn't going to."

"You're welcome." Skinner dropped the cane and rubbed his hands together before crouching down behind Colton's chair and working the knots free in an impressively short time. Colton shot up and quickly took the dart from Gideon's neck.

"What's that?" asked Skinner curiously.

"Some vampire cocktail Rukiel cooked up." Colton tossed it onto the floor with a glance at Rukiel, smothering the twinge he felt at the sight. The shifter had made his own bed.

"He the one who took a bite out of your shoulder?"

The adrenaline had helped smother the pain, and Colton's anger did the rest. He glanced at his shoulder and said, "Werewolf. Rukiel was using his bouncers to turn people."

Skinner's black eyes squinted at Colton. "You're looking very well for a new werewolf."

"I didn't turn," Colton retorted, untying Gideon.

"Intriguing."

Colton slapped Gideon's face, but the vampire remained unconscious. Colton pulled his outer shirt off and held the bloodied shoulder under Gideon's nose. "Wake up."

The vampire's head jerked up, a glazed look in his eyes. "That…was unpleasant," he mumbled, his voice no less precise for being thick with vervain.

"Can he get up?" asked Skinner.

Gideon rose to his feet, graceful if not for the reach toward the back of the chair to steady himself. "Where is Jackson?"

Skata. Colton jogged across the room and scanned the shifter's desk until he saw his phone lying on a stack of envelopes. He unlocked it and checked for a missed call. There were three, plus a message. He listened to the message before calling Skata, who answered on the first ring.

"That'd better be you, Colton," said Skata.

"It is. Did Rukiel call you?"

"Yeah, he told me to stay away, otherwise you and Gideon were in trouble."

"Where are you?"

"Pulling up outside."

Colton glanced at Gideon and Skinner, who were watching him intently. "Anyone with you?"

"I've got Jackson and a puppy named Bonnie. Get out here, and I'll explain on the way to town. Move it."

They moved out the back without seeing anyone—the bar seemed closed for business, which didn't surprise Colton in the least. When a mass murder was going down in town and you were holding two hostages in the office, you didn't want to draw attention to yourself.

The Chevy was waiting in the alley outside, and Skata was leaning against it with his eyes shut.

"Nap later," said Colton, jumping off the back step and hitting Skata on the shoulder.

Skata blinked his eyes open and yawned. "Nice to see you in one piece." When his eyes landed on Skinner, they widened. "What's he doing here?"

"I'm impatient," said Skinner. "Got tired of hanging around and changed. Pretended you'd gotten out and locked the deputy in."

"They fell for that?" Skata asked in disbelief. "That's the oldest trick in the book."

"For a reason," said Skinner simply. "Anyway, my cover's blown. They'll find the remnants of the change and figure it out."

Skata sighed. "Awesome. The truck's only got room for five, unless someone wants to sit all conspicuously in the bed, so who's riding?"

"I am," said Colton, walking around the hood of the car and climbing into the passenger seat.

Gideon said nothing; he had been standing by the back window studying Jackson in silence. Then he said, "Jackson and I will be faster on foot."

The blonde 'puppy' Colton assumed was Bonnie jumped

out of the back seat. "He's not well," she began, but Jackson said, "Calm down, honey, I can make it to the house just fine."

The brothers did not embrace or even exchange greetings. Gideon only gave his younger brother a sweeping glance and nodded, ignoring Bonnie, before the two rushed away in a blur.

Bonnie moved as if to follow them, but Skata barked, "Hey. Not you."

She turned around, looking torn. "But I—"

He lifted a finger. "Back in the car," he said. "Now."

She frowned prettily but obeyed, slamming the door to let him know she didn't appreciate his order. Skinner strolled around the back of the truck and climbed in beside Bonnie, while Skata climbed into the driver's seat and looked at Colton. "Thought you'd want to drive."

"I got hit on the head," said Colton, folding his arms and concentrating on the windshield.

"So?"

"So I'm dizzy, and if you want to get us all in a wreck, then fine! I'll drive."

From the back seat, Skinner chimed in helpfully, "The real cherry on top was the fact he got bitten by a werewolf and didn't turn."

Skata's eyebrows rose. "You've been in the hospital. When'd you have time to take wolfsbane?"

"I didn't," said Colton gruffly.

"That's impossible," said Bonnie.

"Yeah, well, I guess I'm just lucky."

"Not to give a gift horse a dental inspection," said Skinner, "but am I the only one who finds this concerning?"

"Well," said Skata after a brief pause, "it's weird, but we can talk about it later. Does it need stitched up?"

"Naw," said Colton.

"You should disinfect it," said Bonnie.

"I will, later."

Skata started the engine and backed into the side street. "We'll worry about this mystery later."

"Anything new on the Angel front?" asked Colton.

"I have half an update," said Skata.

"Great. I have one, too."

"What's that?"

"I don't think Samuel wants to kill the townspeople," said Colton, gripping his bleeding shoulder. "He's going to turn them all."

Chapter Forty-One

"Freaking hell," said Skata.

"Yep. On earth," said Colton. He jerked his thumb back toward Bonnie. "She from Samuel's pack?"

"Yeah." Skata looked in the rearview mirror. "Is that the plan?"

Faintly, Bonnie said, "I—I think so."

"What's he turning them into?" Colton demanded. "Vampires, werewolves, what?"

"Both. I think it's both," she stammered. "He said he only wants to kill the council members. He says they should pay for the sins of their families."

Skata switched his attention to Skinner and growled, "Did you know about this?"

"Must have slipped my mind," drawled Skinner.

To Bonnie, Colton said, "He might not want to kill everyone, but he's going to kill a lot of them. Thirty-seven percent of human victims die from some part of the process—venom, shock, fever, the attack itself."

Skata glanced at him, bemused. "Anything else you want to tell us, Pie Chart?"

Colton scowled. "Turn right here, it's faster."

Skata turned the wheel, the truck squealing sharply. "Where's it come out?"

"The park across from town hall."

Skata pressed the pedal to the floor, tearing down the street, jumping over the curb, and barreling across the grass before stopping just before they ran into a large oak tree.

Everyone piled out of the truck, following Colton, who led them at a desperately fast clip. The park had been set up for a celebration, with half a dozen ballpark coolers, barbecues, and grills stationed several yards apart. Beach umbrellas shaded picnic tables from the bright, evening summer sun, and a banner tied between two stately trees simply stated 'COOKOUT' in yellow lettering.

It was idyllic, empty, and eerie. "I think we missed the rapture," said Skata.

"Hello! Guys! Over here!"

They turned to see Spencer across the park, waving one hand in the air. The other was wrapped firmly around the wrist of a familiar young, blonde woman, who looked close to murdering him.

"Finally!" shouted Shannon as they approached. "Maybe

one of you can explain why this geek thinks he's the secret service."

"She was trying to go inside," explained Spencer, glaring.

"For the memorial!" Shannon attempted to hit him, apparently not for the first time, since he barely even flinched. "Which has already started without me. I'm the sheriff's daughter; I'm supposed to be there."

"Thanks, man," said Colton, with a grateful look at Spencer.

That seemed to baffle Shannon. "Thank you? Look, can someone tell me what's going on?"

"Where's Maylee?" asked Skata urgently.

"Inside," snapped Shannon, "with her grandfather."

"Let her go," said Colton. Spencer gladly obeyed, and the preacher gripped Shannon's shoulders. "You know Samuel Lemeck?"

"The vampire," she said, fear washing over her face. "Yeah."

"He killed council members so there'd be a memorial. He's got most everyone inside so he can turn them. It's a kill box."

All color drained from Shannon's face. "I have to get her out of there."

"We're on it." Skata hit Skinner, indicating that the doppelganger should follow him. They broke into a run across the park with the others close behind, except Spencer. Skata heard him shout something that included the words "going home," but he ignored the rest. They didn't need him.

Skata raced up the steps of the town hall and rattled the door handles, but they refused to open. "They're locked."

"That means Samuel's guys are already inside," said Skinner, who slammed into the doors. He stepped back with a grimace, rubbing his arm. "They don't make 'em like that anymore."

Colton turned to Bonnie. "Do you know anything that could help?"

"They didn't tell me much," she said, her eyes earnest. "I was basically just an intern."

"Will Samuel know you're missing?"

She nodded.

"We've got to find a way inside," said Skata.

"Then I'd step away, if I were you."

He turned to see the Montgomery brothers standing not far away. For half a moment, Skata wondered if they were in on Samuel's trap—then he noticed they were each holding handfuls of small rocks gathered from the drive.

"They've shuttered the windows inside," Jackson explained. He looked terrible, but his tone was the same as always.

Skata and the others ducked out of the way, and the moroi brothers gave them just enough time before they lifted their arms and—casually, as if tossing a baseball across a front lawn—tossed the gravel at the windows.

The sound of shattering glass filled the air as the windows broke, spraying out like sea foam. The vampires then ran toward the building and smashed through the wooden shutters like they were movie props.

Jackson turned around and held a hand out toward Skata. "Come on."

Within seconds, everyone was inside the foyer. "They'll be in the main room," said Colton, but he was only halfway across the room when there was a muffled shriek from Bonnie.

Skata spun around, gun in hand, to see a man with his left arm around Bonnie's neck and his right hand on the side of her head. His claws drew drops of blood from the pale girl.

"One move and I'll break her," said Nick, grinning.

Something blurred past Skata, and a look of confusion overcame Bonnie's captor. A faint sound, almost a sigh, left him as his hands slipped from Bonnie and he fell to the floor. Jackson stood behind him, his hand slick and bloody, holding the werewolf's heart. He tossed it onto the floor beside its previous owner with a wet thump.

"Come on," he said, as if they'd been hanging back for fun. He moved past Skata with a rush of wind, following Colton and the others.

Skata gestured toward Bonnie. "You okay?"

"I," she said breathlessly, "am fine, yes. I'm fine."

They caught up with the others, who were standing outside the large double doors that led to the main meeting hall.

"Now what?" asked Skata, looking to Colton.

"I vote we go in with guns blazing," said Skinner. "Old-school."

"I vote we send the doppelganger in first," said Shannon. "I need to get Maylee and Dad out of there."

"So we break it down," said Jackson, nodding at Gideon.

"No, man," said Colton, irritated. "We do that, and he'll start massacring everyone before we're halfway inside." He paused, mind racing. "I've got a better idea."

* * * * * * *

Samuel smiled magnanimously into the crowd of horrified faces. "I know what you must be feeling," he said, in his most soothing voice, "but there's nothing to worry about. I promise."

His werewolves prowled around the edges of the crowd, keeping the townspeople in their seats. He gave the room a casual headcount—there were at least three hundred people here. Of course it wasn't the whole town, but three hundred people would turn the rest before nightfall.

A faint sound from the back left caught his attention, and his eyes landed on a middle-aged woman who was looking down. "Please," he said, projecting disappointment. "I said no cell phones—Ethel? It was Ethel, wasn't it?" He motioned to the nearest wolf, who shouldered his way over to the woman and snatched the phone from her hand.

Her voice shook as she said, "The authorities are on their way."

He sighed. "I'm afraid they're not. You see, half of them are here, and the other half at the station are—well, they won't be joining us."

The noise level in the room increased, a mounting swell of whispered terror.

He lifted both hands and gestured as if to push the noise down. "Now, good people, please. You're going to be fine. In fact, you'll be better than ever. I'm going to remake you." He grinned, and the crowd seemed to fall to pieces. "Oh, come on, people, they're only fangs."

From somewhere, a baby began to cry. The sound was hushed immediately, but it was too late. "Do I hear a child?" He scanned the crowd, and his eyes landed on the man who looked the guiltiest. Samuel closed his eyes and took a long breath in through his nose. The room smelled of sweat and the tang of fear, and it calmed his annoyance a little.

"Excuse me." He smiled politely and moved through the people, who willingly stood up to part around him. The man Samuel was after also stepped aside, but Samuel held up a hand. "No, no. Not you. If you don't mind." He looked at the sheriff's jacket bundled in the man's arms and reached forward, pulling the collar away. A toddler, a girl, blinked up at him. "How sweet." He smiled, moving his finger in front of her face. "And what's her name?"

"Maylee," said the sheriff stiffly.

"Is she yours?"

"My granddaughter."

"Hi, Maylee, I'm Sam," he said, in a singsong voice. "May I?" He held out his arms.

"Over your dead body," was the abrupt reply.

Samuel tsk'd his tongue. "You're making a bad example, Sheriff. Weren't you told to respect your elders?"

The sheriff held the little girl closer. It was touching, really. Samuel smiled yet again—he was in a good mood, and today was a good day. He could afford to be generous, but the man was annoying him, and he didn't like being annoyed. "Hand her to me, please."

He could see another refusal on the man's lips, so he sighed and rolled his eyes to the side for half a second before meeting the other man's gaze. "Before I take her from you."

The man blanched. Samuel always liked to see people go pale, to actually watch the color drain from them shade by shade. Slowly, he held the little girl out, and Samuel took her, leaving the coat in the sheriff's arms.

Samuel held the child out at arm's length and inspected her, pleased with what he saw. "Wave goodbye to your grandpa," he coaxed, pulling her to him and walking back to the front of the room.

The room had fallen silent in dread anticipation. "Now I know what you're all wondering," he said, surveying them. They were livestock now—meat and blood, waiting to be made into something better and more efficient. They would be grateful soon; they just didn't know it yet. And who could blame them? "You want to know if I'm going to kill this precious child." He pointed at them. "Right?"

They didn't really need to answer; it was written on their faces. They were prepared to be horrified. They were also prepared to stand by and do nothing, which he found twice as amusing. He looked at Maylee. "Don't you worry, button, Uncle Sammy would never do that to you." He rested a hand on the top of her head. "I'm going to give you a present. Do you like presents?"

She nodded, still silent, still confused. Amazingly well-behaved, he thought.

"Good." He lifted her up again—her neck was too small, too tender. So much risk. She was going to be his first true vampire, if it worked. Maybe he would raise her as his own. She probably wouldn't even remember being human. "The present might sting," he said and opened his mouth.

Something in the atmosphere changed then; a smell, bitter and clear, began to seep into the air. Samuel paused, and his werewolves—every single one—began to snap and howl at the air in a baying cacophony, clawing at their eyes and running up against the doors.

"One diffuser from the church nursery—free. One twelve-ounce jar of concentrated wolfsbane—eighty bucks. The look on your face," said Skata, walking through a side door, "priceless."

Samuel's smile faded. He didn't project the future, he didn't move to any backup plan. He only reacted in the way that made the most sense and did the most immediate thing. He sank his teeth into Maylee's arm.

CHAPTER FORTY-TWO

Skata surged forward and dove at Samuel, taking him to the ground. Maylee rolled away and was scooped up by a woman, free of the trampling feet. Skata slammed his fist into Samuel's nose and felt as if his fist had splintered.

"Nice to see you again, Leslie." Samuel grinned; blood coating his fangs.

"It's Skata," said Skata, punching the vampire again.

Samuel grabbed Skata's shoulders and pushed, flipping Skata onto his back. "I forgot. You'll have to forgive me; Emilia called you Leslie." Samuel pushed his hands down on Skata's throat until he couldn't breathe. "You have been such a pain in my neck, did you know that?"

Skata fumbled for his knife, but it was underneath him, pinned between his back and the floor. He twisted his wrist and arm until he couldn't twist anymore, but he felt the handle; he tugged it free of the sheath, slicing into his own side as he drew it and punched the knife into Samuel's stomach.

The vampire looked down at the knife-handle sticking out of his stomach. "Ow." He continued to grip Skata's throat with one hand as he pulled the knife out of himself with the other. "You know better than that," he said, stabbing the knife into Skata's thigh.

The pain seared Skata's darkening vision, but he had no breath to scream.

"Not your brightest move," said Samuel, turning and pushing the blade down. Skata felt the knife scrape against bone, twisting his leg with it. He gritted his teeth, fighting to concentrate, to forget seeing and feel instead. He reached for his second weapon.

He heard the front doors open, splintered by the furious, desperate werewolves. They would make it into the fresh air and surround the building, if they were smart, attacking anyone else who attempted to leave. It was the wolves outside or the deranged vampire inside.

Skata would have preferred the wolves.

"I would turn you," said Samuel, his breath hot on Skata's face, "but really, I'd rather just kill you."

A shot rang out, and blood splattered across Skata's face, coating his tongue with the taste of copper. The grip on Skata's throat relaxed, then fell away. Skata choked in the deepest breath he could and scrambled upright; he hadn't been able to reach his gun.

Samuel lay where he had fallen, across Skata's legs. The side of his head had been reduced to ground meat, and his remaining eye was wide with surprise.

Skata took the opportunity to shove the vampire away and

grab the knife sticking out of his leg. He hissed a deep breath and tugged it up and out of his leg. The pain made him feel like vomiting, but he couldn't pass out. He couldn't do that yet.

"Hey," said Colton, appearing in Skata's blurry view. "Stay with me, man."

Skata didn't see the slap coming, but the sting helped anchor him in the moment. "Thanks," he choked, spitting onto the floor. The preacher hauled Skata to his feet, but the pressure shot more crippling pain up his body, and his damaged leg buckled beneath him.

"Whoa, whoa." Colton caught him and held him up. "Your leg's in pretty bad shape, man."

"Thanks," said Skata, dizzy. "I couldn't tell. Where's…" He blanked on the name.

"Shannon's got Maylee; everyone's in the foyer."

"They can't go outside." Skata scrambled for the right words, to put them in order. "They'll be killed. The werewolves."

"We figured that out." Colton pulled the bandana off his head and tied it tightly above the gaping hole in Skata's thigh.

On the floor, Samuel groaned and began to twitch as his body healed. Skata drew his gun and pointed it at the prone vampire.

"That won't kill him," said Colton, but Skata interrupted him.

"Damn right it will. I coated the bullets in vervain myself. One shot to the heart, and he's gone."

"We need him alive." Colton grabbed his arm. "Angel needs him."

The sight of Samuel lying helpless on the floor was too much. In that moment, it was simple. "I don't."

The bullet left the gun just as Colton pushed Skata's arm down. It struck the vampire in the ribs, and Skata summoned his remaining strength to shove Colton off-balance before he fell next to the fallen vampire. He had one more weapon, and he knew it would work. He'd picked it up off the ground before taking Jackson's hand.

"Don't!" Colton shouted.

Skata lifted the jagged piece of shutter-wood and drove it up through Samuel's ribs.

For a moment, the room was still, quiet. Skata didn't breathe; he didn't hear Colton. Life held its breath, waiting to see if the vampire would move.

He never did.

Colton pushed his hands through his hair and shook his head. "That ain't gonna work, man. He's a moroi."

"No, he wasn't." Skata swayed, feeling that his grip on the makeshift stake was the only thing keeping him from falling over. "He was a malkavian."

Colton stared at him. "How—"

"I'll tell you later."

This didn't feel right. There was supposed to be more—a surge of victory, a hole filled.

Not this...nothing. Skata didn't feel better; he didn't feel worse. He was as hollow as he had been since Emilia died.

The sound of breaking glass and screaming reached him through the open doors. He felt Colton nudge his arm, heard him say, "Come on."

He stood up, limping after the preacher. The foyer was chaos. People were everywhere pushing to get out the broken widows, bleeding on the jagged glass. Anything to escape the wolves at the door, masses of muscle and fur and ripping, tearing teeth. The people didn't know Samuel was dead, and it was too loud to make it known.

Colton fired at the first wolf outside the window; the creature cried out in pain and surprise, falling back out of sight.

Skata blinked at the shotgun.

"You coat yours in vervain, I coat mine in wolfsbane," said Colton.

Skata turned, looking for familiar faces. The wolves were wary of entering the building and panicked humans were still trying to escape, throwing themselves to the enemy. Gideon and Jackson were nowhere to be seen, and neither was Skinner. He could see Bonnie with her arms around a girl of eleven or twelve who looked terrified.

"Skata!" Shannon ran up. She held a bloody knife in one hand and Maylee on her hip with the other. Maylee's eyes were red, but her bitten arm had been tied up with Shannon's scarf. She saw Skata and Colton looking at the toddler's arm and said,

"I give her vervain. She hasn't turned. I think she's okay."

Relieved, Skata nodded. Adrenaline was helping push the pain back; he felt he could remain standing for just a little longer. "We have to keep everyone inside." He pushed past everyone, toward the doors, raising his voice as loud as he could. "Keep away from the doors and windows! Get back! You're safer inside!"

You'd think they'd hear the screams outside and get that for themselves, he thought, but he had no more time for cynicism. People were idiots, and it wasn't his fault. He lifted his gun and fired at the ceiling.

The shot was like a miracle. The noise reached past the panic and confusion and drew attention like a magnet. Skata lowered the gun and knew he was glaring at them like a principal at a room of seventh-graders. "Shut the door," he barked.

Colton and several people who managed to get past their panic shut and locked the doors.

"That won't do anything," said a deputy from the center of the room.

Skata gave him a sharp look. "It's better than nothing."

"It'll buy a few seconds at most." Jackson's voice sent an equal mixture of irritation and relief through Skata. He turned and saw the vampire and Skinner coming around the hall corner, bloody and irate. Skinner no longer looked like Skata's double—he was back to looking like a lean, keen-eyed inmate.

"A few of the werewolves were holed up in the back room," Skinner explained.

"Where's Gideon?"

"Making sure there are no more inside."

"What are we going to do now?" asked Shannon, glancing from Colton to Skata and back.

Skata rubbed his jaw, trying to think. The situation was impossible to fix, unless…

The hospital.

"Jackson, you and Gideon could do it."

"Do what?"

"Compel them," said Skata.

Jackson leaned against the wall. He looked more normal now—his veins weren't black, and his eyes were gray again—but he didn't look well. "I don't know if I can," he said quietly, shrugging one shoulder.

Someone in the back called, "What do you mean, compel them? What does that mean?"

Someone sobbed hysterically. "What's going on?"

"Where did the wolves come from?" asked someone else.

"They were the people!"

"Who was that man?"

Skata looked at Colton. "You've got to be able to think of something. Use the old 'valley of death' spiel."

"It's the valley of the *shadow* of death, and trust me, they don't want to hear it. They want me to tell 'em everything's fine."

Skata blinked and raised his voice again. "Okay, folks, listen up! I know you're confused and this looks bad, but everything's going to be okay." He was surprised to see that some of them calmed down, and he shrugged, turning back to Colton. "Guess you were right."

Colton grinned, but it faded just as quickly. "What now?"

Skata looked down at his gun. "Don't know. But there's you and me and a few other sorry soldiers, so what do you say we go out there and put a little hell to rest?"

Colton lifted his own weapon and smiled ferociously. "Let's go."

They walked through the middle of the crowd, followed by Skinner, Bonnie, and the Montgomery brothers as Gideon showed up just in time. Everyone backed up, letting them through, and a touch on Skata's arm startled him as he reached the door.

"Dad and I'll try to keep everyone together," said Shannon, still holding Maylee close. "Go get 'em."

Skata looked at Colton. "You take Jackson and Bonnie and take care of the werewolves. I'll take Skinner and Gideon and kill any of the vampires I see."

Shannon's eyebrows rose. "Vampires? There were only wolves before."

"Samuel turned a whole bar just to get at me," said Skata. "I'd be willing to bet we'll find vampires outside, too." He nodded toward his gun. "I've got seventeen rounds."

"Sixteen," said Colton.

Skata licked his lips. "Right. We'll need someone to get more ammo out of the truck."

"I'll do it," said Bonnie.

"It's unlocked," said Colton. "Go out the back and hurry up."

She nodded and ran toward the back doors. Colton and Skata looked long and hard at each other, and Skata wasn't really surprised to see no fear in Colton's eyes. He was ready to die; he was secure.

Skata blew out a deep breath. He wasn't, but right now, he supposed it didn't matter. He was willing, and that felt more important.

Skinner rolled his eyes. "Are we doing this or not?"

"Here goes," said Colton and pushed the doors open.

Skata barely registered them slamming shut behind him as a girl with black lipstick and a dozen piercings jumped off the roof and landed in front of him, fangs bared. He was taken aback only for a second. Then he shot Sophia in the head.

* * * * * * *

"Do you want to talk about it?" Em tilted her head so she could look up at his face. Her arm lay across his chest, her fingers playing with his wrist.

"Nah." He rubbed her shoulder.

"Are you sure?"

"Yeah."

435

"Honey."

"What?"

She pushed herself up onto her elbow. "You just killed someone. Were-wolf or not, that does things to a person."

He opened his mouth to protest, but she shushed him. "I know you. You bottle everything up, and you push it down, and you think you're going to be all right, but all that darkness you keep down there is going to escape sooner or later."

"Make it later."

Her mouth twisted a little, just enough to let him know she understood, but she didn't like it. "I love you. You know that, right?"

He smiled. "Yeah."

"Okay." She leaned forward, an inch away. "When you're ready to talk, I'll listen."

"I'll take you up on that."

"Okay," she repeated and kissed him.

"Now's a bad time to be daydreaming, space man!"

Skata whirled around, something warm dripping down his face. Two dead vampires lay on the ground in front of him, and Skinner stood behind him, also bloody. "Where's Colton?"

"There!" Skinner pointed just as Colton shot at a werewolf who was running across the square on all fours, a streak of brown fur.

"I have more ammo!" Bonnie tore around the corner of the building as fast as she could on two legs. She tossed a sheathed twelve-inch blade, a shotgun, and a loaded bandoleer to Skata. "Take those!"

Skata caught them and did not wait to watch her hand out the rest of the weapons. He turned around and swept the blade through the neck of the vampire behind him. He glanced up and saw Jackson twenty yards away, blood up to his elbows.

Skata got three shells loaded into the gun before he heard a howl and looked up to see a werewolf headed toward him. "Please be wolfsbane," he grunted, pumping the shotgun and firing. The wolf hit the ground and didn't get up. "Hallelujah."

Without Samuel's instructions, the werewolves and vampires were scattered: deadly, but less dangerous for lack of precision. They were easier to pick off, once Skata found a rhythm. His right hand held the shotgun, his left hand held the semi-automatic; it wasn't wise to pump a shotgun with a hand holding a loaded Glock, but he didn't care. When he finished the bullets, he dropped the guns and switched to knives.

He did not keep count of how many creatures he dropped. He did not notice when claws tore or teeth sank into him.

And then, suddenly, there was nothing left to kill.

He turned in a circle, eying every place to hide, expecting something, waiting for it. Instead he saw Gideon and Jackson standing beside each other, Skinner on one knee inspecting a corpse, and Colton, his chest heaving, giving everything a second look.

Skata lifted the knives, stunned. "We done?"

"Think so," said Colton, looking as if he had another battle in him. "You okay?"

"I'll live," said Skata. He lowered the knives, his hands gripping them so tightly he wondered if he'd ever be able to let go. "You?"

Colton looked down at himself. He was torn and bloodied, but still standing. "Guess I'll live, too."

Skata gave Skinner a reluctant once-over. "You look all right to me."

"Thanks," said Skinner.

The Montgomery brothers were joined by Bonnie, all three looking remarkably unharmed. Then Skata turned to look at the town hall, expecting to see it ravaged, everyone dead.

The doors opened, and Shannon looked out. "Is it safe to come out?"

"Safe as it'll ever be," said Skata, and then he was exhausted, and he hurt. He wanted nothing more than to lie down, close his eyes, and sleep.

But Bonnie cried, "Jackson!" just as the vampire collapsed to the ground.

CHAPTER FORTY-THREE

Gideon lifted his brother in his arms as Bonnie hugged herself. "No doubt adrenaline kept the effects of the vervain at bay," he said, by way of explanation. His wore no expression. "Now I must simply hope he is strong enough to survive it."

He turned to leave, aware that his job was done. Skata wondered if he would have stayed even if it wasn't.

"Where are you going?" asked Bonnie.

"I am taking him home," said Gideon.

"I'm coming."

Gideon turned to look coldly at her for a long second, but he said nothing. He only turned around, and Bonnie followed, glancing back at Skata and Colton and the rest before they rushed away.

Colton turned to look at Skata. "Want to tell me now?"

"Tell you what?" Skata wiped his hand across his face, clearing blood and sweat away.

"How'd you know Samuel was a malkavian?"

Skata thought back to when he searched Angel's room, going through the documents kept in his desk. Beneath the picture and mysterious letters was a list of names. At the top were the initials Z. T. and the number 31. Directly below that were the initials S. L. and the number 30. Z. T. was marked with the abbreviation c:strig and S. L. was marked with the abbreviation c:malk.

It wasn't until Easton told him Angel's real name was Zacharia Travalis that he realized it was a list of names, assigned numbers, and vampire classifications.

S. L. – Samuel Lemeck

C:malk – Malkavian.

He tried to condense this explanation, as far-fetched as it might seem, and told Colton. The preacher stared at him for a long moment before saying, "Any idea why he didn't burn in the sun?"

"The same way Angel doesn't."

"How's that?"

"No idea," said Skata. "But I'm going to find out."

"Not to break up the party," said Skinner, "but half the town just saw a bunch of werewolves and vampires fighting outside town hall."

"Gideon took care of it," said Shannon.

Skata squinted, confused. "When? How?"

"He went into the town hall and compelled everyone. Jackson helped. Everyone believes they were at the memorial, and they'll leave and go home. Obviously, there won't be a barbecue."

I must have really spaced out. "Thanks."

"We gotta clean the mess up." Colton looked at the bodies scattered across the battlefield. "Even compelled people'll wonder why there are corpses everywhere."

Skata closed his eyes, just for a few seconds. Then he opened them. "No rest for the wicked," he said, dropping the knives. "Let's load 'em up. We can burn them away from town."

* * * * * * *

Skata pushed open the door to Angel's house. It was good to be home, even at midnight. He heard dishes rattle in the kitchen and called, "Easton?"

"Close, but no cigar. She's asleep upstairs." Angel walked out, drying his hands with a checkered towel. "You look like you lost a fight with a cement mixer."

"And you look…surprisingly okay." Skata studied the vampire. He looked a little pale, but otherwise fine. "I guess the wolfsbane worked."

"Like a charm."

The term 'miracle' came to Skata's mind, but he only leaned against the wall and let out a breath. That breath felt like the last vestige of all strength and energy he had; he slid to the floor.

Angel walked back into the foyer with a first aid kit and crouched next to the fallen hunter.

"Here." He twisted the towel and placed it between Skata's teeth. "What did you do with Samuel?" asked Angel, pouring hydrogen peroxide over Skata's injured thigh.

Skata bit down hard, but lacked the energy even to groan at the pain. He removed the towel. He blinked blearily, his vision fading with exhaustion. "I had to kill him. Self-defense." He shut his eyes to avoid seeing Angel's face. "Sorry."

After a moment, all Angel said was, "Bummer."

"What's a bummer?"

Skata twisted around and watched Easton come down the stairs, her cell phone in hand. When she saw him, she raced down the stairs and crouched down next to him.

"Samuel's dead," Skata mumbled.

Easton shot Angel a stricken look. "But I thought he might be able to cure Angel."

Skata lifted both hands and rested his face against his palms. He inhaled the scent of smoke, cool and acrid against his skin. "I'm sorry."

"Don't worry about it," said Angel. "I like you better, anyway."

Easton kissed the side of Skata's head before asking Angel, "What about you, though?"

He shrugged. If Skata hadn't known better, he might have believed Angel really didn't care. "Keep doing what I've been doing, I guess."

"Hopefully not exactly," teased Easton.

"Well." He grinned.

Skata frowned in confusion. The vampire's pain was real, but so was the grin. Why the heck was he grinning?

He noticed Easton grinning back, just a little.

Well, crap.

The door opened, and Skinner walked in. Easton looked surprised, but Angel seemed used to everyone entering and exiting his house without his permission. Colton followed the doppelganger.

"Figured you had an extra room for him," said Colton to Angel.

"By all means," the vampire said, with a suspicious smile at Skinner.

The doppelganger held up a hand. "I'm one of the okayish guys now."

"Right," said Angel.

"Hey, Skata."

Skata looked at Colton, who looked as tired as he felt. "What?"

"We did good out there today."

"Yeah," said Skata. "So?"

Colton shrugged. "Good job, man."

Something about the gesture, the 'good job' after the preacher had seen him kill Samuel in cold blood, broke something inside

Skata. He only stood up wordlessly, with Angel's help, and left everyone, dragging himself up the stairs and into his room where he could ease his good knee onto the floor. He rested his elbows on the bed and closed his eyes.

He had no grand prayer, nothing to say that felt worth anything. He had only exhaustion and a hollowed-out cavern where his soul should be. That, he supposed, and gratitude. He hadn't fought alone.

"Thanks," he muttered and fell asleep.

* * * * * * *

Easton turned to Angel. "I've got to go to the hospital and see Graham and Dad. Are you going to be okay?"

"Hunky dory," he said with a thumbs-up.

"I can give you a lift," Colton offered.

Easton almost said no—it was midnight, and she could only imagine what had gone down at the town hall. She'd have to wait and ask when the fighters were recovered.

Colton solved her dilemma. "It's on the way."

She gave him a grateful smile. "I'll get my purse and be right with you."

He nodded and headed toward the front door. "See you later," he said, presumably to Skinner and Angel both before he shut the door behind him.

"Nighty-night," said Skinner, before walking up the stairs and out of sight.

The house felt very quiet all of a sudden. Quiet and tired and yet strangely safe.

Easton studied Angel for a moment before asking, "Are you sure you're okay?"

"Never better." His smile was a little too wide.

The truth takes time with this one, I guess. She wrapped her arms around him and hugged him—tightly but gingerly. He'd been dying just hours ago. He didn't lift his arms or hug her back, but she felt his chin rest on her head, like he was too tired to do anything else. She lingered for just a few seconds before pulling away.

"See you later, Zach," she said, backing toward the door.

He snorted softly, but waved his fingers at her. "Take care." His eyes followed her until she shut the door and leaned against the other side, taking a deep breath. *Okay. Okay, then.*

She jogged down the steps toward Colton's waiting car.

* * * * * * *

"Em?"

She did not turn around to look at him, but he saw the subtle shift in her back as she poured her coffee. "What?"

"You were right."

She turned. Not all the way, but enough to see him. "About what?"

He swallowed. Hard. He felt childish, but not enough to keep him from telling her. "I'm not okay."

She set the coffee pot down and faced him. Her eyes were as soft as her hair, curling around her shoulders. "Come here."

He crossed the kitchen. He did not feel guilty, not exactly. Not for killing the werewolf raiding his father-in-law's cattle. It was for killing the human part. The part that had stared at him in pain as he fell back, limbs splayed, dead.

Maybe the werewolf had never killed a human. Maybe it was just a cattle-killer, maybe it was just trying to survive.

Maybe he hadn't deserved to die.

Em stood on the top of his feet and hugged his neck, wordless.

He didn't speak, either; he only wrapped his arms around her waist and held her, breathing in the morning scent of her, coffee and mint.

"I can't do this," he said, his voice muffled. "Not today."

"Well," she told him, "you don't have to, but yes. You can."

"I'm a sinner, Em."

He felt her lips smile against his neck. "If God didn't forgive sinners, heaven would be mighty empty." She kissed the side of his face. "Come on," she said, leaning back to look at him with that same knowing expression that never failed to comfort him, even when he didn't understand why. She ran her fingers across the back of his head, combing through his hair.

He sighed but nodded. "Guess I'll wear something a little more formal," he said, looking down at his drawstring lounge pants.

"Jeans," she said, grinning. "And button your shirt up all the way."

"Yes, ma'am," he said, returning the grin.

She winked. "Don't worry, I won't keep you in them for long."

He paused at the doorway to smile at her, to study her.

"What?"

"Why'd you marry me?"

"For your body," she teased, then took a more serious tone. "Because you're a good man and the man that I love. Till death do us part. Now," she added, snapping the towel in his direction, "go get dressed. We'll be late for church."

* * * * * * *

Skata opened his eyes. A black-and-brown pattern met his eyes, and he straightened, grimacing at the stiffness in his neck. He had fallen asleep on his knee, and gray light now streamed in through the window.

He could always remember his dreams—they were always memories, had been for years. He figured he didn't have enough imagination to create his own. But this memory...when had he forgotten it?

Slowly and painfully, he got to his feet. He needed a hot shower and a massage and a bottle of painkillers—but first things first. "Okay," he said, staring out the window, "we've got an understanding, like I said. Just don't rush me."

He limped into the bathroom and turned on the hot water.

EPILOGUE

The huge black truck was as menacing as the two passengers were unassuming. The man at the gas pump watched as they climbed out, studying their surroundings with interest. The older one was tall and striking, probably somewhere in his late fifties. The younger man of thirty or so didn't look like a relation.

"Excuse me," said the older one, removing his sunglasses as he approached, "but how long have you been here?"

The old man smiled. "Long enough, I should say. Born and raised here. How can I help you boys?"

"We're looking for this man." He took a photograph out of his pocket and held it out for inspection. It was washed out, taken with old film. "His name is Zacharia Travalis; you might know him as Angel."

"Sure, I know him. He's new in town; only been here a year or so."

The stranger smiled. "Would you mind telling us where we

could find him? We've been looking for him for a very long time."

The old man put the pump back, his truck full. "Don't know where he lives," he said, "but stick around long enough, you'll see him. Salvation is a small town."

The younger man climbed back into the truck without saying a word. His companion kept smiling and placed the photograph back in the pocket of his suit. "Thank you for your time."

"Happy to help."

The agent shut the door and released the parking brake.

"The old man said he was here," said his companion. "We'll get him this time."

"Yes, we will," said the agent.

DARK IS THE NIGHT

ABOUT THE AUTHOR

MIRRIAM NEAL is an author frequently masquerading as an artist. When she's not scrubbing paint off her hands, she's thinking about writing (actually, if she's being honest, she's always thinking about writing). A discovery writer, she tends to start novels and figure them out as she goes along and likes to work on several books at the same time—while drinking black coffee. She's a sucker for monsters, unlikely friendships, redemption arcs, and underdog protagonists. When not painting fantasy art or writing genre-bending novels, she likes to argue the existence of Bigfoot, rave about Guillermo del Toro, and write passionate defenses of misunderstood characters. To learn more about her fiction and art, visit mirriamneal.com.